COLD AS ICE

A
LAKESHORE U
STORY

COLD AS ICE

LAKESHORE U

L A COTTON

Published by Delesty Books

Edited by Kate Newman
Proofread by Sisters Get Literary Author Services

LAKESHORE U

Bite the Ice
A Lakeshore U Prequel Story

Ice Burn
A Lakeshore U Story

Break the Ice
A Lakeshore U Story

On Thin Ice
A Lakeshore U Story

Beneath the Ice
A Lakeshore U Story

Cold as Ice
A Lakeshore U Story

Not every victory shows up on the scoreboard

UNKNOWN

CHAPTER 1

AUSTIN

My cell phone vibrated for the fifth time since I arrived at the bar. But just like the four times before, I ignored it.

"Rough night?" the bartender asked, sliding another beer toward me.

"You could say that." I dragged a hand down my face and let out a weary sigh.

It was senior year, my last season with the Lakeshore U Lakers. My final year before I graduated, and shit got real. And I was sitting alone in some bar, nursing my fourth beer of the night while one of my best friends lay in the hospital.

I'd left Connor a couple of hours ago, and I should have done the sensible thing and gone home. But instead, I'd found myself here. Drinking away my sorrows like I was the one who had gotten injured.

Something about seeing him go down on the ice, watching him *not* get back up, had rattled me.

Hockey could be brutal. Anyone who loved the game knew that. Just like anyone who played knew the risks. But witnessing him being stretchered off the ice, seeing him lying in the hospital bed, pain etched into his features, was a stark reminder of how quickly everything could go to shit.

Connor had a family who cared though. He had his girl, Ella, and plans for the future that didn't involve hockey. Sure, it would devastate him to lose out when he was so close to realizing his dreams of going pro, but he'd get over it eventually because he had people.

People who loved him.

People who would be there no matter what.

Hockey was it for me.

Without it, I had nothing.

No one.

Fuck, I was a selfish bastard sitting here, moping about my life, when Con was laid up in the hospital, not knowing whether he'd play again this season. But I wasn't exactly known for my positive mental attitude off the ice.

My cell went off again, and instead of answering it, I switched the damn thing off.

I didn't want to talk to Fallon.

There was nothing to say.

We'd had fun together, but it was done.

Over.

She wanted more, and I didn't.

Watching all my friends fall in love over the last few months, the highs and lows that followed had only cemented in my mind that I wasn't cut out for a relationship.

I liked sex as much as the next guy, sure. But I wanted my sex to come with no strings attached and zero drama included.

Being the Lakers goalie meant I had my fair share of offers. But even the promise of a good time with a puck bunny wasn't doing it for me tonight.

I was restless. Wound tighter than a spring. And the fact I couldn't really put my finger on why—beyond Connor's unexpected injury—had me feeling all kinds of uneasy.

The truth was, nothing had been right since my little sister Aurora had turned up on my doorstep at the beginning of my senior year and flipped my world upside down.

I loved her; she was family—the only family I cared about. But we had too much-unresolved shit between us to just slip into the familial roles of brother and sister. Unresolved shit I couldn't escape now she went to Lakeshore U. Now she was dating one of my teammates, who also happened to be one of my best friends.

Fuck. I hadn't seen that coming.

Noah Holden didn't date. And he sure as fuck didn't date shy, book-smart girls like Rory.

Until he did.

I'd gotten over their relationship for the most part. She was happy, and she deserved it; she did. But I couldn't deny it still stung a little, watching them together.

When it came down to it, Noah had chosen her over his friendship with me.

A commotion over by the door drew my attention, and I watched a group of girls stumble into the bar, singing and laughing. They didn't look like the usual puck bunny crowd, but it didn't stop me from pulling my ball cap lower over my face. I wasn't in the mood for company tonight, and I certainly wasn't in the mood to deal with a group of bunnies hoping to score with the Lakers goalie.

If I had been, I would have gone to The Penalty Box since that's where the team usually hung out.

No, tonight I wanted to be alone.

It had been happening more and more lately. But I guess that's what happened when your friends all fell in love and moved on with their lives.

You got left behind.

Something that bothered me more than it should.

More than I wanted it to.

I turned my attention back to my beer, watching the NHL highlights on the small television screen hanging behind the bar. There had been a time when all I wanted was to play for a pro team. I'd had more than one team interested in me during high school. But I'd been a handful back then. Too pissed at the world and everyone in it to worry about the future. So much so that I'd arrived at LU with no contract, and then one year passed and another, and before I knew it, my eligibility for the draft had passed me by.

I guess you could say I wanted it; I just didn't want it enough.

My fist curled against my thigh. If only I'd had a guiding hand back then. Someone to kick me up the ass and—

"Hey." A pretty blonde draped herself on the bar beside me. "So me and my girlfriends were wondering—"

"Not interested," I grumbled, barely acknowledging her.

"Oh, come on, my girlfriends are trying to cheer me up. It's been a shitty few weeks."

"You a student at LU?" I asked, still not fully looking at her.

"No, but I have friends that go there. Let me guess… you're either a football player or—"

"Hockey." I finally looked at her. "I play hockey."

My head knew she spelled trouble, but my eyes were having a really hard time looking away.

She was gorgeous. Glossy blonde hair tumbled over her shoulders like spun gold, with long bangs framing her face. And her eyes, her eyes were the most intense shade of blue I'd ever seen.

I swallowed thickly, caught off guard by my instant attraction to my unwanted visitor.

"Can't say I'm much of a hockey fan, I'm afraid." She gave me a sloppy grin, confirming what I already suspected.

She was drunk.

"I'm Madison. But my friends call me Madi."

"Austin."

"Well, Austin, be a doll and play along, will you." Leaning closer, she twisted her fingers into my hoodie without hesitation. "My friends think it's time I get back on the horse if you know what I mean."

"They do, huh? And what do you think?" I humored her because, despite what most people thought about me, I wasn't a total asshole.

It had nothing to do with the fact her voice sounded like pure sex.

Nothing at all.

"I think they're full of shit." Her eyes flashed to mine, a ripple of pain there. "But I don't get out much, and my night will go much smoother if they think I managed to score the cute hockey player's phone number."

"Is that so?"

She leaned closer still, and I got a whiff of something sweet. Cherries and vanilla, maybe. "You'd be doing me a huge favor." Her fingers brushed my chest, and the strangest fucking sensation rolled through me.

Oh, who was I kidding?

I was a guy, and she was a hot little thing. I'd have to be dead to be unaffected by her pressed up close against me.

And while my heart might have been buried under a thick layer of ice, my blood still ran hot. With a direct line to my dick, who was more than happy to enjoy this little interaction if the way he twitched behind my jeans was any indication.

"Hand me your cell," I said, playing along.

"Thank you, thank you, thank you." Her laughter made something tug sharply inside my chest.

Who the hell was this girl?

Madison handed me her cell phone, and I typed in my number, changing the last digit. Not that she'd ever know it.

"That should get them off your back for a little while."

"I owe you." She smiled as I handed it back to her.

"Consider it my good deed of the day." I gave her a small nod and went back to watching the highlights.

"See you around, hotshot," she chuckled, and I watched her all the way out the corner of my eye.

She was exactly my type. Petite and slim, with curves in all the right places. But I wasn't good company, not tonight. And I'd learned a long time ago not to give strangers my cell phone number.

So I tamped down the buzz of intrigue I felt and focused on my beer and the television.

I came here for one reason tonight.

And despite my dick's aching protests, it wasn't to get laid.

"This should cover it," I said to the bartender, sliding fifty bucks across the bar.

He gave me an appreciative nod. "Great season so far." My brow rose, and he let out a smooth chuckle. "Recognized you the second you walked in but figured after tonight's game, you probably didn't want to be hounded."

"Thanks, man. I appreciate it."

"Anytime. I hope Morgan's injury wasn't as bad as it looked."

Me too, I wanted to say. But I swallowed the words.

Rapping my knuckles on the counter, I headed toward the restrooms before the walk home. The Saturday night crowd had thinned over the last hour, and I was relieved I'd picked a bar a little further out of town—somewhere, I could fly under the radar.

After taking a quick leak, I washed my hands and headed back into the hall, running straight into

"You," I said, taking a step back from Madison.

"You played me." She narrowed her gaze at me, fisting her hands on her hips. But her attempts at being serious were thwarted by the adorable flush to her cheeks and telling glaze to her eyes.

"Excuse me?" I deadpanned.

"I texted you, and some old man replied. Total creep, by the way." A shudder ran through her. "You gave me the wrong number."

"You texted me?" My brows pinched.

Well, shit. I hadn't expected that.

"Well, yeah, my friends thought... it doesn't matter." She shook her head, looking more than a little irritated. "You made me look stupid."

"Not my problem." I shrugged, moving around her to head down the small hall leading back to the main bar.

"So that's it? You're just going to walk away," she called after me. "And here I thought you were a decent guy."

"Trust me, I'm not," I murmured, but didn't stop.

Until I felt her dainty fingers wrap around my arm. "What the fuck—"

"Sorry, okay." Apology filled her bewitching ocean eyes. "I'm not... good at this. It's been a while, you know." Her shoulder lifted in a small, uncertain shrug that made something soften inside my chest.

"How old are you?" I asked. She couldn't be much older than me, yet she talked like she had years of life experience.

"Don't worry, I'm legal."

"I wasn't... What is happening right now?"

I didn't have time for this shit—these games.

"And here I thought hockey players liked playing around off the ice as well as on it." Madison stepped into my space, her vanilla perfume hitting me like a fist to the stomach.

She smelled fucking delicious, and I was overcome with the urge to bury my face in her shoulder and breathe her in.

Jesus, I really needed to get out of here.

"My friends left," she blurted as I backed up, putting some much-needed space between us.

"They left... why?"

"Because I told them I didn't want to go to a club, and I told them you would walk me home."

"You lied to them." My brow rose, half-impressed, half-confused as fuck.

"I... Yeah, I guess you could say that. They mean

well, but…" She trailed off, dropping her gaze to the floor.

"Where do you live?"

"I'm staying at my friend's place for the weekend." She reeled off an address I knew all too well because Ella lived in the building next to it.

Fuck my life.

"Come on, I'll walk you."

"I'm not going to sleep with you."

My brows furrowed deeper. "I didn't ask you to."

"Good, just putting it out there."

Madison fell in step beside me as we left the bar. It was bitter out, the cold air rolling in from Lake Erie and beyond. But I felt at home in the subzero temperatures.

"So why were you drinking all alone tonight?" she asked, burrowing into her jacket. "Shouldn't you be out celebrating with your team or something?"

"My friend got injured. He's in the hospital and…" I clammed up. "I don't know why I'm telling you this."

"Sometimes it's easier to talk to a stranger." She smiled up at me, and there was that strange tugging feeling deep in my gut again. "Is he going to be okay?" she added when I didn't fill the awkward silence.

"I hope so."

"So Austin…" Her voice had an expectant edge, and I found myself replying, "Hart."

"Austin Hart, I like that." She grinned. "Tell me about yourself."

"Not much to tell. I'm a senior at LU."

"You're a hockey goalkeeper?"

"How do you know that?"

Guilt flashed in her eyes as she murmured, "My friends and I might have looked you up."

"Yeah, I'm the Lakers goalie. Or goaltender as we say in hockey," I corrected her.

"Right. Like I said, I'm not really a fan. I'm more of a football girl."

"Let me guess, it's the tight white pants."

She snorted. "I would never reduce an athlete to his uniform."

Her laughter wrapped around me, tugging at something deep inside me again.

What the fuck was it about this girl?

We'd barely spoken a few words in the bar, but she had my full attention.

Even if I didn't like it.

Ending things with Fallon had clearly fucked with my head. I didn't want a relationship. I didn't want someone to rely on me. I didn't want that burden.

I wasn't good at emotions, at opening up and letting people in. I preferred to keep my walls high and my defenses on high alert.

It was easier that way.

Safer.

But there was something about Madison.

Something I had no intention of exploring.

I would walk her back to her building and then be on my way.

"Are you from Lakeshore?"

"No, Syracuse," I said, even though it hadn't been home for a long time. "You?"

"I live in Olin Bay."

"Next town over, right?"

"Yeah. One of my best friends goes to LU. I don't get to see her much..." She trailed off, but I didn't pry.

I wasn't looking to learn all her secrets.

Madison's cell phone pinged, and she dug it out of her clutch purse, checking the text.

"Everything okay?" I asked, noticing the tension bracketing her mouth.

"Fine." She shoved it back in her purse and gave me a weak smile.

If I had been Noah or Connor, I might have asked her if it was an ex. But I wasn't. And I'd already put myself out to walk her to her building.

"Okay, well, this is me." She pointed to a building up ahead. We were right on the edge of campus, but my place was around the other side.

"I guess this is where we say good night, then," I said, drawing to a stop. I could watch her walk in from here.

"I guess it is." Madison peered up at me. "Or... it doesn't have to be," she said hesitantly.

"What?" I frowned because, surely, she wasn't saying what I thought she was.

"I think you heard me..."

"Yeah, and it sounded a lot like you were propositioning me after you just told me you weren't going to sleep with me."

"I did say that, didn't I?" Her nose screwed up but she looked so fucking cute. "But you could come in for a coffee, or we could watch a movie."

A movie?

Shit. I didn't know what to say. I didn't make a habit of hanging out with girls I wasn't fucking. Fallon was the exception to the rule, and look where that had gotten me.

"Is that code for Netflix and Chill because—"

"Forget it," she rushed out, filling the awkward as fuck silence that had descended over us. "It doesn't matter. It was a dumb idea. Bye, Austin. Thanks for walking me back."

Madison went to leave, but before she could take a step, I grabbed her arm. "Wait."

"Yeah?" She looked at me with big, hopeful eyes.

Alarm bells started ringing in my head. This was a bad idea—the worst kind. But instead of telling her no, or letting her walk away, I found myself nodding.

"Okay, I can come up for a little bit."

CHAPTER 2

MADISON

Austin Hart was a tough nut to crack.

For a second, I thought I'd be walking back to Fawn's apartment with embarrassment and dejection nipping at my heels. But then he'd grabbed my arm and stopped me.

It was apparent the Lakers goalie was an intense guy. In our brief interaction, there had been a dark shadow in his eyes and a permanent frown tugging at his brows. But something about him made my tired, weary soul light up.

Somewhere during our flirty back and forth, I'd gotten a glimpse of the girl I used to be. Before life smacked me in the face and ripped the rug out from under my feet.

And I wanted to hold onto that.

Of course, Fawn and her college friends had been insistent on plying me with enough alcohol to even contemplate talking to the good-looking guy sitting all alone at the bar, hiding under his ball cap.

But she was right. I didn't get many opportunities to be the old Madi. Fun and carefree. A little bit reckless and wild.

As Austin and I walked side by side up to Fawn's apartment, I realized how nervous I was. I'd drawn a line in the sand when I'd declared that I wouldn't sleep with him, but it didn't stop me from imagining what it would be like to let go.

What would it be like to pretend for one night that I didn't have responsibilities and pressures that most twenty-one-year-olds would never have to deal with?

"I apologize in advance for the mess," I said. "We had drinks here before we headed out."

"I've spent the last three years living with a house full of guys. I don't think there's anything behind the door that will shock me."

"Fair point." I smiled, and his gaze dropped to my lips.

Did he want to kiss me?

God, I was so out of touch that I'd forgotten what it was like to have a guy's attention.

Fawn was right; I needed this.

I needed to remember I was still a person. I

needed to remember what it felt like to be desired, to feel my heart race in my chest and butterflies flutter in my stomach. But it had been so long that everything felt strange, unfamiliar, and a little awkward.

There was something about Austin, though.

Something that had made me invite him up before I could do the sensible thing and talk myself out of it.

He hadn't even given me his actual number, for God's sake. Not that I planned to ever call him beyond tonight.

No. This was a one-time thing.

Then, tomorrow, normal life would resume.

I unlocked the door, and Austin followed me inside. Thankfully, the place wasn't as messy as I remembered. Fawn must have cleaned up a little before we left.

"Nice place," he said as I kicked off my heels and made a beeline for the kitchenette.

"Drink?" I asked. "She doesn't have beer, but there's some leftover vodka or tequila."

"I'll have a water, thanks."

"Water it is." I grabbed two bottles and joined him on the couch. "Do you want something to eat? I'm sure she has some chips lying around, or I can make—"

"I'm good."

An awkward silence filled the room, making the butterflies in my stomach beat harder.

I glanced over at Austin, and he looked as uncomfortable as I felt.

"Why does this feel so weird?" I said, and his mouth twitched.

"I can go." He got up, but I blurted out, "Please, stay."

"I'm not sure—"

"I didn't mean stay the night or anything. God, I'm not usually this awkward." I ran a hand through my hair. "I just don't get out much, and I definitely don't meet hot guys anymore."

"You think I'm hot?" Amusement danced in his eyes as his lips curved with a panty-melting smirk.

"Did I say that aloud?"

"I think you did."

"My mistake." I grinned.

"So Madison..."

"Reynolds. Madison Reynolds." I offered him my full name.

"If you're not a student at LU, what do you do?"

"I work."

"Okay... but *what* do you do?"

"Sorry, I'm being vague." I let out a small huff of frustration. "It's just, I have a lot of family stuff I'm dealing with."

"I get it."

"You do?" My brows furrowed.

"More than you know."

Austin gave nothing away, but I saw the flash of pain in his eyes. Whatever it was, he had baggage too.

I didn't push him to explain, though, because that would leave me wide open to his questions.

Questions I wouldn't be able to answer.

"Why did you give me the wrong number back at the bar?" The words were out before I could stop myself.

"I don't make a habit of giving my number out to strangers." He studied me, the intensity in his eyes stealing my breath. "Even one as pretty as you."

"I'm not sleeping with you," I reiterated, trying to remember why that was my rule.

Austin reached for my hand, tugging me up to my feet. "I'm not asking you to. But there's plenty of fun we can have that doesn't involve me getting inside you."

Holy crap.

Heat fired off around my body, places inside me, clenching violently at his dirty words. I couldn't remember the last time a man had talked to me so brazenly.

I liked it.

I liked it far more than I should have.

"Or I can leave, and you never have to see me—"

"A. I choose option A." Tingles broke out over my skin as I stared up at him.

Austin glided his hand along my jaw before

slipping it around my neck and holding me there, massaging gently.

God, it felt good.

So good a small whimper caught in my throat.

"I didn't plan on doing this," his voice dropped an octave, "but I'd be lying if I said I can't wait to taste you."

His mouth came down on mine, hard and demanding. The roughness of his kiss was at odds with the softness in his voice, but it only doubled his sex appeal.

Austin Hart was clearly a master in the art of seduction, and I was all too happy to fall prey to his tactics.

His tongue licked the seam of my lips, teasing little flicks that coaxed me to open for him. He slipped inside, and another whimper crawled up my throat.

Jesus. I was already a puddle, and he'd barely touched me yet.

"Fuck, you're hot," he murmured between kisses.

I'd forgotten how good this could feel. How addictive.

"Can I touch you?" he paused to ask, and there was something so fucking sexy about the fact he was asking my permission.

"If you don't touch me," I breathed, "I'll never forgive you."

Another one of those gorgeous smirks tugged at his

mouth as his hands found the loose material of my blouse, pulling it out of my jeans. His fingers dipped underneath, sliding up my stomach, making my breath hitch. I almost pulled away, a stab of self-consciousness going through me.

It had been so long...

But Austin didn't stop there, going higher and higher until he cupped my breast, toying with my nipple through the thin lace, and all the doubts evaporated out of my mind.

"God, that feels good," I rasped, everything tightening inside me.

He chuckled, nuzzling my shoulder. "I've barely touched you yet."

"Like I said, it's been a while."

He pulled back, his brows pulled into a deep frown. "You're not a virgin, are you?" The expression on his face was so serious I smothered a laugh.

"No, I'm not a virgin."

"Thank fuck for that." He got back to kissing and licking his way along my collarbone.

"Good to know where you stand on the whole virgin thing tho— Ah," I cried when his teeth grazed the sensitive skin beneath my ear.

"Feel good?"

"Mm-hmm."

"Let's get you out of this." Austin had my blouse

unbuttoned and off my shoulders before I could think about how far I was willing to let this go.

Sex was off the table. But I didn't want to stop yet. I wanted… God, I never wanted to stop.

"You, too," I said. "I want to see you, too."

Austin flashed me a smug grin as he pulled off his ball cap and stepped back to tug off his hoodie and t-shirt in one.

His body was utter perfection. Inches upon inches of smooth skin stretched taut over packed muscle, all hard lines and cut angles. I'd clearly not been paying enough attention where hockey was concerned because holy hotness.

"Jesus," I murmured, my throat a little dry.

They didn't make guys who looked like this where I came from. He was so fucking gorgeous.

"I like you looking at me like that," he drawled, and I snapped out of my trance.

"Like what?"

"Like you want to eat me all up."

Another bolt of lust went through me as I pressed my thighs together.

"You want to move this to the bedroom?" he asked.

Yes, would have been the right answer. Fawn could return at any moment. But if I took him to the guest room, I didn't trust myself not to jump his bones.

And sex wasn't in the cards.

At least, that's what I kept telling myself as I

drowned in abs and biceps and that sexy deep-cut V running down either side of his hips.

"You have a little drool." His laughter made my heart flutter.

"I do not." I scowled, trying to regain the upper hand. But it was impossible.

I was starved, and he was a delicious snack laid out on the all-you-could-eat buffet.

"Come here." Curving his arm around my waist, Austin pulled me closer. He gazed down at me, and my heart went crazy in my chest. "There's something about you…"

He kissed me again. Laying siege to my mouth as his hand ran over my skin. His fingers moved lower, teasing the waistband of my jeans. Deftly, he popped the button and gently eased down the zipper.

And I let him.

A little foreplay wouldn't hurt. So long as I kept a level head and didn't end up under him.

No sex. I repeated those two little words over and over in my head, but it became increasingly difficult to focus as he stroked me through my damp panties.

"More," I breathed, giving him permission.

A faint smile traced his mouth; then he was kissing me again. Devouring me with his teeth and tongue as he hooked my underwear to the side and pressed two fingers inside me.

It felt so good. The slow curl of his fingers,

stretching me, and the way his thumb played my clit in small precise circles.

"Oh God," I cried, so deliciously overwhelmed at the feel of him there. "Don't stop."

"Didn't plan on it." He chuckled, finding a rhythm that made my legs quiver and shake.

My gaze flicked over his shoulder to the door. Fawn could come back at any moment. Maybe I should—

"Ah." Air punched from my lungs as Austin upped the pace, and I tumbled headfirst into a riot of sensations.

"You going to come for me, pretty girl?" he rasped in my ear before grazing my lobe with his teeth.

"I'm close," I murmured, clutching onto his arm, pressing my face into his shoulder.

He was so freaking good at this. Or maybe it had just been that long I'd forgotten how it was supposed to feel.

Nope.

Pretty sure Austin Hart knew his way around the female body.

I shut down those thoughts, though. Thinking about him with other girls while he had his fingers inside me was definitely enough to ruin the mood.

And I was too close to lose it now, burning from the inside out.

My hips rocked against his hand, searching for more friction. More everything.

"Mmm, needy little thing, aren't you?" Austin cupped my face and kissed me hard, invading all my senses.

"Yes... *Yes.*"

His thumb pressed down on my clit, and pleasure splintered through me.

Holy shit.

It was intense, standing here, in my friend's apartment, with a stranger's hands all over me.

Except, Austin didn't feel like a stranger.

I shook off the strange thought and inhaled a steady breath. "That was... Thank you."

"You know, you could show me how grateful you are." He smirked, and despite coming only seconds ago, it did something to me. Tightening and twisting some part deep inside me that made me grow a little lightheaded.

"Maybe I will," I sassed, dropping my heavy-lidded gaze to the obvious bulge in his jeans.

"No pressure," he added, but I sank to my knees, returning his smirk.

"Fair turnabout and all that."

His gruff laughter rumbled through me, heating my blood again.

I liked him.

I liked the way he didn't treat me like glass but didn't treat me like dirt, either. It was transactional, sure. But there was no reason it couldn't be a mutually satisfying transaction.

A night I wouldn't forget in a hurry.

My heart galloped in my chest as I tucked my fingers into the waistband of his jeans and inched them down. Austin buried one of his hands in the back of my hair, winding it around his fist, but he didn't wrest control. Instead, he waited, letting me take my time and find my stride. It had been a while, and it probably showed as I hesitantly leaned in, flicking my tongue over his crown, teasing and tasting.

"Fuck," he hissed, his fingers tightening in my hair.

I smiled, remembering how good it felt to have a big, strong guy at your mercy.

Wrapping my hand around his shaft, I took him into my mouth, dragging my tongue along the underside. He tasted salty and a little bitter, but I liked it.

I wanted more.

I wanted everything he was willing to give me.

Except sex.

I couldn't go there.

Because something told me if I did, I'd want so much more than one night.

And that simply wasn't an option.

"Shit, what time is it?"

"W-what?" I cracked open an eye, trying to get my bearings. "Uh, hi."

Heat crept into my cheeks at the sight of the Lakers U goalie lying beside me, looking every bit as gorgeous as he had last night.

"So... last night was..."

"Pretty wild." A faint smirk traced his mouth. "We must have fallen asleep."

Somewhere after the third or fourth orgasm, I suspected.

Jesus. The things I'd let him do to my body.

He'd kissed, touched, and tasted every inch of me, and not once had he tried to sleep with me. Although, I guess technically, we had slept together.

"Yeah. Sorry about that." I untangled myself from his arm and sat up, clasping the sheet around my body. "I..."

"Hey, this doesn't need to be awkward," he said, throwing his legs over the side of the bed. "I had fun, and I'm pretty sure you did, too. It doesn't need to be any more complicated than that."

"Right. Good. That's... good." Silence filled the space between us, but weirdly, it didn't feel awkward.

It was heavy, though. Thick with expectation and something I didn't want to acknowledge.

"Do you want coffee or—"

"No," he said, quick enough that my stomach dipped. "I should probably get going."

"Of course."

He made quick work of locating all his clothes and getting dressed. At some point after orgasm number one, we'd moved things into the bedroom to avoid an awkward scene with Fawn when she got home.

I could only imagine what she was going to say about this.

"I'm going to—" Austin thumbed to the small en suite bathroom, and I nodded.

The second he disappeared inside, I leaped out of bed and pulled on some lounge pants and a tank. By the time he reappeared, I looked somewhat awake and composed.

"So, I guess this is goodbye," I said as he moved to the door.

"I guess it is." He lingered, and for a second, I thought he might say something else.

And for a second, I wanted him to.

But he was a college student. A hockey player, no less.

Our worlds couldn't be further apart.

So, no matter how much I wanted to ask him for his *real* number, I didn't.

Because once he discovered the truth about me, Austin Hart would run in the other direction and never look back.

CHAPTER 3

AUSTIN

I LEFT Madison feeling lighter than I had in months.

And I hadn't even fucked her.

Sure, we'd done pretty much everything except have sex, but after she drew that line in the sand, I was determined not to go there.

Besides, something told me if I had, I'd want to break all my own rules to go there again and again. Because, holy shit, she was something else.

"Austin," someone called, and for a second, I thought it might be Madison chasing after me.

So color me fucking confused when I spotted Connor's girlfriend, Ella, waving at me across the way.

"El?" I paled as I remembered her building was right next door.

Shit.

"What are you doing here?" Her brows crinkled as her curious gaze darted from me to the building I'd just come from.

"I… Fuck." I ran a hand down the back of my neck, looking anywhere but at her.

She gave me a soft, knowing smile but, to my relief, changed the subject. "I'm heading in to see Connor."

"How is he?"

"I wish I knew. His replies this morning have been mostly one or two words." Worry bled into her expression. "The doctor should be around soon with his results."

"He'll be okay," I said.

"Yeah. Well, I should probably go." She thumbed toward her car. "See you soon."

"Tell Morgan…" I hesitated because nothing I could say or do would fix this. But I felt compelled to say something. "Just tell him I said hi."

She gave me a small nod, waving as she headed to her car.

It felt like a lucky escape, but I didn't doubt she had questions about where I was coming from and would probably tell Connor the second he was up to it.

As far as I was concerned, though, there was nothing to tell.

It was fun. Madison had been great. Eager and

willing and so fucking hot, she'd blown my mind —twice.

But that's as far as it went.

I didn't need any distractions, and she had *distraction* written all over her.

It's why I hadn't offered up my correct phone number before I left. Not that she tried to give me hers, either.

It was better this way.

After Fallon, I didn't need any more complications of the female variety.

I needed to focus on hockey. On getting through the rest of my senior year and graduating, and then figuring out what the hell I was going to do with my life.

Everything else was just white noise.

"Austin, it's me," Rory called.

"In here."

She appeared a few seconds later, cheeks flushed from the cold. "I brought brunch." A brown paper bag I recognized from a local coffee shop dangled from her fingers.

"Nice, thanks."

She moved around the kitchen with the ease of

someone who had once lived here, pulling two plates out of the cabinet and placing the bagels onto them.

"Ham, egg, and cheese. Your favorite." She slid it across the counter to me.

"Thanks."

Shit, this was awkward.

Since she'd started at LU, the time we spent together, alone, was minimal. But every time we did, an overwhelming sense of guilt flooded me.

Aurora was my little sister, and I'd let her down.

I'd failed her so fucking much that I was surprised she could even look at me.

"What's wrong with it?" Rory asked, noting the untouched bagel.

"Nothing." I tried to snap out of it, but it was hard.

Being around her was a reminder of how shitty our childhoods had been.

I'd abandoned her. I hadn't seen her cries for help because I was so wrapped up in my own anger and resentment. I spent my teenage years believing our mom loved her more and that she was the favorite. I didn't know...

I didn't—

"Have you given it any more thought?" she asked, and I stared at her. "Christmas with Mason, his mom, and Scottie?"

"Oh, that," I said. "I'm not coming."

Her expression fell, and I felt like a giant shit. But surely she didn't expect me to say yes.

"Austin, please. It's our first Christmas together in a long time. I'd really like it if—"

"I can't, I'm sorry."

"I see." Her mouth twisted as she ate the rest of her bagel. But I felt her frustration in every bite, with every chew and swallow as she watched me.

Rory was pissed at me, but no more than I was pissed at myself.

"Come on, Sis." I tried to lighten the mood. "You wouldn't want me there anyway, playing the fifth wheel."

"Don't do that." The quiver in her voice fucking gutted me. "Don't act like this is funny. You're my brother, Austin. I don't want you to be alone for Christmas."

She didn't get it.

She didn't get that being there with her and Noah, and Mason and Harper would only remind me of how fucked up I was.

She'd found her happily ever after. Despite what Mom had put her through, despite all the heartache and pain, the years of trauma that led to her developing an eating disorder, Rory had found happiness. Something I would never resent her for. But it didn't stop me wondering how she'd done it.

How she'd trusted Noah to care for her heart after

everyone around her—myself included—had let her down.

Fuck.

I dragged a hand back and forth through my hair, the tension between us turning so thick and heavy that I wanted to make an excuse and leave.

To escape.

I didn't do this—I didn't sit around and talk about my feelings.

I couldn't.

"So I heard you ended things with Fallon?" Rory peeked over at me.

"Yeah, so?"

"I don't know, I just thought maybe…" She trailed off, letting out a weary sigh. "It doesn't matter."

"Look, I appreciate you coming over here, bringing me breakfast, I do. But you don't need to coddle me, Rory. I can look after myself."

Hurt flashed in her eyes. "Is that what you think I'm doing? Coddling you?"

"Aren't you? Just because you're with Noah now, and everyone else is shacked up together, doesn't mean—"

The blare of her cell phone cut through the room, and I was relieved. I was so fucking relieved for the distraction.

She dug it out of her purse and hesitated.

"Let me guess, Holden."

It wasn't a question. I could tell it was Noah by her expression. That flicker of longing in her eyes. Complete adoration.

"I'll text and tell him—"

"You should answer it. I have shit to be doing anyway." I started to walk away, but she called after me, "Austin, wait."

"Yeah?" I looked back at her.

"Just think about it. Christmas, I mean. I'd really like it if you came. We all would."

I gave her a noncommittal nod. But we both knew the truth.

Come Christmas Day, they would be in Pittsburgh celebrating, and I'd be in Lakeshore.

Alone.

Just how I liked it.

Two days later, my mood hit rock bottom.

I couldn't step outside the house without being reminded that Christmas was right around the corner.

Lakeshore had become holiday central, and there wasn't a store window or house not covered in mistletoe or holly. So even though I'd decided not to join Rory and Noah when they visited Mason and his family on Christmas Day, there was no escaping the festive season.

No matter how much I wanted to.

I had a rocky relationship with the holidays. It was a time to celebrate with family. To give thanks and reflect. But a childhood full of shitty Thanksgivings, Christmases, and birthdays, meant I would much rather let them pass me by with as little thought as possible.

Rory was disappointed I'd turned them down, I knew that. But I didn't want to play the fifth wheel. And the truth was, there was still too much left unsaid between us: wrongs I needed to right and truths I needed to come to terms with.

Part of me wondered if our mother had tried to contact her, but I didn't ask. That was one call or visit I would avoid at all costs.

Susannah Hart might have wanted to smooth things over with her daughter, but she had never been interested in fixing things with me.

My feelings about the holidays didn't stop me from venturing downtown to buy my sister a gift, though. Except the minute I walked into the store, I realized I had no idea what to get her.

"Can I help you?" the assistant asked as I browsed the displays.

"I'm just looking, tha— You," I said, coming face-to-face with Madison and another girl.

"Austin." Her gaze darted to her friend, and I could sense her surprise.

Maybe even a little bit of panic.

"I'm going to leave you two to... talk." The friend gave Madison a calculated smirk, and she murmured something under her breath.

"Don't mind Fawn," she added, a slight flush to her cheeks.

Ah, the friend who lived in the building next to Ella.

"I won't," I said. "I didn't expect to see you here."

"You shop for ethically made soaps and shampoos a lot?" Amusement danced in her eyes.

"I'm hoping to pick up some gifts."

"For your... Mom? Aunt? Or the girlfriend you didn't tell me about?" I frowned, and her expression dropped. "Shit, I don't know why I said that. It's none of my business if you—"

"Relax." I let out a strained chuckle. "I don't have a girlfriend."

But I didn't know how to feel about the fact she'd brought it up.

Any other time, I would have run a mile. But I kind of liked the words coming from her mouth.

Even if I'd never planned on seeing her again.

"Oh, thank God," Madison sighed.

"You're still in town?"

"Oh, yeah. Only until tomorrow, though. I have to get back home then."

"Well, I should probably leave you to your shopping."

"Yeah." She glanced at Fawn, who was busy pretending to look at one of the soap displays. Fawn gave her an obvious as fuck head nudge toward me, and I fought a smirk. "Unless you want to hang out tonight?" she blurted.

"Hang out?"

"Yeah, we could get a drink or some food." Her cheeks flushed. "If you have plans, then it doesn't—"

"I don't."

"Okay, good. That's good. So where do you want to meet?"

"Same bar as the other night?"

It was discreet. On the edge of town. There was little to no likelihood of running into anyone from or associated with the team, especially since a lot of people had already left for winter break.

And why the fuck was I even entertaining the idea of meeting her again?

But before I could find a way out of it, I had my cell phone out, and we'd exchanged numbers—*real* numbers.

Fuck me. Madison had worked some voodoo magic shit on me because it was hard to believe what had just happened.

I'd been so adamant that she was a distraction—one I needed to avoid at all costs. But I also knew how sweet she tasted. The tiny little whimpering noises she made, the way she cried my name when she came.

How could I pass up the chance to get my hands on her again?

The answer was: I couldn't.

She was only in town for another night. And I had no plans, given that one of my best friends was boning my sister, and my other best friend was laid up in the hospital, his future hanging in the balance.

Damn.

When I put it like that, maybe Madison was exactly the kind of distraction I needed.

"Austin." Madison waved me over. She'd already gotten comfortable in a booth at the back of the bar, which was fine by me; the less prying eyes, the better.

I ordered a beer and made my way over.

"You came." She smiled.

"You thought I wouldn't?"

Madison gave me a half-shrug. "You did give me a wrong number the first time. Honestly, I didn't know what to think."

"I guess I deserve that. But being a Laker isn't

always straightforward. I've had to change my number twice since freshman year."

"For real?"

"Yeah. One of the senior players thought it would be funny to attach my number to a tutoring advert. Once people"—mainly girls—"found out it was me, I was bombarded with calls and texts."

"So you're kind of a big deal on campus."

"Is that a trick question?"

"What do you mean?" Her eyes crinkled.

"Your friend goes to LU, right? She knows—"

"Fine. You got me." Madison fought a smile. "I've heard the stories."

"Should I be worried?"

"Actually, I think it's kind of perfect. Neither of us is looking for anything serious, and I'm not a puck bunny, so you can rest assured I won't be blowing up your phone every two minutes."

Her words should have comforted me, but a strange pang of disappointment went through me.

"By the way, I'm still not sleeping with you." Madison took a sip of her beer and clinked it against mine. "So don't get any ideas."

"I think we discovered the other night that I don't need to be inside you to make you scream my name."

Her breath caught, and a slow smirk tugged at my lips.

God, she was so fucking beautiful. I'd hooked up

with Fallon for months, but I'd never once looked at her and felt my heart tumble into overdrive.

What the fuck was that about?

The guys constantly joked that they couldn't wait for me to get knocked on my ass by the right girl. And I wasn't saying Madison was the one or anything—I didn't believe in any of that bullshit—but she did make me feel things.

Things I didn't want to look too closely at.

Still, I knew the deal.

Fun.

She wanted a bit of fun while she was in town, and after the other night, I just so happened to like her brand of fun.

Even if sex was off the table.

"You just say it how it is, don't you?" She studied me with those soulful blue eyes of hers.

"No point beating around the bush." I shrugged.

"I feel like I should be mildly offended that you think I'm such a sure thing... but oddly, I'm not. I needed the other night."

"Happy to be of service." I chuckled, taking a long pull on my beer.

"How's your friend, the one who got injured?"

"He's going to be okay, but it's looking like he'll be out for the rest of the season."

Ella had texted us earlier to say it wasn't good news.

Connor needed the surgery, which meant a long and painful recovery.

"That sucks."

"More than you know."

"Do you have any plans for the holidays?" she asked.

"Nope. I'm more of a Fred Claus type than Nick."

"I love that movie. I'm a huge Vince Vaughn fan."

"Let me guess, you love Christmas."

"I don't hate it." A faint smile traced her lips. "But it's different now."

"Different, how?"

"Oh, you know. We're older. Fewer gifts." Her smile didn't reach her eyes, a shadow there that wasn't before, and I wondered what secrets Madison kept.

After all, we all had them.

Some were darker than others.

"Will you stay in Lakeshore or go home?" she added.

"I'm staying."

Something passed over her expression, but I didn't look too closely. No matter how at ease with her I felt, how much the chemistry fizzed and crackled between us, burning away some of the ice around my heart, it wasn't headed anywhere. I didn't have the capacity to let someone into my life like that.

Sometimes, I wondered if something inside me was broken, damaged beyond repair, all thanks to a mother more concerned with her modeling career than her children and a father who just didn't care enough to stick around.

I loved my sister. I loved my teammates and the team, but it wasn't the kind of love that consumed you. The kind of love I'd witnessed my friends all fall prey to over the last few months.

I didn't believe in *that* kind of love.

It's why I'd walked away from Fallon before things got too messy. She started to talk about the future, and I knew my future didn't include her. It was only fair to cut her loose.

Maybe that made me a bastard, but it's better to be honest than a liar.

But Madison was different. She was a nice distraction. One who didn't only want a bit of fun with me because I was a Laker.

It was a refreshing change.

One I'd enjoyed far more than I anticipated.

"Then I guess that's lucky for me. To us." Lifting her beer, she waited. I matched her movement, and our bottles clinked together.

"To us."

"Oops." Madison tripped as we stumbled out of the bar sometime later, but I caught her right before she went down.

We drank and talked and drank some more. It was the most fun I'd had with a girl in a long time: no expectations or ulterior motives. Just two people enjoying a beer and a good conversation.

We'd even watched some of the NHL highlights, and I'd tried—a*nd failed*—to teach her the rules of hockey.

But all good things came to an end, and now the air had shifted between us.

"My hero." She grinned, gazing up at me through slightly hooded eyes.

"You good there, pretty girl?"

"I'm fine." She hiccoughed. "Okay, maybe I'm a tad drunk. But I had fun tonight."

"That was the deal, wasn't it?"

"So it was."

Madison laced her arm through mine as we walked toward her friend's building. "I think Fawn's home tonight," she said.

"Is that your way of telling me I'm not welcome back at her place?"

"It would be kind of awkward." She peeked up, her lips pressed into a cute smile.

"I'd invite you to mine, but..."

"You can't." Her smile dropped.

"I guess this is where we say goodbye then." Disappointment welled inside me.

Fuck.

Why hadn't I thought this far ahead? But there was no way I could take her back to the house and risk us getting caught by one of the guys or, worse, one of the girls.

"Maybe I can visit again over the holidays," she said, insinuation heavy in her words.

Tension sizzled between us. Like the other night, I didn't want to say goodbye yet, and if I was reading the glint in Madison's eyes right, neither did she.

Scanning the street, I spotted a dark alley between two buildings and tugged her toward it.

"Austin, what are you— Oh," she huffed out as I pushed her up against the wall.

"I wanted to kiss you goodnight." I toyed with the ends of her hair, staring down at her with a kind of possessiveness I wasn't used to feeling.

Shit. I was in over my head here.

"And you couldn't do that outside Fawn's building?"

I brushed my thumb along her jaw, reveling in the way she shuddered, and leaned in to whisper, "Not the way I plan on kissing you."

CHAPTER 4

MADISON

Austin Hart was dangerous.

I realized that now. My heart was pounding in my chest as he stared down at me, his thumb caressing my jaw.

Part of me was sorely disappointed there would be no fooling around at Fawn's place or his. But the other part—the part I couldn't afford to lose—was a little bit relieved.

Because I suspected another night with him would blur the lines of our arrangement.

Fun.

It was just a bit of fun.

So why did I feel all giddy at his touch?

"Why aren't you kissing me yet?" I said, my chest rising as I inhaled a shaky breath.

He crooked a grin and lowered his head, taking his time to brush his lips over mine. A slow tease that had my toes curling in my boots.

God, the guy could kiss. I didn't want to think about how he'd perfected his technique—the long line of puck bunnies before me. I only wanted to think about him and me and the way he made me feel.

Our tongues slicked together, Austin's body pressed up against mine in the most delicious way. I slid my hands under his hoodie, unable to resist mapping his warm skin. The impressive slab of muscle I knew lay beneath.

His body was a work of art, one I was all too happy to discover.

"Fuck," he breathed. "That feels good." A smile tugged at my mouth as he touched his head to mine. "But now I have all kinds of ideas, and this is where we say goodbye, remember." He gave me a playful smirk.

"I really wish Fawn wasn't home right now," I murmured, desire pulsing through me.

"Too bad."

A beat passed, the air thick and heavy as the air stretched taut between us.

Then snapped.

We crashed together, all lips and hands, grabbing

and touching. His kiss consumed me, made me feel alive and like me again.

The me *before*.

Beautiful and confident and worthy.

If nothing more ever came of this moment, I would forever be grateful to Austin for giving me back a piece of myself.

"You are so fucking sexy," he rasped between kisses trailing his mouth up and down my throat.

It didn't matter that we were in some dark alley, hidden in the shadows like a dirty secret. Or that we'd both laid out our intentions for this to be nothing more than a bit of fun.

"All I can think about is making you come again."

"Yes," I whispered. "God, yes."

Austin didn't wait. He found the waistband of my thick leggings and pushed his hand inside.

"We should—"

"Shh. I got you." He licked the seam of my mouth, angling his body so that anyone looking down the alley would see his back and not me, arching into his touch.

His fingers found their target, and he thrust two inside me.

"Austin," I gasped, pressing my lips together and trapping the moan building in my throat as he curled them deep.

His thumb passed over my clit, again and again, and I clutched his arm, my head falling back against the cold brick wall. I'd never done anything like this. Not in public. Not with a guy I barely knew.

But there was beauty in that, in living and embracing the moment in taking something for me and only me.

When you had the kind of responsibilities I had, when you carried the type of weight on your shoulders I did, it was hard to let go.

But Austin did that.

He made me soar.

"God, it feels so good," I murmured, my fingers drifting to the hair at the back of his neck. His dark, hooded eyes found mine, and I smiled. "Kiss me."

He did. Hard and bruising as if he couldn't get enough.

And when I came, trembling against him, he held me tight and dropped a kiss on my head, and for a second, I imagined that this wasn't temporary. That maybe he could be the guy I leaned on.

But he didn't know everything about me, and if I told him...

No.

I couldn't trust him with that.

"We should probably go," I said as soon as the feeling had returned to my legs. He gave me an indecipherable nod, but I felt the wall go up between us.

Did he feel it, too? The inexplicable connection

between us? The connection neither of us would acknowledge, let alone act on.

"Yeah," he murmured, a hint of something in his voice.

Regret?

Shame?

I didn't regret it.

I wouldn't want everyone to know what I got up to in the dark with Austin, but I wasn't ashamed either.

Thick silence enveloped us as we stepped out of the alley and continued down the road toward Fawn's building.

It was on the tip of my tongue to ask what he was thinking, but I swallowed the words.

Some things were better left unsaid.

And I wasn't under any illusions that this was the start of my happily ever after.

"So... how did it go?" Fawn asked me the second I slipped onto her apartment.

I'd been hoping she might have already gone to bed, but I should have known better.

She was heavily invested in my love life, or more specifically, my sex life.

"It was... nice."

"Nice?" Her expression betrayed her voice. "You went on a date with the infamous Austin Hart, and you're telling me it was just nice?"

"First of all, it wasn't a date. And second of all, I'm not talking with you about this."

"Oh shit." Her eyes almost bugged. "You like him." She practically jumped over the back of the couch. "You actually like the guy."

"No more than I like you or Jeremiah."

"Damn, Madi, you weren't meant to catch feelings for the guy. He's supposed to be your chance at getting back on the horse." She gave me a sympathetic smile, but it felt a lot like pity.

I winced. "Don't do that. Don't look at me like you feel bad for me."

"I do feel bad for you." She scoffed. "It's been almost five years, and the only action your lady garden has seen is at your gynecologist appointment."

"Bitch," I snapped. "You know it isn't that easy."

"So, your life didn't turn out the way you thought. It doesn't mean you have to stop having some fun occasionally."

"I have fun."

"Going to Lemonade with Jer every other month does not count."

"I like Lemonade," I huffed.

"You would because it's full of gay men, and no one is interested in hitting on you."

She had a point. In the two years Jeremiah had been dragging me to his favorite bar, Lemonade, I had never been hit on. It felt safe there. Safe with Jeremiah and his man of the moment and their friends.

But Fawn was right; it had been almost five years.

I'd had no dates. No casual hookups.

No sex.

Nothing until I let Fawn, and her college friends talk me into approaching the hockey hottie at the bar the other night.

My vagina was a frozen-over wasteland occasionally brought back to life by my battery-operated friend. Until the gorgeous hockey player who had teased and tasted every inch of me but respected my boundaries without question.

"I just think you deserve some good D."

"Good D, seriously?" I almost choked on the words. How could I not? She was such an idiot.

"At least tell me you're seeing him again?"

"Maybe." I shrugged. "He's staying in Lakeshore for the holidays. And if Jacqueline and Ken get their way, I'll have some free time."

Her expression turned somber at the wobble in my voice. "You know they only want to help."

"I know... It's just hard."

"So this is perfect. Austin can be your distraction, and I'll give you my key so you can use my apartment while I'm gone. You know, *if* you finally decide to dust off your vagina."

"Fawn! Oh my God."

"Made you laugh though, didn't I?" She chuckled, making her way over to me. "You deserve good things, Mads."

"It can never be anything more…"

"And that's okay, babe. Sex doesn't have to be a committed, long-lasting relationship. You tried that, and look where it got you, babe. Shit, I didn't mean—"

"I know what you meant." My mouth twitched even though my heart ached. "Fine. I'll take your key. But only if you don't mind."

"Mind? I'm freaking ecstatic for you. Madi's going to get the D," she sang. "She's going to get dicked down real good."

"I hate you right now."

"No, you don't." A grin played on her lips. "You love me."

"Yeah, I do."

"Just remember the cardinal rule. This is about sex. Don't make it complicated, and whatever you do"—she gave me a stern look—"don't fall for the guy."

Fawn's words rang through my head as I lay in her guest bed, staring up at the ceiling.

She was right. Of course, she was.

But I couldn't stop thinking about what happened in that alley. The sheer possessiveness and desperation in Austin's touch. The way he'd pulled me off the sidewalk and into the shadows as if he had to get his hands on me that instant.

That feeling was addictive. I remembered how good those early days could feel, where everything was fun and easy, exciting and wild.

It was what came after that was the problem. When the novelty wore off and the excitement dulled.

Texting him should have been the last thing on my mind, but still, I found myself reaching for my cell phone.

Madison: So funny story… Fawn said I can have the key to her place over the holidays.

I hesitated. It was a bad idea. The worst. But if I ended up home alone over the holidays, that wouldn't be fun either.

I would need a distraction.

And Austin was very good at that.

Before I could talk myself out of it, I hit send and gnawed my bottom lip as I waited to see if he would reply.

My phone bleeped, and I almost jumped out of my skin with excitement.

God, I was pathetic.

> Austin: That's very accommodating of her.

>> Madison: I thought so. Maybe we can hang out again if you can fit me into your busy schedule. I know how much you love the holidays, after all.

> Austin: I might be decorating Christmas cookies or out making snow angels, but I can probably squeeze you in. When's good?

>> Madison: I'll have to let you know. I need to figure out things with work first.

The lie came easily enough, but it didn't feel good. But I could keep the two parts of my life separate. Here, when I visited Lakeshore, I could be the fun, sexy Madison. Austin didn't need to know about the other side of me.

He probably wouldn't like her anyway.

I shut down the little voice whispering cruel, spiteful things in my ear. I was proud of the young woman I'd become. All I'd endured and continued to endure. And I loved my life; I did.

But it didn't mean I didn't yearn for things.

Things I knew would never come easily for me.

Austin: Just let me know. I liked
hanging out with you tonight.

I smiled, feeling all giddy inside.

Don't run away with yourself, Madi. It's a bit of fun, remember? FUN.

Madison: I liked it too. Night Austin. xo

Austin: Night, pretty girl.

For the first time in a long while, I fell asleep with a smile.

"Wake up, wake up, sweepy head."

The bed shook beneath me as I peeled my eyes open. "Imogen Grace." I smiled. "What are you doing here?"

"Grammy Cara and Pops said we coulds surprise you."

"They did, huh?" I wrestled the four-year-old ball of energy off me and sat up. "Well, I'm definitely surprised."

She smiled at me, her little dimples making my heart flutter. "I missed yous, Mommy."

"I missed you too, baby girl. Come up here." I held open my arms, and she dove into them, smushing her face against me and wrapping her little pudgy arms around my neck.

I hadn't seen her in four days, hadn't held her or breathed in her cute little toddler smell.

I thought I knew love until the bundle of sunshine curls came along and stole my heart, and I realized everything I thought was a lie.

Imogen Grace was my whole world, and I hated being apart from her. But my parents had insisted on taking her on their annual trip to Frankenmuth, and they'd insisted I take a trip to see Fawn.

The opportunity didn't arise enough for me to turn it down, but now my daughter was back in my arms, clinging onto me like she hadn't seen me in years and the mom guilt set in.

"Did you have fun with Grammy and Pops?" I gently nudged her out of my neck. She nodded, her big blue eyes full of wonder and innocence.

"I wiked the Christmas store."

"I bet you did, baby. And do you know, I think you've grown. Look at you; you've gotten so big."

"Don't be silly, Mommy. I was only gone for four days. I didn't grows any."

"Oh, I think you did. You must have grown at least an inch or two, just like a sunflower."

"Silly, Mommy." She giggled. "People don't grows wike sunflowers."

"Sure, they do. Give them enough love and hugs and tickles." I grabbed her waist and started tickling.

"No, no, not the ticky monster."

Her laughter rang out through the room, and I smiled to myself.

I was a twenty-one-year-old single mom working two jobs just to make ends meet. I'd done a lot of things I wasn't proud of. But Imogen was the one good thing in my life. My biggest achievement and greatest joy all rolled into one. Even when things hadn't been easy with her father, she was the light of my life.

I smothered her with kisses, tickling her until she shrieked and writhed with laughter. A second later, a knock at the door came, and my mom poked her head inside.

"Sorry for the unexpected visit." She gave me a smile, but I saw the strain there. "She was desperate to see you."

"It's okay. Come on, you." I plucked Imogen into my arms and climbed off the bed with her wrapped around me like a tiny spider monkey. "Let's go see Pops. I bet he's thrilled you guys had to drive to Lakeshore." I shot Mom a withering smile, and she rolled her eyes.

My parents were a godsend where Imogen was concerned, and they loved her dearly, but Mom had struggled to let me forget my teenage mistake.

I was their daughter. Full of hopes and dreams, and, in their eyes, I'd thrown it all away when I'd fallen in love with the wrong guy.

I was forever grateful for their help and support in raising Imogen, but things weren't the same between us as they once were.

"Fawny," Imogen sang as we joined her and my father in the living room.

"Hi, Princess Immy. You got some hugs for me?" Fawn held out her arms, and I put Imogen down. She skipped toward my best friend, and Fawn scooped her up. "You hungry?"

"I wike pancakes."

"Sure thing, princess. Pancakes it is."

"How was the trip?" I asked my parents.

"Good. Immy was a dream. Asked for you a lot, but we kept her busy," Dad said.

"Jacqueline called," Mom added. "They want to take her over the holidays. You know, Madi, you don't have to agree."

"They're her grandparents too, Mom." I glanced over at Fawn and Immy mixing the batter and smiled. "She loves spending time with them."

And I needed to keep them on my side in case their son ever decided to show up again.

"Yeah." She let out a weary sigh. "I know. It's just hard watching you send her to his family after everything."

"I know, Mom, but I won't punish them for his actions."

She gave me a begrudging nod. "Anyway, how was your long weekend? Did you enjoy some time with Fawn and her friends? I hope you didn't party too hard."

Her words struck my heart. Even now, even after raising Immy for the last four and half years—four of those alone—she thought I was still the wild party girl from my past.

It hurt, but I locked it down.

"Nothing too crazy, Mom. We went for drinks on Saturday night. Had a pizza and movie night. It's been nice."

"That's good. You deserve some time occasionally. Just don't go getting too used to it." She laughed. They both did.

But I didn't laugh.

"I'm going to help Fawn and Immy with the pancakes." I brushed past her and made a beeline for my daughter.

CHAPTER 5

AUSTIN

Madison: How's Fred Claus today?

I smiled at her taunt and typed out a quick reply.

Austin: Hungry. Just making breakfast.

Madison: I've got a long shift at the coffee shop. Maybe you can keep me company with your festive humor?

Austin: I can try my best.

Madison didn't reply, so I dropped my phone on the counter and added milk to my cereal. I was almost done eating when the back door opened.

"Hey," Ella said as she let herself in.

"How is he?" I asked.

Connor had gotten the surgery a couple of days ago, and I'd heard from Noah that he was struggling with his new reality.

"I'm sure he's fine."

I frowned. "Are you okay?"

"I'll be fine." Her expression darkened, and it didn't escape me that she wouldn't look me in the eye.

"That's a whole lot of fine going on there." One of my brows lifted, and she let out a weary sigh, finally meeting my gaze.

"Mr. Morgan is a very difficult man."

"Are you sure it's a good idea for you to go stay with them?"

I'd heard that was the plan. I wasn't surprised Connor had let his old man talk him into going back to Dayton with them, but I was surprised he'd asked Ella to go, especially after how badly things had gone when he took her home for Thanksgiving.

"Connor wants me there." Ella shrugged.

"And I get it. I do, El. But it doesn't seem very fair to you."

She looked at me funny, studying me a little too hard. "You're in an awfully good mood."

"What? I can't ask how you're doing now?"

"No, that's not... Sorry, I'm just tired and cranky."

"Yeah, I'm fucking exhausted."

"Someone keep you up all night?" she teased, and my defenses went straight up.

I was a private person. I didn't fuck around and then divulge all the dirty details to my teammates, like some of the guys. My private life was just that—private. Even my best friends knew very little about that side of me. It was how I liked it.

Low-key and drama-free.

But apparently, Ella saw right through me, and that was a problem.

"Nah, I couldn't sleep. Bad dreams." I locked down my expression, hoping to give nothing else away.

There was no way in hell I was about to tell her I'd spent most of last night and the night before texting Madison.

"Well, I'm just going to grab a few things of Connor's to take with me." She headed for the staircase, but I called after her, feeling like a giant shit.

"I know I've been a miserable ass the last few months, but Connor is a good friend. If you need anything..."

"Thanks, Austin. I appreciate it." Ella took off toward the stairs, and I sent out a quick group text.

"Got everything?" I asked when she reappeared ten minutes later. Ella nodded, and I added, "Come on. I'll carry those out to your car."

Grabbing the bags off her, I made for the front

door, smiling when I saw the cavalry had already arrived.

"What is this?" Ella said, emotion coating her voice.

"We wanted to come and say bye."

"Guys"—she inhaled a shuddering breath—"we're not leaving forever."

"We know. But this whole thing is shit," Noah said. "And we wanted you to know that we're here for you, El. Always." He pulled her into a hug, setting off her emotions.

"I'm really going to miss you guys." Tears coasted down her cheeks.

"As soon as he feels up to it, just say the word, and we'll be there."

"His dad will love that," she murmured.

"Fuck his dad. Connor needs us. He needs you, El." Noah squeezed her arm before releasing her.

"Thank you." Ella dried her eyes with the back of her hands. "Whew. I didn't realize this would be so hard."

"You can do this, babe." Aiden's girlfriend, Dayna, pulled her in for a hug. "I'll text you every day."

"You don't need to do that."

"Hush. You're important, too, El." She kissed Ella's cheek, gently shoving her into Rory's arms.

"Dayna's right. We're all here for you." She nodded, pulling away.

"Okay, I'm going. I'll text when I get there."

"You'd better, Henshaw," Noah chuckled. "Or else."

"Drive safe," I said, and she gave me a half-smile, her gaze lingering long enough to make me shift on the spot uncomfortably.

The girls walked Ella to her car, and we stayed back, watching as Dayna opened the driver's door. "We're only a phone call away," she said.

"I know." Ella slipped inside, visibly trying to hold it together.

"You think she'll be okay?" I asked no one in particular.

"It's Connor and Ella," Noah said. "They'll get through this. They have to."

Yeah, I thought to myself. Because if any couple had a shot at going the distance, it was the two of them.

And if they couldn't... then there was no hope for the rest of us.

Later that afternoon, I was doing a whole lot of nothing when my phone bleeped.

> Noah: How is it being back at Mommy and Daddy's house?

> Connor: Asshole.

My mouth twitched at Connor's reply. He was in the pits of hell but still managed to keep up with our group chat antics.

> Austin: He has a point, Con. Is your mom going to give you a sponge bath and comb your hair?

> Connor: I hate you both.

> Noah: Did Austin hit a nerve?

> Rory: Don't be mean to him…

> Connor: Thanks, Rory, baby.

Something bitter, like jealousy, snaked through me. Connor and my sister had hit it off the second she stepped foot in Lakeshore.

I wasn't surprised. He was a good guy—the best of us—and Rory had that damsel in distress thing going on that guys gravitated toward. She was the sister he'd never had, and she was all too willing to step into that role while I stood in the shadows, unsure how to bridge the distance between us.

It was good for her to have people in her corner. But it only reminded me of what we didn't have.

> Rory: Is Ella there yet?

Connor: Not yet but she shouldn't be
long.

Rory: Promise me you'll look out for
each other. I know this is really hard on
you, but it's going to be hard on El too.

Noah: Yeah, don't do anything to
screw it up!

Connor: I'm leaving this chat now.

Austin: Don't be a pussy.

Connor: At least I have regular pussy.

Rory: Connor Morgan! Take that back.
Take that back right now.

Noah: Relax, shortcake. It's just a little
five lettered word. P U S S Y

Rory: You'll be getting NO PUSSY if
you carry on.

Jesus. I scrubbed my eyes, wishing like fuck I hadn't been dragged into this. Nobody wanted to witness their sister and her boyfriend talking about this shit.

Austin: Sister, remember. SISTER.

Noah: Oh, fuck off, Austin. If you
haven't already accepted that I'm
regularly petting Rory's pussy, then
that's on you.

Rory: Oh my God. You're all pigs.

Austin: And you're the one who fell for
Noah's bullshit.

Connor: I think Ella is here. I'll catch
you assholes later.

Noah: Stay strong, Con. And don't let
your parents cockblock you. It's not
good for your recovery.

Connor: Not sure it's my parents I
need to worry about.

The conversation went dead, and I chucked my cell onto the coffee table. I could have texted Rory and asked how she was. But I didn't.

I couldn't.

Because I wasn't Connor or Noah or even Mason. I wasn't sure who the fuck I was anymore. It felt like everything was beginning to slip through my fingers. My friends. The team. Hockey. Every day that passed was a day closer to the rest of my life.

A life I wasn't sure I was ready for.

Being in Lakeshore alone for the holidays was a new kind of torture. Last year, Noah had stuck around, and the two of us hung out, hit up some bars, and met plenty of local girls.

But this year, he had my sister. Aiden had Dayna, and Mason had Harper.

I told myself it didn't matter—that I chose to be alone. And I did. But it didn't make it suck any less.

I kept myself busy, working out, going for a daily run down by the beach, catching the highlights at The Penalty Box.

Texting Madison.

Even she'd been quieter the last couple of days, in the thick of her own Christmas plans with her parents.

I'd learned she was an only child and lived in the same town she'd grown up in. She had her own apartment and worked two jobs. But we hadn't really delved much deeper. Instead, we talked about our likes and dislikes, shared silly memes, and generally teased each other.

She made it easy. Simple.

Fun.

There was no constant hinting at more like there had been with Fallon.

I didn't even know if I would get to see her again,

and I was okay with that.

Oh, who the fuck was I kidding. I really wanted to see her again, but I wasn't going to be *that* guy begging a girl to make it happen.

I grabbed a bag of chips and made my way into the living room to settle down and watch a movie. The second I got comfortable, my cell phone vibrated.

> Connor: Ella just left to go sleep... in
> the fucking guest room.

Laughter vibrated in my chest. I could just imagine what a hardship that was for Connor, a guy who was self-proclaimed obsessive with his girl.

> Noah: I thought we talked about this.
> Don't let your parents cockblock you.

> Austin: Dude, he's just had surgery.
> That shit has got to hurt.

> Connor: Not as much as my aching
> dick right now.

> Austin: TOO MUCH FUCKING
> INFORMATION.

> Noah: You've got a right hand, use it.

> Connor: I can't get to the bathroom
> unaided yet and I don't have any
> tissues on hand.

Fuck's sake, they were too much.

Austin: Make it stop.

Noah: Quit being a baby. Con needs
our help in his hour of need.

Austin: Yeah, I'm out. Assholes.

I threw down my cell phone and started the movie, leaving Connor and Noah to it. I drew the line at giving him sex advice. It was fucking weird.

My cell bleeped again, and I snatched it up, ready to tell them all to fuck off, when I noticed Madison's name.

Madison: That was a killer shift. The
holiday crowd is no joke.

Austin: Rough night?

Madison: You could say that. My feet
are burning. I can't wait to get home
and stick them in an ice bath.

Austin: Shame I'm not there to help
you out…

A faint smirk traced my lips. Sometimes, our back and forth turned flirty, but on the whole, we kept it innocent enough. But it had been a few days since I'd seen her, and I hadn't forgotten how fucking hot she'd been.

Not when Madison had starred in all my fantasies since then. Still, it wasn't as half as good as the real thing, and I was as horny as fuck.

Madison: Oh yeah, and what would you do exactly?

Austin: Do you want the PG-13 or the R rated version?

My smile grew. Hopefully, my day was about to get a whole lot better. Phone sex wasn't usually my MO, but I'd make an exception for her.

Only five minutes later, she hadn't replied.

Shit, had I read her all wrong?

I waited another ten minutes until my frustration got the better of me.

Austin: Too much?

Madison didn't reply.

And I went to bed with a bad case of blue balls and the strange, unwelcome feeling of dejection in my chest.

The next morning, I woke to a text from Madison, but it didn't make me feel any better.

> Madison: Sorry about last night. Something came up. I'll probably be out of action for the next couple of days, but I hope Christmas isn't too lonely for you. xo

I didn't reply. What was there to say? She obviously had better things to do over Christmas than text me.

Dragging my grumpy ass out of bed, I went through the motions. Coffee. Breakfast. A morning jog through the neighborhood. Fielding two calls from Mom and another from Rory.

Mom was the last fucking person I wanted to talk to. No doubt I'd have to deal with her eventually, but today was not that day.

By the time I got showered and changed into some clean clothes, it was almost midday, and I still had hours to kill.

Funny how my own company had never really bothered me before. Before my friends all went and got themselves wifed up.

Or maybe it was meeting Madison.

No denying there was something between us. But *something* didn't equal permanent. And it sure as shit didn't mean I wanted to pursue something with her.

The ding of my cell phone pulled me from my thoughts, and I grabbed it off the dresser.

Fallon: How are you?

Fuck. I'd told her not to text me. It was done. Over.

Fallon: I really miss you, Austin. Maybe
we can talk after winter break. We can
keep things casual.

Austin: We both know that isn't going
to happen.

Fallon: Don't you miss me at all? It's
Christmas Eve, Austin. I know you're
all alone in Lakeshore. I could drive
down and keep you company…

I missed the sex on tap, sure. But I didn't miss *her.* Maybe that made me a heartless bastard, but I refused to be guilted into a relationship. Casual or otherwise.

I ignored her, and thankfully, she stopped texting. The last thing I wanted or needed was a clingy ex, not that we'd ever gotten that far. Fallon had never been my girlfriend, but in the end, she'd wanted to be. That's why I'd ended things because I didn't want commitment.

I didn't want permanent.

I didn't want the responsibility of looking out for someone else's heart.

Not when I was pretty sure mine was nothing more than a cold, dead thing inside my chest.

Christmas came and went. There was no tree. No presents. No Christmas dinner.

There was just me, a six-pack, and my favorite takeout.

Rory tried to call. And when I wouldn't answer her call, Noah started blowing up my phone. But I didn't want to let my dark mood spoil their trip.

They deserved to be happy.

Rory deserved it.

I wasn't so sure about me, not after everything I'd done—and hadn't—over the last few years.

So I hunkered down in the house with my meager supplies and let myself wallow.

I didn't hear from Madison again except for a GIF of the Grinch wishing me a 'Merry Fucking Christmas.' I'd smiled briefly but then remembered how quickly she'd dropped me the other night.

It was two days after Christmas when I finally pulled my head out of my ass and joined the land of the living again.

Noah: You alive asshole? Rory has been worried sick.

Austin: Yeah, I'm alive. She knows I hate Christmas.

Noah: Still, you didn't have to ignore
her calls for two days.

Austin: I'm sure you were taking good
care of her.

Noah: Damn straight.

I'd walked right into that one, but it didn't stop the sting.

Noah: Call her back. Before I have to
drive back to Lakeshore and kick
your ass.

Austin: You couldn't take me.

Noah: Don't make me try…

I snorted. He wouldn't do a damn thing to hurt Rory, and pretty sure, despite deserving it, that extended to beating my ass.

Austin: I'll call her soon.

I hit send, knowing he wouldn't reply.
We both knew the truth.
I wouldn't call.

CHAPTER 6

MADISON

"Madison," Jacqueline greeted me with a hesitant smile.

"Jacqui, Ken, come in," I said, welcoming them into my parents' house.

Mom and Dad preferred to do these meetings at their house instead of my apartment downtown.

I think she just liked the opportunity to size up the competition, which was ridiculous to me. They were both Imogen's grandparents and the more people my baby had looking out for her, the better.

"Did you have a nice Christmas?" she asked, the two of them a little guarded as they followed me further into the house.

But I didn't blame them.

The Hovens were the enemy as far as my mother was concerned. Dad and I had more of an understanding approach, but my mother could be a formidable woman when she set her mind to something.

"We did, thanks. Immy was a lucky girl."

"Did you tell her Santa left her some gifts at our place?"

"I did. I—"

"Yay, Granny J is here." Imogen barreled into the hall, almost losing her footing on the parquet flooring.

"Oh, sweetheart. Look at you. I think you've grown again."

"Mommy said I hads. She said I grow wikes sunflowers."

"You sure do, baby." Jacqui scooped her up and smothered her in big, sloppy kisses that made Immy roar with laughter.

"Your turn, Grampy." She held out her little arms for Ken, and he took her.

"Hasn't she grown," his wife said.

"Oh, she has. So big."

"Hears that, Mommy." Her proud little smile was everything.

"Why don't we go get your things and say goodbye to Grammy and Pops?" I took her from Ken and motioned for them to follow me into the kitchen.

Mom stood the second we entered. "Jacqui, Ken," she said stoically.

"Cara."

"Okay then," I said over the lump in my throat. "I've packed everything she should need. You've got my cell phone number. The number of her pediatrician. And—"

"Madi." Ken gently squeezed my shoulder. "We've got this. We'll send you plenty of updates, and I'm sure Immy will want to call you."

"I will, Mommy. I'll calls every day."

"I know you will, baby." I hugged her tight, pressing a kiss to her cheek. "You be a good girl for Granny J and Grampy Ken, okay?"

"I promise. Cross my heart, hopes to die, sticks a needle in my eye."

"Did you teach her that?" Jacqui mouthed, and I shook my head.

"One of the kids at pre-K. Go get your bag." I lowered Imogen to the floor and watched, my heart tugging at my chest as she eagerly grabbed her little bag off my father.

Tension rippled through the kitchen as Jacqui took my daughter's hand. "We'll see you in a few days," she said.

"Okay," I echoed.

"If you need anything—"

"We've got it."

Dad moved beside me, a steel fortress at my back. He knew how hard I found this—trusting them with her. Even though I knew it was the right thing. Even though I knew they were on my side.

Letting my parents take her was different. I trusted them implicitly. But Jacqui and Ken were *his* parents. And despite demonstrating their loyalty to me during the separation, Warren was still their son.

Their blood.

I couldn't guarantee they would send him on his way if he showed up. Or better yet, report it to the authorities.

"Bye, byes Mommy. Bye, byes, everyone."

I helplessly waved as I watched them take her. Wondering if they knew how precious she was to me, how important.

"God, I hate this," I murmured, tears sliding down my cheeks.

"I thought this was what you wanted?" Mom scoffed.

"It was." I shot her a derisive look. "But it doesn't mean it isn't hard."

"If you ask me—"

"That's the thing, though, I didn't ask you, Mom. Imogen deserves to know her grandparents. She deserves to know that that side of her family aren't all narcissistic abusive assholes."

I followed them out to wave goodbye to Imogen.

Three days.

It was only three days.

I could survive that. I just needed to keep myself busy.

It took me a whole afternoon to pluck up the courage to text Austin.

Our conversation had ground to a halt after I abandoned him mid-text the other night. But Imogen had woken up after a bad dream and needed a cuddle. And the wave of guilt I felt for texting Austin and giving myself a moment had hit me full force. Then Christmas came and Imogen didn't give me so much as a second to breathe.

I was allowed time for myself, I knew that, but apart from an occasional night out with Jeremiah, I rarely let myself indulge. But I had three nights to myself now. Jeremiah was out of town visiting family, and I wasn't due back to work until after the holidays.

I could sit at home and drive myself sick with worry over Imogen being at her grandparents, or I could do something for myself.

Shoving down all the little thoughts that said this wasn't a good idea, I opened my message thread with Austin.

> Madison: So turns out I have some
> free time over the next couple of
> days…

> Austin: And here was me thinking you
> were trying to blow me off.

> Madison: Sorry about that. Christmas
> is always a really busy time for me.

> Austin: Relax, I'm joking. You don't
> owe me anything.

Ouch. His words struck harder than they should have. But I couldn't really blame him. I had pretty much pulled back, and I couldn't tell him why.

Austin and my daughter were two paths that never needed to cross.

She was my world, and he was a temporary distraction—a fleeting moment for just myself.

> Madison: I'd like to make it up to you,
> if you'll let me.

Crap, I sounded desperate. Putting myself out there like that. But there was no use beating around the bush, pretending that this was something it wasn't.

I liked how he made me feel, and now that I'd had a little taste, I wanted another. I could own that. I *deserved* that.

Austin: Let me know when you get to
Lakeshore.

My brows pinched. It wasn't quite the response I expected. Gone were his flirty, teasing replies, his sharp-witted humor, and something cold and indifferent was left in its place.

I wanted to ask him what was up with that, but I didn't. Because I was a coward and so out of my depth that I knew if I pushed him, he might retreat altogether.

Besides, this was what I wanted, wasn't it?

Hooking up with the gorgeous hockey player without the risk of catching feelings.

Too late. I ignored the little voice.

So what if I liked Austin? I couldn't imagine fooling around with someone I *didn't* like, and besides, I knew it couldn't go anywhere. I didn't have the time or the emotional capacity for a relationship, and he'd made it clear where he stood.

He was the perfect distraction.

One I planned on enjoying.

"What time is he getting there?" Fawn asked as I paced her living room, clutching my cell phone to my ear.

"In like twenty minutes. If he shows."

"He'll show."

"How can you be so sure?"

"Because he's a guy, and you're offering—" She stopped herself, and I muttered something about this being a terrible idea.

"It is not a terrible idea," she huffed. "It's sex, Mads. Hot, no-strings, drama-free sex. It doesn't need to be any more complicated than that."

"Just sex. Right. I can do that."

"Mads..."

"I can't do that, can I? I have a four-year-old child, for God's sake. I'm a *mother*."

"You're also twenty-one, Mads. You deserve to get laid occasionally. Choosing to put yourself first for once doesn't mean you're neglecting your responsibilities to Immy. She's with her grandparents. She's safe and probably eating way too much candy. It's okay to do something just for you."

"He is very nice to look at."

"And a good kisser. Don't forget that part." Her soft laughter eased some of the tension inside me.

"Actually, I think I said, 'Great kisser.'"

"Even better."

"Okay. Okay." I released a steady breath. "I can do this."

"Yeah, you can. Go get that D, babe. And then call me tomorrow and tell me all about it."

"Pervert."

"And proud. Love you, babe."

"Love you too. Laters."

We hung up, and I checked the time again.

Ten minutes.

Oh God.

I was so freaking nervous.

Rushing over to the refrigerator, I poured myself another glass of wine. I didn't want to get drunk, but a little Dutch courage never hurt anyone.

I looked good. I smelled goddamn amazing. And I'd shaved and plucked myself within an inch of my life. But when the buzzer finally went, I almost jumped out of my skin. Draining the rest of my wine, I smoothed down my dress and went to let Austin up.

By the time he knocked, my body was vibrating with nerves.

"Hey—"

Austin was on me instantly, his hand curving around the side of my throat as his mouth crashed down on mine.

The door slammed shut somewhere in the distance, and I figured he'd kicked it closed.

"Tell me I don't have to stop," he murmured between kisses.

"Don't stop," I breathed, clutching his shoulders as he walked me back into the room.

"Thank fuck."

My verbal permission turned him feral. He devoured me, his hands practically clawing at my skin, trying to find their way under my dress. He managed to get it hitched around my hips and ran his hands down the back of my thighs, squeezing.

"Same bedroom?"

I nodded, a little breathless and stunned.

This was happening.

It was really happening.

A little quicker than I anticipated, but the truth was, if I had too much time to think, I would hesitate. I would deny myself this because I'd forgotten how to put myself first.

Even before Imogen—my gorgeous, sweet Immy— came along, I'd lost sight of my hopes and dreams.

I'd lost sight of who I was.

Austin picked me up, and I squealed, wrapping my legs around his waist. "This doesn't mean anything," he said.

"I know. It's just a bit of fun." I nodded, unsure who I was trying to convince more—him or myself.

My heart galloped in my chest, every breath laced with anticipation. I hadn't done this in so long... too long.

"Austin, I—"

"Shh." He lowered me to my feet, his hands gripping my hips a little too roughly as if his control was a thin restraint on the verge of snapping.

Part of me wanted him to snap. But the other wasn't sure I was ready.

"It's been a while," I said, repeating the words I'd whispered the first time he got me naked.

"I won't hurt you, pretty girl."

But it wasn't my body I was worried about.

"I've jerked off so many times in the last few days to this memory." His big hands shaped my waist, my ass, and my breasts.

"Thanks, I think." My nose crinkled, and a smirk tugged at his mouth.

"Trust me when I say it's a compliment." Austin tugged my sweater dress up my body and over my head. The urge to cover myself, the soft swell of my stomach, and the silvery lines along my hips were overwhelming, but I stood proud.

He thought I was beautiful, and with his heated gaze on me, I felt it.

"I want to see you, too," I said boldly.

"It would be my pleasure." Austin stripped out of his hoodie, t-shirt, and jeans, leaving him in nothing but skintight black boxer briefs that left absolutely nothing to the imagination.

He threw his wallet down on the bed. "Get on the bed, Madison," he ordered, sending a thrill through me.

I liked him like this. All dominant and in control.

As seductively as possible, I shuffled backward

onto the bed. His hungry gaze continued to track my movements as he grabbed his wallet and retrieved a foil wrapper.

The guilt coiled in my chest tightened, but I shoved it down.

I could have this. It didn't mean anything beyond tonight. I was on birth control, and Austin clearly took precautions.

It was fine.

"You good?" he asked, noticing the strain in my expression.

I nodded, running a hand up my stomach, letting my fingers flutter over the curve of my breasts. His nostrils flared as he watched—fixated—on the movement.

The way he looked at me made me feel so beautiful.

I'd missed that.

I'd missed it so much. Wondered if I'd ever feel that way again after giving birth to my daughter.

"Take it off," he said, his throat rippling as he swallowed hard.

I unclasped my bra with ease and pulled it off. Austin inhaled sharply, his knee hitting the end of the bed. He crawled over me, hovering there, staring down at me with such intensity that I couldn't breathe. My lungs smarted as I tried to catch my breath, to break his hold over me. But he was so freaking intense.

"Aus—"

He crashed his mouth down on mine again. My hand slipped around his neck, fingers slipping into his hair. His body pressed down on me, all hard lines and raw, unfettered power.

Things moved fast then.

He teased me, grinding his pelvis against me, his hard length almost impaling me through the thin layers of materials separating us.

Whimpers and moans spilled from my lips as I arched into him, wanting more.

Needing it.

His fingers dipped between our bodies, slipping into my panties and toying with my clit in a way that made me pant.

"God, Austin... It's... Fuck."

He didn't stop, and I climbed higher. Everything inside me tightened as the pressure built.

"I'm close..." I breathed. "Don't stop."

My fingers twisted into the sheets, and my toes curled as I hovered on the precipice. So, so close that I—

Austin pulled away, ripping the orgasm just out of my reach.

"What the—"

He tore my panties aside and filled me in one smooth stroke.

"Oh God," I cried.

I hadn't even realized he'd gotten the condom on. But it didn't matter because the sudden intrusion, the exquisite feel of him stretching me, was everything.

I hitched my legs around his waist, urging him to go harder. Faster.

"Fuck, you feel incredible." He brushed his hand along my collarbone, chasing his fingers with his tongue, licking and nipping the skin there, heightening the sensation.

Austin slid his hand under my ass, slightly changing the angle. It made everything deeper. Somehow more. And I tumbled headfirst into an earth-shattering orgasm.

It crashed through me in waves. Unrelenting and vicious. Tearing me apart and building me back up.

"Fuck, you're choking my dick," he rasped, upping his pace.

"I-I… It's…" My voice shook as I fought to catch my breath.

It felt like a revelation.

The rebirth of my sex life.

Fawn would be so freaking proud.

I choked on a laugh, and Austin stared down at me.

"That's a first," he said, stilling inside me.

"Oh my God, I'm so sorry. I'm not laughing at you. I was just thinking about Fawn."

"Fawn…" His brow arched, and he started to pull away.

"No, not like that. This is coming out all wrong." I let out a frustrated sigh. "I was just thinking she'd be proud of me."

"Proud?"

"I told you." I tried to glance away, but I couldn't. "It's been a while."

"How long exactly?" He searched my eyes, and I realized I had completely ruined the moment.

"A while," I said, refusing to give him a number. "Sorry, I didn't mean to ruin things." I started shoving him away, shame burning my cheeks. "Maybe we should—"

He circled his hips, and a moan slipped out of me. "I'm not done with you, pretty girl."

"Y-you're not?"

Something glinted in his eyes, sending a shiver through me.

"Not a fucking chance."

CHAPTER 7

AUSTIN

Fuck.

Madison felt goddamn perfect beneath me, staring up at me with wide eyes full of emotion and surprise as her pussy fluttered around my dick, the aftermath of her orgasm lingering.

She'd said it had been a while, but there was something about her mid-sex ramble that made me wonder exactly how long we were talking.

She wasn't a virgin. But she had been clear that this wouldn't happen.

A smug sense of satisfaction swelled in my chest. Not because I'd gotten across her line, but because I was so fucking thankful I'd gotten to experience her like this.

She felt incredible. Soft and feminine under my hands, her thighs cradled mine like we were two pieces made to fit.

It didn't make any fucking sense to me. All these new and unfamiliar feelings racing through me as I fucked into her, chasing my own release.

But at that moment, I didn't care.

I'd had a shitty couple of weeks, wallowing in the house all alone, while my sister was shacked up with Noah and our friends, celebrating all the good in their lives.

When Madison had finally texted me to say she had some spare time, I'd been like a junkie craving their next hit. Not my finest moment, but worth it.

She felt too good.

So fucking good that I already knew once wasn't going to be enough.

That was a first for me. I'd casually hooked up with Fallon because it was easy. But with Madison, it was somehow different.

More.

Something I refused to look too closely at.

"Austin," she mewled, dragging her fingertips down my back as our bodies found the perfect rhythm.

"Shit, Madi. You feel perfect. So fucking good."

"I think I'm going to come again."

Male pride spiked through me. I wanted her to

come again and again. I wanted her desperation and breathless and wrecked all because of me.

I was good at hockey... and I was good at this.

Pulling one of her arms from around my neck, I threaded our fingers together, pressing them into the pillow beside her head as I thrust into her. Over and over.

"Oh God," she cried. "Yes... yes... Ah." She came again, her inner walls rippling around me, milking me.

It was enough to tip me over the edge, and I came hard, spilling into the condom.

"Fuck." I rolled away, flopping down beside her. "That was..."

"Yeah." She glanced over at me and smiled. "You're really good at that."

"I've had a lot of practice."

Shit.

Fuck.

The blood drained from her face, the temperature in the room dropping as cold as ice. "I suppose I walked right into that one," she pursed.

"Madison, I didn't mean—"

"Yeah." She gave me a sad smile. "You did."

"Guess you're not the only one who says inappropriate things during sex." I tried to laugh it off, but the damage was done. "For what it's worth," I murmured, "I've never done this."

"This?"

"Yeah, this." I brushed my thumb over her bottom lip, capturing her chin and leaning down to kiss her. "Turning up at a girl's place like this."

"You haven't? But I thought—"

"Madi?"

"Yeah, Austin?"

"Stop talking."

She did.

But only because I kissed the words right out of her.

The next morning was a perfect reminder of why I never did this.

I woke up to an empty bed and the smell of bacon. My stomach grumbled, but an icy sensation slid down my spine.

Climbing out of bed, I pulled on my clothes and ducked into the small bathroom before I went in search of Madison.

"You're awake." She smiled at me over her shoulder. Her blonde hair was pulled up into a messy bun on top of her head, loose strands framing her face, and her long legs were on full display, given the oversized shirt she was wearing only reached her mid-thigh.

"I thought I'd make us breakfast."

"I…"

Her expression dropped. "You can't stay?"

"It's not that. I just didn't think—"

"You didn't expect to do the morning after thing." She turned around, but I didn't miss the sharp breath she took.

"It's not you," I added, trying to ease the tension. "I just think this could blur the lines."

"It's bacon," she scoffed. "Hardly a marriage proposal."

"We agreed."

"I didn't think it meant I couldn't make you breakfast. We had fun, didn't we?" She gave me her eyes again, trying… failing to hide the hurt there. "It's only bacon, Austin. It doesn't come with strings."

Didn't it, though?

In my experience, women were pretty fucking good at reading into signs that weren't there.

But you'd said you didn't make a habit of turning up like this, asshole. You *said that.*

I'd been inside her then, though, totally overcome by how good she felt—how right. I couldn't be held responsible for any of the shit that came out of my mouth.

"Just sit down." She rolled her eyes. "You fucked me twice last night and once again this morning. I think you can eat bacon with me."

My brow arched. "Fair enough."

I sat down, surprised at how much I liked her feistiness.

Madison was... Well, she was a fucking mystery still. A pretty package with secrets. Secrets I wanted to know but had no right to ask about. Because that shit went too deep, and we'd agreed to keep things uncomplicated.

She plated up the bacon and pancakes and shoved one toward me. "Help yourself to syrup, and there's juice or coffee."

"Thanks, this looks great." My stomach growled in agreement, and she chuckled.

"See, your stomach thanks me even if you didn't want to stay." She peeked up at me through those long lashes, a hint of a smile playing on her lips.

"It wasn't even like that."

"Sure, it wasn't, hotshot."

We ate in comfortable silence, stealing little glances at each other, sizing each other up.

It felt like a battle of wills.

A game of who would break first.

I needed to leave. To walk out and keep the line intact.

Fun.

It was... fun.

But I couldn't stop myself from obsessing over the way she ate her bacon. How cute she looked, nibbling on the perfectly cooked strips. The way her lips moved, the shape of them.

Jesus. She was in my head and under my skin.

What was it about her that got to me so much?

"What?" she asked, the question ripping me from my thoughts.

"Uh, nothing."

"If you say so." She gave me a teasing smile.

"Well, this was nice and all," I said, shoving my plate away to stand. "But I really should go."

"Okay."

"Okay?" I frowned.

"Sure, I mean, we had fun. You placated me and stayed for breakfast. My work here is done." She got up to collect our breakfast plates and move them to the sink.

"So, I guess I'll see you around," I said.

I hadn't wanted to stay for breakfast, but now that I had, it felt weird to just leave.

Jesus, I was fucked.

Completely out of my depth.

"Yeah. Maybe when I'm in town next, we can—"

I was on her in a second.

One minute, she was standing there, smiling at me; the next, my hand was curled around the back of her neck, my mouth devouring hers.

"Austin," she breathed, blinking up at me with surprise. "I thought—"

"Change of plans, pretty girl." I smirked, hoisting her up against me.

Madison clung on, laughing as I carried her back through her friend's apartment. "You're crazy."

That was one word for it.

But I wasn't about to overanalyze it. Not when she was like putty in my hands.

Wanting her didn't mean anything beyond the fact the sex was off the charts.

So long as we both knew the deal, we could enjoy this without it getting complicated.

I wasn't like my friends. Falling at the first sign of good pussy.

At least, that's what I kept telling myself.

New Year's Eve was as underwhelming as ever.

I'd stayed in and gotten takeout, falling asleep before the clock struck twelve. I had woken up to a text from Madison, though. That put a rare smile on my face.

We'd been texting daily, sharing small parts of our routines. But neither of us brought up what had happened or the possibility of seeing one another again.

The sex had been intense, the memory of her

warm and willing beneath me imprinted on my mind like a brand I could never erase.

I'd choked the morning after, though, and now she'd put up a wall between us.

Maybe it was for the best for the both of us.

My cell bleeped again, and I snatched it up, hoping to see Madison's name. But it wasn't.

> Connor: Just checking in. PT was a bitch, but I survived.

> Noah: Wondered when you were going to pull your head out of your ass and text us back. You're lucky Rory has your best interests at heart because I was one more day away from driving to Dayton and checking for proof of life.

> Connor: You're such a drama queen.

> Noah: And you're full of shit.

> Austin: Have you spoken to Ella?

I might have retreated into my anti-holiday bubble, but I'd read their texts. I knew all about Connor fucking things up with Ella and her leaving Dayton to go see her mom.

Poor bastard wasn't handling things well.

> Connor: A few texts back and forth.

Austin: What's up with that?

Connor: Things got a little claustrophobic at my parents' house.

Noah: Is she there for the rest of winter break?

Connor: I don't know.

Noah: I hope you know what you're doing.

Austin: Holden has a point, Con.

Connor: Since when do you give a shit about our relationship?

Austin: Dude, you were going to propose. Now she's with her mom and you're stuck in Dayton.

Connor: Some space will do us both good.

Noah: You don't think you'll have enough of that when she's back in Lakeshore and you're not?

Connor didn't reply, and Noah sent me a text to our separate chat.

Noah: Do you think we should be
worried?

Austin: He'll pull himself out of it.

Noah: Yeah, and if he doesn't?

Austin: It's Connor, Holden. He's the
best of us.

If anyone could get through this, it was him.

But as I re-read my words, I wasn't so sure anymore. Everything was different now.

Connor was injured.

Ella was hurting.

And I couldn't get a girl I barely knew out of my mind.

I didn't get to see Madison again. But it was probably for the best, considering Ella returned to Lakeshore unannounced after Connor, the idiot, fucked things up again.

She looked half-asleep as I banged and slammed around the kitchen, grabbing everything I needed.

Noah had texted to say she wasn't in a good way,

and I saw it the second I opened the door to her, looking red-eyed and hungover.

"Here you go," I said. "It's the best I could do."

She lifted her head to find me pushing a plate of pancakes and bacon toward her. "I'm impressed." She gave me a weak smile. "It smells good."

"Yeah, well, I'm not completely useless." I moved back to lean against the counter. "So you haven't talked to Con?"

"Nope. I'm not sure I'm ready to hear all his excuses."

"But you're not going to do anything."

Her eyes flashed with pain. "Would you care if I did?"

"Come on, El. I'm not heartless." I sighed. "Connor is one of my best friends. You're his girl. If the two of you don't make it, there's no hope for the rest of us."

I didn't like the way she narrowed her eyes, studying me.

"What?" I snapped.

"What's going on with you?"

"Nothing, why?"

"I think you're lying."

"Because I took pity on you and made you breakfast?"

"You're acting weird."

Fuck this. I'd tried to do something nice for her in her hour of need and—

"You met somebody," she said.

"No, I didn't," I replied too hastily, the defensiveness obvious in my voice.

"I think you did." She huffed with arrogance.

"You don't know what the fuck you're talking about. I didn't meet anyone."

"Okay, but I'd put money on you hooking up with someone new. Someone you like."

I scoffed, trying to hide the truth because I had met someone.

I just didn't know what the fuck to do about it.

"I never kiss and tell." My mouth twitched.

She shook her head with a chuckle. "Oh, you've got it bad, goalie."

"I have not."

"Whatever you say, hotshot. But you know, it's nice to see you smile."

Everything went still inside me. "Yeah, well, don't go gossiping to the girls. Especially Rory. It's just a bit of fun."

I shrugged like it was nothing. But I had a feeling she saw right through me.

"I won't breathe a word of it." She mimicked, zipping her lips, and I rolled my eyes.

"Why are you here again?"

Ella's expression fell. "I didn't want to go back to my empty apartment."

"Well, I'm headed out soon, but you're welcome to stick around. I'll be back later."

"With your 'bit of fun?'" She grinned, but I didn't return it.

"Not funny."

"Oh, come on. It was pretty funny."

She began tucking into the pancakes, taking minute bites at first.

"Good?" I asked.

"So good, thank you." She cleared the plate, and I offered her a small nod.

"You going to be okay if I head out?"

"I'll be fine. Thanks for brunch."

I nodded again, heading for the door, but her voice stopped me dead.

"Austin?"

"Yeah?" I glanced back.

"You deserve to be happy, you know."

Her words cut deep, but I ignored the sting and strolled out of there as if nothing happened.

Hitching my bag over my shoulder, I grabbed my water bottle and headed out of the gym.

It had been unsurprisingly quiet; most of its

regular clientele was home for winter break. So I'd enjoyed having the free weights to myself.

My cell phone vibrated, and I dug it out of my pocket, smirking when I saw Madison's name.

Madison: How's your day?

Austin: Just finished at the gym. Do you like to work out?

Madison: I don't go to the gym and train or anything, but I try to eat healthily and get my steps in.

Austin: It shows.

Madison: Austin Hart… was that a compliment?

Running a hand through my damp hair, I chuckled to myself as I flagged down the approaching bus. I boarded and found a seat, finding another text from Madison.

Madison: So I've been thinking… Maybe soon we can get together.

Austin: Yeah, maybe.

Madison: What are you doing with the rest of your day?

Austin: Just on my way to meet a teammate for a drink.

Madison: In that case, I'll leave you to it. Chat soon hopefully.

Austin: Definitely.

I hopped off the bus and hit the sidewalk, following Ward's directions to the bar.

"Watch it, Misters," a stern little voice said as I turned the corner and almost tripped over a child.

I looked down to find a little girl glowering up at me. "My bad."

"That's not a 'pology. Mommy says you should 'pologize when you hurts somebody."

"I didn't mean—" Her scowl deepened as she planted her fists on her hips, and I had to resist the urge to laugh at her. "I'm very sorry. Where is your mom, by the way?" I glanced around, frowning.

"She's just— Oh, here she is. Wook Mommy. I mades a new friend."

Fucking hell, the little hellion gave me whiplash.

"Immy, what are you— Austin? What are you doing here?"

"Madison." Her name echoed through my head as she stepped up behind the cute kid and laid her hand on her unruly curls. "What— Fuck."

"Austin." She sucked in a breath, the blood draining from her face. "I can explain. I can—"

"She's..." *Yours*. The word got stuck in my throat.

Because no way.

No. Fucking. Way.

"Yeah." Guilt shone in her eyes, but barely touched the ice hardening around my heart.

A kid.

She had a fucking *kid*.

A daughter with the same ocean eyes. Same golden hair and bow-shaped lips.

I'd been inside her. I'd been fucking desperate to know her secrets, to learn what put shadows in her eyes. But I thought it was a toxic ex or something.

I didn't think—

Fuck.

"We should probably talk but now... It isn't a good idea." She dropped her gaze to the kid.

"Who is Austins, Mommy? Is he your friend?"

"He's a... friend, yeah." Her lips pressed into a thin smile as she peeked up at me.

Friend.

Fuck that.

She had a *kid*.

"Hi, Mr. Austins, Mommy's friend. I'm Imogen Grace, but you can calls me Princess Immy." Imogen held out her hand and stared up at me expectantly.

I didn't know what the fuck to do.

I had zero experience with kids, none.

A beat passed as the two of us stood there, glaring at each other until her little brows furrowed.

"Mommy, what's wrong with him? He's wikes a statue."

"Austin," Madison pleaded.

"I… Shit— I mean, sorry. I'm just really tired. You and your mom probably have things to do, and I… I need to be somewhere." The words spewed out as panic began to build inside me.

"But ifs you're Mommy's friend, you can comes with us," she pouted. "We're going to see Jer."

Jer?

Who the fuck was Jer?

"Oh no, princess. Austin has plans. He can't come with us."

"That's right. I have to go now." I started to back up, ready to get the fuck out of there.

"We'll talk later?" Madison's eyes drilled into mine, all the things she couldn't say hanging between us.

A small nod was all I managed before I moved around them and took off toward the bar.

Ready to drown my fucking sorrows and figure out how the hell I missed this.

CHAPTER 8

MADISON

"You know, babe. If you watch your phone any longer, it might spontaneously combust," Jeremiah said as we sat in his apartment, watching Immy terrorize his cat Vader.

"Want to talk about it?"

"Yes... no." I peeked over at him. "Oh, I don't know."

"I'm guessing this has something to do with the cryptic text Fawn sent me the other day."

"She didn't!"

"Mads, come on. It's been five years. Of course, she was going to tell me. Hell, you should have told me." He gave me a disappointed look.

"I wasn't sure there was anything to tell."

"Did you sleep with him?" He lowered his voice.

Not that Immy was paying us any attention, too busy chasing Vader around the kitchen.

"I..."

"Oh my God, you did. Good for you, babe. It's about time you dusted off your va—"

"Jer!" I scolded, casting my gaze back to Immy.

"Was it good? Fawn said he's a hockey player. I've seen their pre-game workouts on the ice. All those stretches. Gets me hot just thinking about it." He fanned himself dramatically.

"I didn't think men in skates were your thing." I smirked.

"They're not, but it doesn't mean I can't appreciate their dedication to the game." He winked, and we both laughed.

But mine quickly subsided when I remembered the absolute look of horror on Austin's face when he realized Imogen was my daughter.

I should have told him.

God, I should have come clean and told him so he heard it from me first.

It was too late now.

He would probably never speak to me again, and if he didn't, then it was his loss. I didn't need somebody in my life who couldn't accept us as a package deal.

Still, it didn't make me feel any better about the fact I hadn't told him before he found out.

He wasn't supposed to find out.

With a little sigh, I checked my cell phone again.

"Mads." Jeremiah took my hand in his. "What happened?"

"He saw us. Earlier at the store. Austin saw us," I admitted, unable to meet his eye. "He saw... Immy."

"You didn't tell him?" There was no judgment in his voice, just mild surprise.

Jeremiah knew what Imogen meant to me. He knew she had saved me in ways she would never know.

Lips pressed into a thin line, I shook my head gently. "It was just a bit of fun. I didn't think—"

"You didn't think it would become more?"

"Come on, Jer." A soft, bitter laugh spilled out. "He's a senior in college. A hockey player with a shot at going pro if the rumors are to be believed. He isn't going to want to take on me and Immy."

"Then he doesn't sound like the kind of guy who deserves you."

My gaze flicked to him as a wave of sadness washed over me. "I wasn't supposed to catch feelings."

But I had.

I'd known after that first night there was something about Austin Hart. But instead of ignoring all the alarm bells, I chased that addictive feeling I got every time his icy gaze found me.

"Oh, babe. Come here." Jeremiah pulled me into his arms, hugging me.

"Hug time." Immy shrieked, running over to us and climbing onto my lap. She looped her little arms around us both, and my heart swelled.

She deserved so much. She deserved a father who loved her, a father who led by example, who taught her never to expect half-measures.

"I wove you, Mommy. You too, Jerrykins."

I snickered, knowing how much he hated her latest nickname for him. But Jeremiah would never complain, not to Imogen. He loved his goddaughter almost as much as I did.

"Love you, princess," he said, ruffling her curls. "And don't tell your momma. But I think I love you a little bit more than her."

She giggled. "Hears that, Mommy? Jerry woves me the most."

"I'm sure he does. Thank you." I mouthed at him over the top of her head.

"I got you." He grinned, but I felt the sincerity in his words.

I was lucky. I knew that.

Lucky to have people like Jeremiah and Fawn in my corner. My parents and even Jacqueline and Ken, too. Imogen had a whole circle of people who would go to bat for her. So it shouldn't have mattered that Austin had looked at her like she was a contagious disease.

But it did.

It mattered.

Because for the first time since she was born, a guy had made me feel something. And deep down, all anyone wanted was to find somebody who cared.

I pulled away from them, unable to resist a glance at my phone again. But I knew I'd find no new messages.

Austin's silence spoke volumes.

He knew the truth now.

He'd seen it with his own two eyes.

And just like I expected him to—he'd decided I wasn't worth it.

I finally got Imogen down a little after eight. After all the excitement of meeting Austin and then terrorizing Vader and Jeremiah she was a bundle of hyper energy when we'd gotten back home.

Austin didn't text. But then, I knew he wouldn't.

I'd dropped a bomb at his feet, and he'd responded the way most college seniors would.

He ran at the first sign of trouble.

But I still felt guilty over the whole thing, and I couldn't let it go until I apologized for my part in it.

Getting comfortable on my couch with a hot mug

of milk and a sprinkle of cinnamon, I grabbed my cell phone and started typing.

> Madison: Hey, so… today was awkward. I'm so sorry you had to find out like that. I wanted to tell you, but how do you tell the guy you're fooling around with that you have a four-year-old daughter?

I hit send and waited a few minutes. He didn't reply; I didn't really expect him to.

> Madison: Listen there's no hard feelings on my end. I just wanted to apologize and explain myself. This is all new to me. You're the first guy… Well, I guess it doesn't matter now.

Worrying my lip between my teeth, I kept typing as the thoughts and emotions kept pouring out of me until silent tears slipped down my cheeks.

> Madison: Thank you for reminding me that I'm still in here somewhere. It's been a really long time since I felt desired, Austin. So thank you! I guess this will be the last time I text. So have a nice life, Austin Hart. I hope all your dreams come true. Madi xo

I felt better, lighter, getting all that off my chest. It

still hurt knowing that we were done. But it's what I'd wanted—what we'd both wanted.

A little fun without the strings.

Austin had reminded me that Imogen's father hadn't completely destroyed me, and I would always be thankful for that.

There had been a time—when I was a terrified, sleep-deprived seventeen-year-old holding my newborn baby in my arms—when I didn't think I could do it. That I would never be everything she needed. With the staunch support of my parents, Jeremiah and Fawn, and Jacqui and Ken, I'd done it, though. I'd learned how to change diapers, burp her, and keep healthy routines.

I'd learned how to become a mother.

It gave me something to focus on. I couldn't fall apart because my sweet little Immy needed me. So, I forged myself into someone new. I became strong for her. But I lost sight of myself.

I guess, in some ways, after Warren, I shut down. I became numb.

Gradually, with a lot of encouragement from Jeremiah and Fawn, I slowly began to live again. To let myself be Madison, the girl, and not just Madison, the mom. But I'd never allowed myself to get close to anyone until Austin.

And now that he knew the truth, I would likely never see him again.

Maybe it's for the best. Before you got in too deep.

It wasn't like I didn't have a lot to focus on in my life already without the added complication of a guy. At least, with work and Imogen, it would keep my mind from wandering to Austin. Wondering what if…

I shook those thoughts out of my head, maybe in another life.

"Mommy?" Imogen murmured, and I almost jumped out of my skin.

I hadn't heard her come into the room.

"Goodness, baby. You almost gave me a heart attack." I got up and went to her. "What's wrong?"

"Can I sleeps with you?"

"Immy, we talked about this."

"But I had a bads dream, Mommy."

"You did, huh?"

"Yeah, I dreamed that you weft, and I was all alone."

"Oh, sweetheart. Come here." I scooped her up and carried her back down the hall to her room. "Let's get you tucked in, and I'll lie with you for a little bit. How does that sound?"

Imogen nodded, chewing on her fingers. She did that sometimes when she was anxious.

I made her comfortable, grabbing a couple of extra stuffed bears off her shelf, and laid down beside her, brushing her soft curls out of her face.

"You know Mommy will always be here for you.

Always." I bopped her nose. "I love you so, so much, sweetheart."

She snuggled closer, gripping her favorite stuffed animal—a bunny Jeremiah had given her for her second birthday—between us.

With his torn ear and missing eye, Mr. Hopsy had seen better days, but she loved that bunny something fierce.

I stroked her hair, hoping she would fall to sleep quickly. But she murmured, "Mommy?"

"Yeah, baby?"

"Why don'ts I have a daddy?"

"You do have a daddy, Immy. You know that." I managed to get the words out over the lump in my throat.

"So wheres is he?"

"Well, baby. He got sick and had to go away for a while."

It was a lie mixed in with the truth, but we'd all decided she didn't need to know that, not yet.

"Daddy loved you very much, baby."

"What about you, Mommy? Did Daddy woves you? Cos Sierra says her daddy weft because he doesn't woves her mommy anymore."

God, she was four.

Four, and she had so many questions.

I wasn't prepared for this—not so soon. But my girl

was too smart for her own good, and we already had to watch what we said around her.

"It's complicated, baby." I pressed a lingering kiss to her head again. "All you need to know is that Mommy loves you very much. And Daddy loves you, too."

Tears stung my eyes, but I blinked them away, refusing to cry. She was better off without him in her life—we both were. And one day, she would know that. She would know the truth.

But I'd protect her from that for as long as possible.

And when the day finally came when she was old enough, I would do everything in my power to make sure she knew her worth. That she knew she never had to settle for less than she deserved.

It was a promise I'd made to myself after I'd finally gotten us away from Warren.

She would not fall prey to the mistakes I did. Not if I could help it.

"I woves you too, Mommy. So, so much. The mostest in allll the land."

"I love you too, princess." I bopped her nose. "Now close your eyes and try to go to sleep, okay?"

"Sweet dreams," she murmured, closing her eyes.

"Sweet dreams, baby."

I watched her fall into a peaceful slumber. I watched her chest rise and fall, her eyelids flutter as she dreamed what I only hoped were happy things.

The hard questions would come eventually; I just hadn't expected them quite so soon. But Imogen was forever surprising me.

I hated that she would have to one day discover the truth about her father, about the kind of man he was. I hated that she might never get to experience the sturdiness of a good man—a good father. My dad tried to be that for her, but it wasn't the same. He was her grandpa, and no matter how much he tried to fill that void, he would never quite achieve it.

It seemed silly now, lying here with my daughter sleeping in my arms, to ever think that I could just pursue a no-strings arrangement with a guy. Being a mom was who I was—ingrained into the very fiber of my being. Everything I did was for Immy, to give her a better future. She wouldn't be little forever. I could worry about dating when she was older, when I had the emotional capacity to let somebody in.

The right person.

Definitely not the college hockey player with a dangerous smirk and dirty mouth.

Austin didn't reply.

Another day rolled by, and my last texts to him

went unanswered, so, much to my disappointment, I did the sensible thing.

I deleted his number.

Mom and Dad offered to watch Imogen an extra night a week so I could pick up some overtime at the bar. I worked the late shift so I could put Imogen to bed before I left. Tips alone made it worth it.

"Hey, girl," one of the dancers called as I headed into the staff room to drop my purse in my locker.

"Hey, Jada. Is it busy out there tonight?"

"Ain't it always?" She flashed me a bright smile before adjusting her bralette and sauntering back out front.

Before I had Imogen, I loved to dance. I loved to party and cut loose. I envied the girls who danced up on the stage. How, for those few minutes, they held the crowd in the palm of their hand.

When I'd taken the job at O'Shea's, I'd promised my parents I would never strip for money. But what they didn't know was I couldn't even if I wanted to.

Giving birth and nursing Imogen for the first year of her life had changed my body. Changed the way I saw my body. Changed how I felt in my skin.

The men and women who frequented O'Shea's wanted sexy and seductive. Something I hadn't felt in a long time.

Until Austin, a little voice whispered. But I shut it down.

Sure, Austin had made me feel beautiful and desired, and all the things I imagined Jada and the rest of the girls felt with the spotlight beaming down on them. But that was different.

And now that he knew the truth, it didn't matter anymore.

CHAPTER 9

AUSTIN

"This is a surprise, Hart," Danny Mac, the facility's caretaker, smiled over at me as he tinkered with the Zamboni. "I thought practice started back up next week."

"It does. But I thought I might get ahead of the game."

"You know Coach is pretty strict about—"

"Come on, Danny. Do me a favor. I really need to get out there." I glanced at the rink, anticipation zipping through me.

"Fine, fine." He waved a dismissive hand at me. "Just go steady, yeah. We already lost Morgan. We don't need to lose our best goalie, too."

"Relax, old man. I'm only going to do a few laps."

The Lakers facility had been my home for the last three and a half years. I knew this place better than the house I'd grown up in.

The ice was solid under my skates as I hopped through the gate. I'd worked out consistently over winter break; it wasn't like I had much else to do. But this was different.

Skating required everything from you: strength, endurance, flexibility, and power. It was a complete mind and body workout, pushing you to your limits and testing your resolve. But I'd been skating since I was a kid. It was muscle memory now—as easy as breathing.

I closed my eyes and took a leisurely lap of the rink, breathing in the crisp, clean air.

Out here, during practice or a game or even just right now, alone on the ice, everything stopped. To skate your best, you had to empty your mind and focus on every glide, every breath, and every turn.

After a couple of days' laps, I picked up speed. Pumping my legs hard, I flew around the rink. It wasn't enough, though. I needed more. So, I added in some turns, zig-zagging from one side of the rink to the other.

Being a goalie, I had to have excellent game awareness, a strong gloved hand, and impeccable puck-handling ability. But what a lot of people didn't realize was that skating was key for my position.

I had to be able to move quickly in all directions; I had to react and recover, to make abrupt, balanced transitions from one move to another, all while being ready to make the save... wearing fifty pounds of protective gear.

But I thrived on the pressure. On knowing that it was my responsibility to keep the opponent's puck out of the back of the net.

Coach Tucker constantly told us not to bring our personal lives onto the ice, and I was an expert at compartmentalizing.

Not today, though.

I couldn't get Madison out of my head. I couldn't stop thinking how the initial shock and betrayal I felt at discovering her secret had quickly morphed into something else.

Something that felt a lot like disappointment.

But that was only because it had cut short our little arrangement, right?

It should have been a blessing in disguise. I knew the truth now, and I could stay far, far away from her.

I hadn't replied to her apology text. What was there to say?

But I wasn't doing a very good job of forgetting her either.

I didn't like it.

Having my thoughts consumed by piercing blue eyes and a gorgeous smile.

I thought coming to the facility, getting out on the ice and skating my ass off would clear my head, let me refocus on what was important. But as I whipped around the rink, pushing myself to the limit, the frustration only intensified.

Which only made everything ten times worse. Because if I couldn't forget about her. If I couldn't get Madison out of my mind, then I wouldn't be able to play our first game back with a clear head.

Maybe I needed some closure—a face-to-face conversation.

Or another thought hit me out of left field.

Maybe we could just be friends.

It wasn't difficult to track down the bar that Madison worked at. Olin Bay was a small town and she'd mentioned she worked at a local bar.

Probably not my best idea ever, turning up at her place of work unannounced. But after three days of radio silence, I had to see her, and I wasn't sure she'd welcome my offer to meet.

So here I was, like some creep, stalking her at work.

Jesus, I really had stooped to a new low. But I was a Laker, a hockey player who wanted to win. And winning didn't come without the kind of single-mindedness and dogged determination that flowed through my veins.

I shoved open the door and entered the bar, taking in the dimly lit room. It was quiet, only a few people milling about at dark stained tables with a sultry beat pouring out of the hidden speakers.

It screamed strip club.

I knew I'd been to a few over the years with my teammates. But there was no dancer on the small stage positioned at the far side of the room.

A sticky sensation went through me. Did Madison strip? She was a single mom, after all. I already knew she worked two jobs, probably to make ends meet.

Scanning the room, I found her behind the bar, serving an older man his beer. She smiled up at him, laughing at something he said.

A lick of jealousy went through me.

Shit.

Maybe this was a bad idea.

I hadn't planned what I was going to say to her or even—

"Austin," she mouthed, her eyes finding me across the room over his shoulder.

Like the idiot I was, I lifted my hand in a small wave and made my way over.

"W-what are you doing here?" She stared at me with those hypnotic blue eyes, and my heart went fucking haywire.

"I... can we talk?"

"I'm at work. How did you even find me here? What are—"

"Everything good here, Madison?" the guy asked, giving me the once over.

"Yeah, I'm fine, Julian. Austin is... a friend."

I bristled, pinning *Julian* with a 'fuck off' look.

He snorted, not even bothering to acknowledge me and focused his attention back on Madison. "I'll be at my usual table if you need me."

She gave him a small nod.

"That was rude," she snapped the second he was gone.

"The guy was sizing me—"

"Austin." She let out an exasperated sigh. "What are you doing here?"

"I came to see you."

"Why?"

I raked a hand through my hair, feeling all kinds of awkward. "Because... because I wanted to talk."

"To talk..." Bitter laughter spilled out of her. "So, ignoring my attempt to talk to you and explain, what was that exactly?"

"Come on, Madi. It threw me for a loop. I didn't—"

"I don't have time for this. I'm two hours into a five-hour shift, and it's about to get real busy in here."

"I can wait."

"You're going to wait three hours for me?" She stared at me with disbelief.

"I have nowhere else to be." I shrugged. "And looks like the entertainment is just about to start."

A single spotlight had fallen over the stage, illuminating a chair.

"Shit," Madison muttered under her breath.

"Problem?" My brow arched, and she pursed her lips.

"It's Jada. She's... a favorite with the crowd." Something passed over her face. It looked a lot like jealousy, but that couldn't be right.

Madison was drop-dead gorgeous. And from her displeasure at seeing me again, I couldn't imagine she cared much whether or not I watched some stripper do her thing.

Unless...

"I'll have a beer, please."

"You're really staying."

"I am."

"And you're going to watch Jada's performance?"

"Seems like it." I hopped up onto a stool and got comfortable.

"Fine. Whatever. I'm sure you'll love it."

Oh, she was jealous.

Interesting.

Madison stormed off to get my beer, and I fought the urge to track her every move.

I'd never felt possessive over anyone before. It was unnerving, to say the least. Especially given that Julian, or whatever the smug asshole was called, was watching her. He was at least twenty years her senior with a head full of salt and pepper hair. But he had that Eric Dane in his McSteamy era thing working for him.

I only knew because sometimes Fallon liked to watch Grey's Anatomy re-runs, and I usually didn't have the energy to tell her to change the channel.

A group of guys poured into the bar, taking up the tables nearest to the stage. Madison grabbed a notepad and headed over to them. I didn't like it, watching them leer at her, letting their hungry gazes trail all over her soft curves.

Thankfully, the uniform wasn't anything too revealing, but it didn't stop the flood of jealousy saturating my veins.

As if she felt my heavy gaze, Madison glanced over at me. I quickly ducked my head, dragging a hand over my face.

Jesus. This was going to be a fucking shitshow.

I probably should have stayed away. But I never claimed to be smart, and until I'd exorcised whatever spell she'd cast over me, I knew I couldn't walk away.

"Austin, was it?" McSteamy stepped up to me.

"That's right."

"So, how do you know Madison?"

"Like she said, I'm a friend."

Who the fuck did this asshole think he was?

"She's a good girl," he said, glancing in her direction. She was busy taking the table's order still, paying us no attention. "After everything she's been through, she doesn't need—"

"I'm sorry, who are you again?"

"I'm a friend too." He came closer, snarling. "You'd do well to remember that."

He brushed past me. The asshole might as well have pulled out his dick to see whose was bigger.

Madison approached me, wearing a frown. "What was all that about?"

"McSteamy?"

"Mc— What?"

"Yeah, you know Dr. Sloan—"

"I know who Dr. Sloane is, Austin." Frustration coated her words. "I just don't understand what's going on right now."

"I'm about to watch the show and enjoy a beer." I snatched up my bottle and waved it in her face.

Irritation glittered in her eyes, but to my disappointment, Madison didn't take the bait.

Offering me a tight smile, she said, "Good for you," and stormed off, which gave me a perfect view of her ass in her skintight black pants.

The bar went quiet, darkness falling over the entire place. A ripple of anticipation went through the air, making the hairs along the back of my neck stand on edge. The spotlight reappeared, illuminating a single figure. The opening beats of a slowed-down version of *Crazy in Love* played out, and a cheer went up around me.

Madison wasn't wrong. The stripper was clearly a favorite with the regulars.

But I wasn't watching her.

I was watching Madison out of the corner of my eye. The way she watched the stage, eyes fixated on the dancer, brimming with envy and a hollow sadness that sucker punched me right in the chest.

She felt me staring, and our gazes clashed.

The room around us fell away until everything ceased to exist except her and me.

Me and her.

I'd never experienced anything like it.

It was like a clap of thunder in my chest. Waking me up. Bringing me to life.

Madison had a kid.

A kid.

Yet, I was finding it really hard to remember all the reasons why pursuing her was a bad fucking idea.

Madison avoided me like the plague. My next two beers came via another server, who I learned was named Hannah, and I barely got a glimpse of Madison as she worked the tables on the floor.

The bar was crammed now. Full of men all looking to see a few naked pairs of tits and maybe the money shot if they were lucky.

I'd switched off an hour ago. I could appreciate the female form, even going as far as to say I enjoyed a good strip show. But I only had eyes for Madison.

I realized how creepy it was to sit uninvited and watch her work, but I needed to talk to her, to clear the air, and set the record straight.

I don't know why it was so important. She was no one to me, not really. But there had only ever been one person in my life I cared about—really cared about—and I'd let my sister down in more ways than I ever thought possible.

Sometimes, I was surprised Aurora still talked to me after everything I'd unknowingly put her through back in high school.

My hand curled into a tight fist against my thigh as I drained my beer. I hadn't been there for Rory because I'd been a hotheaded, angry teenager with abandonment issues.

I didn't know how to fix my relationship with my sister, how to smooth the cracks that had splintered and fractured over the years. But I could apologize to Madison.

I could prove to myself that I wasn't the cold-hearted bastard everyone thought me to be.

And, then maybe, it would be a step toward figuring out how to make peace with the past.

The bar began to empty; a few stragglers moved on by security. But I lingered. Even McSteamy left. Not before he sought Madison out and said goodbye, though.

The second his mouth grazed her cheek, I'd almost cracked a molar. But she wouldn't appreciate my alpha possessive bullshit, so I forced myself to remain seated, biding my time.

She couldn't avoid me forever, and I had no plans to leave without her hearing me out.

The other servers watched me, shooting Madison knowing looks, but she brushed them off. Until, finally, the staff began to disperse.

"You need to go," she said, coming to a stop in front of me.

"I'm waiting for you to finish."

"Don't bother. I—"

"You're pissed."

"I'm not pissed, Austin, I'm disappointed. Which is ridiculous," she huffed. "I knew how you'd react if you found out the truth. I knew and still let myself— No." She inhaled a shaky breath, tucking a stray curl behind her ear. "I'm not doing this."

Madison would barely look at me, and it fucking stung.

"It was fun while it lasted, Austin, but that's all it was. A bit of fun. As you know now, I have my hands full, and you have... college."

"You caught me off guard." I hadn't expected to come face-to-face with a tiny blonde hellion with Madison's smile, let alone discover she belonged to the girl I was fucking.

"And I apologized, and you ghosted me," she said humorlessly.

"Not my finest moment."

"You're telling me." Bitter laughter spilled out of her.

Damn, she was beautiful even when she looked like she wanted to kick me in the balls.

"So you've got a kid."

"Yeah, I do. And she's pretty amazing."

"I'm not surprised."

Her brows furrowed. "You're not?"

"She takes after her mom."

"Austin..."

"Yeah, I know. Our fun is over." I got up, and Madison stepped back, keeping a safe distance between us. "But that doesn't mean I don't want to see you again."

Her brow lifted, doubt shining in her eyes. "What are you saying?"

"We could try being friends."

"Friends?"

"Yeah."

"Austin, I'm pretty sure you don't want to be my friend."

Shit, why was I so bad at this?

Why couldn't I just let her go?

She'd given me the perfect opportunity to walk away. But I couldn't do it.

Not again.

Not when all I ever did was turn my back on people.

The truth was simpler than that, though. I wasn't ready to give up my time getting to know Madison.

But she was right.

We couldn't be more either.

CHAPTER 10

MADISON

Austin Hart was proving to be a giant thorn in my side.

It wasn't that I wasn't flattered by his unexpected visit. I was. It just didn't change anything, not really.

He was still a senior in college with big dreams of playing for the NHL if the rumors were to be believed, and I was still the twenty-one-year-old single mom working two jobs just to make ends meet.

But he wouldn't leave.

And I didn't have the energy to try and make him.

"Fine," I huffed, giving him a little shake of my head. "I get off at half past. You can walk me home."

"You're walking—"

"Wait, or don't wait." I shrugged. "I've got work to do."

It was late. I was tired and cranky, and I smelled like stale beer and cheap cologne, thanks to the handsy group of guys who showed up to celebrate their friend's birthday earlier.

Not exactly my idea of a fun time but the tips were good, and I needed the money.

O'Shea's could get a little wild sometimes, especially on the weekend, but the safety and security of the staff—floor staff and dancers alike—was a top priority for Jack O'Shea, the owner.

My parents would have preferred I didn't work at a strip club, but there weren't many jobs out there where you could tuck your daughter into bed before your shift, then get home and manage to cram in at least six hours of sleep before she woke.

Besides, it was only three nights a week unless I took on extra shifts.

"Looks like you've got a new fan club," Kingsley said. "You need me to tell him to take a hike? You just say the word, Mads."

"It's all good." I gave him a warm smile as I wiped down the last of the tables. "He's just a friend."

He scoffed, folding his giant arms over his chest. "That's what they all say. You need a ride home, or is your *friend* taking you?"

"I'm a big girl, Kingsley." I tapped his shoulder. "But thanks for the concern."

"Just looking out for my favorite." He winked, but there was no heat there. Kingsley was happily married with three gorgeous children. Sometimes, his wife Yolanda invited me over so Imogen could play with their daughter Kyra.

"You're a good man. I'll see you tomorrow."

He gave me a nod and went back to his position by the door, where he would stand vigil until the last member of staff left for the night.

I slipped into the staff room and grabbed my jacket and purse. Austin was waiting when I went back into the main room.

"All set?" he asked, and I brushed past him, making a beeline for the door. "So do you have all the guys in this place wrapped around your little finger or just—"

"Unbelievable," I snapped.

"Joke." Guilt flashed in his eyes. "I was joking."

"Well, your joke sucked."

"You're really going to make me work for it, huh?" I glared at him, and his eyes went wide with realization. "Shit, I didn't... fuck, you're right, I suck at this."

"Relax, hotshot." Nudging his arm, I smiled up at him as we spilled out on the sidewalk. "You don't always suck."

"I am sorry, you know. About how I reacted the other day."

"I get it. But if I'd have fessed up that first night we met, I'm pretty sure we wouldn't be standing here now."

He opened his mouth to argue but quickly thought better of it.

We both knew the truth.

It stung, but I couldn't blame him, not really.

"But we are ... standing here, I mean." His eyes burned into mine, and I could still feel it. That spark between us, the magnetic pull that I couldn't seem to resist.

It didn't matter though. We were done. Our temporary fun was over.

Austin needed to realize that.

"So this is where you were born and raised?" he asked as we walked toward my neighborhood. It was late—almost one. Usually, I grabbed a ride home with one of the other servers.

"Yep. Olin Bay is home."

"I like it; it has that small seaside vibe."

"I like that everyone looks out for each other. The world needs more of that." I stared off at nothing, trying to ignore Austin's scrutiny.

A heavy silence descended over us, only adding to the tension already crackling between us.

Chemistry or not, things were different now. Fantasy and reality had collided and reminded me why

I didn't pursue dating. Because things got too complicated. And my daughter became a scapegoat.

I didn't want that.

I didn't want her to be an inconvenience to the guys who might come and go in my life, not when she was my priority—the center of my entire universe.

And always would be.

"You know you really didn't have to walk me home," I said, eventually breaking the silence.

"I wanted to."

"Well, consider yourself absolved of whatever guilt you're still feeling once we get there."

Because I couldn't do this.

I couldn't have him pity me or whatever the hell this was.

It didn't feel nice.

"I'm getting the feeling I screwed up by coming here."

"You think?" I asked, failing to keep the incredulity out of my voice.

Austin stopped abruptly and dragged a hand over his jaw as if he was contemplating what to say next. How to dig himself out of the giant hole he'd found himself in.

"I'm sorry, okay."

"Austin, we already did this part." I blew out a frustrated breath. "You're sorry, I get it. But it's just words. It doesn't change anything. Look, you should go. I only live on the next block over, and my parents are there watching Imogen."

"So that's it, huh? You're just going to kick me out of your life?"

"Don't tell me you want to stick around and be friends."

"Is that so hard to believe?"

"I have a daughter, Austin. I work two jobs. I barely have any time to myself. Even if you wanted to be friends—and I don't believe you do—I don't have the emotional capacity to let you in."

It wasn't the whole truth, but he didn't need to know that. He didn't need to know that the fact he was even here, that he'd tracked me down, meant something to me.

And it was because of his little gesture that I knew if I gave him this, if I agreed to his offer of friendship, I wouldn't be able to stop myself falling for him.

"You don't believe me." His expression was crestfallen.

"I know I said I wanted to have fun." My voice was barely above a whisper as I dropped my gaze. "But it's different now. I don't think I could—"

"Stop, please." His fingers slid under my jaw, cupping my chin gently. Austin tilted my face up to his, staring at me with an intensity that made my heart ache. "I didn't come looking for sex. I came to apologize and say that I'd like to hang out occasionally. It's kind of nice having someone around who doesn't care about the fact that I'm a Laker."

"Perhaps you need to widen your social circle if that's the case."

"That's what I'm trying to do." His mouth twitched at the corners, and my stupid, traitorous heart fluttered.

God, he was insufferable.

"You came, you apologized, now please go."

"Fine. I'll leave." He held up his hands. "If you agree to hang out with me again soon."

He kept saying those words.

Hang out.

Like they didn't mean anything.

"Austin, I—"

He started walking off in the direction of my building. "Guess I'll just walk you to your door then."

I hurried after him, grabbing his arm. The second my fingers grasped his wrist, sparks zipped through me. Our eyes clashed again, and he arched a brow.

Dropping his arm, I stepped back. "You're not going to let this go, are you?"

"I'm goalie for one of the best teams in the NCAA. What do you think?" His mouth twitched, and I remembered what it was like to kiss him. How thoroughly he had devoured me.

"I think you need to leave." The words came out muffled, thanks to the giant lump in my throat.

"Can I at least text you?"

"You're starting to sound desperate."

Something flashed in his eyes, but it was gone in an instant. "Fine. You win. I'll watch you go in."

"You don't need to do that," I sighed.

"Good night, Madison."

"Night, Austin."

I lingered for a second, wondering whether I was making a giant mistake. But then I remembered the little girl waiting at home for me and walked away from him.

Austin watched me the entire way to my door.

"How was she?" I asked the second I entered my apartment.

It wasn't much. A modest sized two-bedroom with an open plan living area and kitchen and a small communal yard at the back where Imogen could play. I was saving everything I could for a down payment on a house, but it was going to be years before I had enough.

"An angel, of course." Mom already had her jacket on.

I didn't take it personally. She wasn't one to sit around and make small talk. But still, I found myself saying, "You don't have to leave straight away. We could have—"

"It's late, and we have Pilates first thing."

"Before we go though, sweetheart, we wanted to run something by you." Dad looked at Mom, and she nodded.

"What's wrong?" Dread snaked through me at the strange, silent conversation they seemed to be having.

"The Creedys invited us on vacation with them. A cruise around the Caribbean. All expenses paid."

"Wow, that's kind of them."

"It's Derek's fiftieth birthday. They want to celebrate big."

"Well, you should totally go. I'm sure Jer can help me out with Immy. And I can ask Jacqui and Ken. If you let me know the dates, I can figure something out."

It wasn't ideal, but they deserved a vacation. They gave up a lot to help me with Imogen. If it came down to it, I'd ask for some leave days.

"Well, that's the thing, sweetheart. We leave next week."

Next week?

Crap, that didn't give me long to make any arrangements.

"Oh, I see. Well, it should be okay. It's only a couple of—"

"Three and a half weeks," Mom said.

"What?"

"The cruise. It's for three and half weeks."

She might as well have told me it was for six months.

Two weeks, I could maybe get all my shifts covered. But three and a half weeks? That was going to be virtually impossible.

"We know it's short notice," Dad started, but I cut him off.

"It's fine. Like I said, I'll figure it out."

From Mom's tone, it was apparent they had already made their decision.

He gave me an apologetic smile before coming to kiss my cheek. "If it wasn't Derek and Marie—"

"It's fine, Dad. You deserve a break." I backed away and wrapped my arms around my chest, waiting for them to leave.

Mom didn't comment, but then I didn't expect her to.

"Thanks for watching Immy tonight," I said, filling the awkward silence.

"Good night." She gave me a cursory smile, and I hated it—the icy void between us.

She loved me and Imogen. I didn't doubt that. But she had never forgiven me for messing up my life in the name of young love.

"Night, Dad. Mom."

"Night, sweetheart." Dad held the door, and she slipped out. "If you need some money to cover—"

"I got it, Dad. It's fine."

"You don't always need to be so self-sufficient, you know. It's okay to lean on your old man every once in a while."

"Thanks, Dad. You should probably go before she comes looking for you."

"Your mother loves you, Madison. I know she doesn't always—"

"Greg?" Her voice drifted down the hall.

"Go," I said, ushering him out of my apartment. "I'll see you tomorrow."

He gave me a kiss on the cheek and hurried out after my mother. I closed the door and slid the chain into place, letting out a heavy sigh.

Tonight had been... Well, it had been mightily confusing.

I hadn't expected Austin to show up. And I definitely hadn't expected him to want to make amends.

It didn't make any sense.

He'd learned the truth.

He knew I couldn't keep up with anything more than casual.

Yet, he'd still insisted on getting me to agree to see him again.

Friends.

Did he really want to be just friends?

Frustrated with myself, Austin, and my parents, I padded down the hall and checked in on Imogen. She was fast asleep, clutching Mr. Hopsy like her little life depended on it.

Pulling her door closed, I headed into my room and stripped out of my dirty uniform. I snatched my oversized t-shirt off the back of the chair and yanked it on, before loosening my hair out of its messy bun.

Usually, I showered after a shift at the bar, but I was tired and cranky, and I just wanted to curl up in bed and sleep.

But the second I was comfortable, my cell bleeped.

Austin: I just got home.

Madison: Err, thanks

I bit my lip, fighting a smile. This version of Austin was endearing. If not, a little irritating.

Madison: How did you get to Olin Bay
by the way?

Austin: I took the bus.

Madison: The bus?

Austin: Yeah, is that so hard to
believe?

Madison: You don't drive?

It occurred to me then how little I knew about the Lakers goalie.

Austin: I do, yeah. But everything in Lakeshore is pretty local so I don't have a car right now.

Madison: It's late, I need to sleep before Imogen wakes me.

Austin: Is she a good sleeper?

A trickle of unease went through me. I could deal with him asking *me* questions and the strange banter that existed between us. But I couldn't deal with him pretending to care about her.

Madison: Good night, Austin.

Austin: Night, pretty girl.

I dropped my phone on the nightstand and tucked my hand under my pillow, closing my eyes.

It wouldn't be all that difficult to keep Austin at arm's length. He would grow tired eventually and move on to his next conquest.

Because that's all this was to him.

A challenge.

A game.

Like he said, he was the goalie for one of the best teams in college hockey. He wasn't used to losing.

But I wasn't some trophy or prize he could win.

My life was complicated and messy. And the sooner Austin realized that, the sooner he would walk away and never look back.

CHAPTER 11

AUSTIN

Good question.

But I was trying not to look too closely. The bottom line was I wanted to see her again. Any way I could get her.

> Austin: Because I like spending time with you.

Madison: I'm not sleeping with you again.

> Austin: I'm not asking you to.

Madison: You really want to be just friends?

> Austin: I said I did, didn't I?

Did I want to have sex with Madison again? Of course, I did. She was gorgeous, and now I knew how hot she was between the sheets; I couldn't stop thinking about it.

But this was about more than sex. It was me doing the right thing for once.

I could be a friend to her. Someone she could lean on. I could prove to myself that I wasn't the asshole everyone mistook me for.

It had never seemed important before, but everything was different now.

My sister was in love with one of my best friends. They were living together, for fuck's sake. Connor was out for the rest of his final season with the Lakers, reminding us all how we were only one injury away from never stepping foot on the ice again. And it was less than six months until graduation.

In one way or another, everybody's lives were moving forward.

Except mine.

I still had no real plans beyond graduation. Despite a few conversations with NHL teams in my sophomore year, I had no one chomping at the bit to sign me. There was still time, but the cold, hard truth was I didn't know if hockey was in my future.

And if it wasn't…

I didn't want to think about that.

My phone bleeped again, and relief skittered down my spine. For a second there, I thought she might ghost me.

Madison: Fine. Tuesday? My parents are taking Immy for the night.

Austin: It's a date.

Shit. That sounded all wrong. I quickly texted her again.

Austin: I didn't mean, it's a date date. It's just two friends hanging out.

Madison: Austin?

Austin: Yeah, pretty girl?

Madison: Shut up.

"So let me get this straight," Madison said as she tucked into her bacon and cheese fries. "You left for the night so your roommate could win back his girl?"

"Something like that."

"Where are you going to stay?"

"I'll probably just stay at the team's frat house."

"The team has a frat house?"

"Most of us aren't pledges, but Lakers House is a long-standing tradition."

"Sounds like my idea of hell." She chuckled. "I've never really understood the whole Greek life thing."

"It's not my idea of fun either. But it comes with being a Laker." I drained my soda and motioned for the server to bring me another. "You know, I'm surprised you agreed to meet with me."

"So am I." A hesitant smile played on her lips. "But I knew you weren't going to let it go, and I had no plans tonight." She shrugged.

"Your parents have Immy for the night?" I asked.

"Yeah, they want to spend some time with her before they leave for their vacation."

"Are they going anywhere nice?"

"A three-and-a-half-week cruise around the Caribbean."

"Nice."

"Yeah," she murmured, her expression dropping.

"You're not happy about it?"

"It isn't that." Frustration coated her words, and I saw the torment in her eyes. "They deserve a break, and their friends are paying for the whole thing. But it was last minute, so it didn't leave me much time to make childcare arrangements."

"I take it they help you out a lot."

She nodded. "I don't know what I'd do without them."

"Must be nice to be close to your parents."

"Oh, it isn't all sunshine and rainbows." Her lips pursed. "They're great with Imogen and absolutely adore her. But things between me and my mom are complicated."

"I know a thing or two about difficult mothers."

I didn't talk to people about this stuff with anyone, but it came easy with Madison.

"You said before you have a sister," she said.

"Yeah, just the one."

"Are the two of you close?"

My chest squeezed. For as easy as it was to talk to her, that was a whole can of worms I wasn't ready to open. "It's complicated."

Madison lifted her milkshake in a toast. "To complicated families then." I clinked my glass against her with a smile, and she added, "So winter break is over soon, huh?"

"Yeah."

"Do you have to practice a lot?"

"We have daily practice on the ice, then there's training and conditioning off the ice. We play two games a week, Thursdays and Fridays, and we stand a real chance at making it to the Frozen Four this year. If we do, that means extra games."

"Sounds intense."

"It is. But it's all I know."

It wasn't the grueling schedule I dreaded; it was standing still. Being left with too much time to think. Reflect.

Regret.

"Bet it doesn't leave much time for a social life." Something sparked in her eyes, and I wanted to believe that she meant her.

That I wouldn't have much time for *her*.

But Madison had made it clear where we stood. Even though she was here, something had cooled between us. Like she'd put up a wall.

I couldn't blame her. She had to think about Imogen. But it didn't stop me from wanting to be around her.

"In case you haven't noticed, I'm not exactly a sociable guy," I replied, shoving my almost-empty plate away.

"Oh, I don't know. You don't do so bad." Madison smiled at me, and the air heated between us.

Was she imagining how good it had been between us? Because I sure as fuck was.

"Austin," she warned, and I had my answer. But she had to hammer home the point. "Friends, remember."

"Yeah, I know." I fought a smile.

Friends were safe. Uncomplicated and less messy.

But it didn't stop me from wishing that, for once, that things were different.

That I was different.

"You're sure about this?" I asked when we reached Madison's building.

I'd been surprised when she offered to let me stay. But I wasn't about to decline the chance to spend more time with her.

"You need a place to stay. I have a perfectly good couch going spare."

"I don't want to make—"

"Austin?"

"Yeah?"

"Shut up." Her lips quirked as she unlocked the door and ushered me inside.

The second I entered her apartment, I was aware that this was a family space. Toys littered the floor. Children's artwork decorated the sideboard and hung in frames on the wall. Imogen was everywhere even though she wasn't here.

And I didn't know how to feel about that.

"Don't look so terrified; it won't bite." Amusement coated Madison's words as she caught me staring at some kind of papier-mâché animal. Except it didn't look friendly in the least. It looked positively terrifying.

"It's... cute."

"It's a horror show." Madison chuckled. "But Immy was so proud of herself for making it, I couldn't bear to throw it out. I'm hoping she'll bring home something a little less scary to replace it soon.

"Can I get you something to drink? Eat?"

"I wouldn't say no to a bottle of water," I replied.

I was out of my depth here. But after dinner, we'd gotten a drink. One drink led to two, and then Madison offered to let me stay here for the night.

"I have soda or hot chocolate?"

"Water is fine."

She motioned for me to follow her over to the kitchen. It was a compact design with room for a small table at the end of the breakfast counter. More artwork decorated the refrigerator, and there was a homemade calendar hanging on the wall that looked suspiciously like a reindeer made out of a little hand.

"She's a budding artist," I commented.

"Aren't all four-year-olds?"

"I really have no idea. My entire experience with

kids amounts to my friend's little brother. And he's twelve."

She glanced over at me, those big blues of hers softening.

"What?" I asked.

"Nothing. It's just been a while since I made a new friend."

It was on the tip of my tongue to tell her we could be more than that, at least, in the physical sense.

There was no reason we couldn't continue to enjoy each other. It didn't have to mean more than that. She had a busy life, and so did I.

But I swallowed the words, not wanting to ruin the precarious truce we'd reached.

"I'll get you some sheets and pillows. The couch isn't much but—"

"It's fine. I've slept on a hell of a lot worse."

"Sounds like one story I don't want to know."

"Probably not." I smirked. "Did you have plans for college?"

"I was seventeen, Austin. I had all kinds of plans." Her demeanor shifted, sadness bleeding in her pretty face. I wanted to hold her, to pull her into my arms and make it all better.

It was an unfamiliar feeling.

One I wasn't wholly comfortable with.

"Do you want to talk about it?"

"Not unless you want things to go from a little

awkward to hella awkward in sixty seconds flat." She smiled, but it didn't reach her eyes.

"Fair enough."

I wouldn't push, though, because it sounded like there was a story there. One I probably wasn't ready to hear.

"It's late, and I'm tired," she said, reinforcing her walls. "Make yourself comfortable, and I'll grab those pillows and blankets."

She brushed past me, but I grabbed her wrist. "Madi—"

"Don't Austin, I'm begging you, don't." She stared up at me with pain-filled eyes. "God, don't look at me like that."

"Like what?"

"Like you want to do more than be my friend."

"Maybe I do."

The words surprised us both.

"Shit, sorry. That's not—"

"It's fine." Her soft laughter eased the giant fucking knot in my stomach. "We're both adult enough to not act on our reckless desires."

"Are you saying that kissing me would be reckless?" My brow lifted, my heart crashing against my chest because she was flirting back with me.

Madison felt it, too.

And it shouldn't have mattered because I wasn't

here for that. But I was still a guy, and it felt good to know I affected her as much as she affected me.

Fuck, I was turning into a pussy.

"Get some sleep, Austin. I'll see you in the morning." She gave me another smile before shrugging out of my hold and disappearing down the hall.

I doubted sleep was going to come easy tonight.

Not with her sleeping down the hall.

"Austin, wake up."

"W-what?"

"Aust—"

"The fuck?" I bolted upright, almost head-butting Madison. "Shit, sorry."

"It's okay. You were out for the count."

"Guess your couch was comfier than it looked." I rubbed a hand through my hair and down the back of my neck.

Madison dropped her eyes to my bare chest, and a lick of heat went through me.

"Sorry, I got hot at night."

"It's fine. But I start my shift at ten, and I want to call in and see Imogen before I start."

"Fuck, yeah. I should go."

"Relax, hotshot. There's time for coffee and breakfast. Come on." She motioned for me to follow her, so I got up and pulled on my jeans and t-shirt.

"Can I use the bathroom?"

"You know where it is. I'll go turn on the coffee maker."

It should have felt weird, waking up in her apartment on the couch.

Oddly, it didn't. And when I finally joined her in the kitchen, we worked seamlessly together to get coffee and plate up the stack of pancakes she'd cooked.

"This looks great, thanks."

"Figured you'd be hungry."

We ate in comfortable silence, stealing glances at one another.

I wanted to pick her brain, to know what she was thinking and whether she'd laid awake for hours like I had, remembering how good it had felt to be inside her.

"What?" she asked.

"Nothing."

Her brow lifted with suspicion, but I didn't confess. Some things were better left unsaid.

Besides, the thoughts running through my head were anything but 'just friends' right now.

She looked beautiful. Effortless in her thick black leggings and baggy pale blue sweater. She'd pulled her hair into a loose braid over one shoulder, letting a few strands remain loose to frame her face.

I imagined going to her, wrapping that tempting braid around my fist and—

"You need to stop looking at me like that," she whispered, heat creeping into her cheeks.

"Yeah, sorry." I drained my coffee.

The tension was palpable. The tether between us stretched and frayed. But I couldn't act on it.

So I ate my pancakes and drank my coffee, and told myself that I could do this.

That I could be just friends with Madison Reynolds.

Everyone turned up to see Connor and Ella.

"It's so good to see you." Dayna pulled Ella into a bone-crushing hug. She whispered something to her, giving her another little squeeze.

"Hey, El. Looking good." Aiden gave her a small nod.

Dumfries was my kind of guy. Aloof. A little bit guarded. He'd been the Lakers untouchable, hotheaded captain until he spent last summer in Dupont Beach with Assistant Coach Walsh. Now, he was completely smitten with his girl Dayna, but he still kept to himself.

"Did you enjoy the holidays?" Ella asked them.

"It was nice, but I'm glad to be back in Lakeshore. I won't have to share Aiden with Carson every waking minute."

"Coach Walsh and Dumfries got a little bromance going on?" Connor teased.

"We're friends." Aiden shrugged. "It's not a big deal."

"Hey," Harper and Mason joined us. "Welcome home," Ella said.

"That sounds strange." Harper's eyes crinkled, and Mason wrapped his arm around her waist.

"Sounds pretty good to me."

I tried to ignore the flash of irritation I felt about Harper and Mason moving in. I didn't care that they had taken Rory's old room. It was that their presence reminded me of Noah's absence... because the traitor had moved in with my little sister.

"No regrets about moving out of Lakers House?"

"Fuck no," he deadpanned.

The guys all chuckled. All except me.

"Hey, maybe you should move in, Austin," Noah suggested. "Take Mase's old room."

"Fuck off," I murmured, making a beeline for the refrigerator.

Of course, he thought I should go live in Lakers house. They probably all did.

"Don't push him," Rory chided.

"Come on, shortcake, I was only playing." The two of them began making moon-eye faces at one other, but thankfully Mason changed the subject.

"How does it feel to be back?" he asked Connor.

"Could have been under better circumstances."

"The team's surely going to miss you," Aiden added.

Connor sucked in a sharp breath, and I noticed Ella comfort him. He gave her an appreciative smile and mouthed, "I love you."

"I love you too."

God, they were so disgustingly in love.

I'd never been jealous before around them, only slightly nauseated. But something felt different now.

Thankfully, the guys turned the conversation to easier topics.

Connor was quiet, but I didn't blame the guy. He had a lot on his mind.

"So, where'd you go last night?" Noah asked, and I blinked when I realized he was talking to me.

"None of your business."

He smirked. "Well, according to Cutler, you didn't stay over at Lakers House, and I don't remember seeing you on our couch. So where were you?"

Fuck.

Why didn't I consider that someone would ask around after me?

"Noah," Rory hissed, cutting through the tension as we remained locked in a stare off.

"I have other friends outside of the team, and you four idiots, you know," I said.

"So you were over at a friend's?" Mason asked.

"I am not talking about this."

"Was said friend a girl friend or a guy friend?"

"You're an asshole." I pinned Noah with a dark look.

"Come on." He grinned. "We're only busting your balls. If you've got a new *friend*, it's all good."

"Fucking idiot," I muttered, grabbing a bottle of water and walking straight out of the kitchen.

I didn't owe him an explanation, and I certainly wasn't going to give him one in front of everyone.

I didn't get all up in their business, so fuck knows why they assumed they could stick their noses into mine.

Grabbing my earphones on the way out, I headed for the door and didn't look back.

I needed to burn off some steam before I said or did something I couldn't take back.

CHAPTER 12

MADISON

"Whew, that lunchtime rush was really something." Kayleigh, the owner of Sugartown Coffee Shop, was one of the best people I knew.

A real entrepreneur, she'd built Sugartown from the ground up with nothing but sheer grit and determination and a bank loan that gave her hives every time she thought about it; her words, not mine.

But business was booming, and thanks to a prime location right on the edge of Olin Bay and Lakeshore U, she drew a year-round crowd of tourists and students who couldn't resist her homemade bakes and uniquely flavored iced coffee and cold brews.

"It's the student crowd trickling back after winter break. They can't resist," I said.

"Let's hope so." She beamed. "I want to expand the gluten-free and vegan menu as well as introduce some more plant-based items, so I'm thinking of doing some free taste-testing evenings before we unleash it on the masses."

"That sounds amazing. If you need any help, just let me know."

I liked working at O'Shea's, but I *loved* working for Kayleigh. She was a ray of sunshine, constantly striving to better herself and her business. And at twenty-seven, she was the kind of strong, independent woman I looked up to. The kind of woman I'd always imagined myself becoming.

Before I got swept up in the chaos of young love.

"I will," she said. "Maybe I can arrange something on a night you're not working at the bar. I'll look at some dates."

"That would be amazing. Thank you." I wiped down a couple of tables and tucked the chairs underneath.

Sugartown was an eclectic mix of the old and the new. Modern and chic. I loved it.

It hosted open mic and slam poetry sessions on the weekends, a monthly book club, as well as cat-and-chat therapy sessions once a week for adults with dementia.

I'd just made it back to the counter when the door chimes tinkled.

"Hi, welcome to Sugartown," I said to the unfamiliar girl.

"Hi." She unwrapped her knitted scarf and smoothed the ends down the front of her jacket. "Wow, these look so good."

"The red velvet is my favorite."

"A friend recommended this place to me. I don't know how I've never found it before now."

"Let me guess. Student at LU?"

She nodded. "Freshman. Is it that obvious?"

"Not at all." I smiled. "We get a steady trickle of students passing through, but we could always use more."

For a second, I was tempted to ask if she knew Austin. But I tamped down the urge, pretty sure I wouldn't want to hear anything the female cohort of LU had to say about him.

He was an athlete, after all. Their reputations usually preceded them for a reason.

"I'm glad to be here."

"Well, you're in for a treat," I said. "And everything's homemade."

"You make all of this?"

"God, no, not me." Laughter vibrated in my chest. "My boss, Kayleigh. She's probably out back whipping up another batch of brownies as we speak."

"I heard the gluten-free menu is really good." She

eyed the glass cabinet reserved for our allergy-friendly options.

"They're all good."

"I'll take an almond milk macchiato and one of the gluten-free brookie bars, please."

"Good choice." I rang through her order, and she paid before moving to the end counter to collect her drink and sweet treat.

A minute later, I pushed a tray toward her. "One almond milk macchiato and one dark chocolate brookie bar. Enjoy," I said.

"Amazing, thank you. My boyfriend usually picks me up gluten-free brownies from my favorite coffee shop on campus, but if this tastes as good as it looks, I might have to tell him that's not going to work for me anymore." Her whole face lit up as she let out a soft laugh.

I knew that look.

She was in love. That all-consuming, heart-racing kind of love I'd been in once. But maybe, unlike me, she would get her happily ever after.

My stomach dipped, but thankfully, she added, "Well, thanks for this. I'm going to grab a table and start on some pre-class reading." Grabbing her tray, she headed off to find a seat.

With the lunch rush over and nothing else to do, I watched her discreetly from across the room, making her story up in my head. I bet she studied English or the Arts. Her boyfriend was probably an academic, too. Intelligent but in that sexy nerd kind of way. They probably spent their days discussing the classics and visiting museums. And the sex was off the charts because he was an overachiever and made it his mission in life to learn exactly how to please her.

God, I needed to get out more.

I shook the silly thoughts out of my head and distracted myself by organizing the eco-friendly coffee cups. By the time the pretty blonde returned her mug and empty plate, I'd fully restocked the cups and moved on to the cake boxes.

"Good?" I asked, taking the tray from her.

"So good. I'll definitely tell my boyfriend I have a new favorite."

"Well, here's a card so he doesn't forget." I plucked a business card out of the stand and handed it to her.

"Perfect. And I'll grab some of the brookie bites to go, please." She paid up, and I handed her the bag.

"Enjoy."

"Oh, I will unless my boyfriend eats them all first. He's impossible to fill up when he's practicing all the time."

"Practicing?" I asked.

"Oh yeah, he's a hockey player."

"A hoc—"

Her phone began to ring, and she dug it out of her pocket, glancing at the screen. "I need to take this. But thanks again." She gave me a small wave and hurried out of the shop.

A hockey player.

Her boyfriend was a hockey player.

Interesting.

Sitting down with a mug of coffee, I grabbed my cell phone off the arm of the couch and pulled up my message thread with Austin.

> Madison: I think one of your teammate's girlfriends stopped by the coffee shop today.

> Austin: Oh, really?

> Madison: Cute, blonde, ordered gluten-free brookies.

> Austin: Brookies?

> Madison: Yeah, you know. It's a layer of brownie and cookie smushed together to create a little slice of heaven.

> Austin: Sounds like Mason's girlfriend Harper. Did you talk to her?

I frowned at his reply. You couldn't always interpret someone's tone via text message, but if you could, I had a feeling Austin's would be full of apprehension.

> Madison: I didn't talk about you if that's what you're asking.

> Austin: Shit, Madi. I wasn't… Fine. You got me. I haven't talked to my friends about you yet.

I wasn't at all surprised to hear that.

> Madison: Relax, I'm just busting your balls.

> Austin: You can't say shit like that to me…

> Madison: Why not? Isn't that how FRIENDS talk?

Laughter spilled out of me, causing Imogen to poke her head up from her den. "What's funny, Mommy?"

"Just adult things," I said, fighting a smile.

"Is it Uncle Jerrykins? Cos he's funny," she asked.

"No, baby. It's not Jer."

"Fawny thens?"

"Nope."

"Oh, oh, I know. It must be Mr. Austins."

My heart stuttered in my chest. I hadn't anticipated she would remember him, but then, it was Imogen. She was practically four going on fourteen.

"I think it's time for your bath before Granny Jacqui comes to pick you up." She and Ken were taking Imogen for the night since I had a shift at the bar, and my parents were on their way to board the Caribbean Princess cruise ship.

"Why dids Grammy and Pops weave?"

"They've gone on vacation, remember?" I climbed off the couch and scooped her up out of the pillow fort we'd expertly crafted.

"Will they come back?"

"Of course, they will, sweetheart. They'll miss you so much. I bet they'll bring you a gift back with them."

"Oh, oh, maybe they'll gets me a friend for Mr. Hopsy."

"Maybe so."

"Yay, yay, Mr. Hopsy will haves a friend."

I carried her into our small family bathroom and set her down on the floor.

"Mommy?"

"Yeah, baby?" I asked as I drew her bath, checking to make sure it was the right temperature.

"Will you finds a new daddy for me?"

My heart tumbled. "That's..." Oh God. Icy, cold dread swam in my veins as she stared up at me with hope and expectation. "It doesn't work like that, sweetheart."

"But you can meets a nice young man. Pops said so."

"Did he indeed?"

Dad and I would be having words about what he and Mom talked about around little ears when they were back.

"Mr. Austins—"

"Okay, princess." I started undressing her, hoping to distract her. "Let's get you in the bath before all the bubbles melt."

"Bubbles don'ts melt, silly. They go p-p-pop."

My cell vibrated again, but I ignored it, gently splashing Immy while she enjoyed the water.

She was growing too fast and becoming more aware of herself and the world around her. It wouldn't be long before she had more questions about her father.

I dreaded that day—the day she learned that he was a monster. But until then, I would smother her with as much love as possible. I would remind her every second of every day of how special she was.

Imogen deserved the world, and I would find a way to give it to her.

Even if I had to work myself to the bone to make it happen.

O'Shea's was already crowded when I arrived. Kingsley greeted me, his mouth slashed with a reassuring grin as he warned me there was a bachelor party in.

That usually meant one of two things: a big tip or a lot of inappropriate banter, groping, and not nearly enough tips to cover the privilege.

As I eyed the rowdy group seated at one of the VIP tables at the side of the stage, I hoped it was the former.

"VIP table is yours if you want it, Mads," Hannah said.

"You got it." I never turned down the opportunity to serve a big table.

"Knock 'em dead," she added with an encouraging smile.

I grabbed a notepad and pen and headed toward them.

"About time the entertainment showed up." One of the guys grabbed my ass, squeezing hard.

"Actually, I'm just here to take your drink orders." I sidestepped his grabby hands but kept my smile polite. "What can I get y'all?"

They rattled off their orders, throwing in the odd comment about my tits or ass. The words rolled off me, though; it was nothing I hadn't heard a hundred times before.

"I'll get those brought right over, and we'll throw in a little something extra for the bachelor."

"How much for a private dance with extras?" Ass-grabber drawled.

"It's not that kind of bar, and I'm not a dancer."

"Shame." He huffed, running his hungry gaze up and down my body.

Suppressing a shudder, I headed back to the bar and rang their order through.

"They give you any trouble, and you just let Kingsley know, okay?" Hannah said.

"I can handle it."

"Well, don't be—Mads?"

"Sorry, what?" I dragged my gaze from the door, right where Austin stood, and gave her my attention.

"Isn't that the guy from the other night?" she asked.

"He's just a friend."

"Well, your *friend* better not come around causing any trouble."

"I'll handle it." I cast a furtive glance toward him.

What the hell was he doing here?

We hadn't agreed to see each other again.

"Hey," he said, sliding onto one of the barstools.

"Now would be a good time to fess up to any stalker tendencies." My tone was light, but the wild beat of my heart was not.

"I figured I could walk you home again."

"Austin, I'm at work," I sighed. "You can't just turn up here and sit vigil all night."

"Maybe I came for the entertainment." His gaze

flicked to the stage, and jealousy churned in my stomach. "Madi." He reached across the counter for my hand, but I stepped away. "I... I'm joking. It was a joke. A lame one, apparently."

"Can I get you a drink?" I changed the subject because this was easy.

It was safe.

"I'll take a beer," he said, studying me in a way that made my palms sweat and my heart ratchet. Jesus, if I didn't calm down, there was every chance I might pass out.

With a swift nod, I went to get his drink and put some much-needed space between us.

This was... unexpected. And while I didn't hate that Austin was here, I did hate the way my body responded to seeing him.

He looked good. Too good in his jeans and dark sweater, his hair falling a little over his eyes.

Austin Hart was a visual treat. A total snack as Jada would say.

Jealousy curdled in my stomach again.

I looked good, but everything was a little softer and looser since having Imogen. Certainly not tight and toned and centerstage-worthy.

"He looks at you like he doesn't see anyone else," Hannah whispered as I brushed past her, and my eyelashes fluttered as a shiver ran down my spine.

This was what I was worried about. Austin said he

wanted to be friends, but how was that possible when every time I looked at him, something tugged between us.

He's in college, Mads. College. *He isn't looking to settle down and take on you and all your baggage.*

I delivered Austin's beer with a casual smile. He slid ten dollars toward me and said, "Keep the change."

"Aus—"

"Hey, sexy," Ass-grabber approached us. "Me and my boys need another round of drinks. And maybe that dance, if you've removed the stick from your—"

"Watch your mouth." Austin stood, shooting daggers at him.

"Who the fuck are you? Her keeper?"

"I said watch your fucking—"

"Everything good here, Mads?" Kingsley appeared, and my shoulders sagged. The last thing I needed was Austin getting into a fight over me.

"Everything's good, Kingsley." My smile was tight. "If you could kindly escort this gentleman back to his table, I'll get that fresh round of drinks right over."

Austin didn't move; his jaw clenched so hard I was surprised he didn't crack a molar. Ass-grabber took the hint and shoved past Kingsley, swaggering back to his table.

"I like you, brother." Kingsley chuckled, giving Austin a small nod of respect... appreciation. I couldn't figure it out. I was too livid. "But I handle things around here." He winked and strolled off.

"Seriously?" I balked the second we were alone.

Austin sat down, dragging a hand down his face. "Does that happen a lot?" he gritted out.

"It's a strip club. What do you think?" I rolled my eyes, trying to keep my cool, given Hannah and Kingsley were both watching us.

"I think you need to get a better job."

"Yeah, well, some of us don't have the luxury of options." Indignation burned through me as I marched away from him.

How dare he.

How fucking dare he.

"Mad—"

I kept going, moving right to the other end of the bar.

Rationally, I knew he didn't mean it in the judgmental way I'd taken it. But Austin's presence confused me. His unwillingness to walk away when he had the chance made me wish and want and hope.

It was a dangerous game, though.

One I wasn't sure I wanted to play.

I'd lost part of myself before to a guy who said and did all the right things.

I vowed I wouldn't do it again.

CHAPTER 13

AUSTIN

I watched Madison storm away from me and had to fight the overwhelming urge to go after her.

This was her place of employment. She was right. I couldn't just turn up and act like I had some kind of claim on her.

But hearing that asshole demean her had ignited a violent storm inside me. And if the hulk of a security guy hadn't stepped in, I was pretty sure I would have done something reckless.

I didn't make it a habit of fighting. Not even on the ice, where every game was full of testosterone, competitiveness, and anger. Aside from getting into trouble a couple of months back for fighting before the puck dropped, I usually kept my cool.

Not tonight, though.

Tonight, I wanted to go to war with every fucker who so much as looked at Madison.

Which was a bit of a problem, given she worked in a strip club and the place was crowded, not to mention the fact she wasn't mine and didn't look all that happy to see me here.

Fuck.

Deciding to give her some space, I grabbed my drink and headed for one of the booths at the back of the room. The majority of the male patrons were seated up front, with a clear view of the stage. But I wasn't here for the entertainment.

I was here for her.

I couldn't explain it; all I knew was I couldn't stay away.

Friends. More than friends. I'd take any scraps of what she was willing to give me. Because for the first time in my life, I felt at ease around someone.

It occurred to me that maybe I liked her so much because she didn't know me, not really.

I could be someone else with her. The guy who didn't keep people at arm's length. Who didn't hate himself and the person he'd become.

With Madison, I could push all that shit aside and just breathe.

So I sat there in a darkened corner of the room and watched her. Soaking up every smile and laugh as she moved from table to table, taking orders and delivering drinks.

Some people might have judged her for being a young, single mom working in a strip club. But all I saw was a mom who would do anything for her daughter.

Something I'd *never* experienced growing up.

My mom had chosen her modeling career—*herself* —over me and Rory time and time again. And when our father grew tired of her selfish bullshit and left, she didn't only abandon me; she *hated* me.

All because I looked like him.

I reminded her of what she'd lost, what she'd willingly sacrificed for her career.

Mom might have held Rory to impossible standards and forced her onto a path that crushed her self-esteem and gave her an eating disorder, but she acted like I was dead to her.

Damn. I was a special brand of fucked up to be mentally comparing who'd had it worse at the hands of our mother, but I hadn't realized back then the true extent of the damage she had inflicted on my sister. I'd been too busy trying to escape my shitty existence. Fucking and fighting my way through high school. I channeled all my anger and frustration into hockey, constantly trying to prove to myself and everyone around me that I was worth something. That I didn't need anyone in order to get where I was going. Least of all, my parents. The two people meant to love me unconditionally.

I shut down *those* thoughts. I wasn't some hotheaded kid full of teenage angst and emotions anymore.

"You look like you could use this," Madison said, handing me another beer.

I hadn't even noticed her approach. But now that she was here, right in front of me, and I wanted nothing more than to reach for her and pull her onto my lap.

"Thanks."

"Not enjoying the show?" She tipped her head toward the stage, the scantily clad dancer there, working her spell on the crowd.

"I think we both know I'm not here for the entertainment."

Her lips pressed into a thin line as she studied me. Trying to dig into my psyche.

I didn't tend to worry about what people, especially girls, saw when they looked at me.

But I cared what Madison thought.

That spark I was becoming so used to feeling around her crackled between us, the air turning thick and heavy. Full of delicious anticipation I wasn't supposed to act on.

My gaze dropped to her mouth, and her tongue darted out, wetting her lips. A move that drove me fucking crazy. "Stop looking at me like that," she hissed.

"Stop teasing me with that perfect mouth of yours." The words were out before I could stop them.

"We can't do this again," she said weakly.

"Do what?" I played dumb, trying to cover my mistake.

But it was too late. The words were out in the open, hovering between us. A spark waiting to catch.

"Austin, we can't. I have a daughter, and you have… hockey."

"I'm not asking for anything you can't give me."

I didn't really know what I was asking for.

All I knew was I didn't want it to be the end. I liked her. I liked spending time with her. And I wasn't ready to give that up.

"Friends," she deadpanned, still her expression was as unconvinced as her tone.

"Friends… but more," I countered.

"You mean fuck buddies." Distaste washed over her.

"No, I mean friends with benefits."

Fuck.

Did I?

I'd tried that with Fallon, and it hadn't ended well. But Madison wasn't Fallon. And things weren't the same between us.

"No, thanks." She scoffed. "I've got more self-worth

than to be just another girl in your long line of puck bunnies."

Madison went to walk off, but I snagged her wrist, tugging her back to me. "*Exclusive* friends with benefits."

Fuck, did I really just say that?

"Why?" Her eyes flashed to mine, full of fire and wrath. She was pissed, and rightly so. But I wasn't good at this.

"Because we're good together," I said. "Because you make me feel good. And I think I make you feel good, too."

If I pushed too hard, I would lose her. But I didn't want to keep dancing around the electric chemistry between us. Pretending that I didn't want to touch or kiss her every time we were close.

I wanted Madison.

And I'd made up my mind I would have her any way I could get her.

Even if it was on her terms.

"I can't give you more than that, Austin. I have responsibilities, and Imogen will always come first. Always."

I nodded. "As she should."

Madison chewed her bottom lip, glancing around at the nearest tables. "I need to get back to work."

"Later, then?" I asked, hoping I didn't come off as an overeager idiot.

But the prospect of having her again...

I inhaled a shaky breath, trying to rein in the lust firing off around my body.

"Later," she whispered as she walked away so quietly I wasn't sure I'd heard her correctly.

Until she looked over at me, and I saw it then.

The longing in her eyes.

She wanted what I was offering.

But was she brave enough to take it?

"God, I can't believe I'm doing this," Madison murmured as I licked a path down her jaw, sucking and nipping along her collarbone.

We'd barely made it into her apartment before we crashed together.

"Feels good, doesn't it?" I ran my hand down her spine, curving it over her hip to drag her closer. More, I needed more.

"Yes, so good. So— Ah," she cried when I rolled my hips against her, letting her feel exactly what she did to me.

I'd been hard for most of the night, my gaze following her as she worked the floor. Every time our eyes caught across the room, it was like lightning in my veins.

Madison Reynolds was my kryptonite, and I was a weak, weak man around her.

"I want to feel you," she rasped, snaking her hand between our bodies to find my belt. She worked it open and popped the button before dipping her hand inside.

The second her warm, slim fingers closed around my length, a moan rumbled deep in my chest.

"Fuck," I hissed as she pumped me lazily, swirling her thumb across the slit on the upstroke.

"You're so hard," Madison preened, kissing me harder.

"Are you wet for me, pretty girl?"

"Why don't you find out."

Game fucking on.

I backed her up until she was trapped between my body and the kitchen counter. Madison blinked at me, her lust-drunk eyes blown wide, her lips forming a perfect *O* as I raked my gaze down her body. Her hand didn't stop working me, but she wasn't in control right now.

I was.

And I planned on making her scream.

"That's enough." I gently removed her hand from inside my jeans and took a step back. She pouted, her eyes heavy-lidded as she stared at me.

"Strip for me."

"W-what?" She gulped, the column of her throat bobbing at my demand.

"You heard me." I smirked, dragging my thumb over my bottom lip. "Strip for me."

"Austin, I don't..."

I closed the distance between us. "I watched you tonight, watching the girls up on stage."

"I didn't..." Madison's eyes grew wide. "That's not—"

"Do you know what I was thinking?"

"What?"

"I was thinking, I wish you were up there, dancing for me. Stripping... for me."

"You're being ridiculous." She rolled her eyes away from me. "I'm not going to strip for you."

Refusing to let it go, I dug my cell out of my pocket and opened the music app, selecting a slow song with a sexy beat.

Madison's breath caught, her eyes snagging on mine again. "Austin..."

I saw the spark there, the slight flush to her skin. She wanted to do it. She wanted to strip for me.

"Nobody is watching but me," I encouraged, "and Madi, I really fucking like what I see."

Her eyelashes fluttered as she pushed off the counter a little, letting her hands slide down her stomach. She began swaying her hips, slowly at first, hesitation shining in her eyes.

"Take it off," I urged, desperate to see all of her.

I half-expected her to stop, but she didn't. Instead, she surprised the fuck out of me by peeling her t-shirt off her body with a sexy as fuck little flick of her hair.

Jesus.

My body hummed with anticipation, my dick was hard and aching. I was desperate to get my hands on her. Desperate to explore every inch of her with my hands and mouth and tongue. But the anticipation was addictive. Like a wildfire racing through my veins.

I mirrored her actions, pulling off my own hoodie and t-shirt, discarding it somewhere behind me.

Madison knew how to move her body, letting her hips ripple and dip and pop to the sultry beat. I tracked every movement, the soft rise and fall of her chest, the way her fingertips danced over her pebbled skin as she moved.

"Fuck," I hissed as a whimper spilled out of her.

I needed her.

Now.

Stalking forward, I pressed her into the counter again, sliding my hands behind the backs of her thighs to lift her. Madison gave a little shriek as I dropped her on the countertop. "Ready to get fucked?" I drawled, reinforcing the boundaries between us.

This was sex.

Exclusive friends with benefits.

A clear line was drawn between us.

I gently pushed Madison down on the counter and stepped back, shoving my jeans down my hips and suiting up. Then I moved between her thighs, wrapping her legs around my waist, and pushed in slowly, filling her inch by inch.

My heart kicked up a notch, my body vibrating with need, with something much more than simple lust.

This didn't feel like friends with benefits.

And I didn't know what the fuck to do about that.

"Look what the cat dragged in," Connor said as he caught me slipping into the house via the back door.

"Shit, you scared me." I dragged a hand down my face. "It's early. I didn't think—"

"Couldn't sleep." He shrugged, nursing a mug of coffee.

"Ella upstairs?" I asked.

"Yeah. Mason and Harper are still sleeping." I gave him a small nod, went over to the refrigerator and helped myself to a bottle of juice.

"How was Millers?"

"Good. But we missed you."

I scoffed, "I find that hard to believe."

"Austin, come on."

"It's not exactly my idea of fun playing the seventh wheel." Leaning back against the counter, I ran a hand back and forth over my head.

"So bring your new friend next time." Accusation clung to his words as he pinned me with a knowing look.

"It isn't like that," I said a little too defensively, trying to lock down my expression.

"Is it Fallon?"

"Fuck no."

"Okay, keep your secrets."

"I like her okay, Con," I admitted. "I really fucking like her."

I wanted to tell him the truth. To get his advice but what was the point?

Last night had been amazing; the way Madison had come apart for me. How she'd clawed my back up as I fucked into her over and over. But we'd both agreed.

Friends.

Friends with benefits. That was all it could be.

I wasn't cut out to play the happy family. And she didn't trust that the college hockey player could be the kind of guy she needed in her life.

"That's great," Connor said, but his expression fell when I pressed my lips into a thin smile. "It's not great?"

"I don't know. She's got me all twisted up inside. We

have a great time when we're together, but she's keeping me at arm's length."

There had been no lazy morning sex. No breakfast this morning. No goodbye kiss.

Madison had prodded my shoulder at the ass crack of dawn, told me it was time for me to leave, and watched me walk away.

Because she had a child.

She had a little person who depended on her for everything. I couldn't even pretend to imagine what that was like.

"Well, don't lose your head over some girl you barely know," he said. "The team needs you to focus."

"Asshole," I murmured.

"What?" he chuckled but I wasn't joking, and I was pissed that he saw straight through me.

More than that—I was pissed he was right.

"I'm just saying, I've never seen you like this. And I'm happy for you, man, I am. But just keep a level head, yeah?"

No way I could fess up now. He would think I'd lost my damn mind all over a girl I'd known for a few weeks.

"Don't tell anyone, okay," I urged. "It's nobody's business, and I know what you're all like."

"I'll take it to the grave."

"What are we taking to the grave?" Ella walked in still half-asleep. "Morning."

"You look like you need a strong coffee," I said, turning on the coffee maker.

"Yes, please."

"Last night was fun?"

"The funnest," Connor teased, and she poked her tongue out at him.

I made Ella's coffee, and she went to perch on his knee. Connor wrapped his arm around her waist.

"And I guess that's my cue," I said, pushing the coffee mug toward her.

"You don't have to leave at the first sign of PDA every time you're around us."

"And yet, here I am. Leaving. Tell Mase not to be late for practice." I gave them a salute before grabbing a bottle of water and a banana out of the fruit bowl.

It was strange being back on the ice, especially without Connor.

"Okay, bring it in," Coach Tucker yelled, and we all glided over to the bench.

"Now I know things didn't end the way we hoped before winter break. Losing Morgan will be hard on everyone. But we have a season to win, so I expect everyone to pitch in and pull their weight. Now is not the time to lose morale.

"Leon, son, it's your time to shine."

He gave Coach a humorless nod. He was a rookie, but he had more than proved himself on the ice as one of the team's strongest defensemen.

"There's no game this weekend, but I want us to be ready."

A chorus of 'Yes, Coach' filled the air.

"Okay, Coach Walsh will kick off today's drills. Aiden, a word, son."

The rest of us moved onto center ice, awaiting our instruction from Assistant Coach Walsh.

"What do you think that is about?" Noah asked me and Mason.

"Probably just wants him to keep an eye on the team," Mase said. "Connor was a big presence. A lot of the team look up to him."

"He's not dead," I pointed out.

"Nope, asshole. But he is out of action until Coach clears him to attend practice."

Aiden skated over, stick in hand. "Ready to do this?" he asked, all business.

"Born ready, Cap." Noah grinned. "Lead the way."

CHAPTER 14

MADISON

"You're awfully smiley today," Kayleigh said as we worked side by side to stock the counter and get ready for another busy day.

"Am I?" I played dumb.

"Yep. It wouldn't have anything to do with whoever is on the end of all those text messages, would it?"

Damn, she was observant. Or I was really freaking obvious.

"I have no idea what you're talking about." My mouth twitched as I ducked my head and continued filling the glass cabinet with a freshly cooled batch of brownies. They smelled so good my mouth watered, but I had to be strict with myself after gaining almost five pounds when I first started working at Sugartown.

"There's been an extra bounce in your step lately. If I didn't know better," she went on, "I'd say you got laid."

"Kay!"

"What? It's just sex, Mads. We're all doing it."

"And who might you be doing it with?" I arched a brow, deflecting her attention.

Kayleigh was married to the shop. She was the first one here every day and the last one to leave. She came in on the weekend to prep the following week's bakes and rotating menu. She poured her heart and soul into her business. Something I'd deeply admired while working for her over the last two years.

I'd never heard her talk about a special someone. Never known her to go on anything more than the odd date here or there.

Sugartown was her life, her baby, the way Imogen was mine.

"Todd."

"Todd?"

"Yep." She flashed me a secretive smile. "He's a teacher and cares for his mom. Doesn't have time to date so we... you know." Her shoulders lifted in a playful shrug.

"No, I'm not sure I do."

"God, Mads, don't make me spell it out for you. We're fuck buddies. Friends with benefits. Each other's booty call."

"And is this little arrangement you have with Todd exclusive?"

"I'm not sure. We haven't had *the talk*."

"And that doesn't bother you?" I asked.

"Not really. I mean, he doesn't seem the kind to be dating a string of other women, but if he is, we're safe, and it's consensual." I must have pulled a face because she added, "Hey, don't knock it until you've tried it."

Her soft laughter didn't ease the knot in my stomach. It only made me more tense, replaying last night over in my head. How easily my resolve had cracked.

I liked him.

I liked Austin a whole lot, and I really liked the way he made me feel. Maybe a little too much.

Enough that I didn't want to lose it.

But exclusive friends with benefits?

There was no harm in that, was there?

He had the team. His practice schedule was intense. And I was a single mom working two jobs. It wasn't like there was time for the spark between us to catch fire and turn into something... more.

"You know, Mads, if you are texting someone, that's okay," Kayleigh added with motherly concern despite being only a few years older than me.

"I know. But it isn't like that," I forced out the words over the silly little lump in my throat.

She just smiled, leaving me to fill the rest of the cabinet while she went out back to fetch more cakes.

I tried all morning to forget about Austin, but he wasn't making it easy, probably because the sex was that damn good.

Sure, I felt a speck of guilt at the fact I'd brought him into my home again, but my friends were right; I was entitled to a life outside of being Imogen's mom.

Kayleigh reappeared and placed the final tray of cakes on the counter, then went to open up. Not even a minute had passed before people filed inside, all looking for their early morning coffee and sugar fix.

I spotted the blonde from the other day before she spotted me. "Good morning," I said. "Back for more?"

"What can I say? I have an unhealthy attachment to brownies." She smiled, her kind eyes running over the glass display full of today's offerings. "And those brookie bars were so freaking good."

"Well, I'm glad you enjoyed them."

"Thanks for the recommendation. I'm Harper, by the way."

"Madison." I smiled, a trickle of uncertainty going through me.

Austin didn't want to tell his friends about me, and that was okay. We weren't together—he didn't owe me anything. But Harper seemed like a nice girl, and I couldn't deny part of me was intrigued about what she would say about the Lakers goalie if I asked her.

"Did you give your boyfriend the business card?" I asked.

"I did. Now practice has started up again, most of his spare time is spent at the facility."

"You said he plays hockey?"

"Yeah. He's a left-winger."

"I don't know much about hockey."

"Then you're missing out." Her eyes crinkled with laughter, but I heard the pride in her voice.

"What can I get you this morning?" I asked.

"I think I'll have the same as before. Almond milk macchiato and a dark chocolate brookie bar, please, and one to go."

"Coming right up."

I got her order ready and added it to her tray when I noticed Kayleigh pinning up the poster about the new menu taste testing night.

"So this might sound a little strange," I said, "but my boss is hoping to launch some new gluten-free and vegan options soon. She wants to test them out on a willing group of customers first. I don't suppose you'd be interested?"

"Free samples?" Her face lit up. "Count me in."

"Great, I'll add your name to the list. Harper—"

"Harper Dixon. Can I invite some friends?"

"Sure, the more the merrier. Here's a flyer with some more information." I plucked one off the pile in Kayleigh's hands.

"Got your first guinea pig," I said.

"Excellent. You're a student?"

Harper nodded, and the two of them started talking while I moved on to the next customer.

Harper was pretty. Kind and grounded. And she went out with a hockey player.

She'd *tamed* a hockey player.

The urge to drag her to one of the quiet tables in the back of the shop and quiz her went through me. But I couldn't do that without giving away mine and Austin's little secret.

So I trapped the words behind my lips and focused on my job.

Telling myself that it was better this way.

Austin: Long day?

Madison: The longest. Imogen bumped her head at my friend's place. I had to take her to the medical center to get checked out. We only got back an hour ago.

Austin: Shit, I'm sorry. Is she okay?

I glanced down at the sleeping ball of curls tucked into my side and smiled. She was okay now, but it had been touch-and-go there for a while. Pretty sure my t-shirt was still damp from all the tears and snot.

Madison: She's fine. She's got a nasty bruise, but her brain isn't going to melt out of her ears.

Austin: Let me guess, she has a super active imagination?

Madison: You wouldn't believe the half of it. How was practice?

Austin: Strange without Connor. But it's good to be back on the ice.

Madison: How is he doing?

Austin: Better now he's back in Lakeshore and has fixed things with his girl. Being stuck in the house is going to drive him insane though.

Madison: That's good. I should get some sleep. I've got a double shift tomorrow.

Austin: At the bar?

Madison: Yeah.

Austin: Hope it goes okay. Good night, pretty girl.

My heart fluttered. That little sensation setting off warning bells that I was in over my head. That being just friends would never be good enough for me.

Madison: Good night, hotshot.

Without upsetting Imogen, I reached over and dropped my cell phone on the nightstand. It was late, and after a stressful day, I was tired. But my mind was also busy.

It wasn't unusual, though. When you had so much to balance, a moment's peace didn't come easy. There was always something.

I was always thinking about work or whether I could afford my next round of bills. Trying to arrange Imogen's childcare or worrying about leaving her at pre-K. The constant little voice in the back of my mind whispering that one day, Warren would come back.

Being a mom was hard.

Being a twenty-one-year-old single mom to a strong-minded four-year-old was really freaking hard.

But I did my best. I leaned on the people around me. I spent time with my daughter. I made sure that what I couldn't give her in materialistic things, I gave her in love and patience and understanding.

I wanted her to know that she came first, always.

But it was exhausting shouldering the burden

alone. I hated Warren for what he'd done to me—to our daughter—but there was no denying I missed the connection. The feeling that someone had your back no matter what.

Old emotions rushed to the surface as I stroked Imogen's hair, but I swallowed down the tears. I wouldn't cry. I couldn't. Because if I started…

It had been so long since I'd had anything for myself. It was hard not to latch onto those pesky little butterflies that soared every time I saw Austin's name flash up on my cell phone. But I couldn't afford to lose myself to the addictive feelings.

The thrill.

Because for as much as I hoped to meet somebody one day, Austin Hart was not a forever type of guy.

And I couldn't afford to lose my heart to Mr. Right Now.

"Jerrykins." Imogen bolted toward him, but like always, he caught her, bundling her up into his arms.

"How was your day, princess?"

"It was okay."

"Only okay?" His brows furrowed as he held tightly. "Uh-oh, whose butt do I need to kick?"

"Keenan Jackson said I'm a little miss knows-it-all."

He glanced at me, and I smothered a smile. "It's true. Miss Lauren confirmed Keenan did, in fact, call her that."

"Sounds like Keenan doesn't have any manners."

"I'm not a knows-it-all."

"Damn straight. You're a very intelligent, confident four-year-old. Nothing wrong with that, princess."

"That's what I told him," she fumed. "And he said that nobody likes a smart aleck. So I told him that my mom and Uncle Jerrykins and Fawn and Grammy and Pops all woves me just the ways I am and that he's just jealous because he doesn't have all of you."

"And how did Keenan take that?" Jeremiah flashed me a bemused look, and I shrugged.

Imogen was a force to be reckoned with, but so long as she wasn't being outwardly mean or difficult at pre-K, I made a point to try and not dull her sparkle.

"He wents crying to Miss Lauren and called me a bully. Me, Uncle Jer."

"Wow, what a little ass—"

"Okay, why don't we see if Jer has a snack you can have." I wrestled Imogen out of his arms and lowered her to the ground. "Go wash up, and I'll make you something quickly before I leave."

"Okay, Mommy." She skipped off down the hall, almost as familiar with his apartment as our place.

"Rough day?" he asked as I let out a weary sigh, rubbing my temples.

"You could say that. Miss Lauren asked me to talk to her about using her kind words."

"Sounds like Keenan was being a whiny little bitch."

"Jer!" I smothered a laugh.

God, I was so lucky to have him, especially while my parents were on vacation.

"So she's wise beyond her years. It's not a bad thing."

"No." I glanced down the hall, lowering my voice. "But I worry."

"Hey now"—he leaned over and squeezed my hand—"Immy is perfect just the way she is."

"But she has questions, Jer. Questions I don't always have the answers to."

"You mean Warren." His expression hardened, and I nodded.

"I can only withhold the truth for so long."

"She's four, babe. There's time—"

"You just said it yourself. She's four going on fourteen."

"Well, I wouldn't go that far—"

"Jer! Not helping."

"Shit, I'm sorry. Come here." He came over and pulled me into his arms. "You know I've always got your back, right? Both of you."

"I know." Taking a second to compose myself, I inhaled a deep breath and stepped out of his embrace. "I don't know what I'd do without you."

He constantly went above and beyond to help me and Imogen out. Like tonight, he'd agreed to babysit so I could work my shift at O'Shea's.

"Wook who I founds." Imogen appeared, carrying Vader baby-style in her arms.

"I wondered where she'd gotten to." Jeremiah smiled, mouthing, "We'll be fine," at me.

"It looks like you'll be getting pizza," I said after inspecting his sparsely filled refrigerator.

"Nothing but the best for the princess."

"You spoil her."

"I try." He winked.

"There's some crackers, baby, and some juice on the counter. I need to go if I'm going to make it."

"Go, we've got this, right, Immy?"

"Mm-hmm," she murmured, barely looking up from that damn cat.

"Remember, Vader isn't a toy, Immy. If you keep petting her like that, she'll get cranky."

"She wikes it. Bye, Mommy."

"Love you too," I muttered to myself, grabbing my purse off the counter. "I'll see you in the morning, okay?"

But not too early, I was looking forward to a rare lie in.

"Okay, Mommy."

"Okay, then. Guess I'll go."

"I'll text you updates," Jeremiah said.

"Thanks." I grabbed my bag and headed for the door, telling myself that he was right.

Telling myself that my baby would be okay.

"How's my favorite girl?" Kingsley asked when I arrived on shift.

"I'm good. How's Yolanda and the kids?"

"They're a pain in my ass as usual."

"But you wouldn't have it any other way." I smiled, slipping my notepad into my back pocket.

"Damn straight. How's that man of yours?" My brows furrowed, and he gave me a knowing laugh. "Don't be looking at me like you don't know exactly what I'm talking about."

"What are we talking about?" Hannah joined us.

"Just checking in on Madi's new guy."

"Ooh, yes. How is the new guy?" Her mouth twitched with amusement, and I flipped her off.

"There's nothing to tell." I brushed past them both and made myself busy organizing glasses behind the bar.

"Can we expect to see him tonight?" she asked.

"I don't think so."

"Shame. A bit of eye candy makes things around here run a little faster." Hannah flashed me an amused wink before turning her attention to the tables.

Kingsley's deep chuckle reverberated through me as I shook my head at their antics. Hannah was... well, she was Hannah. And Kingsley was one of the best guys I knew. He treated most of the female staff at O'Shea's like family. It's why Jack kept him around.

We felt safe with him watching over us, and he had that firm but fair approach that usually nipped altercations in the bud before they could get out of hand.

He was one of the reasons I'd stuck it out here for so long.

"You just make sure he respects your boundaries and treats you like the queen you are," he called across the bar, making my cheeks flame.

If only it was that simple.

But I couldn't tell them the truth.

I couldn't tell them that what Austin and I had was nothing more than a casual arrangement. A family man like Kingsley wouldn't understand. And Hannah knew me better than that.

Still, it didn't stop me from hoping that Austin might show. Even though I knew it was dangerous territory.

Austin Hart was becoming a high I couldn't stop chasing.

And like any true addict, I was already craving my next hit.

CHAPTER 15

AUSTIN

"You good?" Noah glided up to me and grasped my shoulder.

"Yeah." I rotated my other arm, a streak of pain skittering through my muscles.

Fuck.

He'd gotten me good. But somewhere between thinking about Madison and thinking about my sister's wounded expression this morning when we'd bumped into each other at Joe's Coffee Shop, my head wasn't in it.

"You want to talk about it? Rory said—"

"Nope." I shook him off me and put a little space between us.

"She's worried, Austin. We both are."

"I'm fine."

"You're distant. You've always been guarded, but this feels different."

"You need to quit it with the *Dr. Phil* routine. I'm fine. I'm still adjusting to the fact that one of my best friends is banging my sister."

"Come on, man, you know it's not like that. I fucking love her. She's it for me."

"You think I want to hear that shit?"

Thankfully, Coach called us into the bench, so I skated past Noah, hoping like fuck he'd get the memo.

Of course, the guy was worse than a dog with a bone.

"Austin, come on, bro, will you just wait a second." He reached for me just as I whirled around to tell him to back the fuck off. The motion took his skates out from under him, and Holden went down like a sack of bricks.

"Fuck," he breathed, glaring up at me.

"Shit, Holden. I didn't mean that."

"Yeah, yeah. Help a guy up, will you." He held out his hand, and I pulled him to his feet. "I wasn't trying to get under your skin. I thought we were past this stuff with me and Rory—"

"We are. I'm just tired."

His brows furrowed. "You'd tell me, right? If something was up."

There had been a time I might have before he got with my little sister. Now, I couldn't trust him not to run off and tell her my business.

The same went for all the guys, really. Noah. Mase. Connor. They'd all found their person. They all had someone to share everything with now. I was the outcast—the odd man out.

"Austin, son," Coach called as we approached the huddle. "A word."

"Sure, Coach." I skated around to him. "Not here. My office in ten."

I nodded and headed off the ice toward the locker room.

"What did Coach want?" Mason asked me as we hit the benches.

"I'm assuming he wants to talk about my plan."

"You have one of those?" He smirked, and I jabbed him in the side with my elbow as I moved ahead of him.

It was no secret I didn't have my future all mapped out. And although I'd always wanted a future in professional hockey, lately, I wasn't sure. The draft had always seemed so far away, but it was fast approaching, and I knew Coach wanted to know my intentions.

But the truth was, I didn't like to think beyond life at LU. Past losing my friends, the teammates forged some semblance of a family with me. Maybe I didn't wear my heart on my sleeve or open up over a beer or two like the rest of them. But my days at Lakeshore U were some of my best.

I'd found purpose here.

A home.

The idea that it was almost time to say goodbye to that left me feeling bitter. Reopened old wounds, wounds I'd worked hard to keep closed over the years.

"Hey, Austin, you good?"

I blinked over at Mason and nodded.

Was it that fucking obvious that something inside me had changed?

I mean, aside from being a grumpy asshole since Noah had declared his intentions where Rory was concerned.

I made quick work of changing and headed to Coach's office, knocking once before I slipped inside.

"Ah, Austin, just the man I wanted to see."

"What's up, Coach?"

He leaned back in his chair, steepling his fingers. "I had an interesting chat with the head of recruitment up in Vancouver yesterday. Their second goalie has been struggling this season, and they're looking to bring in some fresh blood. Your name came up."

"The Canucks, wow. That's... I don't know what to say."

"You don't have to say anything yet. I know Vancouver is on the other side of the country, but this is the NHL, son. You'd be a fool not to think about it."

"I will, Coach, thanks." I stood, needing some air.

I couldn't really explain it, but my skin suddenly felt too tight, and I couldn't quite get air into my lungs.

When I was a boy, I'd dreamed of playing for the Blue Jackets or the Penguins. I hadn't imagined moving three thousand miles across the country to Canada.

But it wasn't like I'd be leaving much behind. I didn't have anywhere to call home—hadn't ever since I'd left Syracuse, moved to Lakeshore, and never looked back.

Lakeshore was the home I'd made for myself. But what would I do when everyone else eventually moved on? Bum around? Get a shitty job and watch the rest of the guys go off and chase their dreams?

Hockey had always been my constant. The one thing I could count on. In a lot of ways, it had become my crutch and a form of therapy over the years. A way to hone my anger, and to take all my frustrations out in a controlled manner. It taught me how to deal with unwanted emotions, and how to direct my negative thoughts and funnel them into skill and determination on the ice.

Maybe a fresh start would do me good. Somewhere where no one knew me—where I had a chance to finally leave my past behind me and become the man I'd always wanted to be.

Only, I had no idea who that was.

The house was empty when I got back from practice. The guys had gone to The Penalty Box to meet the girls for dinner. But I'd declined, not wanting to play third or fifth or even seventh wheel.

I made myself something to eat and worked at the breakfast counter to finish up an assignment, making the most of the peace and quiet.

After washing up my dishes, I headed upstairs for a shower. I'd planned to go to the bar and see Madison, but my chat with Coach had left me feeling all kinds of off-kilter, and I didn't expect I'd be good company tonight.

But as if the universe heard my strife, my phone vibrated in my pocket as I stripped out of my clothes.

I smiled at the sight of Madison's name.

Madison: How was your day?

Austin: Pretty standard. Yours?

Madison: Same old.

Austin: I thought you were working tonight?

Madison: Already here. It's pretty dead
though. I'm just taking a break.

Austin: And you thought you'd
text me?

It was fucking stupid, and part of me didn't like how much a simple text from her affected me so much, but I immediately felt lighter.

Leaning back against the bathroom vanity, I waited for her reply, barely able to keep the grin off my face.

I couldn't remember the last time I'd had so much fun with a girl. In fact, come to think of it, it had never been like this. It probably had something to do with our upfront arrangement.

Friends with benefits.

Exclusive friends with benefits.

All of the perks. None of the drama.

Madison: I could always text
somebody else if I'm inconveniencing
you…

Austin: Cute.

Madison: Well, my ten minutes is up.
Maybe talk later?

Austin: Yeah, maybe. Don't work too
hard!

Madison: Don't study too hard xo

I tried not to read too much into her sign off. But for some reason, it irritated me that she'd pointed out our very stark differences. I was a college student, and she was a single mom busting her ass to make ends meet.

For the next hour, I tried to focus. I tried to keep my mind on the paper about the impact of public policy on sports and not the handsy, drunken assholes that frequented O'Shea's.

Throwing my pen down, I ran a hand down my face, accepting defeat. I couldn't get Madison out of my head, no matter how much I tried.

And I knew only one thing would soothe the restlessness churning through me.

Seeing her with my own two eyes.

O'Shea's was quiet, which only made the handful of leering patrons stand out like a sore thumb.

But none of them seemed to care, too transfixed by the half-naked dancer working the pole with her toned, lithe body.

Madison didn't spot me right away, but the hulk-of-a-security guy did. He gave me a subtle nod, which I returned before sliding into a booth along the far wall.

Content sitting for a little bit, I alternated between scrolling absently through the team's upcoming schedule and watching her work. When she finally spotted me, her brows furrowed into an adorable scowl.

Madison made her way over and placed her palms flat on the table. "This is a surprise."

"Is it?"

Her lips pressed into a thin smile as if she had trapped some sassy retort on her tongue. "You didn't say you were going to stop by, so I thought…"

"Because I wasn't going to stop by."

"Oh."

The air crackling between us cooled, turning a little icy.

"Shit, that came out wrong." I dragged a hand over my jaw. "I just meant, it's been a crappy day. I was going to stay home and wallow, but…"

"But?"

"You texted and said the place was dead."

"You know, people are going to start talking. I already have one security guy," she flicked her head over to the guy watching us, "I don't need another."

"I can go?" I went to get up, but she blurted, "No, stay. I'm glad you're here, Austin."

"Yeah?" A small grin played on my lips.

She shook her head, but I saw the laughter and heat in her eyes.

"Can I get you a drink?" she asked.

"I'll take a water."

"One water coming up."

Madison sauntered off, and I really fucking hoped the extra little swish to her hips was for my benefit.

The vibration of my cell pulled my thoughts out of the gutter. I dug it out of my pocket and grimaced.

Connor: Where are you?

Austin: Out.

Connor: Hot date?

Austin: You wish.

Connor: Come on, Austin, don't be like that. You deserve to find your happily ever after too, man.

Fucking idiot. Just because he and Ella had finally figured things out didn't make him some kind of relationship expert.

I didn't reply. I didn't have anything to say to him. But, of course, the goofy asshole couldn't let it lie.

Connor: If you're not ready to share
her with the world, that's fine. But you
can always talk to me. I know I like to
turn everything into a joke. But I can
be serious when the mood
demands it.

Austin: Appreciate the offer, but there's
nothing to tell.

Madison was cool. We had fun together. But that's all it was.

Fun.

She had a daughter, for fuck's sake. Real-life responsibilities. And I had... Well, I had a hockey championship to focus on. The rest I would deal with later.

Connor didn't reply. But then, I didn't expect him to.

I was used to keeping people at arm's length. Letting them get close but not *too* close. A therapist would probably say I had abandonment issues. But I liked to think of it as common fucking sense.

If you didn't let people in, they couldn't hurt you.

They couldn't disappoint you.

Madison returned with my water and a bowl of chips. "In case you're hungry," she said with a playful smile.

"The only thing I'm hungry for is—"

"Madison, how lovely to see you." The pretentious asshole I'd dubbed McSteamy pressed his hand to the small of Madison's back and leaned in to kiss her cheek.

"Julian," she said with nervous laughter. "I didn't expect to see you tonight."

"What can I say? I can't seem to stay away." His eyes, sharp and assessing, flicked to mine. "Looks like I'm not the only one."

I tipped my head in acknowledgment, trying my best to keep calm.

"Madi," another bartender called, a woman I recognized from my previous visits. "A little help."

"That's my cue." She gave me a hard look. "Play nice. Julian is one of O'Shea's best customers."

I had a hundred replies for that, but I kept them all to myself.

Thankfully, he didn't stick around, but he did make a point of escorting Madison back to the bar.

Smug asshole.

The security guy arched a brow in my direction, a faint smirk tracing his lips.

At least someone agreed with me.

McSteamy was a total sleazeball.

Over the next hour, the place got a little busier, and Madison barely had a chance to come talk to me. But that was okay. I was a patient guy.

At least, the influx of men meant that she didn't

have time to pander to McSteamy, either. He'd moved to a table off to the side of the stage, sipping his top-shelf whisky like he owned the damn place.

"You're going to crack a molar if you keep that up." Madison pushed a new bottle of water toward me.

"Thanks." I unscrewed the cap and poured it into the glass.

"He's harmless, you know."

"Famous last words," I muttered.

"Austin." Madison glowered. "Please don't start—"

"Relax, I can behave."

"I have to go in the back and help restock. You'll be okay out here for a little bit?"

"I think I can handle it."

"Are you staying until I get off?" She hesitated, looking up at me through her thick, dark lashes. "My shift ends at eleven-thirty."

"I'll be here." The words came out heavy, laced with anticipation.

"Imogen is staying overnight with my friend again."

"I should probably walk you home and make sure you get in okay then."

"That sounds like a good idea." Lust swirled in her eyes, and heat pulsed under my skin. But the moment was broken when a group of guys spilled into the bar.

"Later," she mouthed, pushing a stray curl behind her ear.

"Later," I murmured.

Hoping like fuck it came sooner rather than, well, later.

CHAPTER 16

MADISON

"So what's happening with you and McHottie?" Hannah asked me as we emptied crate after crate of beer.

"It's nothing."

"So you aren't screwing each other's brains out, because let me tell you, Mads, the way he looks at you... I figure the sex has to be off the charts."

My lips twisted as I tried to smother my laughter and my embarrassment.

I wasn't ashamed; it wasn't that at all. But I didn't do this.

I didn't have no-strings sex with gorgeous guys. I played it safe. I kept guys at arm's length. I shored my defenses and buried my heart under a layer of impenetrable ice. Because I couldn't ever afford to let myself be vulnerable again.

"Oh, you are so getting some." She began dancing around the storeroom, gyrating her hips like the dancers out front.

"Han, will you stop, already. It's just a bit of fun."

"Well, good for you, girl. It's about time you got back on the horse."

"He's a hockey player at LU."

"No shit. I bet he knows all those indecent stretches they do." She waggled her brows, but I gave nothing away.

What was between Austin and me was just that.

Between us.

"Enjoy it while it lasts, Mads. We all need to burn off a little steam sometimes. It's just a shame we can't all find men as good looking as your guy out there.

"I bet McSleazy doesn't like the fact you have a new admirer."

"Julian is harmless."

She gave me an incredulous look. "Watch yourself with that one, babe. Men with more money than sense seem to think they're entitled to take whatever they want. And he's always had a thing for you."

"He's always been polite," I pointed out. But I couldn't shake the creeping sensation of dread.

Something about his constant attention did make me feel uncomfortable at times. But I worked in a strip club. Feeling uncomfortable came with the territory.

"Let's hope it stays that way." She grabbed a small crate of beer and headed for the door. "You good here if I go back out there?"

"Of course."

It didn't take long to finish the restock. Jack liked us to stay on top of things throughout the week so that the place was ready to go come the weekend when things usually got a little crazy.

After stacking the empty crates in the corner of the room, I hit the light switch and left, ducking into the staff restroom.

My shift was almost over, and while there would be no time to freshen up before I headed home, I managed to tidy up my hair and slick some gloss over my lips.

He came.

Those two little words flitted through my mind again.

I'd wondered if he would, but I didn't want to pin my hopes on seeing Austin again tonight. Not when this thing we had was supposed to be nothing more than a casual arrangement.

Still, I didn't want to have sex—casual or otherwise—with a guy who treated me like dirt. I'd had enough of that with Warren, and we'd started a family together.

That familiar sense of guilt rose inside me; the little voice of trust whispered I was selfish for pursuing something for myself when I had Imogen to think about.

The little voice that had turned me off dating ever since I got away from Warren.

But life was better now. I was better. And I deserved this—I deserved to have something that wasn't defined by my label as a mother.

With a weary sigh, I washed my hands and checked my reflection one last time. It wasn't perfect, but it would have to do.

I'd barely made it back into the main bar area when a voice said, "There you are."

"Julian." I gave him a polite smile. "Is everything okay?"

"There's a mess in the male restrooms." He stepped closer, and everything inside me went on high alert. "So they said I could use the one back here."

My gaze darted over his shoulder, but the nature of the hall meant that our position was secluded from the rest of the bar.

"You're scared." He stopped suddenly, his brows furrowed with concern.

"I... No." I forced a weak smile, my eyes darting to the archway again. "I really need to get back to work, though."

"Of course. I didn't mean... Madison, I hope you

know how much I respect you." He reached for my arm, gently grasping my shoulder. "It can't be easy raising your daughter alone. Working two jobs."

"Madi? Are you—" Hannah rounded the corner and stopped dead. "What's going on?"

"Nothing." I moved past Julian. "I was just heading back."

"And I'm about to use the restroom," he said smoothly.

So smoothly, I wondered if I'd misread the entire thing. But there had been something in his voice—maybe not a threat, but a strange kind of reverence that set my teeth on edge.

"Hey," Hannah caught up with me. "Is everything okay?"

"Yeah, fine."

"You seem a little shaken up. If he said or did something—"

"He didn't. He was just being polite, but I got a little spooked." In part thanks to her unnecessary warning earlier. "That's all."

She studied my face, but I locked down my expression. It wasn't that I was defending him. I wasn't. But I didn't want to make a fuss out of nothing.

He'd always been nothing if not nice to me. And yes, maybe he did seem a little overfamiliar at times, but that didn't mean anything.

It didn't mean I had to worry.

Do my job. Smile. Make the patrons feel like a friend of O'Shea's. That's what Jack always told us. And if anyone did step out of line, Kingsley would be there to show them the door.

I followed her back to the bar and risked glancing over at Austin. The second his eyes found mine, he frowned.

"Okay?" He mouthed, and I nodded a little ardently.

I didn't want him to lose his cool again. It wasn't good for business or my fickle heart.

"Give me twenty," I mouthed back.

Austin's eyes stayed on me the whole time, and by the time we left the bar together, my encounter with Julian was the farthest thing on my mind.

"What happened tonight?" Austin asked me the second we got into my apartment.

"What?"

"When you came back into the bar, you looked... spooked."

"I don't know what you're talking about." I made a beeline for the kitchen. I needed a drink, something strong.

Between Hannah and Kingsley, and now Austin quizzing me, I felt on edge.

Or maybe that was just my strange encounter with Julian. He hadn't bothered me again, hadn't so much as looked in my direction. But I couldn't shake Hannah's warning.

"Okay," he said coolly. "I must have been mistaken."

"Must have," I murmured, pulling a bottle of vodka from the freezer. "You want a drink?"

"Sure." He watched me closely.

A little too close.

I spun away from him and set about making our drinks: a cube of ice each, a generous pouring of vodka, topped with some lemon juice and a dash of sugar. I wasn't a mixologist by any means, but I'd picked up a few tricks from Bryn, our resident cocktail maker.

When I turned back to hand him his drink, Austin was still watching me.

"What?" I asked.

"Nothing."

Silence stretched before us, heavy with insinuation. He knew I was lying. Yet, he didn't push me for answers.

I slid the drink across the breakfast counter. "It shouldn't be too sweet."

"Thanks."

The air shifted. That cool, strained tension between us melting into something warmer—a simmering heat that seemed to exist whenever we were in close proximity.

Whenever he turned his hazel eyes on me.

"It's good," he said, taking another sip.

"Mm-hmm." I practically drained my glass, wiping my mouth with the back of my hand.

Suddenly, I was parched. My skin vibrated with delicious anticipation.

"What do you want, Madi?" The low, rough tone of Austin's voice sent shivers racing down my spine, and I licked my lips, trying to focus on anything but the erratic beat of my heart.

Austin made me nervous. He made me feel desired and beautiful and strong.

All things I hadn't felt in so long.

I'd been so cold. So lonely. So starved of attention that I forgot what it felt like to *feel*.

But there was another feeling buried underneath it all. A kernel of hope. A little seed of yearning.

A little voice whispering to me that this, what we had here and now, wasn't enough.

"Kiss me," I said, hoping to erase the dangerous thought.

Because *more* wasn't an option.

I wasn't ready to bring a guy into Imogen's life. Especially a college guy I knew had no intentions of sticking around once he grew bored of our little arrangement.

Austin finished his drink and placed the glass down before moving toward me. He took his time, letting his eyes rake over every inch of my body.

"You are so fucking beautiful." His hand slipped into the back of my hair so he could curl his fingers around my neck.

"You're pretty nice to look at, too."

His mouth twitched. "I'm glad you think so."

Our mutual laughter was drowned out by teasing kisses and desperate sighs.

Austin mapped my body with his hands, exploring every curve and swell, letting his fingers linger at the waistband of my skintight work pants.

"Your ass looks phenomenal in these." He gave it a greedy squeeze.

"I really need to shower," I pointed out.

"Good plan. I am a little dirty." Austin lifted me into his arms and carried me down the hall to my bathroom.

He wasted no time stripping the clothes from my body, taking his time to touch and caress every inch of my skin before shoving me into the shower while he got out of his own.

He didn't join me straight away, though.

Instead, he watched me through the glass as I stood under the spray and slowly worked my hair free.

Grabbing my loofah, I added a little soap and began trailing it over my body. His eyes flared, tracking my movements, his long, thick, and utterly perfect dick standing to full attention.

He was so gorgeous, standing there like a sculpted Adonis, that I should have felt a pinch of inferiority. I felt nothing but beautiful and confident, though, as his heated gaze drank me in.

So confident that I crooked my finger at him and backed up against the tiles.

Austin came at me with fervor, but before he could reach me, I dropped to my knees and gazed up at him.

"Fuck," he breathed, sliding his fingers deep into my hair. His back protected me from the shower spray, making it easier for me to lean forward and flick my tongue out to taste him. I curled my fingers around his shaft and guided him deeper into my mouth.

"Oh, fuck yeah." Austin's hand went to the tiles above my head as I alternated between my mouth and hand to make him feel good.

"Hollow your cheeks, babe," his gruff command rumbled through me, making my body sing. "Take me as far as you can."

God, his dirty commands did something to me. They unlocked a part of me that I thought had died a long time ago.

But she was stirring back to life, completely addicted to the way she felt in his presence.

I sucked him deeper, loving his salty taste, the velvety smooth slide of him as I swallowed to the back of my throat.

"Shit, pretty girl." Austin rubbed his thumb over my jaw. "You look so good with my dick in your mouth."

A whimper worked its way up my throat, and the vibrations made him buck against me.

"Fuck, fuck, Madi. You've got to stop, or I'm going to come."

I pulled off him and licked my lips. "Good, I want it."

"And I want to come," he pulled me to my feet and crowded me against the tiles, "with my cock buried deep inside you.

"Wrap your arms around my neck." I did, and Austin grabbed the backs of my thighs, lifting me up. "Line me up."

I reached between us, grasping his length and notching against my entrance.

"Look at me," he ordered, and our gazes collided. For a split second, my heart fluttered with silly, traitorous thoughts. "You good with me fucking you bare?"

"I... Yes, yes. I'm on birth control."

"I'm clean."

I nodded, my eyelashes fluttering at the feel of him right there, slipping and sliding against my clit. Close but not close enough.

But then he said, "I want your eyes on me as I fuck you."

Sex.

It was just sex.

Austin impaled me on his dick; our collective moans were drowned out by the shower.

"More," I cried as he lifted off again and slowly pulled me back down right as he thrust upwards.

It felt incredible.

The slip and slide of our bodies as he fucked me slow and hard in the steam.

"I'll never get enough of this," he said, capturing my lips in a bruising kiss.

He didn't mean it. They were just words spoken in the heat of the moment. But my heart snagged on them, nonetheless.

Because while I knew it couldn't be more—for my sake and his—I was still only human.

And hearing the guy you were casually sleeping with say those words made me wish there was a tiny bit of truth to them.

"Mommy, Mommy."

The familiar voice circled my dream, pulling me

from the darkness. Confusion swam in my head as I tried to get my bearings.

"Mommy, I'm home. Jerrykins brought me to say good mornings."

My eyes flew open.

"Mommy where—"

"Shit. Shit, shit, shit." Panic slammed into me as I threw off the covers and turned to the sleeping hockey player beside me. "Austin, Imogen is here."

"W-what?" he murmured, voice heavy with sleep.

"Imogen is here."

"MOMMY, WHERE ARE YOU?"

"Fuck." He scrambled out of bed, tripping on his own feet and landing with a resounding *thud*. "What do I do?"

"I don't know. Jeremiah is here too."

"Jeremiah, who the fuck is Jeremiah?"

"My friend." I snapped, frantically trying to pull on some appropriate clothes. "And that's not important right now. If she sees you—"

"Shit, yeah. Okay. Maybe we can say I'm a plumber or something, here to fix your pipes."

"Is that supposed to be funny?"

"I thought it had merit." He smirked, clearly less concerned about the four-year-old currently making her way through our apartment.

But when she called out again, his expression quickly sobered. "I'll hide in the bathroom."

"Good idea. She'll probably want me to take her for breakfast now, so I might have to leave you here while I'm gone."

God, what an absolute disaster. But I couldn't think about that right now. Imogen was almost at my door, and I had bigger worries than offending Austin.

"It's fine. I can see myself out."

A pang of guilt went through me, and I found myself saying, "I'll make it up to you. Maybe I can get Jer to—"

"Mommy, Mommy! I'm here." The door burst open, and Imogen spilled into the room in a curly blonde whirlwind. She made a beeline for me, wrapping her little arms around my waist and hugging me tight.

My heart was in my throat as I glanced over to where Austin was.

But relief sank into me.

He was gone. The only hint that he'd ever been here in the first place was the soft click of the bathroom door closing behind him.

CHAPTER 17

AUSTIN

Fᴜᴄᴋ ᴍʏ ʟɪfe.

They seemed like the only apt words to describe the absolute shitshow I'd woken up to. I'd barely even gotten my eyes open before Madison was snapping at me to hide.

Hide.

Where the fuck did she want me to go?

I was a six-foot-three hockey player, for Christ's sake.

I guess the bathroom was as good a hiding place as any. She could steer her daughter away from me and keep her distracted while I waited for them all to leave.

So much for lazy morning sex before and after breakfast.

Pressing my ear against the door, I waited and waited, their voices barely audible beyond Madison's bedroom.

At least she'd wanted me to hide and hadn't decided it would be a good time for me to meet the kid.

Something inside me tightened.

Shit, did I want to meet her daughter?

I mean, technically, we had already met. But I didn't want to cross that line.

I liked our little arrangement.

It was nice. Simple. Good company and great sex with a clear understanding that we were both too unavailable for anything more.

Still, I hadn't planned on ending up in the fucking bathroom like some dirty little secret.

Time seemed to slow to the point of stopping as I waited... and waited.

Until a knock cut through the thick silence.

"Madi?" I whispered, stepping away from the door as it clicked open.

"Sorry to disappoint." The guy slipped inside, plastering himself to the door.

"Let me guess, Jeremiah?"

"And you must be the college guy." His brow arched with mild curiosity, and there was something about the way he said it that rang the *dirty little secret* bell louder.

"Austin."

"Well, Austin. We need to get you the hell out of here before Princess Immy catches you."

"I thought Madi was going to take her for breakfast?"

"She is. She left me behind to do clean up."

My brows knitted. That's not what she'd said a minute ago. But I guess plans changed, and maybe her daughter's unexpected arrival had hit her with some home truths.

"Come on, hot stuff." He clapped his hands together. "Time to go."

"Fine, yeah. Whatever." I made quick work of grabbing the rest of my things and followed the friend out of Madison's apartment.

"My car's over here," he said, nodding toward the parking lot.

"Actually, I think I'll walk."

"Listen, I don't want to be that guy, but do you know what you're doing here?"

"Excuse me?" I bit out.

"Having some casual fun is one thing, but that was a close call this morning, and Imogen is—"

"Madison's priority. Got it." I ran a hand through my hair. "It was reckless, and it won't happen again."

"Good because I love that girl like she's my own. Both of them." He pinned me with a warning look I didn't appreciate. "And something tells me you're not looking to jump feet first into a relationship with a single mom and enough emotional baggage to last her a lifetime."

"What—"

"Shit, I probably shouldn't have said that." Guilt skittered over his expression. "It was nice meeting you, Austin. Let's hope next time is under different circumstances."

He gave me a small salute before heading back toward Madison's building. But his words stayed with me long after.

No matter how much I didn't like hearing him say them, he was right.

I wasn't looking to get involved with a single mom.

I wasn't looking to get involved with *anyone*.

It was sex.

At least, that's all it was supposed to be.

Madison was fun to be around, and the sex was off the charts. But maybe it was time to cool things a little and put some distance between us.

This morning was a wake-up call.

And a very lucky escape.

"You don't live here anymore," I said, entering the kitchen to find my sister propped against the breakfast counter.

"Good morning to you, too."

I arched a brow, waiting for an explanation as to why she was in my kitchen at this hour.

"I'm waiting for Harper." She shook her head a little, clearly irritated at my attitude.

But I wasn't in the mood to talk, least of all, with her.

Rory, though, had other ideas.

"So," she said. "How are things?"

"Fine."

"Good. And practice? Noah said Connor's left a big hole to fill. But he thinks Leon can—"

"I need coffee." I cut her off and moved around her to get to the coffee maker.

"Guess you don't want to talk. You know, it's been months, Austin. Yet, you seem to be punishing me more now than before." She grabbed my arm as I passed her to get a mug. "Hey, look at me."

Our eyes clashed, and that bitter taste of regret burned my throat.

"What's going on with you?" Hurt flashed in her eyes, but it only made me double down on feelings.

"I'm fine."

"You're not—"

"Sorry, I'm ready." Harper breezed into the room. "Oh, Austin. I didn't know you were here. Mason said you were out."

"I'm back."

"Good, that's good, isn't it?" She glanced between me and Rory. "What's going on?"

"Nothing." Rory smiled, but it didn't quite reach her eyes. "We were just talking."

"Oh, well, in that case, shall we?"

"Sure. I'll speak to you later?" Hope glittered in my sister's eyes, but I couldn't do it. I couldn't give her what she wanted.

"Yeah," I murmured, more interested with the label on my bottle of water.

"Remember, we have that thing at the coffee shop tonight."

"That's tonight?" Rory followed Harper down the hall. "I could have sworn…"

Their voices trailed off, and I ran a hand over my face. Rory didn't deserve my cold shoulder, but things were different.

I was different.

And after the close call this morning, I felt off-kilter.

What the fuck did I know about raising kids? I'd been Rory's big brother, and I'd let her down at every fucking turn. If she never talked to me again, it would be more than I deserved. But Aurora always had been too soft, too forgiving.

The vibration of my cell phone jolted me from my thoughts.

Madison: I am SO sorry about that. I
had no idea that Jeremiah would bring
Imogen home early. It's probably a
sign we need to be more careful.

Right. Because I was just a college fuck boy who didn't have the emotional maturity to handle the fact the girl I was fooling around with had a daughter.

Austin: Or a sign we need to cool
things.

I hit send before I could temper my anger.

Fuck.

I braced myself for her reply, the three little dots taunting me.

Madison: If that's what you want.

Austin: I think it's for the best, don't
you? Before things get messy.

Madison: Okay.

I pocketed my cell because what else was there to say? Our little arrangement had run its course, just like we both knew it would eventually.

Exhaling a little huff of frustration, I tensed when I heard footsteps.

"Austin, what's wrong?" Connor asked.

"Nothing." I snapped out of it, forcing a weak-ass smile he saw right through.

"Did something happen? Rory—"

"Nothing happened. Just need another coffee or three to kickstart my motivation."

He studied me, looking a little too closely. "If you want to talk—"

"I don't."

"Yeah, figured you'd say that." Frustration rolled off him. "But sometimes it helps."

"How's PT going?"

"It's going. Fucking kills me that I'm not playing with the team, but it could be worse."

"That's the spirit."

"You figured out your plan yet?"

"Huh?" I gawked at him.

"Come on, Austin. I'm heading to the Flyers, Aiden is heading to the Red Wings, and Mason is in talks with the Blue Jackets. We're all waiting for you to make a decision."

"I didn't know my future was that important to you guys." I gave him a dismissive shrug.

"Jesus, you're a tough nut to crack. We're your friends. As good as family. It wouldn't hurt to let us in."

He was right. Maybe talking things over would help.

"Coach pulled me into the office yesterday."

"Mase mentioned something."

Of course, he had. Fucking bunch of girls.

"The Canucks are interested. Their second goalie is having problems, and my name came up."

"The Canucks, wow. That's… a long way away."

"Yeah, I know. But it isn't like I have offers lined up."

"You're considering it?" His brow arched in that accusatory way of his.

"You don't think I should?"

"It's not my decision to make. But Vancouver, Austin? That's… a big step when we'll all still be local."

"It's the NHL, though."

"Yeah, it is. So long as you're doing it for the right reasons."

"What the fuck's that supposed to mean?" Everything inside me tightened.

"So long as you're not… running."

"You don't know what the fuck you're talking about." I glanced away from him, trying to get my emotions locked down.

Connor didn't know; nobody did. Because I'd spent years, *years* shoving down all those feelings from my childhood, my teenage years.

But when I finally gave in and looked at him again, I saw it.

He knew.

Somehow, Connor knew. And I suspected it was

because the loveable, lighthearted joker of our group saw far more than we realized.

"You've been different ever since Rory came to Lakeshore."

"Yeah, well, watching one of your best friends fall in love with your sister—"

"This isn't about Noah. It's about you."

"I don't know what you think you know, but you're wrong." I barged past him, heading for the hall.

"Austin, come on. It's me, you don't have—"

"Do us both a favor, yeah?" I cut him with an icy stare. "Stay out of it."

And then I got the fuck out of there.

I headed to the gym to burn off some steam but barely managed twenty minutes before my cell started blowing up.

Muttering to myself about my overbearing friends, I snatched my cell off the bench and paused, my stomach curdling at the sight of my mother's name.

For a second, I contemplated ignoring her. She never called unless she needed something. And after she'd sent Rory a box of weight loss pills and supplements, I'd made damn sure to give her a piece of my mind.

That had been months ago, and apart from a couple of calls I'd ignored, I hadn't spoken to her since.

Fuck her. I dropped my cell like a hot potato.

Nothing good could come from talking to her right now.

But she didn't give up, and the shrill of my ringtone echoed around the empty gym.

"Fuck's sake," I grumbled, grabbing it again and bringing it to my ear. "Yeah?"

"Really, Austin. Is that any way to greet your mother?"

"You called. I answered."

She scoffed, the line thick with tension. "We haven't spoken in weeks. I thought—"

"Yeah, well you thought wrong."

"Rory said—"

"Rory is a fool for giving you even a second of her time after the bullshit you pulled last year."

"Aurora and I can work through our differences like adults, Austin. Unlike you and your man-sized tantrum. Really, it's quite ridiculous."

Go to hell, I wanted to scream. But despite being a selfish bitch Susannah Hart was still my mother, and there was part of me that was still a young boy desperate for his mother's attention.

God, I hated her for that.

For ruining me just enough to be able to cut her off, but deep down, I still craved her attention.

Talk about Mommy issues.

Unlike Rory, I'd never talked to a shrink about my issues. I'd pushed them down and down, right down enough until I could tell myself that I was okay.

That it didn't matter that my dad left and then my mom spent years acting like it was somehow my fault.

I reminded her of him, and she made sure to remind me in turn that while he might have walked away from her, he didn't care enough about me and Rory to stick around, either.

"I'm going to hang up now," I said with a weary sigh.

I didn't have time for her bullshit.

"Wait, Austin, please—"

I hesitated.

Fuck.

Even now, I couldn't do it. I couldn't fully slam the door in her face.

"What?" I practically snarled the word, unsure if I was more pissed at her or myself.

"I know I haven't always made things easy." *Understatement of the fucking century.* "But I'd like for me, you, and Aurora to get together. There's something I wish to discuss with you both."

"So tell me now."

"No, this needs to be done in person."

"I've got a busy few weeks coming up. The team has

a real shot at going into the playoffs. I won't be able to get to Syracuse any time soon."

"Not even a couple of days? You know I wouldn't ask if it wasn't important."

It was on the tip of my tongue to argue, but I didn't have it in me. Something about talking to her again sucked the life right out of me.

"I don't think I'll be able to make it work. Sorry." I hung up, frustration coming off me in angry waves.

How dare she.

How fucking dare she act like I owed her a visit.

Dropping down onto the bench, I inhaled a shuddering breath, trying to rein in the tumultuous emotions raging inside me. I wanted to rage, to scream and lash out. But I wasn't that guy now.

I controlled my emotions—they no longer controlled me.

As far as I was concerned, moving to Lakeshore had been a one-way ticket.

And until Rory showed up, I'd made my peace with putting my childhood behind me.

Fuck.

Fuck. Fuck. Fuck.

I slammed my fist down on the bench, reveling in the shock of pain skittering up my arm.

Everything had been fine until I opened my door and found Rory standing there. And slowly, day by day, week by week, her presence—the truths that came to light—unraveled my carefully constructed world.

Rory and I had talked shit over. We'd done the heart-to-heart, awkward as fuck conversation where I apologized for my sins, but nothing changed.

If anything, the truth—learning about her eating disorder and the years of trauma at the hands of our mother—broke something inside me.

Something that had festered and grown and leeched the last shreds of decency from my soul.

Rory might have forgiven me, but I would never forgive myself for abandoning her.

The vibration of my cell phone startled me, and I read the incoming text, hardly surprised to see my sister's name.

Rory: You really can't find a couple of days to come home with me?

Austin: I'd rather swallow glass.

Rory: Austin, don't say that. You haven't been back in so long and she sounded kind of… desperate.

Austin: There is nothing that woman could say to me to fix the last ten years.

Rory: For me, then? Please.

Fuck. How could I deny her when I owed her so much. But I'd vowed I would never set foot in that godforsaken place again.

> Rory: It doesn't matter. Noah will come
> with me.

Ouch. I knew she didn't mean it maliciously, but it cut deep all the same. I'd let my sister down, and now she'd found solace—found comfort—in my teammate. One of my best friends.

She didn't need me anymore.

And it was a fitting punishment for how badly I'd let her down.

But part of me couldn't let it go. Maybe I never would.

My fingers flew furiously over the screen, and I hit send.

> Austin: I'll go with you.

Even though stepping back in that place will destroy me.

CHAPTER 18

MADISON

"Okay, out with it," Kayleigh said, nudging me with her elbow as we worked side by side to get the shop ready for tonight's taster session.

"What?" My brows furrowed.

"You look like someone kicked your puppy."

"I don't have a puppy."

"Mads." She rolled her eyes at me. "What's wrong?"

"Nothing." Her expression turned skeptical, and I struggled to hold in my sigh. "Something happened."

"With the guy you've been texting?"

"Maybe."

"If you're trying to *not* talk to me about this, you're doing a great job."

"Oh, hush." I whipped her with a towel. "It wasn't like it was serious or anything…"

"Okay, back up and start from the beginning because I feel like I'm missing some of the important facts here."

"Austin. His name is Austin."

"Okay, and where did you meet this Austin?"

"It's not important."

"A college guy, really, Mads?" Her laughter did little to quell the nervous energy zipping through me.

"How did you… No, never mind." I didn't want to hear how obvious I was being. "He came over last night after I got done at the bar."

"Bringing him back to your place, that sounds pretty serious." Her expression sobered. "And so not like you."

"I know, I know." When she said it like that, it sounded bad. Reckless. And it made me wonder if I'd made a huge mistake. "We agreed to keep things casual, and it isn't like I can go to his place. He lives with his friends, it's weird. And Immy was over at Jer's. Or at least, she was supposed to be."

"Oh my God, tell me they didn't catch—"

I nod slowly. Internally cringing as I remember the sheer panic that had struck me when I'd realized Imogen was in the apartment while Austin and I were naked in my bed.

"She wanted to surprise me, and Jer didn't think to check that I was home alone."

Because Kayleigh was right—I didn't do that. I didn't bring guys back to my place.

Except, with Austin, I had.

More than once.

"Thankfully, he hid before she burst into my room, but I swear to God, Kay, my life flashed before my eyes."

"Would it really have been that bad?" She frowned. "I mean, sure, it's probably not the way you want your daughter to meet your... *friend*." A smirk teased her lips. "But it could have been worse. You could have been mid-ride—"

"Kayleigh!"

"What? Come on, that's funny. So she didn't see anything?"

"No, thank God."

"Everything's good then."

"Actually, we decided to cool things."

"We?" Her brow arched, and I didn't like the insinuation in her voice. "Or him?"

"It was a mutual decision."

I'd promised myself when I left Warren that I wouldn't be the kind of mom who brought a string of guys around Imogen, that I'd focus on her and us, and rebuild our lives together.

"So why the glum face?"

"I don't know." I shrugged, turning away from her to avoid any more scrutiny.

It wasn't like I expected Austin to want to get to know Imogen. We'd both made our intentions clear about things. But I guess I didn't expect him to end things so abruptly after one close call.

"You like him," she said.

"Well, yeah." I glanced back at her with a sad smile. "I wouldn't be sleeping with him if I didn't. You know me better than that."

"I do, and this sad girl act you've got going today tells me all I need to know about your casual arrangement with College Guy."

"Oh, babe." She dropped the box of coffee cups and pulled me in for a hug. "You *really* like him."

"I—"

Was that it?

I mean, sure, I liked the way he made me feel. How easy it was being with him. But our relationship—if you could call it that—was surface-level only. We hadn't even gotten to sharing the deep stuff.

But I'd wanted to.

Crap, I'd wanted to go there with him.

What an idiot.

"I'm so stupid." I sighed with frustration. "He's in college. He made it perfectly clear that—"

"Stop, stop." Kayleigh grasped my hands between us, offering me a pitiful smile that only made me feel ten times worse. "You're only human, Mads. And this is the first guy you've let in since Warren. It was always going to be complicated, even if you both laid your cards on the table.

"You should be proud of yourself, though. Look how far you've come." She squeezed my hand. "You trusted a guy again after everything you've been through."

Inhaling a shuddering breath, I nodded. "You're right. God, you're so right. I'm being ridiculous. He didn't promise me anything, and I did act kind of crazy this morning. I made him hide in the bathroom, and then just left him there."

"You were protecting Immy. No one can blame you for that."

But Austin did.

Or maybe he didn't.

Guess I'd never find out now.

"This might sound a bit odd, but do you think that maybe you picked Austin *because* he's a college student?" My brows knitted, and she continued. "I just mean, maybe some part of you knew he was a safe bet. A bit of fun to test the waters."

"Yeah, maybe."

But if that was the case, then why did I feel so hurt by his dismissal?

And why did part of me wish things had gone down differently this morning?

"All set?" I asked Kayleigh sometime later. She looked a little nervous as we waited for the taste testers to arrive.

But she had nothing to worry about.

She'd spent the afternoon whipping up a storm in the kitchen, and the place smelled so good my stomach had grumbled nonstop for the last thirty minutes. So much so that I may have snagged a couple of tasters off the cooling rack.

"I hope they all show up," she said, spying out of the blinds.

"They will. You have nothing to— See, here they come." My smile grew as Harper and a group of girls appeared at the door.

Kayleigh welcomed them inside, flashing me a relieved little smile as she helped them get settled.

"You came," I said, approaching Harper's table first.

"Free drinks and snacks? Hell yeah, we came." She chuckled as I handed around some complimentary drinks. "Madison, these are my friends Rory and El. Girls, this is Madison. She works here and got me hooked on the brookie bars."

"It's nice to meet you," Rory beamed at me.

She seemed familiar; there was something about her green eyes or maybe it was her smile.

"This place is incredible," she said. "Coffee and books. Two of my favorite things."

"Have we met before?" I blurted.

"I... I don't think so." She gawked at me. "I've never ventured this far across town.

"Odd. I have the strangest feeling we have."

"Really?" Harper said, glancing between us.

"Sorry, I didn't mean to be all weird. I don't get out much, can you tell?" Strangled laughter bubbled out of me.

What the hell was wrong with me?

Harper was a nice girl, and now she was looking at me like I'd grown two heads.

"Make yourselves comfortable; you're in for a real treat."

I hurried away, cheeks burning with embarrassment. But there was something so familiar about Rory. Maybe I'd seen her around Lakeshore the few times I'd hung out with Fawn there.

Kayleigh moved the platters she'd prepared to one of the empty tables set up along the wall, and I began getting them ready to serve while she welcomed everyone and explained the new menu.

Out of the corner of my eye, I watched Harper and her friends, a pang of jealousy going through me.

I'd missed out on all of that. College. Girlfriends. The parties and hookups.

Imogen was my world, and I couldn't imagine life

without her, but Kayleigh was right; I was only human. And watching Harper and her girlfriends made me wonder *what-if.*

What if my life had turned out differently?

Shaking the pointless thoughts out of my head, I waited for my cue from Kayleigh and began handing out the first tasters.

"Ooh, these look so good," Harper said, helping herself to a piece of olive and feta bread. "I think it's so great Kayleigh wants to incorporate more gluten-free options into her menu."

"Everything tastes great, too," I confirmed.

"This is such a great find," Rory said. "I love Joe's and Roast 'n' Go, but it's nice to leave the regular crowd behind."

"You're both students at LU, too?"

"English majors," El replied. "I graduate this year, though."

"What are your plans?"

"I'm moving to Philadelphia with my boyfriend."

Harper and Rory shared a secretive look, and I suddenly felt very much out of the loop.

"Seriously." El quirked her brow. "It's not a big deal."

"Babe, come on, it's a huge freaking deal." Harper grinned. "Her boyfriend is signed with the Philadelphia Flyers."

So she was another hockey girlfriend.

"Wow, that's… impressive." I hoped my expression looked less strained than my voice sounded. "You must be so excited."

"Connor and Ella have had it tough over the last few months. So we're all stoked for them."

"Connor? You're Connor Morgan's girlfriend?" The words were out before I could stop them.

"You know him?"

"Yes, no…" Crap. "I saw the news. He got injured, right?"

Guilt lodged itself in my throat. I didn't owe these girls anything, but it felt deceitful, somehow, to pretend I didn't know Austin or anything about the team.

"Yeah, he did." Ella studied me closely. "Do you follow hockey?"

"Oh no, I'm not really much into sports. Between working two jobs and taking care of my daughter, I don't have much time for hobbies."

"You have a daughter?" Harper asked, and I nodded. "You look too young to have— Crap, I'm sorry. That was rude."

"It's fine." I covered the awkwardness with a strained laugh. "I get that a lot. She's four going on fourteen, and I'm twenty-one but feel forty some days."

Jesus. Why was I telling them all this?

"Sorry, I should go help Kayleigh." I darted away

from their table and found my boss over by the trays of tasters.

"Everything okay?" She frowned at how flustered I was.

"Uh, yeah. Fine. It's going well?"

"I think so. Hopefully, we'll start to attract a bigger college crowd if word spreads. Can you hand out the feedback forms, and I'll start with the dessert tasters."

"Of course." Grabbing the pile of sheets, I made my way around the room. Everyone seemed to be enjoying themselves, and there was a lot of positive chatter about Kayleigh's new items.

Not that I'd expected anything less.

Kayleigh was an excellent baker. An even better businesswoman. It was so wonderful to see her flourishing and chasing her dreams, and I was grateful to play even a small part in her success.

It made me wish I had my own dreams beyond being the best mom to Imogen I could be, though.

But between losing my head to young love and then falling pregnant, I'd never had time to discover what I wanted to do with my life. And, now, my number one priority was attending to her needs.

"Madison," Harper said as I reached their table again. "This might seem a little strange, and you can totally say no, but we're heading to a bar after we get done here, and we wondered if you'd like to join us. I feel just awful for what I said earlier, but figured I could apologize properly with a cocktail or two."

"I… I'm sorry, I can't."

"Oh, that's a shame. Maybe another time?" She gave me a warm smile. Genuine and full of hope.

"I have a friend at LU, actually," I said. "I'm due to visit her soon. Maybe next time I do, we can meet up."

"Oh, that would be great. Here, take my number." She grabbed a napkin and wrote it down. "Mason, my boyfriend, has a kid brother. Well, Scottie is thirteen, but he has autism, so things can get pretty intense. I volunteer with his group and help out with Mason's inclusive hockey program at the center over in Rushton."

"That's so cool."

"It doesn't compare to being a full-time parent, but I love kids, and I know how hard it can be…" She trailed off, the air turning thick between us. "Sorry, I'm overstepping again."

"Not at all. You're right. Being a single mom is the hardest thing I've ever done. But one of the most rewarding, too." I smiled, a strange mix of pride and melancholy swirling inside my chest. "Kayleigh is about to bring around the sweet tasters. I'll collect your feedback sheets as soon as you're done."

I went to walk away, but Harper stopped me in my tracks.

"My number." She held it out for me to take, and I took it, offering her a polite nod.

"Thanks."

I walked away, wishing I could make use of it and call her.

Harper seemed like the kind of girl I could hang out with. But her boyfriend played hockey with Austin. And that was reason enough for me to drop it in the trash out back.

No good would come from me befriending her, which was unfortunate because I liked Harper. I did.

And something told me we could be good friends.

CHAPTER 19

AUSTIN

"You're quiet," Rory said as we pulled into our old neighborhood.

"Don't have much to say."

"Austin…"

"Just leave it, yeah, Sis." I turned off the engine to Connor's truck, whipped off my ball cap, and ran a hand through my hair.

"Six hours, and you've barely spoken a word."

"You slept for half of it," I pointed out.

We'd left early to get a head start. I wanted to get in and out as quickly as possible.

The season had started but the team had a bye week this weekend, so I'd reluctantly agreed to come with Rory to Syracuse.

I already regretted it.

I'd vowed never to step foot in this place again after I left for college. But I owed it to my sister. And for some unknown reason, she still held onto the hope that our sorry excuse for a mother could somehow be redeemed.

"Austin…"

"Look, I don't know what you want me to say. I'm here. I came. Isn't that enough?"

"You didn't have to come," she said. "Not if it's going to cause you so much discomfort."

"Why do you care so much?" I blurted, and Rory frowned. "About her."

I flicked my head toward the house, letting the emotions pushing their way to the surface settle. I'd always known coming back here would be difficult. It's why I'd avoided it for so long.

But still, I hadn't expected this.

A crushing weight so heavy I felt like I couldn't breathe.

"After everything she's done," I seethed. "How can you want to spend any time with her?"

"I know it's complicated, but she's our mom, Austin. The only mother we'll ever have."

"She never wanted us around," I scoffed. "Pretty sure she resented us for ruining her modeling career."

Rory inhaled a deep breath, studying me in a way

that had spiders crawling under my skin. "I had it all wrong, didn't I?"

"What?"

"Back in high school," she said quietly. "I thought you'd abandoned me. I thought... I guess it doesn't matter now. I see it now. You were just doing whatever *you* needed to do to survive."

"Don't. Don't try and absolve me, Rory. I should have realized. I should have—"

"Austin." She leaned over, gathering my hands in hers. "She hurt both of us. In her own way, I think she hurt you more."

"You've got to fucking kidding—"

"Just... hear me out." Her expression softened, but it did little to ease the guilt churning in my gut.

The guilt that had been growing and festering ever since she turned up on my doorstep.

"She hurt me, yes. But I think, in her own way, it was out of love. She wanted me to be her protégé, to follow in her footsteps."

The muscles in my jaw worked overtime as I tried to fight the urge to punch something.

"What?" Rory asked.

"There isn't a single thing wrong with you, and I hate—fucking loathe—the fact she ever made you feel like there was."

"But I don't think she knew the impact she was having on me."

"That doesn't make it okay, Rory. That doesn't make *any* of it okay."

"I know. Trust me, I know. But with you"—her sad smile dropped—"it was different. She didn't like the way I looked, but she hated you."

I scoffed, giving a little shake of my head. "Thanks for the reminder."

"It seems stupid now. But back then, I thought you didn't care. I didn't know."

"Let's not do this." I went to shoulder the car door open, but Rory squeezed my hand tighter. "She can't hurt us anymore, Austin. Coming here isn't about forgiving her or making amends. It's about closure. About finally letting go."

Fuck. She made it sound so simple.

Maybe she was just a better person than me, a bigger person. I didn't want closure. I wanted Mom to fucking rot for the way she'd treated us—especially Rory.

I stared up at the house, a hundred and one tainted memories looping through my mind. "I don't know how you expect me to go in there and listen to whatever bullshit she has to say."

"You don't have to come in," Rory said. "I can go in alone. But honestly, I think you'll regret it. Our childhood wasn't the best, Austin. But it wasn't the worst, either.

"We got out. We moved on. We didn't let her

completely ruin us. That has to count for something."

"I'm so fucking proud of you." Pulling her into my arms, I held my sister tight, trying to tell her everything I couldn't say.

I'm sorry.

I'll try and be better—to earn your trust and forgiveness back.

I love you.

This version of my sister wasn't the same girl I'd met back at the beginning of the year. Gone were the hesitation in her eyes, the crippling self-doubt, and anxiety. She stood tall now. Owning her flaws and embracing them.

I knew Noah was partly responsible for the sparkle in her eyes. But it was more than that. It was Connor and Ella, Harper, Dayna, and the rest of the guys.

Rory had found her place among my friends and their girlfriends.

And she deserved it.

Even if her acceptance had become my alienation.

It wasn't her fault. But watching Rory flourish after everything our mom had put her through only made me more convinced than ever that Susannah Hart had broken something irreparable in me.

"Oh, Austin." Rory hugged me back, and I swallowed over the ball of emotion lodged in my throat.

I could feel things, that wasn't the issue. I just didn't know what the fuck to do with those feelings.

"Come on, let's get this over with."

"For real?" She pulled back, smiling through the tears she didn't let fall. "You'll come in with me?"

"I came this far; might as well go all the way."

I only hoped I didn't live to regret it.

The house was exactly as I remembered.

It had been over three and a half years since I'd stepped foot inside the place, but it could have been all of a minute.

Portraits and framed magazine covers littered the walls, countless younger versions of Mom staring back at me. Everything was pristine, from the clinical white walls and polished marble surfaces.

Susannah Hart's home looked as sanitary and flawless as her image.

Even though there were slightly more lines around her eyes, she still looked immaculate in a fitted midnight blue skirt and blouse. Her hair was pulled into a tight ponytail that hung down her back, tight enough to act as a natural facelift.

I smirked to myself.

Some things never changed.

"You came," she said, pulling Rory in for an awkward hug. "Austin."

Barely a glance in my direction.

Lovely.

My sister flashed me an apologetic smile, but I didn't need her fighting my battles. Not here.

Not with the woman who hated me almost as much as I hated her.

"You had something to tell us?" I said, hoping to move this little family reunion along.

"Really, Son." She pursed her lips. "You can't just—"

"Why don't we all get a drink and sit down?" Aurora suggested, flashing me a pleading look.

"Fine." I moved ahead of them, hoping like fuck Mom had something stronger than soda lying around.

Just being here, in these four walls, made my skin crawl. There were too many bad memories. Raised voices. Glass smashing. Her bitter, hateful stare following me around the house.

"Hey, you okay?" Rory caught up to me and squeezed my hand, but I wrenched it away, too angry. Too frustrated.

Too everything.

"Austin, I—"

"It's fine," I gritted out. "Let's just get this over with."

"I'll make us all some coffee."

Coffee?

I wanted vodka or whisky. Something to take the edge off, to settle the pit in my stomach.

"You look well," Mom said from behind me. "That little seaside town suits you."

Rory gave her a tight smile. "I'm very happy."

"Good, that's... good."

"What? No compliments for me?" I spat.

"Austin," Rory quietly warned, but it was too late. I was a teenager all over again.

A hotheaded fifteen-year-old living up to the reputation as the wayward son Susannah Hart wished she'd never had.

"Austin," Mom started, a crack in her polished veneer.

"Don't. I don't want to hear whatever bullshit you're about to spew. I came here for Rory, nothing more."

"Well, then. I guess I should tell you..."

"Are you sick?" Rory blurted.

"Sick?" Mom frowned. "Gosh, no, Aurora. I'm... moving."

"Moving?"

Mom nodded. "I've decided to sell the house and move back to Rochester. I recently reconnected with an old childhood friend, and well, I think there's something there worth exploring."

"You dragged us all the way up here to tell us you're moving?" I asked, failing to keep the annoyance out of my voice.

"I thought you might take the rest of your things. Say goodbye."

"G-goodbye?" Rory's voice wobbled. "What do you mean?"

"Oh, Aurora, let's not fool ourselves." Mom had the audacity to brush Rory's hair from her face.

Softly, tenderly, the way of a mother who actually gave a fuck.

"Your life isn't here in Syracuse anymore. And I need a fresh start. Away from…" Her eyes flicked to mine, and my heart plummeted into my fucking toes.

"Yes, well." She swallowed whatever bullshit she'd been about to spew and composed herself.

Even now, in the privacy of her own home with her children, Susannah Hart wouldn't break. She wouldn't show so much as a shred of human decency because appearances—her beauty—were always more important than anything.

"Garth has contacts in the industry. He thinks he can help me relaunch myself."

And there it was.

Mom hadn't turned over a new leaf. She hadn't reconnected with an old flame and finally decided there was more to life than fame and fortune.

An opportunity had presented itself that was too good to resist.

"When do you leave?" I asked.

"The movers will be here next Wednesday. The realtor is going to handle everything else."

"That's... I don't know what to say." Rory glanced around the house, emotion rippling over her features, and I couldn't help but wonder what she saw.

Did she hate this place as much as I did? Or did she still cling to the foolish notion that we could be a family again?

Like that would ever happen.

Mom hadn't been my family in a long time. And although I loved my sister, she had Noah now. She didn't need me.

"If you want some time to sort through your things. Whatever isn't gone by the time the movers arrive Wednesday will be donated to Goodwill."

A bitter laugh spilled out of me, and both of them looked over at me. "Surely, you can see the irony," I said.

"I didn't expect you to understand," Mom said with the same disappointment and resentment she'd only ever leveled in my direction.

"So why did you want me here then? Why invite me at all?"

"Because I knew it was what Aurora would want."

"Mom!" Rory gasped.

"And because I thought some closure would be good for all of us."

"I took everything I wanted when I left. Take whatever time you need," I said to my sister, "but I'm done here."

"Austin—" she called after me, but I was already out of the door.

Unwilling to give even another second of my time to a woman who would never change her ways.

"I thought I might find you here." Rory slid into the booth beside me. "What are you drinking?"

"Whisky."

She lifted her hand and flagged down a server. "Can I get a whisky on the rocks, please? And another for my brother."

"Coming right up."

"You don't drink whisky." I narrowed my eyes.

"No, but that was... a lot. I could do with a drink."

"You could have ordered one of those sugary cocktails you and the girls like so much."

"One whisky won't hurt." She smiled. "Besides, it looks like it did a great job of improving your mood." Her eyes rolled, and I chuckled.

"Touché, Sis. Tou-fucking-ché."

"For what it's worth, I am sorry I made you come with me."

"You didn't make me do anything. I came because you shouldn't have to deal with her alone. And yeah, maybe part of me wondered…" I trapped the words, inhaling deeply through my nose.

"You wanted to see if she'd changed."

I shrugged, draining the rest of my drink. The server arrived then, and I snatched the new glass up, forcing myself to sip instead of down the thing in one.

Fucking hell, I was a mess.

Rory didn't push. She sipped her whisky in silence, making a disgusted little sound after every mouthful.

"You can get something else," I said.

"No, we're doing this."

"This?" I gave her a sideways glance, arching a brow.

"Yeah. Drinking away our issues. Drowning our sorrows at the bottom of a bottle of whisky. Getting ass over skates drunk."

"You sound like Connor."

"I'm glad he worked things out with Ella," she mused.

"Yeah." My blood heated, the liquor already working its way into my system. "Can I ask you something?"

"Always." Rory smiled.

"How did you know Noah was the one?"

"Somebody hold the phone. Are you finally admitting you know that he's—"

"*Don't* push it," I warned, but I was smiling, too.

It was probably the whisky and not the fact that I was happy for them.

Nope. Not that one bit.

"Because he made me happy." She shrugged, running her thumb around the rim of her glass.

"Happy?"

"Yeah. It sounds silly, but I spent so long hating myself, Austin. Wondering what was so wrong with me that people continually hurt me... It was so easy with Noah. He loves me. And he helped me to love myself again."

"He's a good guy."

"He is. The best." She nudged my arm. "Why do you ask?"

"No reason."

"Wouldn't have anything to do with this mystery *friend* you've been hanging out with, would it?"

"Yeah, that's over." I swirled the amber liquid in my glass, staring at nothing. Mentally recounting all the reasons why cooling things with Madison was a good idea—the *only* fucking idea.

"What? Why?"

"Because I'm broken." I drained the remnants and flagged down the server to order another.

"How many of those did you drink before I got here?"

"Not nearly enough."

"I know things have been strained between us." Rory laid her hand on my arm, and my eyes flicked up to meet her concerned expression. "But you can talk to me about this, Austin. I won't run off and tell Noah or Connor or the girls. You can trust me."

A harsh laugh rumbled in my chest, and she let out an exasperated sigh.

"What?"

"I'm a fuckup."

"Did something happen? With your friend?"

"What do you think?"

"Austin—"

"I fucked it up, Sis. Because I am fucked up. I don't know how to let people in. I don't know how to get close. When shit gets real, I run. It's what I do."

"It's worth the risk, you know," she said. But I didn't have a fucking clue what she was saying because my head felt a little fuzzy.

"What is?" I drawled, downing the rest of my glass.

Another.

Another would fix everything.

Maybe get Madison out of my head because nothing had worked yet. I'd tried. Fucking tried my hardest to forget her.

But nothing worked.

Whisky, though, whisky felt like a sure thing.

"Love, Austin."

"Love?" I barked out. "What the fuck do I know about love?"

"Exactly," she said softly. "Maybe it's time you open your heart to the idea."

CHAPTER 20

MADISON

"Thanks for helping me out this afternoon. I really appreciate it," Kayleigh said as we wiped down a couple of tables.

"Anytime. I think she's enjoyed it far more than me." I glanced over to where Imogen was busy stroking a gorgeous Tabby cat.

Kayleigh's weekend girl had been sent home sick, and since it was the shop's monthly Cat 'n' Chat session, Kayleigh needed an extra pair of hands. We just so happened to be stopping by when Florence left, so I offered to stick around for a bit.

Mrs. Owens, the organizer, had been more than willing to have an extra pair of hands, and Imogen had spent the last hour wooing the attendees and Mrs. Owens' rather impressive collection of cats.

"They all love her," Kayleigh remarked.

"Yeah." A burst of pride went through me as I watched her chatter away to her new friends.

Imogen was like a ray of sunshine, and it had been humbling to watch her interact with the small group of dementia patients attending the session.

The ding of the doorbell drew my attention, and I watched as Harper, her friend Rory, and a teenage boy entered the shop.

"Madison," Harper beamed. "We were hoping you'd be here."

"I'm actually just about to go off shift."

"Really? Maybe you can join us?"

"I—"

"Mommy, Mommy. Mrs. Owens says I'm the bestest helper she evers had."

"She did, huh." I leaned over the counter and gave Immy my full attention. "Well done, baby. Go wash up, and I'll see if I can find you a cupcake."

"One withs sprinkles?"

"One with sprinkles, baby. Now go wash up so I can serve these customers."

"Oh my God. She's adorable," Rory said, watching Imogen bounce off toward the back.

"I'm hungry," the boy said. "You said we could get a cake."

"And we can," Harper said. "Which one do you want?"

He studied the glass cabinet, his brows furrowed with concentration.

"The red velvet is really good, or maybe the cookies and cream," I offered. "What do you like?"

"I like cake. But it can't have the cross-taminations."

"Cross-tam—"

"It's okay, buddy. Madison and her boss Kayleigh are very good for people like me."

"People like—"

"I'm celiac, so Scottie knows how important it is for me to avoid gluten."

"She gets sick. Once she got so sick my brother had to carry her into the house, and then they had the sex in—"

"Excuse Scottie." She gently covered his mouth with her hand. "Why don't you and Rory go see the cats, and I'll order for us."

"Come on, bud. You can tell me all about your latest collector cards. I heard you got some for your birthday." Rory guided him toward an empty table.

"You'll have to excuse his lack of filter. He's autistic," Harper explained.

A shriek filled the shop, startling us. But when I looked over toward Rory and Scottie, the blonde whirlwind at their table was smiling excitedly.

"Oh God, I apologize. Imogen can be a handful."

"It's fine. Scottie is surprisingly good with young kids. Look."

We both watched with rapt fascination as Imogen tugged Scottie down onto a huge beanbag, and the two of them began petting the cats.

"What can I get you all?"

Harper rattled off their order, and I set about preparing it, keeping one eye on Imogen. But she was all too happy chatting away to Scottie and Mrs. Owens, holding court like she owned the damn place.

Gosh, I was going to have my hands full when she was older. She was so headstrong and confident.

"Thanks, this all looks amazing," Harper said when I shoved the tray toward her. "Tell Kayleigh the new menu is going to be a big hit."

"I will. She's around here some— Ah, here she is." Kayleigh appeared to look calmer than she had when I'd first got here.

"You can take off now," she said. "Thank you so much for helping me out today."

"Anytime, you know that."

"You'll join us for a little bit?" Harper asked.

"I..."

"Go. I've got this." Kayleigh ushered me out from behind the counter.

"I'll see you Monday," I said.

"You will. Now go," she mouthed. "Make friends."

I rolled my eyes before following Harper to their table.

"Mommy, wooks. I made a new friend. His name is Scotties."

"Scottie," he corrected.

"That's what I said."

"No, you said Scotties. There's only one of me. I'm not a plural."

"What's a plural?"

"She's only little, buddy," Harper intervened. "She doesn't know—"

"Hey, I'm not wittles. I'm a big girl. I'm fives this year."

Rory and Harper smothered a laugh, but I saw no judgment in their eyes.

"Immy, baby, no one meant any harm."

"I am a big girl, Mommy. Tells them."

"We know, princess."

"Princess?" Scottie frowned, looking her over. "You're not a princess."

"I am so sorry," Harper mouthed as she quietly explained the rules of role-play to him.

But I was smiling, too.

There was something so pure about watching kids interact. Experiencing the world through their eyes.

I wanted to treasure every moment.

"Scottie, time to go, bud," Harper said.

The Cat 'n' Chat session had ended almost an hour ago, but Scottie and Imogen were having so much fun with Mrs. Owens, she'd agreed to stay longer.

"I want to stay here. With Immy and the cat lady."

"But we're meeting Mason soon."

"Can they come?"

"I don't think Madison and Imogen want to hang out with a bunch of hockey players, buddy."

"Why not?" He looked genuinely horrified. "Hockey is the best thing ever."

"Is nots." Imogen pursed her lips, and I braced myself for another argument. But Scottie merely rolled his eyes. "Princesses," he muttered, and the three of us struggled to stifle our laughter.

"It would seem she's won him over," Rory said.

"I think she won the entire place over," Kayleigh said, collecting our empty mugs.

"You want me to help—"

"No, I want you to stay on this side of the counter for once." She gave me a hard look. "You've helped me enough today."

"They could come with us," Scottie argued again.

"Yes, Mommy. We coulds go and meet the hockey players."

"I don't think so, baby. Not today."

"But Mommy, we—"

"I said not today, Imogen."

Her lips wobbled, and I felt like the monster Mom. But I couldn't hang out with Austin's teammates—his friends. What if he was there? What if he thought I was trying to encroach on his life?

No, I couldn't do that.

No matter how much we'd enjoyed hanging out with Harper, Rory, and Scottie this afternoon.

"Are you sure you won't come?" Harper asked, and I nodded, beckoning for Imogen to climb onto my lap.

She wrapped her arms around my neck, and I ran a hand over her head. "Mommy has our evening all planned. We're going to do face masks and watch a movie, and I even thought I could paint your nails. Just like a princess."

"Pink, I wants pink."

"Pink it is." I smiled, peppering her cheeks with kisses. "Say goodbye to Scottie, Harper, and Rory, baby."

"Bye-bye."

"It was nice to meet you, Princess Immy," Rory said, making her beam.

"Thank you," I said over the lump in my throat.

We got ready to leave, but Imogen pulled away from me at the last second and ran toward Scottie, throwing her arms around his waist.

"Oh my God." Harper inhaled a sharp breath, obviously concerned about his response. But to our surprise, Scottie tapped her on the head and said, "I guess hockey players can be friends with princesses."

That put a bounce in her step as she came back to me and took my hand. "Sees you soon." She waved at them all the way to the door.

I didn't have the heart to tell her she probably wouldn't see them again.

"Mommy, can we gets a cat?"

"No, baby. We talked about this. I have enough to think about without looking after a cat."

"But Uncle Jerrykins has a cat, and he's a man."

"But Uncle Jer doesn't have you to look after." I hauled her onto my lap, tickling her waist.

"Can I haves a big brother then? Like Scottie?"

"Uh, it doesn't quite work like that, baby. If you had a brother or sister, you would be their big sister because you came first."

"Hmm." Her brows crinkled as she contemplated my words. "I knows." She held a finger up. "Scottie cans be my boyfriend."

Silent laughter bubbled inside me.

She was something else.

"Don't you think you're a little bit young for a boyfriend?"

"I ams not," she huffed. "And you won't gets one, so maybe I should."

God help me.

"It's not that simple, Immy. You don't just decide you want a boyfriend and go to the store and pick one."

Was I really having this conversation with my four-year-old?

"But you is really pretty, Mommy." She toyed with my hair. "I bet Mr. Austins would wikes to be your boyfriend."

Jesus. Talk about kicking me when I was already down.

"I don't think we'll see Mr. Austins again, baby," I said with as much indifference as I could muster.

"Whys not? Does he have another girlfriend?"

It would have been a damn sight easier if it were that simple.

But no, Austin didn't have another girlfriend. At least, not that I knew of.

He just didn't want me and all my baggage.

The worst of it was I didn't blame him. He was nearly done with college; he had his whole life ahead of him. Why the hell would he want to be tied down to a girl like me?

What we had was temporary. Fleeting. It always

had been. So this ache I felt in my chest, this sense of loss, was silly.

He'd blown me off when he'd first found out I had a daughter; it should have been no surprise he got cold feet when she almost caught him in my apartment.

A sigh rolled through me, and Imogen's nose crinkled. "What's wrongs, Mommy?"

"Nothing, baby. Nothing." I hugged her closer, silently reminding myself that she was all I needed.

Risking my heart again wasn't worth the inevitable fallout.

Imogen deserved people in her life who would show up for her. People who would be there no matter what. That was my priority, my focus.

My own needs were secondary to that—they had to be.

So why the hell had I let Austin in? Brought him into my home and given him a glimpse into my life with Imogen?

Because you wanted him to care. You wanted him to prove you wrong.

No, that wasn't right. It couldn't be. It was just sex. I liked him, sure. But I knew it couldn't be anything more.

"Mommy!" Imogen grabbed my face in her little hands and scowled at me. "You're ways with the fairies again."

"Sorry, princess. I'm really sleepy today."

She climbed off my lap and crawled across the couch to grab the blanket. "We can have a naps, Mommy."

My heart almost burst with love as she snuggled into me and pulled the blanket over us.

I may not have done many things right in my life, but I'd gotten it right with her.

"I love you, Imogen Grace," I whispered, pressing a kiss to her hair.

"I woves you too, Mommy. Soooo much." She closed her eyes, and I held her tight.

Just like I always would.

"What, Jer?" I asked him Monday afternoon as we watched Imogen and Vader run loops around his apartment.

"Nothing. Nothing at all."

"Just spit it out."

"You just seem... different. And I can't help but wonder if you're missing a certain hockey player?"

"I'm not." I kept my eyes on Imogen, hoping he couldn't see the truth on my face.

"Shame. He was a gorgeous specimen of a man."

"If you need reminding"—I tossed him an acerbic look—"he cooled things, not me."

"You didn't exactly fight for him."

"Fight for… seriously?" Incredulity dripped from my words.

How could he say that?

"I didn't mean it like that," he said softly. "I'm just saying he can't have been that concerned about bumping into Imogen if he was at your apartment. And he had the perfect opportunity to walk away when he found out about her. But he didn't."

The look he gave me didn't make me feel any better.

Was he right?

Was Austin giving me subliminal messages that my having a daughter wasn't a deal breaker?

Laughter bubbled up my throat. "Nice try. You almost had me there for a moment."

"Mads, that's not—"

"Mommy, wooks at Vader."

"Oh my God, Immy." I bolted up, rushing to recuse Vader from her current predicament of being strapped into Imogen's baby stroller. "Sweetheart, we can't do that to Vader. She's a cat, baby. Not a dolly."

"But she wikes it, Mommy. She tolds me."

"She told her?" I mouthed to Jeremiah, who could barely contain his laughter.

"Your phone is vibrating," he said, coming over to us. "You take that, and I'll deal with Princess Immy and her cat baby."

I scanned the screen, smiling. "This is a surprise," I said.

"What? I can't call my bestie anymore," Fawn said over her laughter. "How're things going?"

"Imogen currently has Vader strapped onto her stroller like a doll."

"Oh my God, that girl is something else. Listen, I can't talk long, but I wondered if you wanted to come out Friday."

"I can't. My parents are still away and—"

"Hi, Fawn, love." Jeremiah smushed his cheek against mine. "Madi says she would love to come out."

"Jer," I hissed.

"She needs a pick me up after Mr. Hockey Player ditched her."

"Oh, Mads, I'm sorry," Fawn said.

"It's fine. I'm fine. And I really can't make it. I have no one to watch Imogen—"

"She'll be there. Text her the details. K, love you, bye." Jeremiah snatched the phone out of my hand and hung up.

"What the hell was that?" I gawked at him.

"I'll watch Immy. Or Jacqui and Ken will take her. A night out with Fawn will do you good."

"You said that the last time, and look where it got me." I sighed.

"I think you'll find it was a one-way ticket to orgasm town."

"Jer!" I whisper-shrieked, swatting his arm.

"What?" Laughter pealed out of him, his eyes twinkling with amusement. "I know you're bummed things didn't work out with Mr. Hockey Hotshot, but you can't let that stop you."

"Oh, I don't know. You know how Fawn and her friends can get."

"You're going." He leveled me with a meaningful look. "Even if I have to drag you there myself."

CHAPTER 21

THE CINCINNATI U CAVALIERS came out determined to make us work for it. After two early goals—goals I was still kicking myself for conceding—I was beginning to think that our luck had turned.

We'd had a solid run leading up to winter break. But we were missing Connor on defense. Leon had worked hard to pick up the slack, but things weren't as seamless with a rookie as they were with a senior player with three years of experience under his skates.

Coach had let Connor sit on the bench, though, and by half-time, he was yelling at our players almost as much as Coach Tucker and Assistant Coach Walsh.

"Come on, let's go Lakers," I yelled, trying to hype up my teammates. The last thing we needed was a loss.

Another setback going into the final few games before regionals.

Aiden gained the puck, racing down the ice toward the Cavaliers' goal. "Go, go!" seemed to echo around Ellet Arena, stoking the fire in my veins as I watched our O line fly toward the Cavaliers' goal.

"Take the shot," I muttered under my breath.

Aiden was on target to do what our captain did best, but a defenseman closed in, and at the last second, he changed direction and sent the puck sliding across the ice toward Noah instead.

Noah managed to evade his D-man, and with a little flick, he sent the puck hurtling into the net.

The buzzer sounded, and the home crowd went wild. Even Connor leaped up, celebrating with the rest of our teammates.

One to two.

We were back in the game. But there was still a long way to go.

When the final whistle sounded, we'd won the game seven to five. And in true Lakers style, we all filed off the ice and high-fived Connor as if it was his win as much as ours.

"Good game." He gave me a small nod.

"Thanks. It was close there for a second."

"Nah, knew you could do it." His mouth twitched as I moved past him into the locker room.

I was beat. Every inch of my body, achy and sore. It hadn't just been a tough game; it had been a dogfight, and we'd had to claw for every puck and every goal.

The fact I'd let five goals slip past my glove pissed me off, but we got the win, and that's all that mattered.

"Hey, Hart, you looked a little tired out there," Abel Adams called with a cocky smirk.

"Fuck you, asshole."

"Ignore him," Noah said, coming up beside me. "You know he likes to live up to his reputation as the dumbest motherfucker on the team," he said the last part loud enough for Adams to hear.

"I don't understand why Coach doesn't just kick his ass to the curb."

"Because other than a bit of banter, he plays by the rules, and he's a decent enough player."

"He's an asshole." I pinned him with a dangerous look.

Noah's hand slid between us, and he shoved my chest. "Don't let him bait you. He isn't worth it."

"Hmm." I began pulling off my protective gear, but Coach Tucker had other ideas.

"Okay, team, listen up. We got the win"—a group of cheers went up around me—"but you made it look like hard work. Austin, son, you looked a little distracted out there tonight. Anything I need to be worried about?"

"No, sir."

Noah's eyes drilled into the side of my face, but I didn't acknowledge him.

I knew Rory had probably filled him in on our trip to Syracuse; the fact I'd drunk myself stupid at the bar after pouring my heart out to her.

We didn't talk about it the next day. We'd simply grabbed her shit from the house and gotten the fuck out of there.

I didn't want to talk about it. As far as I was concerned, it was done.

Over.

Mom could burn the house to the ground for all I cared.

"Well, okay then. You need to keep showing up. Especially if you're going to talk to the Canucks."

A couple of the guys whistled, but I waved them off.

I hadn't decided anything yet.

"I know it's going to take some time to adjust to not having Connor." Coach went on, "But if we want to go all the way to the Frozen Four, we don't have forever to get our shit together. Okay, good game. Hit the showers and get out of here."

I grabbed my towel and toiletry bag and headed for the showers, but while my teammates were eager to meet their girls and celebrate, I was only thinking of one thing.

The blonde with sparkling blue eyes that I'd walked away from.

Sometime later, I followed the guys out of the arena to the small group of fans waiting in the parking lot.

I was hardly surprised to see my sister, Dayna, Ella, Harper, and Scottie. But I was surprised to see her practically growling at the group of puck bunnies hanging around.

One of them flashed me a playful smile, but I ignored her. I wasn't in the mood. And I sure as shit wasn't in the mood to tangle with a bunny.

Aiden broke rank first and moved ahead of us teammates, making a beeline for his girl. He pulled Dayna straight into his arms and kissed her.

"Whew, did it just get a little hot in here," Rory said.

Aiden flipped us all off over her shoulder, and they laughed.

I didn't feel much like laughing, though.

"Where's Connor?" Ella searched the crowd for him.

"He's in with Coach Tucker," someone said.

"Is everything okay?" She chewed on the end of her thumb, clearly nervous.

"Think he's getting an earful for not staying in his seat," Mason said, Scottie already glued to his big brother's side.

"He's not hurt, though, right?" Ella asked.

"Relax, El," I said. "Your guy is good."

A second later, Connor appeared, and she hurried over to him. He hauled her close, lowering his head to kiss her deeply.

Somebody wolf-whistled, and everyone laughed again.

I remained silent, something akin to regret curdling in my gut.

"We heading to TPB?" Noah asked, hands all over my sister like I wasn't fucking standing right there.

"It'll be full of bunnies," Rory pointed out, nose wrinkled with distaste.

"Can't we get food and then head to Zest? I told Jordan we'd stop by."

"It's the first game back. We've got to put in an appearance at TPB." Aiden hugged Dayna to his side, whispering something into her ear. "We can eat at TPB, then join you at Zest later on."

"Fine."

They discussed the finer details of the plan while I watched Connor and Ella. Lost in their own world, whispering sweet nothings to one another.

I'd never wanted that. Not for one second. And yet... No, fuck that.

A girlfriend was a complication I didn't want or need. One I was almost certain I couldn't handle.

So why the fuck couldn't I stop thinking about Madison?

Wondering if I'd made a huge fucking mistake.

The Penalty Box was swarming with Lakers fans, and the second we filed inside, a huge chorus went up.

"Fuck, it's good to be alive," Leon chuckled before slipping into a group of awaiting bunnies.

"Fucking dog," Noah whispered.

"You don't miss those days?" someone asked, and my sister's boyfriend didn't miss a beat.

"Like hell I do. Rory is all I'll ever need."

"You hearing this, Austin? Holden's all—"

I moved past them and melted into the crowd.

I loved Rory, and yeah, we'd gone some way to clearing the air between us after our short trip to Syracuse, but I didn't need to listen to that shit.

It was bad enough I got to witness Noah with his hands all over her on the daily.

"Austin." A set of perfectly manicured nails slid over my arm.

Fuck.

"You look good." Fallon gazed up at me, and I felt... nothing. "I was hoping we could—"

"Not going to happen."

"But I've missed you. I've missed us, Austin." Her hand found mine and she threaded our fingers together like she had some fucking claim on me. "Didn't you miss me?"

Why?

Why the fuck did girls do this?

I didn't want to be an asshole. I didn't want to hurt her feelings. But what part of *we're over* didn't she get?

"Look, Fallon—"

"Is there someone else?" She blurted. "Because if there is, I'll understand."

"No, there's no one else." The words felt wrong.

They felt like a lie.

Fuck.

Fuck.

"You sure about that?" Her expression hardened. "Because you don't look sure."

"Fallon," I let out an exasperated sigh. "This isn't the time or place."

"We could go somewhere. My place—"

"No."

Hell no.

"I'm here with the team, and I meant what I said, this—us—it's over."

Her expression crumpled, tears glistening in her eyes.

"Look, I'm sorry—"

"Don't, Austin. Just... don't." She backed away from me, shaking her head as the crowd swallowed her.

"What's that look for?" Mason joined me.

"How do you do it?" I asked.

"Do what?"

"Deal with the drama?"

He spotted Fallon making a beeline for the door and smirked. "Ah, I see. She wants to start things back up?"

"Something like that."

"You know, I never thought I'd say this, but it's worth it. For the right girl, it's all worth it." Mason squeezed my shoulder and left me to it. Like me, he wasn't one to talk about his feelings and all that mushy shit.

I flagged the server down and ordered a beer. Just one to take the edge off.

Bringing the bottle to my lips, I surveyed the room —my teammates and our adoring fans.

There was a clear divide now—those in relationships and those not. And I was somewhere stuck in the middle. I hadn't done the casual hookups or fucking a different girl each weekend for a long time. But I hadn't wanted to put a label on what I had with Fallon either. All I knew was when I was with her, I didn't look into my future and see her.

She was safe and familiar, and I thought I could trust her not to go and catch feelings.

I was wrong.

Pulling out my cell phone, I opened my chat thread with Madison, and read our last text exchange.

It was the right call.

She had a daughter.

Her number one priority would always be Imogen.

Something I could respect. Because unlike Susannah Hart, Madison was a good mom. The kind of mom who would bust her ass to make sure her daughter had everything she needed.

She was everything I'd never had.

Everything I would never have.

It was a good thing I was surrounded by my teammates, or else I might have done something stupid, like drowning my sorrows in the bottom of a bottle of whisky.

"Yo, asshole, where are you going?" Noah called as I began to head in the opposite direction.

The guys were done at TPB, ready to move on to Zest and see their girls.

"I'm heading home," I said.

"Like hell you are." He came over and slung his arm around my neck. "We're celebrating. And you're bringing your grumpy ass with us."

"Holden has a point, Austin," Aiden chimed. "We're already a man down; you're not escaping, too."

"Besides, we've brought the rookies along for the ride." Noah flicked his head toward Ward and Leon. "You won't be playing third wheel."

"You can play wingman, though, if you want," Leon laughed.

"You'll be needing all the help you can get with that new haircut."

"What's wrong with it?" Leon ran a hand over his buzzcut.

"You're practically bald." Mason smirked.

"Yeah, so? The ladies dig it."

"What are they supposed to hold onto when you're... you know, kissing the kitty."

"Kissing the kitty?" We all gawked at Ward. "What are you, twelve?" Noah burst into laughter.

"Oh wait, I know," Mason added. "She can hold onto his ears."

"Fuck off. You're all fucking idiots. I'm telling you, I'll be fighting them off."

"Big words for a bald man." Mason and Aiden shoved him down the sidewalk, Ward following behind, leaving me with Noah.

"You're not going home," he said.

"Yes, I am."

"No, you're not. You're coming out with your friends."

"Rory—"

"Loves you and will be happy to see you. Just like everyone else."

"Fine," I grumbled. "Just for an hour or so."

"Thank fuck." He relaxed his hold on me as we caught up with the others. "I really didn't want to have to drag you there."

"Like you could take me."

The guys fell into a debate about the team's performance tonight while I tried to empty my mind.

I could manage an hour or so at Zest.

It was usually a bunny-free zone and not the usual college crowd.

But the second we stepped inside, my plans of surviving Noah, my sister, and our friends all went to shit.

Because sitting there nestled between Rory and Harper with a drink in her hand and a smile on her face...

Was Madison.

CHAPTER 22

MADISON

"Fawn, tell me how this happened?" I murmured under my breath as we stood at the bar, ordering another round of cocktails.

"Uh, the hockey girlfriends insisted we join them, and I'm a really bad friend and couldn't say no, but you love me anyway." She peeked up at me through her thick lashes, clearly amused by the whole thing.

"Mm-hmm." I made a derisive sound in the back of my throat, nervous energy vibrating through me.

The night had been fine until Fawn insisted we go to a different bar, and we walked in to find none other than Harper and Rory there.

It wasn't like we could turn around and walk out, so we'd spent the last two hours hanging out with them.

They said the guys were stopping by later, and I'd planned to be long gone. But Fawn, the devious minx, kept plying me with drinks.

And maybe, just maybe, a little masochistic part of me wanted to stick around and see if Austin would show.

The look on his face when he'd spotted me sitting wedged between Harper and Rory had me sorely regretting my life choices, though.

"I should go."

"Hell. No," Fawn fumed. "We were here first, and we're not leaving just because Hockey Hottie looks two seconds from either coming over here to choke the life right out of you or fuck it out of you."

"Fawn." Heat blasted through me, and I blushed.

"He doesn't... That's not—"

"Madi, come meet the guys." Harper grabbed my hand and tugged me back toward the couple of tables we'd taken over.

I liked Zest. It had a chill vibe and clearly wasn't your average college hang out, but my happy vodka-fueled bubble had burst the second Austin had walked in.

"Guys, this is Madison," Harper announced, wiggling past Rory to sit on her boyfriend's lap. He pulled her down and wrapped his arm around her waist, kissing the spot behind her ear.

"She works at the coffee shop I was telling you about on the edge of town."

"I heard you made quite the impression with Scottie," he said.

"Oh no, that was all Imogen."

"Imogen?" one of the other guys asked.

"Madison's daughter," Rory said. "Oh my God, she's just the cutest. She had Scottie wrapped around her pinky."

"He's already asked when we're seeing you again." Harper beamed, but her boyfriend didn't look too impressed.

"He's a sweet kid," I said, hating the attention.

Hating that Austin hadn't even looked twice in my direction.

"The cat café is such a great idea. I'm going to suggest something similar to Jet at the center. We're always looking for new projects."

"If you take on any more projects, I'll never see you," Mason grumbled.

"Who's your friend?" the guy with the buzz cut asked as Fawn approached with our drinks.

"Fawn? She goes to LU."

"She single?"

"Yes, she is." Fawn flashed him a saucy grin.

"Nice. There's a free seat right here." He patted the space next to him, and she got herself comfortable.

"Your friend wasted no time, did she?" Mason let

out a smooth chuckle, earning him an elbow in the ribs from Harper.

I didn't belong with these people.

College students with their assignment deadlines and dreams beyond graduation. I had real-world worries. Bills to pay and mouths to feed.

It hadn't felt so bad sitting with Harper and Rory and their other friends. I almost felt like one of the girls. Minus the fact they talked mostly about sex and studying. But now the guys were here, I was acutely aware of myself. Of Austin sitting across the table from me. So close and yet so far away.

Did he regret being with me?

Did he wish that he'd picked someone with less baggage?

Or did he not care enough to think about it?

From the way he had ignored me since arriving, I was pretty sure it was the latter.

"I'm just going to use the restroom," I said to no one in particular.

I used the moment to text Jeremiah and check in on Imogen.

Madi: Is she sleeping?

Jer: Of course. Uncle Jerrykins runs a tight ship you know. How's girls' night?

Madi: It was great until a certain
hockey player showed up.

Jer: Holy shit. He's there? This is
perfect…

Madi: No, it's really not.

Jer: Of course it is. You can flirt and
dance with some other guys and make
him realize what he let slip through his
fingers.

Madi: I'm a mom, Jer. My daughter is
literally asleep in your guest room. I
don't have the time or energy to play
games.

Jer: Fine, forget I said anything. At
least don't let him ruin your night.

Madi: I'll try.

Jer: Atta girl!

I rolled my eyes at that. Jeremiah was my best friend. My ride or die, but he was also a giant pain in my ass.

Checking my reflection in the mirror, I washed my hands and smoothed the loose tendrils around my face behind my ear.

I hadn't gone over the top tonight, opting for

skintight black jeans and a sparkly off-the-shoulder top. But it was hard to keep out the pang of self-doubt when Austin had barely looked twice in my direction.

No. Screw him.

Jeremiah was right.

I didn't have to let him ruin my night.

With a new sense of resolve, I exited the restrooms, only to walk straight into him. "Austin," I breathed. "Listen, I—"

"What the hell are you doing?" he growled, crowding me against the wall.

"Excuse me?"

"Why are you here, Madison?"

"I... Sorry, what?" I blinked at him, certain I'd misheard him or, at the very least, misinterpreted the anger in his voice. "It sounds like you're saying I shouldn't be here."

"Is this some weird attempt to get close to me by using my friends?" His brow arched with heavy accusation.

"You did not just say that."

Who the hell was this guy?

And why did his words hurt as much as they pissed me off?

"You've got to admit, it looks a bit desperate."

Desperate.

The word ricocheted through me, and I flinched.

"Wow. I'll be leaving now," I said, shoving past him.

"Madison, wait. I—"

"Don't bother, Austin." I glanced back, heart in my throat, pride on the floor. "You've made it perfectly clear where we stand."

I didn't leave the bar.

Instead, I heeded Jeremiah's words and flirted up a storm.

I was annoyed at myself for letting Austin's words affect me so much. But who the hell did he think he was talking to me like that?

The endless stream of cocktails the guys—minus Austin, who had kept his distance all night—kept bringing us might have been slightly to blame for my false bravado.

"Maybe you've had enough," Fawn said as we danced with Harper.

"I'm fine," I said, weaving my hands through the air, letting the music take me over. "Fiiine."

"You sound it." She rolled her eyes, checking her cell phone. "It's late. We should probably head back."

"What happened to Leon?"

"His groupies arrived." Fawn grabbed my finger and pointed over to where Leon and three girls sat, all a little too close to be considered appropriate.

Even for a bar.

"Come on, party girl, let's get you—"

"Oh, I love this song." I threw my arms around her neck and began swaying us to the beat.

"Fine. I guess we can stay a little longer."

A couple of Harper's friends joined us, and we all danced and laughed and danced some more.

I felt good. Austin's blatant rejection was a distant memory thanks to all the vodka in my veins and music in my soul.

Until my eyes found him across the bar, in a heated discussion with—

"Rory."

My heart crashed against my chest as I watched them move into a quieter spot, heads lowered, bodies close.

It didn't make any sense.

She was with Noah. I'd spent the entire night watching the two of them all over each other. But there was no mistaking the tension between Austin and Rory now. Even from all the way over here, I could see the angst in his expression—the pain.

They looked like forbidden lovers hiding in the dark.

Oh my God.

He wanted her.

He wanted Rory, and she was with his friend. His teammate.

Which made me what?

His rebound.

His second choice.

A distraction while he pined after the girl he could never have.

I felt nauseous.

"E-excuse me," I blurted, fighting my way through the sea of people to get to the restrooms. But stupidly, my path took me right past them.

"Madi, what's wrong?" Rory called, and I glanced over.

Big mistake.

Austin looked furious.

Because I'd uncovered his secret.

"Nothing. I'm just… restroom." The room spun, and I reached out, trying—*failing*—to grab hold of something as the world shifted beneath my feet.

"Shit," Austin growled at the same time as Rory shrieked his name.

His strong arms caught me, helping me back to my feet. But he didn't let go.

"How much did you drink?" He scowled.

"I…" I swallowed, acid burning my throat, tears burning the backs of my eyes.

God, I was a mess.

I'd taken Jeremiah's advice, downed a few drinks for Dutch courage, and spent the last two hours doing my best to forget all about Austin Hart, maybe trying to make him a little bit jealous in the process.

All the while, he was lusting after his friend's girlfriend.

"I-I need to go." I wrenched myself out of his hold and took off toward the entrance.

"Madi," Rory called, her voice drowned out by the music, blood rushing in my ears.

I didn't stop until I was outside, the cool air instantly tempering the hot stains of embarrassment on my cheeks.

"Breathe," I muttered, glancing up and down the sidewalk, trying to get air into my lungs. "Just breathe."

I pulled out my phone to text Fawn. I needed to get out of here. I needed—

"If my sister didn't suspect something before, she will now." His voice rumbled through me.

"Just go back inside, Austin." I whirled around and pinned him with the best *fuck you* look I could muster. "We have nothing— Sister?" My brows furrowed. "What are you talking about?"

"You caught that, huh?" His mouth quirked, guilt shining in his eyes.

"I... I don't understand." Except... that sense of familiarity I'd had at Sugartown when I first met her. "Oh my God." Realization slapped me in the face. "Rory is your sister."

"Yeah, and a relentless pain in my ass."

So much made sense now.

Why he'd looked so angry to find me sitting with her and Harper.

Why he'd spewed those angry, hurtful words at me.

"Well, I guess that changes things."

And yet, it didn't change anything at all.

Austin didn't want his sister or friends to know about the single mom he'd been sleeping with.

I don't know what hurt worse. When I thought Rory was the object of his affection, or now that I knew she was his sister.

His family.

And he didn't think to tell me.

"Look, I'm sorry. Seeing you tonight..." He raked a hand through his hair and ran it down the back of his neck, tension bracketing that gorgeous mouth of his. "It threw me for a loop. Especially seeing you hanging out with my sister."

"I didn't know—"

"I know. That's pretty obvious."

My cheeks flamed again. But this wasn't my fault.

"I guess things got messier than either of us planned on," I said, barely meeting his eyes.

I couldn't.

Because when I looked at him, all I could see was him kissing me. Making me come apart with his teeth and tongue and those big hockey goalie hands of his.

Time seemed to stop as his fingers brushed my jaw,

sliding under my chin and tilting my face to meet his conflicted gaze. "Madison, I—"

"There you are." Fawn appeared, and Austin let me go, stepping back.

She laced her arm through mine, completely oblivious to the moment Austin and I were having.

Or completely aware.

I arched a brow at her, and she gave me a calculated grin. "Sorry, was I interrupting something?"

Oh, she definitely knew she'd walked in on something. But maybe that was a good thing.

"No," Austin said before I could answer. "I just wanted to make sure Madi was okay."

"Madi is fine, thank you," she sassed. "I've got this Hotshot. See you around." Fawn led me away from him. "What the hell was that?" she hissed the second we were out of earshot.

I dropped my head on her shoulder and let out a weary sigh.

"Honestly, I have no idea."

"Here, drink this." Fawn thrust a bottle of water at me. "It'll help with the inevitable hangover tomorrow."

It wasn't the hangover I was worried about.

It was that awkward moment with Austin. The awkward moment that had very much felt like *more*.

"Thanks." I uncapped the lid and chugged it down, trying to make sense of the night.

Of my reaction to seeing Austin with Rory—when I thought she'd been someone other than his sister.

"Did you know Austin has a sister?" I asked.

"Above knowing he's the Lakers goalie, I don't really know much about him. Hockey, as you know, isn't my thing."

"So last night was what exactly?" She'd been all over Leon Banks until he'd found the trio of puck bunnies to keep himself entertained.

"What?" She shrugged. "He was cute."

"Rory is his sister."

"No shit. I thought they had a similar look. But for real, they're related?"

"Yep."

"I'm guessing you found this out tonight?"

"Yep."

"Well, that's good, isn't it? Means he isn't hung up on his teammate's girlfriend."

"I didn't know, Fawn. We hung out with her all night, and I didn't... I guess it was really just sex, after all."

"Babe, don't do this. It was sex, remember? Casual, no-strings, get-you-back-on-the-horse sex. You weren't supposed to catch feelings."

"Too late." I gave her a sad, self-deprecating smile.

"Yeah, I figured as much when he walked in. You've got it bad."

"Because I'm an idiot."

"No." She let out a soft chuckle, pulling a fluffy cushion onto her lap. "Because you're human."

"I felt something with him, Fawn. Something that scared me."

"You wanted to trust him."

"Yeah, I think I did." I tucked my hair behind my ear, inhaling a shaky breath, trying to shut down the emotions whirring inside me. "But it isn't fair of me to act hurt. We didn't make any promises to each other. And I have a daughter, that's—"

"Will you stop with that, already. You make it sound like being a single mom is synonymous with having a contagious disease. The right guy will never see Immy as anything less than she deserves. Both of you deserve."

"You think?"

"Babe, I know. There are good guys out there—guys who would be lucky to have you and Imogen in their life. So the first guy you trust isn't the one. They'll be others."

"You're right."

Two words I hadn't been able to believe for a long time. Not after how badly Warren hurt me.

And she was right. Maybe Austin wasn't the one, but he had healed something inside me.

He'd brought me out of the cold and lit a fire inside me again.

But most of all, he had shown me that I could let someone in again.

I would always be grateful for that.

CHAPTER 23

AUSTIN

"Rise and shine, asshole."

Something cold and wet landed on my head.

"The fuck?" I murmured, trying to peel my eyes open—immediately regretting it when the light poured in, and a bomb detonated in my skull.

Holy shit.

That hurt.

"Jesus, you're a mess," Noah said with a smug lilt that would have usually got my back up. As it was, I was too hungover to give a fuck.

"Get cleaned up. Rory made breakfast, and she expects you to be present."

"Can't I—"

"No. Ten minutes, or I'll be back with a bucket of

cold water. Seems like you've got some explaining to do." He stalked out of the room and slammed the door behind him. Asshole.

I gave myself a minute before I pushed up onto my elbows with a pained groan.

Their apartment was a one-bedroom. So if I was in their bedroom, where the fuck had they slept?

Shit.

I managed to sit up, but the room spun so violently, I almost puked all over Rory's pale blue rug.

Once I was sure everything was going to stay on the inside, I dragged my sorry ass into their bathroom and washed up. I couldn't stomach the thought of a shower, but I did swill my mouth with some toothpaste and water to try and wash away the rancid aftertaste of one too many whiskys.

Coach was going to fucking kill me if he got wind of my little pity party for one. But everything had gone to shit after Madison left me standing on the sidewalk without so much as a backward glance.

The suspicious-looking stain on my shirt had me reaching for one of Noah's t-shirts. Then I headed to find them.

"You look relatively alive, considering how unconscious you looked last night."

"I... Shit, Rory. I am so fucking sorry."

"Hey, asshole, it's my apartment too." Despite his serious tone, Noah smirked.

"Here. Drink, then eat something. I'll get you some Advil." Rory's cold shoulder was impressive.

"In case you haven't noticed, she's pissed you didn't tell Madison about her."

"I— You know."

"Of course, I fucking know. Even if Rory hadn't told me, which she did, you wouldn't shut up about it on the ride home. You're welcome by the way." He snorted. "We got you out of there before you could make a total fool of yourself or get yourself reported to Coach."

"Oh."

"Yeah, oh."

"Seriously, Austin. Do you have any idea how hurt she is after that stunt you pulled last summer by not telling us she was transferring to LU."

"I fucked up."

"Yeah, you did." He got up and squeezed my shoulder. "And I'd love nothing more than to stay here and watch her string you up by your balls. But I figure the two of you need to talk. So I'm going to meet the guys at the gym. Sort your shit out and get your head in game mode, yeah."

"Thanks," I said, realizing it was long overdue.

"What for?"

"Being there for her when I wasn't. She's lucky to have you, Holden."

"Not as lucky as I am." He clapped me on the back

and made a beeline for my sister, pulling her into his arms. "Try not to physically harm him; we need him for regionals."

Her gaze flicked to mine as she muttered, "I can't promise anything."

Noah kissed her. Soft and lingering, enough to make me look away before the night's liquor made a reappearance.

"He's gone," she announced, moving closer.

Rory leaned against the counter, staring at me with a mix of pity and sadness that hit me right in the chest.

I knew I'd messed up—I didn't need her to rub it in.

"What?" I bit out, the silence almost too much to bear.

"Oh, Austin." Her expression softened. "What have you gotten yourself into?"

"Better?" Rory asked.

She'd finally sat down at the breakfast counter while I managed to eat two plates of bacon and eggs.

"Yeah, thanks."

"Okay, time to talk."

"Rory, I—"

"No, Austin. I've been patient. I've been

understanding. But the look in Madison's eyes last night... that wasn't fair to either of us."

"You barely know her."

"True. But I like her, and I think we could be friends. Surely you can see how messed up it is that she thought... God, I can't even say it." She shuddered. "How long has it been going on?"

"The night Connor got injured."

"She has a daughter."

"She does."

"Have you met her?"

"Not on purpose," I said, and Rory frowned. "I ran into them at the store before Christmas."

"And yet, you didn't stop seeing her?"

"We agreed to keep things..." I trailed off, realizing that we hadn't kept things simple at all.

Madison continually let me go back to her place. She let me into her and Imogen's space. I didn't think much of it at the time. I figured it was just sex.

But now, it felt different.

"What happened?" My sister pushed, but I saw no judgment there.

"I stayed over, and Imogen almost walked in on us. She was supposed to be staying away for the night but wanted to surprise Madi in the morning." The twitch of her lips had me frowning. "What?"

"I would have paid to see you get found out by that little girl. She's something else."

"Madison panicked, made me hide in the bathroom, and I got cold feet and ended things."

"Do you want to end things?"

"No. Yes." I heaved a sigh, hating that she was doing this. But at the same time, I felt a sense of relief to finally be talking about it.

It was confusing as fuck.

"Shit, Rory, I don't know. She has a kid. I'm still in college."

"I've never seen you like this before," she said, and the words rocked me to my core.

"What do you mean?"

"In high school, you were the popular guy, surrounded by girls and guys all wanting a piece of the Austin Hart pie. I just assumed that's how it was for you here. But I don't know, you're different."

"Three years of college will do that to a guy."

"No, it's more than that." Her expression turned sad. "It's like you're lost, Austin. Or maybe not lost, but stuck. Going through the motions."

"You'd be lost too if all your friends started settling down."

"But this isn't about them, it's about you. What *you* want and need. Why did you end things with Fallon, Austin?"

"What?"

"Just humor me."

"Because I knew it wasn't going anywhere. She

started to talk about the future like we were a sure thing, and I knew my future didn't include her."

"And Madison?"

"I— It's not the same." A long sigh escaped me. "I was seeing Fallon for months. I barely know—"

"Humor me."

"I didn't really let myself think beyond the next time I saw her."

Just that I wanted to see her again.

"Maybe you didn't think about the future with her because it scared you. Because you knew it was different."

"I..." The words didn't come.

I wasn't an idiot. I knew what Madison and I had was different. Sure, it was mostly based on physical attraction. That simmering connection that seemed to flow between us. But Rory was right, there was something more there, too.

Something I didn't let myself look too closely at because the thought of needing someone, of someone needing me, fucking terrified me.

I didn't know the first thing about being in a relationship, let alone a relationship with a single mom.

"You're scared." Rory laid her hand on mine. "Austin, you can't let what happened with Mom, with me, define your future. You're a good person; you deserve to find happiness."

"I let you down."

The words ripped through the tension in the room like bullets.

"You were a child, Austin. A hotheaded teenager—"

"Still, I should have protected you. I should have—"

She got up and wrapped her arms around me. "No, Austin Hart. We are not going to keep doing this. I'm okay. I'm okay, Austin. She didn't break me, and she'll never have power over me again. Because do you know what, I won't give it to her. And you shouldn't either."

"I fucked it up." I didn't expand. I didn't need to. Rory knew exactly what I was talking about—she was there. She saw the look of devastation on Madison's face when she thought... Shit, I couldn't even say it.

"Then fix it."

"Why do you care so much?"

"Austin." She let out an exasperated breath. "You're my brother. My family. I love you. And until you can learn to forgive yourself—to *love* yourself—I'll love you enough for both of us."

Rory's words stayed with me all weekend.

Apart from our second game against the Cavaliers,

where we managed to scrape another win, I kept a low profile, hanging out in my room, going for a run, hitting the gym.

Anything to distract me from what I really wanted to do.

Go and see Madison.

It wasn't fair on her to barge back into her life without being one hundred percent certain I knew what I wanted.

I wanted her.

That was a given. But she came as a package deal, and that was uncharted territory for me.

Then there was the more pressing issue. What if I threw my cards on the table, and she rejected me?

I wouldn't blame her. I'd acted like a fucking coward. But she hadn't exactly fought for me either.

We'd done everything backward, though. Gotten hot and heavy from the start, insisting that it couldn't be more than sex. Keeping each other at arm's length.

But my sister was right; there was a reason we kept coming back for more. A reason why Madison felt safe enough with me to bring me into her home. A reason why I couldn't look too far into the future.

Fuck me.

I liked her.

I *really* liked her.

And I hated the idea that we were done.

I just didn't know what the fuck I was going to do about it.

"Hey, man. Didn't realize you were here," Connor said as he entered the kitchen. "What's that look about?"

"Just thinking."

"Thinking, huh? Watch it, you might hurt yourself." I flipped him off, and he grinned. "What is going on in that head of yours?"

"How much do you know?"

"If you're asking me if Rory and Noah filled me in, what do you think?"

"I think you're worse than a bunch of gossiping old women."

He snorted at that. "They're only worried."

"Yeah, so they keep saying."

"So she's got a kid." I nodded, and he blew out a steady breath. "Got to say I didn't see that coming."

"You and me both."

"It's not a deal breaker for you?"

"It was. At least, I thought it was."

"And now?"

"I don't know. I like her. Really like her, Con. Think we could have something worth exploring but—"

Fuck. How did I explain it?

"You're not sure you can be what they need."

"I don't exactly have a great track record taking care of the people I care about."

"If you're talking about Rory, you need to let that shit go." Connor shook his head. "She loves you, and she's forgiven you. You were a kid, Austin. Dealing with your own shit and finding your own way."

I wanted to heed his words, to accept my sister's forgiveness, but it wasn't going to be easy.

"Your past doesn't define you," he added. "But a little word of advice from someone who let the best thing ever to happen to him slip through his fingers once before: don't go to her until you know what you want and what you're prepared to do to get it."

That was the million-dollar question, wasn't it?

Was I ready to open myself up to that kind of risk? The potential heartache and fallout if it didn't work out.

Just the thought of it made my palms sweat and my pulse ratchet.

But the thought of *not* seeing her again, that made me feel a different way entirely.

"She's really under your skin, huh?" Connor flashed me a knowing grin that usually would have annoyed the hell out of me.

"Fuck you."

"Austin's got bit by the love bug," he sang with a ridiculous lilt.

"Don't start with that shit."

"Oh, come on, humor me."

"I'm serious, Morgan, don't try to—"

"Hello?" Ella's voice flitted down the hall, the familiar click of the front door echoing behind.

"In here," he called. "Austin was just—"

I shot up from my seat. "You're an asshole."

"Ah, don't be like that. You know you really love me."

"Is everything okay?" Ella's gaze bounced between us. "Because I can always go."

"Like hell, you will." He grabbed her by the waist and pulled her down on his lap, nuzzling her neck. "Good morning, Kitten."

"And that's my cue," I muttered, but it lacked its usual irritation.

"You don't have to go," Ella called in our well-practiced routine of them getting all handsy and me making a quick exit.

"Let him go," Connor said as I walked away. "Something tells me he has a lot of thinking to do."

He was right; I did.

But this time, I didn't walk away from them with bitter resentment and frustration.

I walked away with an odd feeling of hope.

CHAPTER 24

MADISON

"I appreciate you taking her," I said to Jacqui.

It was Monday afternoon, and Kayleigh had offered me an extra shift I couldn't refuse.

"Anytime, Madi. We've told you that." She smiled. "And how is Princess Immy today?"

"I mades a new friend."

"You did, huh."

She nodded emphatically, blonde curls bouncing around her face. "He's a hockey player, and he's this tall." Imogen reached high. "And don't tells Grampy, but I'm going to asks Scottie to be my boyfriend."

"Wow, that sounds wonderful, sweetheart." Jacqui gave me a mildly concerned look.

"Don't worry. Scottie is a friend's little brother, and

I've explained to her that boyfriends are for when you're older. Much older."

"I wants Mommy to get a boyfriend," she declared. "But she said it doesn't works wike that."

Jacqui smothered her laughter, and I refrained from cringing. We were all used to Imogen's lack of filter. But discussing my dating life with my ex's mom was one conversation I wanted to avoid for all eternity.

"I should be back around seven."

"We'll be fine, won't we, princess?"

"Of course. Can we bake cakes again?"

"We can do whatever you want, sweetheart." Jacqui held out her hand, and Imogen took it.

"I'll see you later, okay? You be a good girl for Grammy Jacqui."

"I will, Mommy. I'll be the bestest girl evers."

"I know you will." I kissed my fingertips and held them out to her. "See you later."

I let myself out and zipped up my jacket to stave off the cool breeze.

My stomach still felt a little tender after my awful hangover Saturday, but it was nothing that one or two brookie bars wouldn't fix.

I still couldn't believe what had happened at the bar. Couldn't stop dwelling on that moment right before Fawn interrupted us.

What had Austin been about to say?

I guess I would never find out now. It was probably better that way.

The walk to Sugartown only took me fifteen minutes. It was one of the things I loved about Olin Bay—how small the town was.

I couldn't ever imagine leaving. I wanted to raise Imogen here. Wanted her to attend Olin Bay High School, to join the debate club or cheer team. I wanted her to fall in love, chase her dreams, and realize her potential.

But I couldn't stop thinking that she would never truly know herself if she didn't know the truth about her father. And the thought of telling her *any* of that made my skin crawl.

I would do it one day. Later. When she was older and wiser. When I could trust that she could handle it. And I would pray that I'd raised her with enough confidence and forgiveness to understand it all.

"Madison, just in time." Kayleigh looked up from behind the glass cabinet. "I have a batch of muffins in the oven. Take over this for me?"

"Of course. Let me just wash up."

I quickly stowed my purse in the staff room and washed my hands.

The afternoon rush wouldn't start for another thirty minutes or so, so we worked together to fill the cabinets and restock the takeaway boxes.

The sickly-sweet scent of cherries filled the room, tempered by a sharp note of lemon.

"What's on this afternoon's menu?" I asked, perusing the tray in Kayleigh's hand.

"Lemon drop muffins. Dark chocolate cherry brookie bars. And I made an experimental batch of gluten-free chili chocolate cookies."

"How do you look that good when you bake so well?"

She chuckled. "Trust me, after a while, it all starts to taste the same."

"Oh, I don't know about that. I've worked here two years, and I still adore your bakes."

"So how was your weekend?" She changed the subject. "Anything exciting happen?"

"Nope."

I wasn't going there.

Not now. Especially not with Kayleigh.

What happened at Zest on Friday was something I'd rather file away and forget all about.

Fawn had almost convinced me that things between Austin and I weren't over, but they were.

They had to be.

Our lives were on different paths, and that was okay. I could appreciate our time for what it was. We had a spark, yes. But not all sparks burned bright. Some sputtered out before they could catch fire.

"Why do I feel like you're lying to me?"

"I'm not. Do I need to restock the coffee cups?"

"You're deflecting."

"And you're a pain in my ass."

She chuckled at that. "It's a good thing you're one of my best employees." Kayleigh winked before disappearing out back again.

God, was I really obvious?

I needed to lock down my emotions. Focus on work. On *not* thinking about Austin.

Because nothing good could come from that.

Nothing at all.

There was a steady flow of customers all afternoon. It was quieter than the weekend, but enough to keep me and Kayleigh's other part-time girl, Jess, on our toes.

"I'm taking off," Jess said. "See you soon."

"You will." I smiled as I wiped down a table.

It was forty-five minutes until closing, and the place was empty except for a couple enjoying their second cup of coffee.

I delivered the tray of empties into the back for Kayleigh to deal with and went back to start cleaning out the display cabinets. The coffee machine was the last thing we cleaned since there was always a chance of a last-minute customer or two.

The doorbell chimed, and I smiled to myself. But it quickly dropped when I saw Austin.

"Hey," he said a little sheepishly.

"What are you doing here?"

"Can we talk?"

"I don't think so, Austin. I'm at work, and you're—"

"It's fine, Mads. You can take ten," Kayleigh, the traitor, called from behind me.

"I—"

"Please," he implored, his expression lined with guilt.

"Fine. Do you want something to drink?"

"A bottle of water, please."

With a small nod, I grabbed a bottle and another one for myself and joined him at the table furthest away from our two remaining customers.

"I owe you an apology," he said, that icy stare of his fixed right on me. Heating me from the inside out, which made no sense.

We were done.

Over.

"Apology accepted. You can go now."

"Madi, come on, please."

"What, Austin? What do you possibly want me to say? You called things off. You ran the second you were reminded of my situation. You did that." I kept my voice low, but it didn't disguise the hurt there. Because I was hurt.

He had hurt me.

It wasn't supposed to happen. But it had.

"I know... Fuck." He dragged a hand through his hair. "I know, okay. I panicked. I've never been in a relationship before. It's not something I've wanted before."

"What are you saying?" My brows furrowed because hearing that word from his mouth...

Relationship.

I didn't want to deal with this today.

"I... I miss you."

"You miss me?" Bitter laughter bubbled up my throat. "You barely know me."

"Not true." Defiance shone in his eyes as he watched me carefully. "I know you're a great mom. I know you'll do whatever it takes to give Imogen the best life you can. I know you love to dance but don't think you have the body or confidence to get up on stage and do it.

"I know you've been hurt in the past, that there's more to your story. I know you probably had dreams of your own before having Imogen, but you gave them up when she came along. Because you're selfless like that. I know—"

"Austin, stop. Just... stop."

"Sorry." His expression crumpled. "I didn't mean to make you feel uncomfortable."

Pressing my lips together, I fought to compose

myself. "I just don't understand what you want; it's done. You walked away. And I get it, I do. It was just sex."

"Is that what you think?" His eyes darkened. "That I was just using you for sex?"

"I..." I inhaled a quiet, shaky breath, my eyelashes fluttering as I remembered every moment with Austin. The way he'd touched me. Kissed me. He was right. It had never felt like just sex.

But that didn't matter because we both knew it couldn't be more either.

"Madison, I think we both know it was more than that."

"I have a daughter, Austin. A sassy, headstrong four-year-old who is my world. You're in college. *College.*"

"I'm a senior, Madi. There are only a few months left."

"Even if you want to pursue whatever is between us, my priority is Imogen. She will always come first, she's—"

"And she should," he countered. "It's one of the things I admire most about you. I didn't have a good childhood, Madi. My dad walked out, my mom... Well, the less said about her, the better. I only had my sister, and I let her down. I..." He stopped himself, swallowing whatever words he'd been about to say.

God, I wanted to know this man.

Even now, after everything, I wanted to know him.

It wasn't simple curiosity either; it was soul-deep recognition that meeting Austin was more than just happenstance.

"What are you saying?" I asked, my heart crashing wildly in my chest.

"I want you, Madison Reynolds. I want to try...with you."

Oh God.

I didn't know what to say.

Everything inside me, the parts of me damaged and broken by Warren, was screaming at me to tell him no. To run far, far away from Austin and never look back.

But those other parts of me, the parts I'd protected, the parts that Imogen had slowly repaired. That Jeremiah, Fawn, my friends, and work colleagues had pieced back together wanted to say yes. They wanted to grab hold of Austin's words, the hope they represented, and never let go.

"You don't know what you're saying. You have your whole life ahead of you. I'm tethered here, Austin. My life is here."

"And if I want to be a part of it?"

"I... I don't think that's a good idea." I stood abruptly, too overwhelmed at his words.

At the possibilities they offered.

"Madison, please." He stood too, his expression

softening, his eyes pleading with me to give him a chance.

"I appreciate your apology. I do. But I don't think it is a good idea."

"I don't accept that."

"W-what?" I gawked at him.

"I have never felt this way before, Madison. All I'm asking for is a chance to show you I can be what you need. What you both need."

This couldn't be real.

He couldn't be—

"We're all done here." The last customers called over. "Thank you."

They waved and I mindlessly waved back, trying to think of something—*anything*—to say to Austin.

But I had nothing.

I had… nothing.

"Austin, I—"

"Don't finish that sentence, okay," he said. "I'm going to go now. I'm going to give you some space to think about things." He moved closer, lifting his hand to my face and brushing his thumb along my jaw. "I'll see you soon, pretty girl."

Austin dropped a kiss on my forehead and walked out of the store like he hadn't just landed a bombshell at my feet.

Because while my head was saying run. *Run as fast as you can and never look back…*

My heart was saying something else entirely.

"So let me get this straight: he came and professed his love for you, and you still sent him on his way?"

"He did not profess his love."

"Oh, come on, Mads, it was as good as." Jeremiah sipped his coffee while we watched Imogen fuss over Vader. She'd been extra gentle with him since spending time with Mrs. Owens.

"What do I do, Jer? I mean, I can't possibly consider it... can I?"

"Why the hell not?"

"Because!"

"You'd make a terrible defense attorney." He smirked, and I poked my tongue out at him.

Surely, he understood where I was coming from.

"Look, Mads. After you finally got away from Warren, I would have been the first person to warn you off of men and dating and all that stuff. But you're not that girl anymore. You're strong and brave and capable.

"You are a wonderful mother to Immy, and she's so lucky to have you. But it's okay to move on. It's okay to want more."

"College, Jer. He's in college."

"You keep saying that like it really changes

anything. He graduates in a few months, babe. I'm not suggesting you marry the guy or even jump in feet first. But giving things a chance, a real chance, could be the start of something beautiful."

"Or a freaking disaster," I muttered under my breath.

"And that attitude will be the reason you die old and alone with a vagina full of cobwebs."

"Will you stop," I snapped. "This is serious, Jer. It's my life…"

"I'm sorry. You know sarcasm and humor are my way of broaching the heavy topics." He reached for my hand and squeezed it gently.

"I just don't think I can do it." My gaze drifted back to Imogen.

How could I bring someone into her life who might skip out at a moment's notice?

She didn't deserve that.

Not when she already had so many questions about her father.

"But maybe it's time to put yourself out there? You can still show Imogen what a strong, independent woman looks like and have a relationship."

"God, you make it sound so easy."

"Because I think it could be," he said with pure conviction. "Nothing in life is guaranteed, babe. Not a damn thing. Imogen deserves a mom who loves her and puts her first, always, but did it ever occur to you that you deserve someone who puts you first, too?"

"Jer..." Emotion clogged my throat, my eyes burning with tears I refused to let fall. Of course, I wanted that.

Of course, I wanted someone to be there for me the way I would always be there for my daughter.

Who didn't want that?

But the thought of ending up heartbroken again terrified me. I was finally in a good place. I had friends, two jobs I loved, a place to call our own, and I had a life.

A life I had been perfectly content with until Austin came along.

Could I really risk all that on a hockey player with a dirty mouth, icy gaze, and his whole life ahead of him?

CHAPTER 25

AUSTIN

Madison had doubts about me.

But that was okay. I could play the long game.

When I turned up at Sugartown three days ago, I didn't have any expectations beyond her hearing me out.

Okay, maybe a small part of me hoped she would forgive me, and we could start up where we had left off, but I knew it was unlikely.

So now I needed a plan that involved giving her enough time and space so that I didn't come across as a total creep while still making enough effort, so she knew I was serious about her.

Dead serious.

Still, I was out of my depth.

My position as goalie for one of the best hockey teams in the NCAA required a cool head and steady hands. I had to read the game, watch my players and their opponents, see the play as it unfolded at breakneck speed, and, most importantly, never take my eye off the puck.

It was as easy as breathing.

This—dealing with my feelings and relationships and women—was not.

But I refused to let my fear, and my own stubbornness ruin my chances at fixing things.

"Austin, I swear to God, son, get your head out of your ass and keep your eye on the—" The puck went sailing past my glove, and Noah's laughter pulled me out of my thoughts.

"I see you brought your A game today."

"*Don't* say a word," I bit out.

He grinned, slipping past me, and headed back into formation. "Might want to keep your eye on the puck next time."

"Like you don't spend most of your life daydreaming about my sister."

"True, but I don't let it affect my game."

"Asshole," I muttered.

"Sorry, what was that? I was too busy *daydreaming about your sister.*" His brows waggled suggestively, and I flipped him off. Not that he could tell under my glove.

Thankfully, when we ran the play again, I managed

to block the shot. Coach was right, though. I was distracted, trying to figure out my game plan.

Asking the guys wasn't an option. It was bad enough that they kept making snide comments or trying to give me advice.

I didn't want their advice. I wanted to do this on my own.

I needed to.

The only person I trusted enough with my plans was Rory, and things were still shaky between us after the other night.

"Okay, bring it in," Coach boomed across the ice, and we all filed in. "Leon, much better today. You're learning to read the rest of your D line. Good work, son. Austin, I don't even want to know what that was." He cut me with a scathing look. "Just make sure it doesn't happen this weekend."

We had away games in Michigan. Which meant any plans I had for Operation Prove It needed to happen before or after. And I wasn't sure I could hold off seeing Madison until Sunday.

I'd given her three days.

Three days of radio silence. Of stepping back and giving her space.

But I was done waiting.

It was time to turn words into actions.

O'Shea's was busy. Busier than I expected for a Thursday night. But not so busy that I couldn't get a booth.

I slid into one, offering the security guy a nod in greeting. He tipped his head toward a table near the stage, and I saw Madison taking an order.

Fuck. She looked good. Working the simple black uniform like it was made for her. It fit her gorgeous curves to perfection.

A lick of possessiveness went through me at the knowledge that I was the only guy in here who knew what lay underneath. At least, I hoped like fuck I was.

I wasn't here to seduce her, though, not tonight.

This was just step one in my plan to prove to her that I could be the kind of guy she could depend on—that she could trust with her heart *and* her daughter.

Nervous energy zipped through me as she finally lifted her eyes and found me across the room.

A flash of something streaked across her face, but I couldn't decipher if it was surprise, anger, relief, or something else entirely.

She headed for the bar and rang in the table's order, before whispering something to the other server and heading in my direction.

"I didn't expect to see you here."

"I told you I'd give you some space."

"And you decided three days was enough?" Her brow quirked.

"I leave tomorrow. We have back-to-back games in Michigan. I wanted to see you before I left."

"Austin, I—"

"I got something for you. Something for Imogen, actually." I lifted my ass off the seat and plucked the envelope out of my back pocket, placing it on the table.

"What is it?" Madison picked it up and slid it open.

"Tickets for a hockey game."

"Oh, I'm not sure about that. It's so crowded and loud and—"

"Relax." I chuckled. "It's not tickets for my hockey game." *Yet*.

But one day, I wanted her there. Imogen, too, if the little hellion decided I was worthy enough to be with her mom.

"Harper is taking Scottie and some of the kids from the group she works with to see a local amateur game. I thought you and Imogen might like to tag along."

"That's… that's really sweet of you. Imogen hasn't shut up about Scottie, so I know she'll be excited to see him again, but I'll have to check my shifts."

"Of course. You can arrange everything with Harper, her numbers on the envelope. I know they will be happy to have you."

Madison stared at the tickets, a hundred and one questions glittering in her eyes.

Questions I knew she wouldn't ask.

Not yet.

I could still sense her hesitation, the solid wall between us, and I didn't blame her.

"I'm not expecting you to tell her they're from me. I know that's not how this works. I'm not looking to buy her approval or anything. I just thought…" Shit, I was losing her. "Anyway, that's all I came for. So, I'll go—"

"You don't have to go, Austin. Stay, have a drink. Something non-alcoholic." Her lips twisted. "If you have a game tomorrow."

"Lime soda, please."

"One lime soda coming up." She pocketed the envelope and gave me a soft smile. "Just when I think you can't surprise me anymore."

Madison walked away before I could find out whether or not that was a good thing.

"You," McSteamy said as I exited the restrooms.

"Me," I said, staring him down with the same mistrust he afforded me.

"What do you want with Madison?" he asked.

"I don't think it is any of your business, do you?"

He puffed up his chest, quiet rage rippling off him. "I'm making it my business."

Jesus. Who the fuck was this guy?

"You need to back off, buddy," I said over his bullshit. "I'm Madison's friend, and unless she says otherwise, I don't plan on going anywhere."

"We'll see about that." His eyes narrowed, and I arched a brow, waiting for the motherfucker to move out of my way.

He didn't.

"Really?" I scoffed, but he remained completely still, the faintest smirk playing on his lips.

Asshole.

"Fine, have it your way." I shoved past him, his unnerving stare following me out of the hall.

"Everything okay?" The security guy asked as I passed him.

"Someone really needs to speak to McSteamy about personal space."

"Julian causing you trouble again?"

So, he had noticed our previous interactions.

"Nothing I can't handle," I said, "but I don't like his weird fixation on Madison."

"He's harmless enough, boy. But I'll be keeping an eye on him. The name's Kingsley."

"Austin."

"We going to be seeing you around here more often, Mr. Austin?"

"If I have anything to say about it."

"Oh, it's like that, huh?" The corners of his mouth tipped in a knowing smile.

"It's exactly like that."

"I'm sure going to enjoy watching Mads put you in your place. Excuse me, looks like I need to see about reminding a couple of guys about the rules around here."

Sure enough, I glanced behind me to find a couple of guys getting really handsy with one of the servers.

Thankfully, Madison was behind the bar. I couldn't handle watching her getting groped like that. But I had to remember this was her job, and as she'd pointed out to me before, she didn't have the luxury of options.

It was late, almost midnight, and I needed to get up and at it early.

Madison caught my eye as I made my way over to her.

"You didn't have to stick around this long," she said.

"I was hoping we might get to talk some more."

"Sorry, we weren't expecting it to be this busy."

"Not your fault. Will you be okay getting home?"

She nodded, but it wasn't her eyes I was looking at; it was her lips. Soft and pink and begging to be kissed.

"Austin," she snapped, and I jolted out of my fantasy. "You can't do that here."

"But other places?"

"Don't push it." Her amused expression, the slight

flush to her cheeks, was at odds with her stern tone. "Good luck with your games."

"Thanks. I'll be back Sunday." I planted the seed, hoping she'd bite.

To my disappointment, she didn't.

"Well, okay then."

"I'll be seeing you, pretty girl." I rapped my knuckles on the bar and forced myself to walk away.

Not quite the grand exit I'd imagined, but I couldn't hang around all night.

No matter how much I wanted a goodnight kiss.

"So... how did it go?" Noah didn't even wait for the bus to pull out before he started with the questions.

"I have no idea what you're talking about."

"Seriously? You're going to freeze me out? After all the bonding we've done recently." He clutched his chest dramatically.

"Can't you swap seats with somebody so I don't have to endure this for six hours?"

"Oh, I'm sorry. Does it bother you that your best friend, your teammate... your sister's boyfriend, for fuck's sake, cares about you and your happiness."

"What's that about Hart's happiness?" Leon poked his head up over the seat in front.

"Nothing. Go away," I murmured.

"Come on, man. Don't be that way. I thought we were all friends. If you're struggling with the ladies, I can probably—"

"Not struggling with the ladies, but thanks for that glowing self-endorsement." Sarcasm dripped from my voice.

He shrugged and slipped back down into his seat. I shot Noah a hard look, and he mouthed, "What? It's not my fault you're a cagey bastard."

It obviously hadn't occurred to him that I didn't want everyone to know my business, no matter how tight the team was.

Until Madison was mine, I planned to keep a lid on things.

Speaking of Madison... I pulled out my cell phone and opened our messages.

> Austin: Have a good weekend, don't work too hard.

Have a good weekend, don't work—" I smacked Noah upside the head, and he whined like a little bitch. "Was that really necessary?"

"Dude's fucking his sister, and he still doesn't know when to quit it," Leon laughed. But I wasn't laughing, and neither was Noah.

"I'm not fucking her, asshole. I live with her. And me and Austin are on the same page now." He peeked over at me, looking all kinds of sheepish. "We are on the same page, right?"

"Yeah, you're good, Holden." I smiled.

I smiled, and they all looked at me like I was the one who'd lost his mind.

Maybe I had.

Because I sure as shit hadn't felt the same since Madison walked into my life.

"It's Valentine's Day soon," Noah said. "I can't decide whether to make a grand gesture or keep things low-key. What do you think?"

"We have a game that weekend," I pointed out.

"If you think that will stop me from finding time to romance the shit out of your sister, you clearly haven't been paying attention." He had the audacity to grin at me.

"Girls aren't bothered about all that shit, are they? I mean, you're together now." I shrugged. "Rory knows you love her."

"Jesus, you have a lot to learn about women. Please tell me you have a plan to let she-who-shall-not-be-named know you're into her."

What?

I didn't need a special day of the year to do that.

Did I?

"Oh shit, you really are clueless, aren't you?" Noah grinned like an idiot.

"I gave her tickets to that hockey game Harper is taking Scottie and the group to watch."

"No fucking way."

"What?" I balked.

"I didn't know you had it in you. Way to score brownie points with the kid, too."

"I told her not to tell her they were from me."

"What? Why?"

"Because asshole, I haven't even formally met her. It's weird."

"Austin, it's not—"

"Yeah, it is." Dropping my head back against the seat rest, I inhaled a thin breath. "What the fuck am I doing, Holden?"

"I think it's time."

"Time?" I cast him a sideways glance, wondering what the hell was about to come out of his mouth next.

"Yeah, it's definitely time." His mouth twitched.

"I swear to God, Holden. If you don't tell me what the fuck you're talking about, I'll make you sit with Leon."

"Heard that, asshole," he grumbled, lifting his hand to flip me off over the seat.

"Yo, Mase. What do you think? You think it's time we induct our boy into the club?" Noah's eyes twinkled with mischief.

Mase shook his head. "Nah, I'm not sure he's ready."

"Oh, I don't know. I think he's almost there." The two of them continued talking about me like I wasn't sitting right fucking there.

"I'm not listening to this bullshit," I muttered, pulling my ball cap down over my eyes.

"Listen, don't listen," Noah chuckled. "Still doesn't change the fact that you, my friend, have finally joined the dark side."

CHAPTER 26

MADISON

"Madison, over here." Harper waved Imogen and me over. But the second Immy spotted Scottie she took off like a whippet, darting between the sea of bodies to get to him and Harper.

"Princess Imogen," he said, patting her on the head.

"Whens does the hockey start?"

"We have to find our seats first," he said, and Harper and I watched them with wide smiles.

"I'm glad you came." Harper turned her attention to me, a sheepish expression falling over her. "So I probably should have mentioned this sooner, but I didn't want you to change your mind."

"Hi, I made it." I turned to find Rory approaching.

She offered me a warm smile, but it did little to ease the knot in my stomach. "I take it from your expression that you didn't know I was coming."

The look she gave Harper was telling.

"I'm sorry, okay," Harper said. "I really wanted Madison to come, and I didn't know if she would if—"

"It's fine," I said to Rory. "You haven't done anything wrong,"

"No, we can blame my idiot of a brother for that." Her lips quirked. "It's nice to see you again. I was hoping we might get to talk soon."

"You were?"

She nodded. "I didn't like how we left things last weekend."

"Gosh, I'm so embarrassed," I said, keeping one eye on Imogen. But she was entranced by whatever Scottie was showing her on his cell phone.

"Please, don't be. I was so happy you hung out with us and then Austin turned up and ruined everything. I love my brother, Madison? But God, he's a big clueless idiot sometimes. I'm sorry he didn't tell you about me. And I'm really sorry you felt like you couldn't tell us about him."

"It wasn't serious. I didn't want to overstep."

"Perhaps we can start over?" Rory gave me a hopeful expression.

"I'd like that."

"See, I knew it would all work out for the best."

Harper grinned. "Now can we please get the kids in and seated before we lose someone?"

"I'm sitting nexts to Scottie," Imogen declared, and he rolled his eyes.

"We'll see, baby. Scottie is here with all his friends, remember?" We'd talked about it on the ride over and I'd explained that she couldn't monopolize all of his time.

"It's okay Miss Imogen's Mom, the princess can sit with us. *If* she can be cool. You have to be cool at hockey games." He gave her a look that made her beam.

"See, Mommy." She grabbed his hand faster than I could tell her to stop. "Scottie said I cans sit next to him because he knows I is a princess. And princesses always get the bestest seats."

"I am so sorry," I murmured to the girls.

"Relax, it's fine. We'll know when Scottie needs a break. Although something tells me we have nothing to worry about." Harper pointed discreetly to where Scottie was introducing Imogen to his little group of friends.

"We've never done anything like this before," I said. "She has friends at pre-K, but I tend to avoid the parent meet-ups."

I was the youngest mom at Imogen's school. A fact that hadn't escaped a lot of the other parents, so I preferred to keep to myself. So long as Imogen was happy, that's all that mattered.

"Well, you're both always welcome to hang out with us."

It was weird, to feel so accepted, especially by two college girls who didn't have the kinds of responsibilities I did.

"Thank you."

We herded the kids toward the concession stand and got them all a drink before finding our seats.

"Mommy, Mommy, wook." Imogen, seated right in front of me wedged in between Scottie and one of his friends, pointed to the ice where both teams were already warming up.

"You know, my big brother is going to be a hockey player, one day. He's going to be famous just like Alex Ovechkin."

"Maybe, buddy, one day," Harper said. "Here, put these on." She handed him a pair of headphones and he slipped them on.

"Sometimes the noise can trigger him," she explained.

My purse vibrated and I dug my cell phone out.

Austin: Enjoy the game.

Madison: Shouldn't you be getting ready for your game?

Austin: I have five more minutes before
Coach confiscates my phone.

Madison: Good luck!

Austin: I'd take a good luck kiss right
about now…

Heat bloomed in my cheeks, and I suppressed a smile. I didn't want to make it easy for Austin, and I still didn't even know if I was willing to risk my heart on him. But I couldn't deny that I liked this side of him.

Playful. Persistent.

Real.

It didn't feel like a gimmick or some joke to him. Maybe that was more than he deserved.

Only time would tell.

For now, I had a hockey game to enjoy and memories to make with my daughter.

"Did you like the game, Princess Immy?" Rory asked.

She'd been so good with Imogen all night, it made me a little emotional, watching how easily they accepted her.

"I did, especially whens they started beating the craps—"

"Imogen Grace," I gasped. "I know you know we don't say that word."

"Sorry, Mommy."

"Want to pick ice cream?" Harper asked her and Scottie and they nodded, following her out of the booth, my daughter slightly more enthused than the teenager.

The hockey game had been a big success with all the kids soaking up the atmosphere and cheering on their local team. Imogen loved every second, a huge grin on her face the entire time.

Once the rest of the kids were safely returned to their parents, Harper and Rory invited us to get some post-game dinner, so we'd headed across the street to the diner.

"So what's going on with you and Austin?" Rory asked the second the kids were out of earshot. I hesitated and she quickly recovered. "Crap, I'm sorry. I didn't mean to pry. It's just, I don't think I've ever seen my brother this way before."

I let out a strained laugh. "Surely, there's been a long line of girls—"

"There hasn't. He was casually seeing a girl before… and you probably don't want to know that. Sorry."

"Don't be. It would be nice to have a little more insight into his life. We didn't exactly get to all the important bits."

"Did he tell you about our parents?" I nodded, and she continued. "Then you know we didn't have the best childhood. Austin has carried a lot of that around with him. Still does. Our mom is... Well, she can be a cruel, vindictive woman. I think she broke something inside him, Madison. Something that I didn't think would ever heal... until you came along."

"Rory." My breath caught.

"I know, this is weird, and I'm being intense. I don't mean to be. I just think you should have all the facts before you make any decisions about whether or not to give him another chance."

I liked Rory.

It was impossible not to.

She was so different from Austin. Warm and open and accepting. It made me wonder just how bad Austin's childhood had been for them to turn out so vastly different.

"I know what you're thinking, you're wondering how we can possibly be related." She smiled.

"It's like you read my mind."

"Let's just say I found a family at LU, and I thank the universe every day that I transferred here."

"You and Noah seem very happy," I said.

"We are. It sounds silly, but he taught me to love myself again."

"It doesn't sound silly at all."

I know exactly what you mean.

Sunday, Kayleigh convinced me to work an extra shift again. And since Imogen was over at Jacqui and Ken's, I agreed.

It was hard to refuse the opportunity to earn extra money when every penny I made counted.

"So let me get this straight, he ignored you for three days, gave you and Imogen tickets to the hockey game, and now he's ignoring you again?"

"We texted Friday."

"Yes, and now it's Sunday."

"I guess he's staying true to his word and giving me space."

I'd finally filled her in on everything. I needed someone to talk to and Kayleigh offered a different perspective since we were friends on a professional level rather than a personal level.

"And you're okay with that?"

"I mean, it's not like I've agreed to anything yet."

She arched a brow, a knowing glint in her eyes. "And yet, you're fooling nobody."

"Oh hush." I whipped my towel in her direction, but she dodged it at the last second.

"So now wouldn't be a good time to tell you, your guy is heading toward the door."

"What?" My head snapped over to the window and sure enough, Austin was there.

He smiled when he saw me and came inside.

"Hey."

"Hi." I blushed. "What are you doing here?"

"You greet all your customers that way?"

"Sorry, you caught me off guard. You seem to be doing that a lot lately."

The air crackled, the connection between us refusing to be ignored.

"I heard you both enjoyed the game," he said.

"We did, thank you. You didn't by any chance send Rory to support your case, did you?"

He considered my words, then smirked again. "I'm insulted you think I'd do such a thing. But no, I didn't know if she'd go or not. I am glad you two got to hang out though."

"You're not worried she told me all your deepest, darkest secrets?"

"It doesn't give me a warm fuzzy feeling but strangely, I'm okay with it."

"Hmm."

"You can take off," Kayleigh called from the back. "I can manage."

"You want to grab a drink?" Austin asked.

"I really shouldn't."

"Just an hour? No pressure."

"Fine, okay. But I can't stay too long, I have to pick

Imogen up from her grandparents."

"Your parents are back?"

My heart tumbled.

Crap.

Crap.

"Uh, no." I didn't want to lie but I also didn't want to go there yet. Still, I found myself saying, "She's with her father's parents."

"Oh."

And there it was.

The story I had yet to tell him.

The story I *never* wanted to relive.

I inhaled a shaky breath, hoping he would drop it.

He did.

"I'll wait for you to get your things," he said, sticking his hands in his pockets and stepping back, as if he were stopping himself from reaching for me.

"I can't believe he's here," I said to Kayleigh, joining her in the back.

"Really? Because I think this is going to become a regular occurrence until you give him another chance," she chuckled.

"I can stay—"

"No, go. It's quiet and I'll be closing up soon anyway. But promise me, you'll hear him out this time. You deserve happiness, Madison."

All I managed was a nod, too choked up to reply.

I quickly slipped off my apron and hung it on the peg and grabbed my purse.

"Have fun," she called after me, and I waved her off.

"Okay, I'm ready."

"Any preference where we go?"

"Somewhere local. I don't have long, remember." I reminded him.

"So what did Imogen really think of the game?" Austin asked as we walked down the street.

"Oh, she loved it. Had Scottie and all his friends eating out of the palm of her hand."

"Sounds like she's going to be trouble." He glanced down at me with an intense look, sending my heart into a tailspin. "Just like her mom."

"Austin…" I warned.

"Yeah, I know. Come on, this place looks alright." He made a sharp turn and held open the door to the sports bar.

"A sports bar, really?" I laughed as I slipped past him.

"Grab a table, and I'll order our drinks. What would you like?"

"An iced tea, please."

"You mind if I have a beer?" he asked.

"Go ahead."

I found a quiet table away from the giant television screen showing the sports highlights from the weekend and checked my cell phone. There was a message from Jeremiah and one from my parents.

> Dad: We arrived in Grenada. Finally
> have some reception. Hope you and
> Immy are good. We miss you. See you
> soon. xo

I quickly texted him back and opened Jeremiah's message.

> Jer: Whoever decided to schedule a
> Peloton class on a Sunday is evil and
> twisted. My legs are jelly. I swear to
> God, I can't move. If you don't hear
> from me again, send help.

> Madison: You are such a drama
> queen. Was it the hot instructor again?
> What was his name? Christopher?

> Jer: Christian. And he isn't hot, Mads.
> He's the male form perfected.

I laughed at that.

> Madison: And you'll be the male form
> in emergency care if you keep pushing
> yourself to keep up with those crazy
> classes.

> Jer: I'm choosing to ignore that. How's
> your day?

> Madison: Kayleigh let me go early.
> Austin showed up again...

Jer: Kudos to the hockey player, he
really knows how to put in the work. I
hope you plan to reward him for his
efforts.

> Madison: You are such a Slutty
> McSlutterson.

Jer: Get some D, babe. You've been
so much happier since you started
fooling around with him.

With an indignant gasp, I shoved my cell phone back in my purse and watched as Austin brought our drinks over.

"One iced tea for the lady." He slid it across the table to me.

"Thanks."

"Everything okay?" His gaze dropped to my purse.

"Yeah, it was just Jeremiah."

"Ah, the friend. Did you tell him where you were?"

"If you're asking if I told him I'm with you, then yes, I did."

"Did he tell you to run and never look back?" Austin's brows crinkled a little, but I sensed there was something he wasn't telling me.

"No, why would you say that?"

"No reason." He shrugged, sipping his beer.

"Did Jer say something to you the morning they returned unannounced?" His tight expression told me all I needed to know, and I let out a small sigh. "What did he say?"

"Honestly, nothing I didn't already know. But I think it was just another reminder that we were getting in too deep."

"But you don't think that anymore?"

"Oh, I do." He ran a hand down his face. "But I don't care. Me cooling things that morning wasn't about you, Madison. It was about me."

"Because you have trouble letting people in?"

"Something like that. I told you that I didn't have the best childhood and I'm sure my meddlesome sister filled in some of the blanks."

"She did, but I want to hear your side of the story, Austin."

"We don't have nearly enough time for that today," he said. "But let's just say, I spent years thinking I wasn't good enough. That if I couldn't trust my own parents to love and stick by me then I definitely couldn't trust some girl I met in high school or college.

"It was easier to cut off my emotions. To build a wall and keep people out. Then Rory turned up at LU and pulled the rug out from under me. And then I met you..."

He gazed at me with so much hope and hunger, it made me feel weightless and heavy all the same time.

"My life is complicated, Austin," I whispered. "There are still things you don't know. Things that might change your opinion…"

He reached for my hand and threaded our fingers together. "I find that hard to believe."

"Imogen's father." I inhaled a shaky breath, my skin vibrating with nervous energy.

I didn't talk about this. I didn't let myself relive the memories.

The simple fact was, I couldn't.

Every day, all I needed to know was that I got out. I broke free from Warren's toxic hold on our relationship.

But how could I ever move forward with someone else if I couldn't tell them the truth?

The answer was, I couldn't.

Austin squeezed my hand gently and my eyes lifted slowly to his. What I saw staring back at me stole my breath.

He was here. He wasn't running again.

I just had to trust him.

I had to take that leap of faith.

CHAPTER 27

AUSTIN

"I MET WARREN IN HIGH SCHOOL."

Warren.

So the guy who had put the shadows in her eyes had a name.

I already despised the guy.

Hated that he'd had her first. That they had a daughter together. A life. But this wasn't about me, it was about Madison, about her trusting me with her past.

Something I didn't take lightly.

"Things moved pretty quickly," she went on. "I was infatuated, and he was obsessed with me. We were inseparable."

My fist curled underneath the table, rubbing against my thigh. But I managed to get out, "Go on."

"My parents weren't all too happy. Warren hung around with an older crowd. They partied a lot. Got high. Did things teenagers have no business doing. But I was young and in love and nothing could make me see sense."

"What happened?" I asked, hoping I didn't sound as jealous as I felt.

"A few weeks into senior year, I found out I was pregnant. My mom didn't speak to me for almost a month. Warren wanted me to get an abortion. I was a mess. Fawn and Jeremiah held me together while I decided what I was going to do.

"But honestly, there was never any doubt in my mind. I was young, yes. But the second I found out, something clicked inside me. I was going to be a mom and I was determined to make it work."

"And you wonder where Imogen gets her headstrong attitude from." I tried to make light of the situation. Thankfully, it made Madison laugh but her smile didn't reach her eyes.

I knew why.

She hadn't reached the worst part of her story yet.

"Our parents set us up in a small apartment. I managed to take enough classes to graduate early, and Warren got a job on the weekend, and for a while, things were good.

"Until they weren't."

I drained the rest of my beer, bracing myself for whatever was coming.

Madison noticed my worsening mood and let out a steady breath. "Austin, we don't have to do this."

"Yeah, we do. I need you to know, I will never look at you differently, no matter what you tell me. But the idea that anyone hurt you…"

"Warren never physically hurt me," she rushed out. "It wasn't like… that. But he hurt me in other ways." Madison's gaze shifted away from me, anguish rolling off her in palpable waves.

During our time together, I'd picked up the odd clue here or there that she had secrets. But hearing her lay it all out for me made me want to rage at the world.

I was a coldhearted bastard at times. But I didn't ever set out with the intention of hurting someone. It was one of the reasons I kept people at arm's length.

"Warren cheated on me when I was six months pregnant. I was fat and swollen and miserable, and he was an eighteen-year-old guy obsessed with sex. I'm sure you can fill in the blanks." Devastation crept into her expression. "My self-esteem took a huge hit, but I was determined to hold our little family together. So I forgave him. By the time Imogen arrived, I was so relieved, so besotted with her that it was easy to turn a blind eye to his ways."

"Fucking asshole," I muttered.

"Oh, it gets worse." She gave me a sad, defeated smile. "I couldn't do anything right. He constantly put me down. Said that I wasn't attractive anymore. Said that I'd become ugly and boring. But when I finally worked up the courage to leave, he completely lost it.

"I thought he'd turned over a new leaf. Realized that he couldn't live without us. I didn't realize until later that he was manipulating me. Using my own vulnerabilities against me." Madison took a sip of her drink. "Things only got worse after that. I'd threaten to leave, and he would spew all of these vile, hateful things at me. Then, the next day, he would be sorry, smothering me with love and attention.

"I had no identity. No life outside of being a new mom. He was like a totally different person whenever our parents visited. I think my mom always saw past his act, but she was still angry at me for ruining my life. As far as she was concerned, I'd made my bed." She sucked in a shuddering breath, swiping the tears out of her eyes. "I'm sorry. I didn't mean to get upset."

"You have nothing to apologize for. Not a damn thing." I locked down the storm raging inside me. "I'm so fucking sorry you had to go through all that."

"Don't get me wrong, I love my mom, and she and my dad have been there for both of us since I got away from Warren. But things are still strained..."

The words *got away* played on a loop in my head.

She could have said left or walked away from or any number of other phrases.

But she hadn't.

And those two words told me all I needed to know about the kind of man Imogen's father was.

"Does she still see him?"

"No." The change in Madison was almost instant. "There was... an incident. He lost it and smashed up the apartment while Imogen and I were there. It was the final straw. I moved back home, and my dad helped me get a restraining order."

Fuck.

The storm broke, violent anger coursing through my veins. I wanted to ask what happened, what else that fucker did to warrant a restraining order. I wanted a name, an address, I wanted to know where that asshole lived.

But I didn't push.

I wouldn't.

Madison had trusted me with so much that I would earn the rest. Piece by piece, even if it took months, a year... longer.

It made me look at time together in a new light though. Every kiss, every touch and moment I'd spent worshipping her body was a gift.

A rare and precious gift she'd felt safe and comfortable enough to bestow on me.

"You are incredible," I said over the lump in my throat. "Everything you've endured…"

"I don't need your pity, Austin."

"It's not pity. It's awe, I promise. I'm so fucking in awe of you, Madi."

"I did what I had to." She gave me a dismissive shrug, but I refused to accept that.

"Easy to say that now. But you were what? Eighteen… nineteen when you left him?"

Madison nodded, barely meeting my gaze. "I should have ordered something stronger." She drank the remainder of her iced tea. "This conversation got far too heavy for a Sunday afternoon."

"I'm glad you told me."

"Me too."

"Yeah?" Hope sparked in my chest.

"Yeah. But don't look too excited, Austin. I still don't know what this all means for us."

"We can take it slow. I'm not going anywhere."

"So you're not heading off to Vancouver after graduation?"

Shit.

"Who told you?"

"I heard the guys talking about it at the bar. I'd be a fool to start something with you again if you're only going to leave in a few months. It isn't fair of me to expect you to give up your dreams, Austin. I would never ask that of you."

"I guess we're doing a lot of this ass backward."

We hadn't dated or slowly gotten to know one another. We'd jumped straight to the good stuff and worked our way back to the beginning.

"Yeah, I guess we are." She gave me a small smile.

I wanted hockey. I wanted a shot at going pro. But the truth was, I wanted my shot with Madison more.

That was a huge burden to shoulder her with though, so I played it cool.

At least, I hoped like fuck I did.

"Let's make a promise to each other," I said. "If I convince you to give me another chance, we move at your pace. It's important to me that you know I'm serious about you, about this. So whatever you need, however slow you want to take it, that's fine by me."

"And Vancouver?"

"Nothing is set in stone yet. I've still got to sit down with their people, and I haven't decided anything. So what do you say we ignore all the background noise, the what-ifs and maybes, and focus on the here and now?"

"If I remember correctly, we did that once before and it went horribly wrong."

"Firstly, there was nothing wrong about anything we did." A smirk tugged at my mouth. I couldn't help it. Madison was fucking gorgeous, and I knew how good it felt to be buried deep inside her.

But it was more than that.

It was her laugh and her smile and the way she didn't take any shit from me. It was how hard she worked for her daughter. How much she valued family and friendship.

Madison was everything I never knew I wanted. And I would do whatever it took to make her mine.

"And secondly?" she asked.

"Secondly, I will never knowingly hurt you again."

"You're saying all the right things..." She gnawed the end of her thumb, hesitation swimming in her ocean eyes. "But I don't know, Austin. Are we just asking for more heartache?"

"You have reservations and I get it. I do, too. I've never done this, Madi. Ever. But being with you feels good. It feels... right. And I don't want to lose that."

"I don't want to lose you."

"Okay." It slipped off her lips barely more than a whisper.

"Okay?"

"Yeah, okay. But I want to take it slow, Austin. I need to this time."

"I can do that." I grinned, trying to rein in the sheer elation I felt.

Fuck, she wanted this too.

She wanted *me*.

"So what happens now?" she asked, putting me on the spot.

The confidence I'd felt a second ago wavered. Because fuck if I knew.

But one thing was certain, I couldn't wait to find out.

I was nervous.

Clutching the bouquet of flowers in my hand like my life depended on it.

I'd never bought anyone flowers before, but I didn't want to turn up empty handed. Besides, I was hoping it would soften the blow of turning up unexpectedly again.

After leaving Madison yesterday, after giving her nothing more than a chaste kiss on her cheek, we'd made no arrangements. But today, I'd watched my friends. Listened to them talk about their girlfriends, making plans for the future, and there was only one place I wanted to be after I got done with classes.

The owner of Sugartown spotted me first, giving me a bemused smile as I entered.

"Is she here—"

"Mr. Austins," a familiar voice said, and I didn't have time to think before Imogen was in front of me.

"Hello," I said awkward as fuck. Because shit.

Shit.

"Don't yous remember me? We met outside—"

"Immy, baby, what are you—" Madison stopped dead as she came through the door separating the shop from the kitchen.

"Look, Mommy. It's Mr. Austins. And he gots me flowers."

"Oh my God," Madison breathed, sliding her wide-eyed gaze from me to her daughter and back again. "I'm not sure those are for you, sweetheart," she said with a hitch in her voice.

"Actually, they are." I crouched down to the kid's eye-level and smiled. "Beautiful flowers for a beautiful girl."

Fuck. My chips were well and truly in now. But I couldn't regret it when Imogen grabbed the bouquet and beamed, "Oh, I loves them. I loves them sooooo much. Wook, Mommy." She swung around almost hitting me in the face with the dozen red roses and bounded over to her mom.

"Austin is right." She leaned down to study the flowers. "They are very beautiful."

Her gaze found mine again, conveying everything she couldn't say in front of her daughter.

"I'm sorry," I mouthed. "I didn't think—"

"Why don't you go with Kayleigh into the back, sweetheart. I think she's about to take a fresh batch of brownies out of the oven."

Madison gave Kayleigh a meaningful look and she

jumped into action. "Yes, of course. The brownies." She gently grabbed Imogen by the shoulders and steered her away. "Why don't you come with me, princess."

"Fuc— I mean, shit. Jesus." I blew out an exasperated breath. "I'm sorry, I had no idea she would be here."

Madison stared at me with a horrified expression but then her whole demeanor shifted. "It's fine," she chuckled. "Although you might want to lay off the cuss words. Most kids this age soak up and regurgitate everything they hear."

"Lay off the cuss words, got it. Anything else I should know before—"

"Mommy, Mr. Austins, I gots you both a brownie."

We watched her approach, precariously balancing a plate of brownies in her hands.

"Immy, be careful, baby." Madison didn't rush to take it off her, instead, she waited, giving her gentle encouragement.

"Why don't we sits down?"

I smothered a laugh as the little hellion marched right past us to an empty table.

Thankfully, there were only a couple of customers in, and they seemed to find the whole thing as amusing as I did.

"Come on thens."

"Are you sure about this?" Madison whispered under her breath, hesitation written all over her face.

"It's fine, I've got this. I promise." I went to reach for her but caught myself, settling for brushing the back of her hand as I headed for the table.

"These smell really good," I said, sitting down opposite Imogen.

She looked so much like her mom, I couldn't believe I'd missed it the first time we met.

"They are. Mommy says Kayleigh makes the bestest brownies in the wholes of Olin Bay. Try one Mr. Austins."

I helped myself to a brownie and tore it in half offering the remainder to Imogen. She glanced at Madison for permission.

"Go ahead, baby."

"Mmm, so good," she murmured around a mouthful of chewy chocolate goodness.

The Reynolds girls were right. Kayleigh baked some damn good brownies. I could see why Harper had started to come around here.

"Did you wikes it?" Imogen asked once I was done.

"I did, thank you."

"You don't gots to pay for that one. Kayleigh said it's on the houses. Whatever that means."

Madison laughed softly but I kept my focus on her daughter.

"How comes it's been so wong since we saws you Mr. Austins?"

"Well, I go to college and I'm a hockey player so I'm pretty busy."

"Oh my Gods, Mommy. Mr. Austins is a hockey player just wike Scottie. I woves hockey, Mr. Austins. 'Specially when they all starts fighting."

"Imogen!"

"Sorry, Mommy."

"I heard you went to watch a game with Scottie and Harper. You know, Harper's my friend too."

"Oh, I wike Harper, and Rora. Harper gots me and Scottie ice cream."

I debated telling her Rory was my sister, but something stopped me. Madison wanted to take things slow, and I already felt like I'd potentially messed up by coming here again.

"Yeah, I like Harper too." *I like your mom more though.*

I bit the inside of my cheek to stop the words from tumbling out.

"Maybe we can all hangs out one time. Oh, oh, I knows. We can help Mrs. Owens with her cats. I wove her cats."

Jesus. Imogen was something else.

I'd been terrified of meeting her officially, of crossing that line. But just like her mom, she made it so fucking easy.

"And I gots to thinking Mommy," she went on,

barely stopping to take a breath. "I know you said he can't, but he gots me flowers and everything."

Madison caught my eye again and smiled. But it quickly fell when Imogen's next words landed.

"So, I think you should let Mr. Austins be your boyfriend."

CHAPTER 28

MADISON

"Immy, princess, that's not—"

"You know Imogen," Austin interjected, giving me a reassuring smile. "I'd really like to hang out with you and your mom sometime. How does that sound?"

She considered his offer, pushing her finger against her top lip. "Will yous be her boyfriend?"

"I don't know about that, but I do know I would really like to be your mom's special friend."

Special friend.

Oh my God.

This was a freaking disaster.

And yet, there was something so endearing about the way Austin handled Imogen that my heart practically melted inside my chest.

"Will yous be my special friend too?"

"If you want me to be." Austin nodded.

"I'll have to thinks 'bout it, Mr. Austins. I already gots Scottie as my specials friend." She hopped down off the chair and smiled at him. "But I'm sures he won't mind."

"Where are you going, baby?" I asked her.

"To gets a drink and gives you and Mr. Austins some special time."

Austin barely contained his laughter, but I stomped on his foot, turning his amusement into a pained groan.

"Is yous okay?" Imogen frowned at him.

"I'm good, princess."

She skipped off happily and I covered my face with my hands.

"Come on, it could have been worse," Austin said with a chuckle, leaning across to pry my fingers away from my eyes.

"Special friend, Austin. Really?"

"I panicked." He shrugged. "Besides, it's true. I do want to be your special friend."

Humor danced in his eyes, but I wasn't laughing. Not even a little bit.

"She's never going to let this go, you know," I said. "She's worse than a dog with a bone."

"So long as she's in my corner, I'm not complaining."

"Austin, will you be serious for just a second."

"I am being serious. The way I see it is we just ripped off the Band-Aid. She knows we're friends, *special* friends"—God he made the word sound so dirty, I didn't know whether to punch him or pounce on him—"so if she starts seeing me come around more often, she's not going to think it's weird."

"Why are you being so calm about all of this? You're supposed to be the one running at the first sign of all my emotional baggage."

"What can I say, I'm a changed man." He smirked and I finally cracked.

"You are enjoying this far too much."

"I hid out in your bathroom, Madi. It's nice to see you squirm for once."

I poked my tongue out at him because what else could I do?

He'd told me he was all in and I guess if we stood any chance of working out, I had to try and believe him. But it wasn't going to be easy.

I had years of trauma and heartache to unravel.

"Where did you go just now?" he asked with a concerned expression.

"I can't promise this will be easy," I admitted. "That I'll make things easy."

"I don't expect you to. But I need you to trust me, Madison. And I need you to talk to me.

"If I step out of line or do something that doesn't sit

right with you, you have to tell me instead of shutting me out. I'm not a mind reader, pretty girl."

I nodded. "I can do that."

"Yeah?"

"Yeah." I smiled and it didn't feel fake or forced. It felt... real.

"In case you wondered, the flowers were in fact, for you. And they came with an invitation."

"An invitation?" That piqued my interest.

"Yeah. I'd like to take you out one night."

"Like on a date?"

"Yeah."

"Where would we go?"

"It's a surprise."

"It might be a struggle this week. I have an extra shift at the bar, and I'll need Jer or Jacqui to watch Imogen."

God, how was this ever going to work? Imogen needed me. And I had to use my childcare sparingly, prioritizing my shifts at the coffee shop and the bar.

Our relationship would be limited to after-work trysts and the sparse date here or there when I could arrange for someone to watch Imogen.

It wasn't exactly what most guys were used to.

"So we'll take her," Austin said as if it was that simple.

"You want to go on a date with me and Imogen?"

"Why not?

"Sorry, I guess I'm just having a hard time getting my head around that you're okay with this."

"Let me know when you have a free evening and we'll arrange something."

"Wednesday," I said, throwing caution to the wind. Hoping like hell I wasn't making the biggest mistake of my life.

"We're free Wednesday."

"Immy, we've got twenty-five minutes, baby. Are you almost ready?" I called as I fluffed out my hair.

Austin was picking us up at six, but the location of our date was top secret, something Imogen had discussed far too much over the last two days.

"Mommy," she shrieked, turning my blood to ice.

"Immy, what is? What's wrong?" I raced into her bedroom, grinding to a halt to search for any signs of injury.

"My tummy hurts."

"Oh, baby. Maybe you need—"

Imogen vomited all over herself and the pink and purple outfit she'd picked out especially for our date with Austin.

The tears started then as she puked again.

"Gosh, okay, let's get you into the bathroom." I

scooped her up, holding my breath the best I could as I carried her into the bathroom and set her down on the floor.

"Mom—" She projectile-vomited all over the toilet bowl, most of it managing to miss the actual bowl.

Jesus Christ. It was like something out of the Exorcist.

"Okay, new plan," I muttered, stripping off my puke-spluttered sweater and jeans and throwing them in the laundry basket. Then I reached into the shower and turned on the jets. "Come on, princess. Let's get you cleaned off." I scooped her up into my arms and carried her into the shower.

"I don'ts feel so good, Mommy." Imogen groaned, hanging in my arms like a ragdoll.

"We'll get you cleaned up and into bed, okay?"

"But what abouts our special date with Mr. Austins?"

"You can call him Austin, you know, sweetheart." A fact I'd told her at least twenty times since Sunday.

"I wanted to knows the surprise."

"I know you did, baby. But we can reschedule."

She sobbed against my chest as I tried my best to clean her up.

"Mommy's going to have to lower you to the floor, okay? Just so I can undress you and wash your hair."

Imogen nodded but she was crashing fast from the aftermath of vomiting everywhere.

I managed to make quick work of getting her clean and before she knew it, I had her bundled in her favorite fluffy towel. "Let's get you some water and crackers and I'll tuck you up in bed," I soothed.

"I want to stays with you, Mommy." She tightened her arms around my neck as I carried her through our apartment.

"Mommy needs to clean up your room first, so why don't you snuggle Mr. Hopsy on the couch and then we'll snuggle."

She nodded against my chest and gave me a meek, "Okay."

With Imogen safely on the couch, set up with her favorite TV show and a plastic bucket just in case she wasn't done vomiting, I grabbed my cell and quickly texted Austin.

Madison: I'm so sorry to do this last minute but Imogen is sick. Rain check?

Austin: Of course. Is she okay? Do you need anything?

Madison: We're good but thanks. xo

I left my cell on the counter and grabbed some cleaning supplies to go tackle her bedroom. The rancid smell hit me the second I entered the room, and I had to breathe through my mouth as I set about cleaning up the mess.

Not how I'd planned on spending my Wednesday night. But maybe the universe was trying to tell me something.

No, I didn't want to believe that.

Austin had been great with Imogen on Sunday and clearly intended to include her in our relationship.

It took a little while to scrub the carpet, but I got there in the end, right as Imogen called out for me.

"Mommy, Mommy!

"I'm coming, baby." I gathered everything up and shoved it in the trash bag. "Mommy has got to take out the— Austin."

"Hey," he said from the door.

"What are you doing here?"

"I was already on my way when you texted, so I stopped at the store and grabbed some supplies." He held up the grocery bag. "I figured we could stay in."

"Austin—"

"Looks, Mommy. He gots me a new friend for Mr. Hopsy." Imogen clutched the brand-new stuffed rabbit to her chest as she held Austin's hand, and my heart fluttered.

He wasn't playing fair.

Yet, I didn't have the energy to send him away. Because the truth was, it meant a lot that he was here. That he cared enough to stop by and check in on us.

"I guess you'd better come in," I said. "I still need to clean up a little and disinfect the bathroom."

"I can stay with Austins, Mommy." She tugged him toward the couch.

"Are you sure? She's been pretty sick."

"Yeah. We've got this." He gave me a reassuring smile. "Unless you want me to be on clean up duty?"

"No, you handle the princess. I'll be as quick as I can."

I watched with my heart in my throat as they sat down on the couch and Imogen grabbed the blanket, tucking herself into his side. Austin's arm hovered awkwardly along the back of the couch, but he didn't move her away. He just sat there, letting her use him as her own personal snuggle toy.

This time when I swallowed the lump in my throat, it didn't stop the silent tears from rolling down my cheek.

"Sorry, I took so lo—"

"Shh, she just dozed off." Austin said, tucking the blanket over Imogen's sleeping form.

"I am so sorry about all of this."

"Madison, relax. It's fine. I came to lend a hand."

"But you didn't have—"

"Stop. I want to be here." He gave me a meaningful look. "I want to help. So just nod and say, 'Okay, Austin.'"

"Okay, Austin."

"There, that wasn't difficult, was it? Now what do you want to do with the sleeping princess?"

"She'll probably be out for the night, so I'll just take her to bed."

"I can do it."

I wasn't sure my heart—or my ovaries—would withstand watching him carry her to bed.

"No, it's okay. I've got her." I rounded the couch and gently eased her into my arms. She wriggled a little but didn't wake. "I'll be back."

Imogen was out for the count when I tucked her into her freshly made bed. Her room smelled of vanilla and cherries now and I hoped it stayed that way.

"Good night my princess." I gently stuffed Mr. Hopsy and her new bunny in under her arm and kissed her forehead before returning to Austin.

"She okay?"

"Yeah, whatever it was seems to have passed. Kid-puke is no joke." Austin grimaced, and I chuckled. "Sexy, I know."

"Come here." He reached for me, and I took his hands, letting him pull me down half onto his lap. "Hi."

"Hi."

"I know you said we needed to take it slow but how slow are we talking?"

"I think we can probably step it up a gear." My gaze dipped as my heart crashed violently against my rib cage.

He was here.

He was here and he wasn't turned off at the state of me. Of the fact that I'd just spend the last thirty minutes cleaning a four-year-old's vomit from every surface in my bathroom.

"Yeah?"

"Yeah. But let me change first. I must—"

"Madison?"

"Yeah, Austin?"

"Stop talking now." His hand slid up my spine and into my hair, cupping the back of my neck. "I've missed this," he said huskily, leaning in to ghost his lips over mine.

He pulled away, searching my eyes, asking for silent permission. I pressed my lips together, wetting them, and nodded.

"Thank fuck." He crashed his mouth down onto mine, plunging his tongue deep inside and stealing the very air from my lungs.

My fingers twisted into his sweater, anchoring us closer.

God, he wasn't the only one who'd missed this.

Austin kissed me until I was breathless, hot and

desperate for more. But Imogen was right down the hall, and I'd promised myself that we'd take it slow.

"Yeah," he murmured, breaking the kiss, resting his forehead against mine. "We should probably stop before we can't."

"I'm sorry."

"Don't do that." He brushed another lingering kiss against my mouth. "I want this, Madi. I want you and that amazing little girl of yours. I'm in, okay. I'm all fucking in."

His admission made me feel dizzy. Like free falling through the clouds.

"I'm glad you're here, Austin." I traced the lines of his face, before stealing another kiss. "Are you hungry?"

His eyes flashed with lust, and I laughed. "For food, hotshot."

"I could eat. You want to order in? My treat?"

"Or I could cook something for us. I'm not sure what I have in the refrigerator."

"I have to admit, I'm not a very good cook."

"Come on then, hotshot." I got up and offered him my hand. "I'll teach you how to make something."

"A cooking lesson?"

"Let's see what I've got in here." I pulled the refrigerator door open and scanned the contents. "Okay, we've got one beer." I handed Austin the leftover beer from the last time Jeremiah came over for movie night. "There's some leftover wine for me. And we have all the ingredients to make spaghetti. I mean, it's practically a date." I grabbed everything I needed and dropped it on the counter.

"What do you need me to do first?" Austin placed his beer down and came up behind me, circling his arms around my waist.

"Hmm, let's see. You can wash the tomatoes and bell peppers."

"I can do that." He moved my ponytail over one shoulder and pressed a lingering kiss to my neck. I sank into his kiss as a soft whimper spilled out of me. "Or I can stay right here and..." His mouth trailed up and down, making my stomach twist and tighten.

It felt good.

Too good.

"That is... very distracting."

One of his big bands splayed across my stomach. "You're distracting, pretty girl."

"Austin, I smell like Lysol."

"I hadn't noticed." He continued licking a path along my collarbone.

"That is..." I sucked in a shaky breath, my fingers curling into the edge of the counter.

"Mommy!" Imogen's sobs echoed through the apartment and Austin moved away with a pained sigh.

"Crap, I'm sorry," I said.

"Go check on her. I'll get the bucket and the cleaning products."

"Austin, you don't have—"

"Go. I'll be right behind you."

I took off toward my daughter's bedroom with a hundred thoughts running through my mind. But one stood out against all the rest.

I realized that this was the moment I might have fallen a little bit in love with Austin Hart.

CHAPTER 29

AUSTIN

Being knee-deep in puke wasn't how I anticipated my first date with Madison and Imogen going down. But once we'd finally gotten Imogen cleaned up again and into yet another fresh set of sheets, Madison became ill.

It was past two in the morning now, and we were both exhausted.

"You know you'll probably get whatever we have," Madison murmured as she lay in bed, a cold compress on her forehead.

"How do you feel now?" I asked her.

"Like my stomach went through a meat grinder."

"Well at least we can mark off seeing each other covered in vomit off our relationship bingo card."

"I can't believe this happened," she groaned, throwing her arm over her face.

"Hey, look at me." I pried her fingers away wishing like fuck that she never felt the need to hide from me. "I'm here because I want to be."

"You know you're going to be Immy's hero after that move you pulled carrying me into the bathroom."

"Hey, if it scores me some extra brownie points with her, then it's worth it." I brushed the damp hair off her face. "It's late, I should probably take off."

"No, don't go." Madison grabbed my arm. "I mean... what if I get sick again and Imogen needs me."

"I can call Jeremiah. Or her grand—"

Madison inhaled a shaky breath. "I know I said I wanted to take it slow and I do. But I'm also feeling really sorry for myself, and you've been so amazing, Austin. Stay, please."

"Fine. Do you have any more spare blankets? I'll take the couch—"

She shook her head, patting the empty space beside her.

"You're sick," I said. "You don't know what you're saying."

"Just get in here before I change my mind."

She didn't need to tell me twice. I quickly stripped down to my boxer briefs and climbed in beside her.

"Hmm, you're so warm." She pressed in close, laying her head on my chest as I wrapped my arm around her. "Thank you for tonight. I know it isn't what you had planned, and you're probably scarred for life... but it means a lot that you stuck around."

"I'm sure I can think of a few ways you can repay me," I said, pressing a kiss to her hair.

This was new territory for us, but strangely nothing felt weird about it. Vomit aside, I'd genuinely liked being here in their space.

Madison wanted to take things slow but there was nothing slow about the depths of my feelings for her. I wasn't ready to name them yet, but I could acknowledge that I'd never felt this way before.

"Mmm," her soft laughter punched through my chest and wrapped around my heart. "I'm beat. Mind if I go to sleep?"

I tangled my fingers in her hair. "Sleep, Madi. I've got you."

She let out a contented sigh and snuggled closer. My heart was in overdrive, crashing against my chest. A rhythmic thunderclap in the silence. It seemed fitting for the gravity of the situation.

I'd never done this—*any* of this.

There was a little girl down the hall who had managed to wrap me around her pinky in less than a few hours, and her mom curled up beside me like she was born to be there.

It was a lot to get my head around.

But I wasn't scared. Not in the way I thought I would be.

Being around Madison brought me peace. *She* brought me peace. And now that I knew what that could feel like, I never wanted to let her go.

"Austins, Mr. Austins."

Something tickled my face. I swatted it away, cracking an eye open to find a bunny paw coming right at me.

"What the—"

"You is a sleepy heads." The bunny disappeared and Imogen's face came into view. "Why is you in bed with Mommy?"

"I..." Shit. *Shit.* I glanced over my shoulder to find Madison was still out cold.

Clearly, neither of us had thought this through when I'd climbed into bed with her a few hours ago.

"Your mommy is still sick, so why don't we get up and let her sleep a bit longer?" I suggested.

"Okays. Can you makes me breakfast? My tummy is alll empty."

"I... Uh, yeah. Yeah, we can do that. But I'm going to need you to wait in the hall for me, okay?"

"Okay. But don'ts be wong." She skipped off,

obviously feeling a lot better than she had been last night.

"Madi." I leaned over her and brushed my fingers along her shoulder. "Imogen is awake."

"Hmm," she murmured, not really waking.

"I'll get up with her and get her some breakfast. Just promise not to kill me if I poison her." I pressed a kiss to her skin.

Madison didn't rouse. So I slipped out of bed, pulled on my clothes and went in search of the little hellion.

"Austins," she shrieked when I found her.

My mouth twitched. At least it was a damn sight better than Mr. Austins.

"Is Mommy okay?"

"I'm sure she'll be fine. She's just sleeping it off. Why don't we make you breakfast and then we can make Mommy breakfast in bed?"

The guys would fall over laughing if they could see me now. Lakeshore U Lakers goalie Austin Hart playing domesticated families with his girl and her daughter.

My girl.

The thought streaked through me, heating my blood.

We hadn't put a label on anything yet. But I wanted to. I wanted to make Madison mine and declare it for all the world to hear.

Jesus, I was in deep.

So fucking deep, I started opening cabinets and pulling out all the things I needed to make Imogen the best damn breakfast she'd ever had.

"What is all this stuffs?" she asked, her blonde brows bunching together.

"Breakfast things. We've got eggs and oatmeal," I rummaged through the items. "Or I think there's stuff to make pancakes."

"I just has Cap'ns Crunch, silly." Imogen rounded the breakfast counter and opened a low-level cabinet pulling out a box of cereal and a rather worn-looking princess fairy bowl. "Get the milks. Mommy doesn't let me do the milk cos I spills it sometimes."

Locating the carton of milk in the refrigerator, I helped Imogen up onto the stool and together, we covered her Cap'n Crunch in milk.

"Thanks, Austins." She gave me a megawatt smile before diving in.

I made myself a coffee while she chatted about everything and nothing. The cereal became part of her story, her actions becoming more and more animated until she laughed so hard at her own joke cereal and milk sprayed across the counter.

"Oopsie." She giggled some more, and I broke, laughing right along with her.

She was... Well, she was like no one I'd ever met. Which wasn't saying much when my experience with kids was non-existent. But there was something special about her.

"What's going on in here?"

We both looked over to find Madison leaning against the doorjamb.

"Mommy!" Imogen abandoned her cereal and leaped down off the stool, almost causing me a heart attack, and practically tackled her mom. "Is you feelings better?"

"I'm okay, baby." She scooped Imogen up and carried her over to me. "What is all this?"

"Austins was going to makes me breakfast but wike I tolds him, I always has Cap'n Crunch."

"Thank you," she mouthed over Imogen's head.

I gave her a small nod, unable to hide my smile.

"You sit and finish your cereal while I get myself a drink."

"What do you want?" I asked. "Coffee?"

"No." She ran a hand over her stomach. "I still feel a little bit delicate. Water and some crackers for now."

"Sit, I've got it." I had no problem finding a bottle of water and a packet of graham crackers. "Here," I said.

"Thank you."

"We were going to surprise you with breakfast in bed."

"You were?"

"Isn't that right, Imogen?"

"Princess Immy," she reminded me through a mouthful of cereal.

"Sorry, Princess Immy."

She grinned showing me the rest of her breakfast, and Madison smothered a laugh.

"I wikes Austins, Mommy. Next time he sleeps overs can he sleep in my room?"

"I... I'm not sure that's... Eat your cereal." Madison's cheeks flushed firetruck red, and it was my turn to hide my amusement. "I see I had nothing to worry about," she murmured.

"I guess not."

Smug satisfaction swelled inside me. We could do this—move at our own pace as fast or slow as we wanted.

Until Madison said, "Don't you have to be at practice soon?"

Shit.

I did.

"Go. We'll be fine," she said.

"I can text Coach and tell him—"

"Go. We've got this, don't we, princess?"

"We gots it, Austins." Imogen grinned again.

"Okay, but I'll call you later."

"Go!" They both laughed but I didn't.

I was fucking stunned.

Because for the first time in my life I wanted to choose something other than hockey.

"Where the fuck have you been?" Noah hissed as I hurried into the locker room.

"I overslept."

"You over—" He stopped himself and narrowed his eyes at me. "You mean you got laid."

"Firstly, I didn't. And secondly, it's none of your fucking business."

I ran a hand down my face. Exhaustion lingered in my muscles, and the last thing I wanted to do was spend ninety minutes on the ice deflecting my teammates pucks, but I was a Laker and that still meant something to me.

Even if part of me wished I could have stayed with Madison and Imogen.

"So, what happened?" Noah probed.

"We're taking it slow," I said with a dismissive tone.

"Taking it slow. What the fuck does that mean? You were obviously at her place last night. Was her kid—"

"She has a name."

His eyes went wide, and I mentally kicked myself for sounding so defensive. But this was all new to me and I didn't exactly have myself under control where Madison or my feelings for her were concerned.

"Jesus, you have it bad. So is that it now? We can expect to see you attending family hour at—"

"Can you just stop?" I blew out an exasperated breath.

"Yeah, give him a break, Holden." Mason came to my defense. "The guy's in love. He's not used to—"

"Oh, fuck off, both of you."

Their laughter did little to quell the nervous energy skittering around my stomach.

"So when can we meet her? Officially?" Noah asked.

"If I have my way, never," I muttered.

"Oh, don't be like that. You should bring her to TPB one night."

"Millers might be a better call," Mase added. "Less bunnies."

I groaned. The two of them were enough to give me a major headache. And I already had one of those thanks to the lack of sleep.

"It's too early for that," I said.

The last thing I wanted was to overwhelm her.

Madison was already cautious enough about me. About the fact I was still in college and played hockey.

I didn't need these assholes ruining things for me.

"Too early? Nah. You need to introduce her into the fold, give her plenty of time to get her head around what she's getting herself into," Noah grinned but I didn't return it. "Oh, come on, don't be such a—"

"Okay, people. Let's move it along," Coach Walsh

bellowed. "Coach Tucker wants us out on the ice in five. We've got a big couple of weekends ahead of us."

Thankfully, the guys took that as their cue to stop giving me shit and we all got suited up as quickly as we could.

"You know, before I met Rory," Noah said to me as we filed out with the rest of the team. "I thought that hockey was the only thing that mattered."

"And now?"

He looked up at me and grinned as if he was about to let me in on some big secret. "Win or lose, I'm going home to the woman I want to spend the rest of my life with. Nothing will ever beat that feeling."

A few weeks ago, if he said that shit to me, I would have shaken my head in disapproval. But now...

Now I had a feeling I knew exactly where he was coming from.

Meeting the girl of your dreams in the lead up to some of the biggest games in your hockey career to date, was never going to be easy. But after a sloppy win, followed by a draw at home, Coach Tucker demanded more from everyone. More team meetings, more practice time on the ice, and more focus.

It made finding time to see Madison outside of her shifts at Sugartown and O'Shea's even harder.

I'd seen her once in the last five days and she'd had Imogen with her. So there had been no time to show her how much I missed her.

The team was away this weekend, but I refused to leave without seeing her, so as soon as classes got done Thursday, I hopped on the bus out of town and headed to Sugartown.

"Austin, this is really not a surprise." Kayleigh laughed as I approached the counter. "Madi is just out back. Can I get you something to eat or drink?"

"I'll take a cookie of the day and water please."

She rang up my order and I paid.

"Give me one second." Kayleigh got my order and slid it across the counter. "I'll tell Madison you're here."

"Thanks."

I found an empty table and made myself comfortable. A minute later, Madison appeared wearing a huge smile.

Fuck, that smile did things to me.

"You made it."

"I said I would." She went to sit next to me, but I snagged her waist and pulled her down onto my lap.

"Austin, I'm at work."

"I know but I've missed you. I need to say hello properly." I kissed her quick and hard, not giving a fuck if we had an audience.

"Mmm, hello to you too." Madison slid off my lap and sat on the chair beside me. "How was your day?"

"Long."

"Yeah, I know what you mean." She gazed at me with the same intensity I felt.

We'd barely had any time alone. To talk. To do *other* things.

I'd promised we could take things slow, but it didn't change the fact I was counting down the days until I could get my hands on her again.

"Austin," she breathed, electricity flowing between us.

"Yeah." I smirked, thinking of all the downright dirty and delicious things I planned on doing to her at the first possible opportunity.

"Do I even want to know what you're thinking right now?" she whispered.

"Probably not."

"I need to go help Jess. I'll be back as soon as I can."

"Sure, go."

To my endless disappointment, the store only got busier, and I knew I was a distraction Madison didn't need. So after another thirty minutes of watching her work, I spotted my opening and headed over to the counter.

"I'm going to head out," I said.

"Already?"

"Yeah, you're busy and I don't want to get in the way."

"Okay then." The disappointment in her eyes made me feel ten-feet tall. "We'll see you on Sunday when you get back?"

"I should be back around midday."

"Can't wait. Imogen already has our afternoon all planned out."

"I'm looking forward to it." I pressed my hands on the counter and leaned forward a little.

"What are you doing?" Madison's eyes grew wide, but I saw the lust swirling there.

"I need to get my good luck kiss." I reached for her arm, pulling her gently toward me.

"Austin..."

"Just one little kiss, pretty girl, and then I'll go."

Madison relented, twisting her fingers into my hoodie as she leaned in, brushing her mouth against mine.

Heat exploded inside me, kicking my heart and other more southerly parts of me into overdrive but I reined it in, forcing myself not to take more than she was comfortable with.

"I'll see you Sunday," I said, giving her a playful wink before walking out of there.

Wondering if she knew how completely and utterly gone I was for her.

CHAPTER 30

MADISON

"Austins, Austins is here, Mommy." Imogen practically ran through the apartment to get to the door first.

"Okay, baby. Just let him—"

"Austins." She threw her arms around his waist and hugged him tight.

"I've missed you too, princess." He pulled out a small gift bag from behind his back. "This is for you."

"Ooh, a present?"

"A present all the way from Detroit. Why don't you go over to the couch and open it so I can say hello to your mom."

"Look Mommy, Austins got me a present." She skipped off the couch and I arched a brow at him.

"Another present," I said. "You're setting a dangerous precedent."

"Worth it if it gives us a minute's peace," he said, stalking toward me, heat simmering in his eyes. "I missed you." Austin tucked my hair behind my ear and leaned down to kiss me.

"Mmm, I missed you too."

Too much.

But life with two jobs and a four-year-old kept me on my toes, so there hadn't been much time to dwell on his absence.

Still, I couldn't help but wonder what would happen to us if he decided to go off and play for the Vancouver Canucks.

We hadn't talked about it again, and I really didn't want to. Not yet. But it was always there, in the back of my mind—a faint whisper, warning me that this could all go horribly wrong.

Austin slid his hand into the back of my hair and pulled me closer. "God, I want you."

"I know. Maybe I can ask Jer to—"

"Mommy, wooks. Wooks."

I released a soft sigh. "I guess our time is up."

"It's okay, I can wait."

Austin let me go and we both went over to Imogen.

"What do you have in there?" I asked her.

"It's a doggy, Mommy. And there's some princess gloves. Why did you gets me gloves, Austins?"

"Well, the bulldog is the mascot from the team we played at the weekend. But don't tell my teammates I got you one. And the gloves are for today."

"Wheres is we going then?" She frowned at him, anticipation glittering in her eyes.

"How would you like to go ice skating with Harper, Mason, and Scottie?"

"For reals? We're going hockey skatings with Scottie?"

"We are."

"Woohoo, this is the bestest day evers." She began running circles around us.

"I think she's excited," I chuckled.

When he'd suggested it, I knew Imogen would love it. She loved her new friends. Especially Scottie.

"Thank you Austins." She grabbed hold of his leg and hugged it. "You is the bestest Mommy's boyfriend ever."

His eyes snapped to mine, flaring with a rare glimpse of emotion.

"She has a point," I said, knowing my next words would rock his world. "You do make a pretty good boyfriend."

"I can't believe I'm watching Austin Hart play princesses versus hockey players," Harper said as we drank our hot chocolates on the bench.

We'd all been out on the ice but the kids were running circles around us, so Austin and Mason offered to watch Imogen for a little bit while we— mostly me since I hadn't skated in years—caught our breath.

"Are you keeping up with the score because I have no idea what is happening right now," I said.

Austin had his arms hooked under Imogen's shoulders half-carrying and half-gliding her around the ice while she attempted to maneuver the hockey stick. Scottie was guarding the goal and Mason looked to be chasing them or running away from them while Imogen shouted, "Save the princess," at the top of her lungs.

I was grateful that we'd managed to score a private session, thanks to Mason who knew the owner of the ice rink because nobody needed to hear that.

"Nope, but she's enjoying herself."

"She is." I smiled.

She loved Scottie and Austin, and although Mason was a little more guarded, she'd even warmed to the Lakers left-winger.

"So are you the two of you... together?"

"We're seeing where things go." I kept my answer vague.

If there was one thing I'd learned about Austin since meeting him, it was that he was a deeply private person. So while I meant what I said earlier when I'd indirectly referred to him as my boyfriend, I didn't want to rush to put a label on things.

"Well, I don't think I've ever seen him smile so much. So you must be doing something right."

It was hard not to watch him with Imogen and imagine the future—the future I thought I'd have with Warren.

I was older now. Wiser. And I knew nothing was ever guaranteed.

But Austin made me happy.

He made us both so very happy.

"Madison, what's wrong?" Harper gently squeezed my arm.

"Nothing." I gave her a weak smile and she waited for me to explain. "You know when something good happens to you and you're almost too scared to believe it?"

"I know it better than you think."

"Well, it's how I feel." The confession felt like a betrayal of how amazing Austin was, but I couldn't help the way I felt. "Like I'm waiting for the rug to be pulled out from under me."

"No, don't say that. It's obvious Austin is crazy about you and Imogen. He's like a completely different person around you both."

I didn't have time to answer. Mason and Scottie skated over to us, laughing and nudging each other.

"What do you feed that kid?" Mason said, glancing over to where Austin was still swinging Imogen around. "She's like the Energizer Bunny on steroids."

"She's alright," Scottie added. "But she's very loud."

One of the reasons Harper had thought to give him his headphones earlier.

"Mommy, Mommy, wooks, I'm flying." Imogen shrieked with delight as Austin spun her in circles, her little legs swinging out in front of her.

"Wow, baby. That looks fun."

"Maybe Austins can make you flys too, Mommy."

"Oh, I'm sure he will," Mason muttered, earning himself a clip around the ear from Harper.

"Behave," she hissed.

"Why? What did he say?" Scottie asked.

"Nothing you need to worry about, buddy," she said.

"Oh wait, is it a sex joke?"

"Okay, I'm going to get back out there." I didn't wait around to hear what Mason said to his little brother.

I wasn't ready to be the brunt of anyone's sex jokes.

"What was that all about?" Austin asked me as I reached them.

"Nothing." I steadied myself then leaned up to kiss him. "I don't know about you two but I'm getting hungry."

"I could eat," Austin said, his eyes sparking with a different kind of hunger. "What about you, princess? Ready for some food?"

"Can Scottie come?" Imogen asked.

"Yeah, he can come."

"Then, yay, let's goes eat."

"Thank you for today," I said, joining Austin on the couch after putting Imogen to bed. "We both had a great time."

"Is she asleep?"

"Out like a light. I have no doubt she'll sleep like the dead after all that skating."

"Mason's right, she is like the Energizer Bunny on steroids."

"He told you about that?" I asked.

"Lakers don't keep secrets, Madi."

"Only about their *special friends*?" I arched my brow, unable to hide my amusement.

He slid his arm around me and pulled me onto his lap in one smooth move. I adjusted my legs so that I could straddle him, looping my arms around his neck.

"Yeah, well, I didn't know what you meant to me back then."

"And now?" I whispered. "Do you know what I mean to you now?"

"I thought I'd made it pretty obvious. But in case you need reminding." His fingers fluttered around my throat as he gazed right into my eyes, making my breath—my heart—catch. "I am completely"—he kissed the corner of my mouth—"and utterly"—tracing his lips down to the curve of my jaw—"gone for you."

He sucked the skin there, not enough to mark me but enough to send shivers racing down my spine.

"Austin," I whimpered, my skin burning as he continued sucking and licking at my heated skin.

"Fuck, Madi, I don't think I have ever wanted anything as much as I want you right now."

"Let's go to my room." I curled my fingers into the neck of his hoodie.

"Are you sure? What about Imogen?"

"She's out for the count."

"And if she isn't?"

"Kind of killing the mood here," I grumbled.

"I just don't want to rush you." He swept my hair off my shoulder and held me there again. "I can wait, I promise."

"Still, come to bed with me?" Even if he refused to touch me, I wanted to be with him.

I wanted him to stay.

I knew people—my parents and Warren's parents

mostly—would think I was rushing into things. They would be concerned about the impact of bringing a new man around Imogen. But I trusted him with my heart.

With Imogen's.

I would have to tell them soon but tonight, I wanted to take my boyfriend to bed and worry about tomorrow's problems tomorrow.

Climbing off his lap, I stood and offered him my hand.

"You're sure?" he asked, and I nodded.

"Imogen loves you. And I'm pretty sure I do too."

"You love me, pretty girl?" He stood, pulling me into his arms and sliding his fingers into my back pockets.

The air crackled with anticipation as he gazed down at me, his eyes full of fire.

"Yeah, I think I do. Does that scare you?"

"Not as much as I thought it would."

"We're not moving very slow," I said, biting my lip.

"No, we're not. But honestly, I don't give a fuck. I want you. Both of you. And I have something to tell you too actually. Something I haven't told anyone else yet."

"Okay." My heart galloped across my chest as I braced myself for his declaration.

A beat passed and I could hardly stand it.

But then he said, "I'm going to tell Coach Tucker I'm not interested in playing for the Canucks."

"What, why?" I frowned.

"Because I don't want to leave. Not when I've just found you."

"Austin, that's... That's a big decision."

Maybe even bigger than saying the three little words I yearned to hear.

"I know. But honestly, even if you hadn't agreed to give me another chance, I think my answer still would have been the same.

"Hockey will always be part of who I am, but I've come to realize it isn't my dream, it's my crutch. It's the thing I use to switch off from everything else. I don't need that anymore because I have you. I have my sister and Noah and the rest of the guys."

"What are you saying?"

Because I needed to be sure.

I needed him to say the words.

Austin lowered his head and inhaled a ragged breath. "I'm saying, I don't need to run anymore."

I lifted my hands to his face and palmed his cheeks. "You're really staying?"

He nodded, one of his rare but no less beautiful smiles breaking over his rugged face. "I'm staying."

It was better than any declaration of I love you and more than enough to soothe the frantic beat of my heart.

"Now I really want to fuck you," I said huskily.

"Madison Reynolds, you kiss your mother with that mouth?"

"Oh God, you know what this means?" His eyes clouded and I grumbled, "I have to introduce you to my mom."

"At least she can't be worse than mine. And no, I never plan on letting you anywhere near that woman." His quiet laughter reverberated through me.

When he stopped, he fixed his icy gaze on me and smiled. "You make me happy, Madison."

"You make me happy too." I leaned up and kissed him, hoping he wouldn't see the emotion in my eyes.

Today had been a lot, in a good way.

But no matter the high I was currently riding, that little voice of doubt reminding me how quickly things could change, refused to quiet.

"The hockey player looks good on you," Kingsley said with a knowing glint in his eye.

He and Hannah had been teasing me all week, but it was nothing I couldn't handle. I was too damn happy to let their jokes ruin my good mood.

"Will he be in tonight?"

"No," I said. "He's got a game then he's going to his friend's engagement party."

Connor was proposing tonight. On Valentine's Day no less. I was going to head over there once my shift was done.

My first official introduction as Austin's girlfriend. Hopefully, it would go a damn sight better than introducing Austin to my mother.

That had been an hour of my life I never wanted to relive.

But Austin had taken it all in stride.

He and Dad had bonded over hockey and their love for the cute little princess who knew how to wrap the men I cared about around her pinky finger. Mom had been frosty to say the least. But she saved her true opinions until the next day when she berated me for thirty minutes on my 'serious lapse in judgment' where dating a college hockey player was concerned.

I told her I appreciated her opinion but that I was old enough to make my own choices and that was that.

I was happy. Imogen was ecstatic to have Austin in her life and a whole bunch of new friends. And he was staying in Lakeshore for the foreseeable future.

The rest would figure itself out.

"Well, you tell him to keep on doing what he's doing, Mads. It's good to see you smile again, girl." Kingsley gave me a nod as I headed into the back to take some empty crates into the storeroom.

I swapped the crate for the two bags of trash and made my way down the hall to the back exit, to sling them outside. But when I shouldered the door open, I stopped in my tracks.

"Julian, what are you doing out here?"

His erratic gaze darted to mine and a sinking sensation went through me.

Something wasn't right.

"Madison, I—" His eyes moved to the left of me, and fear slid down my spine.

"Julian, tell me what's going on."

"I'm sorry, Madison." His expression dropped right along with my heart. "I'm so, so sorry."

CHAPTER 31

AUSTIN

I CHECKED my cell phone for the fourth time.

Nothing.

Where the hell was she?

Madison was supposed to be here thirty minutes ago. But she wasn't answering my calls or my texts.

"Where's this girl of yours then?" Connor ambled over, still wearing the shit-eating grin he'd been wearing since he got down on one knee in front of a sold-out Ellet Arena and proposed to Ella.

The old me would have branded him a pussy for that move but Madison was definitely having an impact on me, because I'd cheered like an idiot right alongside my teammates and our fans when she'd said yes.

"I'm not sure, she isn't answering me." I checked my phone again, willing her to respond.

"You think something's happened?"

"I don't know. It's not like her to ignore me."

"You should go and make sure she's okay," he said.

"It's your engagement party—"

"And she's your girl. I get it. You won't rest until you hear from her, so go."

"Thanks, and Con?"

"Yeah?"

"I'm so fucking happy for you and Ella, you know that, right?"

"Yeah, I know, man. Come here." He pulled me in for a hug, slapping me on the back a little harder than necessary. "Little piece of advice," he whispered, "hold onto her."

"Plan on it," I said, breaking away before the conversation could get any deeper.

"Hopefully, I'll be back soon with Madison in tow." It was already late, and the party would start winding down soon.

It didn't make any sense. Unless her battery had died, or they needed her to stay longer at the bar.

I ordered an Uber as I headed for the entrance, but Rory intercepted me on route. "Austin, what's wrong?" she asked.

"Madison hasn't turned up yet so I'm going to head

over to O'Shea's and make sure everything is okay. If she turns up, can you text me."

"Of course, I hope she's alright."

"I'm sure she's fine."

Because the notion that she wasn't…

Nope. Not going there.

I met my Uber and climbed in, sending her another text.

Austin: I'm heading over to O'Shea's now. If you're already on the way to me, let me know and I'll double back around. Can't wait to see you.

I hit send and waited.

Like all my other messages before, it went unanswered.

By the time the Uber pulled up outside of O'Shea's I was on edge.

Madison still hadn't replied to me, and Rory had messaged to say there was no sign of her yet.

It didn't make any sense. We were good. Everything was great.

Her mom had been a little frosty with me when I'd met her earlier in the week, but it was nothing I couldn't handle. Nothing that should have worried Madison.

Unless Mrs. Reynolds had been whispering in her daughter's ear, planting doubts.

No, we were solid. I hung out at Sugartown, visited her on her shifts at the bar. I'd even gone with her a couple of times to pick Imogen up from pre-K, and we'd all gone over to Jeremiah's so I could officially meet the best friend and his cat.

We were writing our own story on our own terms.

The only thing I hadn't done yet was give her the three little words she'd already said to me.

She knew I felt them. She had too.

They were in every touch, every kiss and smile. Every laugh we shared.

Madison made me happy.

She made me feel worthy.

I'd declined the Canucks invitation to talk for fuck's sake. She had to know what she meant to me.

Didn't she?

I didn't like second-guessing myself but that's exactly what happened as I walked into O'Shea's, frantically searching for her.

But there was no sign of her.

She wasn't—

"Austin?" Hannah said, and I blinked, realizing she

was right in front of me. "Thank God, have you seen her?"

"What?"

"Madison, have you seen her?"

I spotted Kingsley talking to two policemen and another man I didn't recognize, and a wave of dread crashed over me.

"What's going on?" My voice didn't sound like my own as the pieces started to slowly fit together.

"Julian—"

"What did that fucker do?" I bit out, pure rage flooding my system. If he'd touched her. If that smug fucker had hurt her.

"Austin, perhaps—"

I spotted him, joining Kingsley and the officers, and I saw red.

"Austin, no, wait," Hannah called but it was too late. I was already across the bar with my hand around his throat, slamming him into the wall.

"What the fuck did you do to her?"

"Whoa, easy there, boy." Kingsley's big hand landed on my shoulder. "Julian isn't to blame here."

"I-I... Breathe." His face turned red. "Can't breathe."

"Let the man go," Kingsley warned, his baritone voice reaching the rational part of me.

I let him go, and he slid down the wall, coughing and spluttering.

"You must be the boyfriend," the other guy I didn't recognize said.

"Who the fuck are you?"

"Jack O'Shea. Madison's boss."

"Will someone tell me what the fuck is going on? Where's Madison?" I pinned Julian with a deadly look.

"I didn't touch her, I swear." He rubbed his temples and I realized he was injured, a big bruise blooming across his hairline. "I would never hurt her. It was him. H-he took her…"

"He?" I growled.

"The man who took her."

"Shit," the officer murmured. "We need to check that security footage pronto. And we're going to need a description and a rundown of exactly what happened."

"They knew each other," Julian said. "Madison called him Wa-Warner or maybe it was—"

"Warren." Fear hit me dead in the chest.

"Warren?" Kingsley frowned. "Her ex?"

Everything inside me turned cold.

She was with him?

He'd *taken* her,

What the fuck had happened here?

"Can you get us a photograph?" the officer asked me.

"No." I ran a hand over my jaw, trying to think.

"Any ideas where he might be taking her?" someone asked, and Kingsley snagged my attention.

And my heart plummeted into my toes at the sheer horror in his eyes.

"Imogen," I blurted. "He's going after their daughter."

"Okay, where is she right now?"

"At Madison's apartment. Her parents are babysitting."

Imogen had wanted to be there in the morning to see me and refused to stay over at her grandparents, much to Mrs. Reynolds' annoyance.

"Address?"

Their voices became white noise as blood roared in my ears. I didn't even realize I'd started moving away from them until a hand grabbed me.

"Do you know what you're doing, boy?" Kingsley asked.

"Not really. But I love her. I'm in love with her."

"Go." He nodded once. "I'll make sure someone is right behind you."

I got the fuck out of there before anyone could stop me and started running like my life depended on it.

Police sirens wailed in the distance as I reached Madison's building and yanked the door open. I had no plan other than to get to my girls.

Taking two steps at a time, I darted up the stairs and down the hall, only slowing when I heard raised voices.

"She is my fucking daughter. You think I won't do it," Warren yelled as I moved closer to the door which had been left ajar.

Thank fuck.

"You think I won't punish you all for keeping her from me."

"No one is keeping her from you." Madison said calmly but I heard the slight hitch in her voice. The fear. "But this isn't the way, Warren. You're scaring her. You're—"

"Mommy makes him stop. Makes him—"

"Shut up," he snapped. "Just shut the fuck up."

"Warren, son. Think about this."

"Mommy, Mommy, I don't wants to go with him." Imogen sobbed. "He's not my daddy. He's not—"

It was the pure fear and desperation in Imogen's voice that kicked me into action. I slipped my hand around the edge of the door and worked it open as quietly as possible.

Not quietly enough though because Imogen saw me down the hall and shrieked, "Austins, Austins is here."

Warren swung around and his momentum gave Imogen enough leverage to wriggle out of his hold. She crashed to the floor with a pained cry, and I swooped in to grab her.

"Austin!" Madison screamed right as I stood while Imogen clutched my shoulders, to find the end of a blade pointed right at us.

"Who the fuck are you?" Warren snarled.

I gently cradled the back of Imogen's neck, pressing her close to me, hoping like hell I could keep her out of harm's way.

My heart pounded in my chest as I stared down her father, the man who had broken Madison. "You don't want to do this," I said, keeping my eye on the knife.

"Don't tell me what the fuck I want to do. Are you fucking her, is that it? Did she spread her legs for you like a good little whore."

Imogen sobbed against my shoulder, and I held her tighter, whispering soothing noises in her ear.

"Warren, please," Mrs. Reynolds sniffled. "She's just a child."

"My child. SHE'S MY FUCKING CHILD." He kept the blade pointed at me, but his eyes were burning hatred at Madison's parents. "And you and your husband took her away from me. You made sure she'd grow up never knowing me. Her own flesh and blood."

"We can talk about this. No one has to get hurt, son—"

"Don't call me that. Don't ever fucking call me that. You took everything from me."

I inched backward. Slowly. Carefully. All while my heart threatened to beat right out of my chest.

This was bad—really fucking bad.

One wrong move and someone could get hurt.

I needed to get Imogen away from him.

Where were the police?

Where the fuck was back up?

"Warren." Madison stepped forward and my heart jumped into my throat. She caught my eye and gave me a coded look.

"Warren, look at me. Talk to me."

He glanced back at me, his hand trembling. His eyes were blown, a sure sign he was under the influence of something.

"Seriously, Madi, you fucking this guy?"

"He's not important, baby. This is about you and me. Look at me."

He started to turn, giving her his full attention, and I used Madison's distraction to my advantage, backing up further.

I caught Madison's eye, hating the fear there. The sheer determination. She wasn't thinking about herself. She was only thinking about the terrified little girl in my arms.

Go, she seemed to say. *Get her out of here.*

I bolted for the door and spilled into the hall. "Inside," I yelled at the police officers moving down the hall. "He has a knife."

The officers poured into the room, and I heard one yell, "Freeze," as all hell broke loose.

"Shh, princess, I've got you. I've got you." I held Imogen tighter, trying to protect her from whatever was going down in the apartment.

"Austins, wheres Mommy? I wants Mommy." She started to wail, her body trembling in my arms as I held on and prayed to God that Madison was okay.

Seconds turned into minutes and minutes seemed like hours. But finally, the door opened again, and the officers came out shoving a cuffed Warren between them.

He met my stare and I conveyed everything I wanted to say to his face but never would while I held his little girl in my arms.

I'll take care of them.

I'll protect them.

I'll love them.

And if you ever pull that shit again, I'll fucking end you.

He opened his mouth to speak but one of the officers shoved him down the hall.

"Imogen? Immy?" Madison came running out of her apartment and took her from me. "Oh, thank God. Thank God, baby. You're okay, you're okay now. Mommy's here. Mommy's—" Her composure cracked, and big fat sobs overpowered her.

"Is the bad man gones now?" Imogen sucked in a

shaky breath, and Madison smoothed a hand over her blonde halo of curls.

"He's gone, baby. And he won't ever hurt you again. I promise." Tears streaked down her cheeks, and I couldn't wait a second longer.

I pulled them both into my arms and buried my face in Madison's neck. "I love you, Madison Reynolds. I love you both so fucking much."

And I planned on showing them that every single day for as long as she would let me.

"Thank you, officer," Mr. Reynolds escorted the officer out of Madison's apartment some time later.

"Here, I made us all some hot cocoa."

"Thanks, Mom," Madison said wearily.

"You should let me put her to bed, it's no good for her sleeping out here."

"Not yet." Madison's arm tightened around Imogen who was out cold, one hand curled around Mr. Hopsy and one hand tangled with mine.

Mrs. Reynolds glanced at me and let out a resigned sigh. "It would seem my granddaughter is really quite smitten with you."

"Mom, please."

"It's okay," I said, not wanting to add to Madison's plate. She'd been through enough tonight.

"If you let me finish, Madi, I was about to thank Austin for everything he did tonight."

I looked her straight in the eye and said, "I care about your daughter a great deal, Mrs. Reynolds. There isn't much I wouldn't do for her or Imogen".

"Yes, I think I can believe that. Please, call me Cara."

"They want us to go down to the station tomorrow to finish answering some questions." Mr. Reynolds came back over. "But for now, we can all get some rest now that he's out of the picture."

"Have they notified Jacqui and Ken?"

"I believe so. Do you want me to call them?" he asked, and Madison nodded.

"I can't do it, Dad, not yet. Not until I've had time to..."

"I'll handle it, sweetheart. Do you want us to stay?"

"No, I think we'll be fine." She shifted her gaze to mine, and I nodded.

I wasn't going anywhere.

I'd sent Rory a text message half-filling her in on everything. The rest could wait until tomorrow.

"You're sure? We can stay—"

"We should give them some space, Cara, love." Mr. Reynolds settled his gaze on me. "Austin here can handle it. Can't you, son?"

"I think so, sir."

He gave me a reassuring nod and I felt like I'd passed some kind of test.

"Okay. But if you need anything, you can call. We'll wait up—"

"Mom, you don't have to do that. We'll be fine. Once we get Imogen into bed, we'll probably call it a night too."

Mrs. Reynolds looked less than pleased at the idea of me sleeping over. But I really didn't give a fuck.

I needed to hold Madison in my arms tonight. To know that she was safe.

That nothing could hurt them.

"Take her for me for a second." Madison scooched Imogen onto my lap and got up to see her parents out.

I stroked her hair, my hands still shaking as I tried to process the last few hours.

When she came back, she gave me a weary smile but I saw the fear still in her eyes. "I can't believe that happened."

"You're okay now. Everything's going to be okay." I reached for hand and pulled her down beside me, wrapping my arm around her.

"If you hadn't come—" Sobs overtook her again as she cried into my chest.

"Shh, babe. It's okay. You're both okay." I kissed her head, wishing more than anything that I could take it all away from her.

But I couldn't.

All I could do was be there for her. For them both.

"I was so scared, Austin. When I went outside and saw Julian, I didn't understand. And then Warren stepped out of the shadows, holding a knife. I... I didn't know what to do."

I inhaled slowly, trying to get a hold of the violent emotions raging inside me.

"Austin?"

"I'm okay," I forced out, but Madison sat up, sliding her hands along my jaw.

"I told you I come with all kinds of baggage."

"Yeah, don't give a fuck," I murmured.

"Because you love me. Us...You love us."

"Yeah, I do, pretty girl. I love you so fucking much."

"I love you too. We both do. I don't care what my parents or Jacqui and Ken think. What we have, the way you make me feel, it's real." She leaned in, touching her forehead to mine. "It's real, Austin."

"I love you."

"I loves you too," a little voice said, and Imogen wriggled in my arms, climbing up my chest to wedge herself in between us.

"You were supposed to be sleeping."

"I was Mommy. I was dreaming abouts the brave prince who saved me."

"A prince, huh?" Madison smiled, trying to stave off a fresh wave of tears.

"Yep. And guess whats?"

"What?" I asked.

"He was a hockey player just like you and Scottie."

"He was, that's so cool." I chuckled.

"I love you, Austins." She wrapped her arms around my neck and crushed herself into me. "Thank you for savings me and Mommy."

"Oh, I don't know, princess," I looked at Madison and swallowed the lump in my throat. "I think you saved me too."

CHAPTER 32

MADISON

"Oh my God, Madi." Rory rushed over and pulled me into her arms. "Thank God you're both okay."

"Austins saved us," Imogen announced proudly, and Rory let me go so she could crouch down to greet my daughter.

"He did, didn't he? And I am so, so happy you and your mom are okay. Can I get a hug?"

"Of courses." She threw her little arms around Rory and hugged her tight and I wouldn't ask, but I was sure I saw a tear in her eye.

"You must be the girl we have to thank for thawing our goalie's cold, dead heart." Connor Morgan stepped forward with a slight limp and grinned. "Connor." He held out his hand.

"Madison." I took it but he yanked me forward and pulled me into a bear hug.

"It's good to finally meet you. Thanks for loving our guy," he whispered.

"He makes it pretty easy." My voice cracked but I kept my composure.

Austin was right. This group of people weren't just friends—they were family.

"Hands off my girl, Morgan." Austin came up behind me and wrapped an arm around my waist.

"You is a hockey player too?" Imogen asked Connor.

"We're all hockey players," he said, tipping his head to the other guys crammed into our private little event at Sugartown.

Mason. Noah. And the Lakers captain, Aiden Dumfries.

"Wow. There's so manys," she said with a touch of awe.

"She's going to have them all wrapped around her pinky finger in no time." Harper came up beside us. "I'm glad you're all okay."

"Thank you."

I didn't want to keep talking about it. Warren had been arrested, and according to our attorney, the case against him was airtight. Assaulting Julian outside of O'Shea's, forcing me into his car at knifepoint, and trying to take Imogen weren't his only crimes.

He'd gotten into trouble up in Michigan and there was a warrant out for his arrest.

I'd always worried what I would tell Imogen about her father one day, but he'd sealed his fate the night he pointed a knife at her and Austin.

If I got my way, he would never see Imogen again.

Jacqui and Ken took the news hard, but I didn't feel much sympathy right now given that they had talked to him and not told me or the authorities. Warren was their son, yes, but Imogen was their granddaughter and it devastated me to think they had an indirect hand in what went down.

"Hey, you good?" Austin asked me as Ella showed everyone her ring.

They'd all celebrated Saturday night at the engagement party but since unfortunate events had overshadowed their happy news the last few days, I'd talked Kayleigh into letting us host a small party.

It was nothing too elaborate. Just some cakes and soda and good company.

"Yeah, I'm okay." I laid my hand over his arm and leaned back against him as we watched Imogen soak up the attention.

"This was a nice idea," he added, pressing a lingering kiss to my neck. My eyes shuttered as I sucked in a shaky breath.

"It was the least I could do."

"Okay, everyone." Kayleigh appeared with a tray of

pink plastic champagne flutes. "My license doesn't cover alcohol but since this is a private event and you're celebrating, I figured one glass of champagne couldn't hurt." She handed them around, giving Imogen her very own flute filled with grape soda. "Would anyone like to say a few words?"

"I will." Austin stepped around me. "I know I've been a miserable shit the last few months. I've struggled watching you all find your way and figure out that there is more to life than hockey."

"Don't let Coach hear you say that," Aiden snorted, earning him a round of laughter.

"But I think I can finally say, I get it." He took my hand in his, squeezing gently. "Connor, Ella, congratulations. You deserve a lifetime of happiness together."

"Thank you," Ella smiled.

"And, I may have some news of my own," Austin added.

"We already know you've switched sides," Noah laughed.

"True. But no, it's not that." He glanced down at me, and the air shifted, the tether between us tightening. "I've decided not to pursue a contract after the season ends."

"The fuck?" someone said but I didn't know who because I was too lost in the intensity in Austin's gaze.

Of the love shining there.

The promise of a future together.

"I'm staying in Lakeshore," he said, finally looking at his friends again. "I'm going to talk to Coach Tucker and Coach Walsh about getting into coaching."

"Good for you, man." Mason was the first to congratulate him. "I know a team who would be happy to give you some experience."

"Oh, Austin." Rory hugged him. "I'm so happy for you."

I let go of his hand and gave them a minute, scooping Imogen up into my arms. "How's your special drink, princess?"

"I wikes the bubbles." She smacked her lips together and I smiled, searching her face for any hint of trauma. But she seemed fine.

In fact, she'd barely asked about Warren or what had happened.

"What's wrongs, Mommy?"

"Nothing baby. I just love you sooo much." I kissed her forehead.

"I woves you too, silly. And wook, Mommy. Wook at all our new friends." She grabbed my cheeks and turned my head to the group.

Austin spotted us and frowned. "Okay?" he mouthed, and I nodded, holding back the rush of tears. He said something to Rory then headed in our direction. "What's wrong?"

"Nothing, I'm fine."

"And how's my special girl?" He held out his arms for Imogen and she went to him.

"I wike your friends, Austins."

"Yeah?"

"Yeah. 'Specially Connor Morgans."

"Is that so, huh? Well, they all like you too, princess. In fact, I think Rory and Harper would like to spend some special time with you later."

"They would?" Her eyes lit up, but Austin was looking at me.

"Yeah, would that be okay?"

"Hells yeah," she shrieked so loud everyone stopped dead, staring at her. "Why dids everyone goes quiet?"

Everyone laughed and she frowned at me.

"Never change, my sweet girl." I ran a hand over her soft curls and laid my head on Austin's shoulder.

This was all I needed.

My beautiful strong-willed daughter and the man who had brought me back to life again.

"Oh God, God," I whimpered, my fingers twisted in the sheets as Austin speared his tongue inside me, his thumb rolling tight little circles over my clit.

"Come for me, Madi. Come all over my face."

Jesus.

The tightly wound coil inside me snapped and I went soaring. My legs trembled around Austin's head as he licked me through the waves of pleasure crashing over me.

"Stop, stop." I yanked his hair, trying to pull him up my body.

I wanted to kiss him. To feel his weight pressed down on me.

"Fuck, you're sexy when you come." He crawled up my body, hovering over me. "I love the little sounds you make, the way you whimper my name. How good your pussy tastes on my tongue."

"Austin!" I went to swat his chest, but he caught my wrist, pinning my arm to the bed.

"We still have twenty-five minutes until they're back."

"We should probably use them wisely then," I sassed, lifting my hips a little to try and nudge him to where I wanted him most.

"Patience, pretty girl." He leaned down, nipping at my jaw.

"Stop teasing and fuck me."

"And what about if I don't want to fuck you?" He dropped his weight over me, pinning me to the bed. "What if I want to make love to you? To bury myself so fucking deep in you I don't know where I end and you begin?"

"Jesus," I breathed, every nerve ending in my body on fire.

Austin didn't take his eyes off me as he slipped his hand between us and worked himself to my entrance, pushing in so slowly I felt him everywhere. "Fuck, you feel…"

"I know, don't stop." A violent shudder ripped through me at the intensity of this position. We were so close it felt incredible.

"I'm going to come again," I cried, completely overwhelmed at the sensations he was wreaking on my body.

Austin didn't fuck me.

He worshipped me. Whispered words of love onto my skin as he rocked his body against mine. Slow and deep, hitting that magical spot inside me that made me soar.

"This… I will never get enough of this, of you." He released my wrist and slipped his arm underneath my back, anchoring us even closer as he pressed into me. Over and over.

"I love you." I wrapped my arms around his shoulders, holding on as my body splintered apart for him.

"I love you too, Madison." He came hard, burying his face in the crook of my neck. But I still heard him say, "You're mine now. And I'm never letting you go."

CHAPTER 33

MADISON

Imogen never ceased to amaze me.

Over the next few weeks, she adapted beautifully to our new routine with Austin and his friends. So much so that sometimes, I worried she would get disappointed when it was just the two of us hanging out.

But my girl was gracious and kind and wise beyond her years. She soaked up every second of excitement surrounding us as the Lakers fought for their place in the Frozen Four tournament.

We hadn't made it to any of their games yet. Despite being the Lakers newest—and self-proclaimed biggest—fan, Imogen was still only four and if I wanted to take her to watch him play in the tournament, I needed to save every penny I had for the trip to Pittsburgh.

We supported the team in our own way though. We hung out with Jeremiah and Vader, or Harper and Scottie and tuned in to the games when possible. And Austin and Imogen had the cutest pre-match ritual of a video calling each other so she could wish him luck.

Life was good.

Better than good, it was everything I had never let myself dare to imagine it could be.

"Nervous?" Jeremiah asked me as he joined me on the couch with our half-time bucket of popcorn, our hockey game snack of choice.

"A little. That's silly, right?" I flushed. "It's just a game."

"We both know it's not just a game to these guys." He tipped his head toward the television, the huddle of cyan and indigo players crowded around Coach Tucker.

"The Lakers will wins," Imogen said with a confidence I didn't quite feel.

The Lakers were winning five to three. But according to the commentators it had been a difficult game so far. Leon had taken a nasty hit and Aiden had gotten into it with one of the other players, earning him time in the penalty box.

But Austin had looked calm and composed, doing his best to keep the puck out of his net.

I still didn't know all that much about the rules, but I loved watching him play. His strength and speed and utter determination. I wanted the win for him, for all of the guys who had accepted me and Imogen into their circle without question.

"Wooks, Mommy. Theres is Austins." Imogen clapped with delight as he skated out to his goal. "Go Austins, kicks some Pelicans ass."

"Oh my God," I smothered a laugh. "She's spending too much time with the guys."

"I can always step in. I wouldn't mind spending more time with the guys." He smirked. "Especially, the surly captain."

"Jer! Aiden is with Dayna."

"Shame. Oh, look they're facing off," he said as if he had any more idea what was happening than me.

"Goes Lakers!" Imogen cheered right alongside him, and I smiled, saying a silent prayer for Austin and his team to go all the way.

Madison: Congratulations. I know you'll be celebrating with the guys. But I just wanted to tell you we watched the entire game. Imogen was so excited. We're so happy for you and the team. Go Lakers! xo

"Who knew hockey could be so riveting," Jeremiah said, placing our empty glasses onto the counter.

It was late. But after Noah scored a last-minute goal and secured the Lakers victory and their ticket to the Frozen Four tournament, we stayed up and celebrated.

"Do you regret not going?" he added.

"I mean, I would have liked to be there for him. To celebrate with them. But she wouldn't have understood." I glanced toward Imogen, curled up on Jeremiah's couch fast asleep. She refused to go to bed, insisting on watching all the post-game analysis.

"But at least now you'll get to go watch him in Pittsburgh."

"I hope so."

"If you need money—"

"I appreciate it, I do. But it's not necessary." If I managed to take Imogen to Pittsburgh it would be because I'd worked for it.

"As stubborn as always." He chuckled. "I'm going to take out the trash." Jeremiah headed down the hall and I finished drying the dishes.

"Mads, come here," he called, and I made for the hall.

"What's— Austin." I stopped dead in my tracks. "What are you doing here? You're supposed to be with the team, celebrating."

Jeremiah gave me a knowing wink as he headed back into the apartment, and I moved toward Austin.

"I-I don't understand."

He reached for my sweater and tugged me toward him, wrapping his arm around my back.

"Funny story," he said. "We were all in the locker room celebrating and I looked around at my teammates, some of the best friends I'll ever have, and I realized something..."

"Yeah?" I gazed up at him, so deeply in love with this man that my heart felt ready to burst.

"Yeah, pretty girl." He smiled. "I realized there's nowhere else I'd rather be than here."

EPILOGUE

AUSTIN

"Well, here we are," Aiden said as the five of us sat on the ice after our final practice of the season.

"Five minutes," Coach Walsh shouted, and Aiden gave him a thumbs up.

"Is it me or does he seem more of a miserable asshole than usual lately?" Noah said.

"Probably sad he's losing his bestie," Connor gave Aiden a pointed look, and Dumfries flipped him off.

"I didn't want to say anything because it's not my style," Mason said. "But I think I walked in on him and Emerson having a moment a couple of weeks back."

"No shit, Coach Walsh and the team's PR manager," I said. "That has disaster written all over it. What says you, Aiden?"

"Seriously? You think I want to sit around gossiping about who Coach may or may not be fucking when we're on the precipice of the national championship final." He gave us a look that rivaled the ones Coach Tucker and Walsh regularly aimed in our direction.

"I never thought this day would come." Connor changed the subject.

The lighthearted atmosphere of our last session with the team before the final game tomorrow turned somber.

"Four years, and it all comes down to this moment."

"Jesus. Don't go getting all sentimental on us now." Noah grinned. "Besides, some of us will still be here next season."

"Nobody asked you to be here, Holden," I teased.

"Yeah, right. Like we'd let you have this moment without us."

"I can't speak for Holden but I'm sure as fuck going to miss you guys," Mason said.

"Agreed," Noah nodded.

"Well, this got depressing as shit." I clambered to my feet. "We still have a game to win tomorrow, you know."

The guys followed suit.

"Madison and Imogen are coming, right?" Noah asked.

"I fucking hope so."

It had been a long couple of days without seeing my girls.

"Still surprised you didn't insist on bringing them down earlier."

"Kayleigh needed help with an event and Madison has this thing about paying her own way."

Which I wanted to respect.

She was used to being independent, doing things her way. I didn't want to bulldoze my way in and take over.

Besides, the schedule was crazy and didn't leave much downtime for players to spend it with their friends and family so having them come down tomorrow was probably for the best.

"Any regrets about telling the Canucks you weren't interested?"

I shook my head. "None."

"I always knew you were going to fall harder than the rest of us." He smirked and I flipped him off.

"We should probably head in before Coach Walsh comes looking for us," Aiden said. "But before we do, I just want to say, playing hockey with you all has been the privilege of my life."

"Fucking hell, Cap, you're not dying. Who knows where we might meet in the future. There could be more games in our future, we just might be on opposite sides of the ice."

Aiden shot Noah an exasperated look and skated off toward the tunnel.

"You just can't help yourself, can you?" I shook my head and took off after Aiden.

"What? What did I do?" Noah called after me.

Damn. I was going to miss these guys. But I was excited to see what the future had in store for us all.

Starting with winning the national championship in front of my girls tomorrow.

MADISON

"Wooks, Mommy. Wooks at it." Imogen stared up at the PPG Paints Arena as if it was the most magical thing she'd ever seen. "It's so... shiny."

"It is pretty impressive, isn't it." Rory squeezed her hand gently. "Austin is going to be so happy to see you, princess."

"We can sees him befores the game?"

"We talked about this, remember?" I said. "We'll be able to see him after."

"But I needs to wish him good luck."

"We already did that, baby."

"It's not the sames." She pouted. "I wanted to gives him one of my special kisses."

The girls all laughed.

"Don't forget your new headphones." Harper pulled them out of her rucksack.

"Oh, wikes Scottie has."

"Yes, just like Scottie." Harper helped Imogen fit them, fluffing out her hair around the headband. "Perfect."

"And I gots my special gloves that Austins gots me." She made little fists as we approached the gathering crowds.

I was so nervous.

Not only for Austin and the team but also the surprise we'd put together for him. The girls insisted it was perfect, but I wasn't sure.

Things were great between Austin and me, but it was still new.

We were still finding our way.

"Everything okay?" Dayna asked me as we joined the line.

I'd gotten to know her better in the last few weeks and she was just as nice and kind as Harper and Rory.

"I'm fine."

"It's okay to be nervous," she said. "It's a big night for them."

"Can I ask you something?"

"Of course."

"Do you think he made a mistake not talking to Vancouver?"

Austin was one hundred percent sure of his decision. But there were still moments when I wondered if he would come to regret it.

"Madi, if there's one thing you need to know about the Lakers," she said, "it's that they don't hesitate. And they don't do things unless they want to. Austin loves you, and I don't think there's a single person who knows him well that thinks he made the wrong decision."

I nodded, desperately wanting to believe her.

Imogen dropped back from Rory and Harper and buried herself into my side.

"Sweetheart, what's wrong?"

"There's lots of peoples, Mommy."

"There is." I scooped her up and held her on my hip. "But once we're inside we'll get our seats okay. Then you'll be able to watch Austin and the guys."

"Is Connor Morgans playing?"

"No, baby. Connor can't play but he'll be on the bench, cheering the team on."

"Do you think Austins will like our surprise?" She tugged at her jacket.

"I hope so, baby." I kissed her hair.

I really hope so.

AUSTIN

The air rippled with anticipation as Coach Tucker entered the room.

"This is it," he said, preparing to give his final pep talk of the season. "It all comes down to this moment.

"For some of you, this is the last time you'll ever put on your Lakers jersey. For others, it's the start of a long road ahead. But whether you're a freshman or a senior, I want each of you to know how proud I am.

"This season hasn't been easy. We lost one of our best players." His gaze landed on Connor. "It's not easy to bounce back from that kind of loss. But Connor is a part of this team whether he's on the ice or not.

"Now I could stand here and talk to you about last-minute strategy or give you some long motivational speech that you'll forget the second you get out on the ice and hear the roar of the crowd. But instead, I'm going to tell you what my father told me on the night before my first college national championship.

"Not every victory shows up on the scoreboard." Coach Tucker took time to look at every player in the locker room, letting his words settle. "You all made sacrifices to be here. You all put in the work. You all earned your spot. Now let's go out there and show everyone what the Lakeshore U Lakers are made of."

The atmosphere in the PPG Paints Arena was electric. There wasn't a spare seat in the house and if the noise was any indicator, everyone had come ready to cheer for their favorite team.

"Holy shit," Leon said, whizzing past me as we warmed up.

Holy shit indeed.

"Lap it up, brother." Noah clapped me on the shoulder.

"It's something, huh?" I scanned the crowds, trying to spot my girls. But the lights made it difficult to see anything beyond the swathe of indigo and cyan.

"Any regrets?"

"None. You?"

"Not putting a ring on your sister's finger on Valentine's Day."

"Are you trying to give me a heart attack before I play the biggest game of my life?" I huffed.

Noah's laughter grated on my last fucking nerve. "You should see your face. I'm only half serious. But I figured it can't hurt to get you fired up."

"You're an asshole."

"And yet, you're stuck with me."

"Can you see the girls?" I scanned the front rows again. Family and friends had preferential seats, so they had to be down there somewhere.

"Relax, they're here."

Easy for him to say.

He hadn't watched a mad man wave a knife at the girl he loved.

I didn't let Madison see it, but that shit had messed

with my head. I wanted eyes on them both at all times, especially at something as huge as this.

"I still can't—"

"Hi." Madison mouthed as I spotted her.

I skated in their direction before Coach had a chance to tell me to stay put.

"Austins, Austins." Imogen jumped up and down, banging on the plexiglass.

But it wasn't her broad smile that melted my heart. Or the way Madison looked at me with nothing but love and adoration. It was what they were both wearing that stopped me in my tracks.

"Surprise," she mouthed, giving me a little twirl.

Fuck.

The sight of them both in my jersey, number thirty-one blazed across their chests, did things to me.

Crazy, mad things.

Screw the game. I wanted to burst through the glass, throw Madison over my shoulder, and take her back to my hotel room and fuck her in nothing but that shirt.

Why the fuck hadn't I thought to put my jersey on her yet?

"I fucking love you." I grinned, slowly skating backward at the bellow of Coach's orders.

"We love you too." Madison smiled and I knew at that moment that whatever happened on the ice tonight didn't matter.

I had everything I needed sitting right there.

The woman I loved.

And the little girl who had me wrapped around her pinky finger.

Win or lose, I was the luckiest guy here.

MADISON

"Oh my God, I can't watch."

"You gots to watch it, Mommy." Imogen pried my fingers away from my face. "Wooks. Wooks."

A player in black and yellow hurtled toward Austin in a last-ditch attempt to close their one-point deficit.

"Come on, come on," I murmured, watching as the man I loved track the puck.

If he conceded this, the Stingrays would equalize and have a shot at stealing the win right out from under them.

The player lined up the shot and sent the puck sailing through the air. The entire arena seemed to take a collective breath as Austin moved and stuck his glove in its trajectory.

"Did he get it?" Did he get it?" I yelled right as Austin flipped the puck and dropped it on the ice, sending the crowd into chaos.

"Let's go Lakers," Dayna shouted.

"This is so intense." Rory buried herself into my side as we watched the teams face-off again.

"Ninety seconds left on the clock," I said, certain my heart was going to burst out my chest at any moment.

"Go, go," the crowd behind us roared as Aiden won the puck, taking off toward the Stingrays goal. But their defense covered him, forcing him to try and get the puck to Noah.

"Oh God." Rory grabbed my arm, trembling as Noah broke away with the puck only to be slammed into the boards.

"Noah!"

"He's fine. He's fine," Dayna reassured her. "It's done. It's theirs."

Frenetic energy built in our section of the arena, the realization that unless something went very wrong in the next thirty seconds, the Lakers had done it.

They were champions.

"Twenty seconds," I muttered, jostling Imogen on my hip. "Ten... five..."

The whistle sounded and the Lakers fans blew the roof off the place.

Players pulled off their helmets, throwing them in the air as they all raced toward our section.

But my world narrowed to the goalkeeper skating toward us.

Number thirty-one.

The man who had saved me.

Brought me back to life.

The man who loved Imogen as if she were his own.

"You did it," I cried, pressing my hand against the glass, right over his palm.

"I love you," he said, a lifetime of promises in his eyes.

"I love you too."

"I love you threes," Imogen sang, sliding her hand between mind and the glass.

Then the rest of the guys—Connor, Aiden, Noah, and Mason—piled on Austin. Cheering and celebrating as we laughed along with them.

Five guys that were more than just friends or teammates.

They were family.

One I was forever grateful to be a part of.

BONUS EPILOGUE

AUSTIN

MY HEART CRASHED beneath my ribcage as I drank in the sight of her.

"Fuck," I rasped. "You look…"

"Do you like it?" Madison asked, flipping her wavy blonde hair over one shoulder, letting me get a better look at her in my jersey.

My fucking number.

"Like? I fucking love it." I went to get up, but she wagged her finger.

"I need you to sit right there for a minute."

"Madison, come—"

Music filled her room, some slow sexy bass that made lust swim in my veins.

"I've been thinking about what you said to me that one time. About wishing I could dance at O'Shea's."

"Oh yeah?" I cocked my head, letting my gaze sweep over her sexy-as-fuck body again. Her long smooth legs peeked out of my jersey as she wound it around her fist to give me a glimpse of her little black lace panties.

Holy shit.

I swallowed hard.

I wanted to touch her. To kneel at her feet and lick my way up her legs, along the curve of her knee and up between the soft flesh of her thighs.

I wanted—

"You're right," she said. "I want to dance, Austin. But I don't want to dance for anyone but you."

"You want to dance for me, pretty girl?" I asked, and she nodded, licking her lips.

"Then dance." I placed my hands flat on the bed behind me and tried to think of anything but my raging hard-on.

Control yourself, Hart. Or you'll come faster than a teenage boy watching his first porn movie.

Madison began moving her body. Rolling and popping her hips to the beat.

I loved her like this.

Confident and sexy and willing to put herself out there for me.

She swayed closer, pushing my jersey up her stomach and over her tits.

"Fuck, Madi. That's so fucking hot."

She teased me a few seconds longer, then let the material fall back in place as she spun away from me, giving me the perfect view of her ass.

A low groan vibrated in my chest.

How the fuck did I get this lucky?

"We need to buy your parents a gift," I said, my skin burning up as she continued to dance for me.

"My parents?" She flashed me a questioning look as she ran her hands up through her hair and wove them high above her head.

"For taking Immy tonight."

Her soft laughter was like music to my fucking ears. "She'll be back bright and early."

"Then we should probably make the most of it."

Done waiting, I hooked my arm around her waist and pulled her between my legs.

"Austin," she shrieked. "I wasn't done."

"If I don't get my hands on you right now, I'm not sure I'll survive."

"Ahw, is my big broody hockey player feeling a little needy." She ran her fingers through my hair and leaned down to kiss me.

I wrested control though, plunging my tongue deep into her mouth as I pulled her down on the bed and rolled her beneath me.

"Austin, that isn't fair."

"Pretty sure you'll be thanking me in about ten seconds." I slid off the bed, letting my knees hit the carpet.

"What—oh. Oh god," she breathed as I buried my face in her lace-covered pussy.

"You were saying?"

Madison fisted my hair and shoved my head back down. "Less talking, more licking."

Now there was a plan I could get on board with.

MADISON

"Mommy, Austins." Imogen came barreling through the door but before I could catch her in my arms, she veered around me and headed straight for Austin.

"Good morning, princess." He scooped her up and dropped a kiss on her head. "How was your sleepover with Grammy and Pops?"

"Grammy said it's too soons for us to live togethers. Are we gonna lives together?"

"Oh dear," Mom turned beet red as my heart dropped to my toes. "I didn't think—"

I glanced at Austin, and he grinned. "Behave," I mouthed.

We hadn't even talked about moving in together, but Austin loved any excuse to make my mom squirm.

"I don't know, princess. Your mom and I haven't

talked about it... yet," he added.

"You already stay overs all the time," Imogen replied.

"You're right, I do."

"Yes, well." Mom cleared her throat. "Your father and I wondered if you would like to come over for dinner Sunday?"

"Oh, I'm not sure—"

"That sounds great, Cara." Austin gave her a megawatt smile. "Thanks".

What?

I gave him a pleading look, but he only grinned again.

"We'll see you, Sunday then." She gave him a tight smile.

To say things were still strained between me and my mom was an understatement. She liked Austin, I knew that. But she still had reservations about our relationship.

It wasn't enough for her that he'd decided to stay in Lakeshore, or that he'd come to the rescue when Warren came back.

It was enough for me though.

I'd never been so happy, and Imogen absolutely adored him.

"Thanks again for watching her," I said.

"Honestly, Madison, she's our granddaughter. It isn't any trouble."

"Say bye to Grammy," Austin added.

"Bye Grammy."

"Bye."

Mom left and I breathed a sigh of relief.

"You've got to cut her some slack," Austin said.

"Seriously?"

"Why don't you go set up the tea party," he said to Imogen, lowering her to the floor. "And I'll be there in a minute."

"Can we have a breakfast tea party? With pancakes."

"Hell yeah, we can." He held up his hand and she gave him a high five.

"Don't be wongs," she called, skipping off down the hall.

"It's official." I pouted. "She loves you more than me."

"I am pretty awesome." Austin came over and wrapped his arms around me. "If you don't want to go to your parents on Sunday, we don't have to go."

"No, we can go. It's just... I don't want her to ruin this for us." My fingers curled into his t-shirt.

I was so freaking grateful it was spring. Austin had finally traded his Lakeshore U hoodies for t-shirts that hugged his muscles in ways that made me salivate.

"Never going to happen, Madi." He gazed down at me. "I love you and I love that amazing little girl of yours. I'm not going anywhere, I promise."

"And about what my mom said, us living together, I'm not—"

"We move at your pace, remember?" He touched his head to mine. "I know I'm over all the time, but I still have my place. And this will always be your place."

"I think I might want to, one day. But it's a big step for me and this is still so new."

"We have time, Madi. We have all the time in the world." Austin kissed me, his hands sliding down my spine to grab my ass. "You were so fucking hot last night. I can't stop thinking about it."

"I don't think I've ever come so hard," I admitted. "That thing you did with your—"

"Mommy! Austins! The tea is getting colds."

Austin let out a soft chuckle. "We probably shouldn't keep the princess waiting."

He went to walk away but I grabbed him.

"I love you, Austin."

"I love you too, Madi. So fucking much."

AUSTIN

"Feel okay?" I asked Imogen as I tightened the belt on her floatation vest.

"Feels okay." She grinned. "Will I gets to drive the boat?"

"I'm not sure about that, princess. But we're going to have lots of fun.

"Look at you," Dayna said. "Are you excited?"

"So excited. Can I sit with you and Rora?"

"Of course, princess. Come on." Dayna held out her hand and Imogen went off with her.

"Need any help?" I asked Austin.

"Nah, I'm good. There's beer in the cooler and Dayna packed a bunch of snacks."

"This was a good idea," Noah said, joining us.

"Yeah. It's a shame Connor and Mason couldn't make it though," I said.

"It's going to be difficult getting us all together now."

Graduation was right around the corner. Connor and Ella were already spending more and more weekends in Philadelphia, and Harper and Mason were helping out at the center more.

Our lives were moving in different directions. But the thought didn't fill me with dread anymore because I had all I needed right here.

My eyes landed on Madison and Imogen talking to Rory and Dayna.

"It still gets me every time," Noah said with a hint of amusement.

"What does?"

"The way you look at them."

"Don't start with this shit again." An exasperated sigh rolled through me.

"It's not a bad thing," he argued.

"Will you tell him?" I asked Aiden, but he only smirked.

"Holden has a point."

"Oh, fuck off, both of you."

"She called you daddy yet?"

"The fuck?" I glared at Aiden, and Noah exploded with laughter.

"Shit, that came out wrong. I meant, Imogen. Has she called you—"

"No, she hasn't called me daddy, what kind of question is that?"

She had a daddy, albeit a piece of shit, who had lost his right to be her father the second he held Madison at knifepoint.

"It happens all the time". Aiden shrugged like he hadn't just landed a bombshell at my feet. "Young kids latch onto the new boyfriend and before you know it, they're calling them daddy."

"This conversation is really weird," I said.

But now that he'd said it, I couldn't stop thinking about it.

The same way I couldn't stop thinking about what Cara said about us moving in together.

I would never pressure Madison into anything she wasn't ready for.

But I was ready.

I'd been ready for a while.

I hated being away from my girls. Hated staying at

the house on my own, waking up all alone.

"Oh shit." Noah clapped me on the back. "You're totally thinking about it, aren't you?"

"You don't know what you're talking about," I muttered, shoving past him to go to Madison.

Her eyes lit up as I approached and slid onto the bench beside her.

"She loves it," she said, leaning into me as we watched Imogen with Dayna and Rory.

"I knew she would."

My little princess loved an adventure.

"This is all because of you, you know."

"Oh, I don't know about that."

"I do." Madison kissed my jaw. "You've given us so much to look forward to Austin."

Silence settled over us as the boat cut through the water, and Imogen's excited shrieks only got louder as Austin went faster.

"She's so brave," Madison mused.

"Just like her mom."

"I don't feel very brave right about now," she chuckled.

"Good thing I'll always be here to protect you then." I tightened my arm around her waist and rested my chin on her shoulder.

"You promise?" she whispered.

"I promise, pretty girl."

Always.

PLAYLIST

People Watching – Conan Gray
Don't Blame Me – Taylor Swift
Ocean Eyes – Billie Eilish
Cold Heart – Clementine Duet
My Tears Ricochet – Taylor Swift
Lose Control – Teddy Swims
Wrecking Ball – Boyce Avenue ft. Diamond White
The Night We Met – Lord Huron
Astronomy – Conan Gray
Let Me In – Snowmine
Waiting Games – BANKS
Yours – Conan Gray
Till Forever Falls Apart – Ashe, FINNEAS

ACKNOWLEDGMENTS

This book wasn't easy to write - not because Austin and Madison's story wasn't there, but because sometimes life gets in the way. I'm sorry it took me a little longer than usual, but I hope it was worth the wait.

Writing Cold as Ice was always going to be bittersweet because it's the final full-length book in the series. I've spent the last eighteen months with this group of characters and I've loved getting in their heads and bringing their stories to life.

Thank you so everyone who has fallen in love with my Lakeshore U Lakers, and to everyone who has had a hand in helping me along the way. My editor, Kate; my proofreaders, Darlene and Athena; my graphic and PR girl, Sammi; my audio producer, Kim; my alpha reader and all-round cheerleader, Jen; and to every single reader, blogger, bookstagrammer, and booktokkers who has taken the time to read, review, and share their love for the series.

Thank YOU!

The final story will be coming later in the year... any guesses who it will be?

Until next time...

L A xo

ABOUT THE AUTHOR

Reckless Love. Wild Hearts

USA Today and *Wall Street Journal* bestselling author of over forty mature young adult and new adult novels, L. A. is happiest writing the kind of books she loves to read: addictive stories full of teenage angst, tension, twists, and turns.

Home is a small town in the middle of England where she currently juggles being a full-time writer with being a mother/referee to two little people. In her spare time (and when she's not camped out in front of the laptop), you'll most likely find L. A. immersed in a book, escaping the chaos that is life.

L. A. loves connecting with readers.
The best places to find her are:
www.lacotton.com

www.ingramcontent.com/pod-product-compliance
Lightning Source LLC
Chambersburg PA
CBHW061049210726
48294CB00001B/71